"War is hell, but WORLD WAR III is a riot!"

WORLD WAR III

Starring **SARGE**

with Pvt. E-2 Ernest Youngman, Charlie Brown,
Louie, the Greek; Lt. Commander Ju-Chao, Li Ming,
and a horde of blood-thirsty warriors

See
Squad C-323
go ape!

S0-APQ-755

WORLD WAR III

JOHN STANLEY

 AVON
PUBLISHERS OF BARD, CAMELOT, DISCUS, EQUINOX AND FLARE BOOKS

WORLD WAR III is an original publication of Avon Books.
This work has never before appeared in book form.

AVON BOOKS
A division of
The Hearst Corporation
959 Eighth Avenue
New York, New York 10019

ISBN: 0-380-00487-9

First Avon Pinting, January, 1976
Third Printing

Printed in the U.S.A.

1
Napalm Sunday

This is the story of a miracle.

It began, as miracles tend to begin, in a humble, almost mundane, fashion near the ammunition and ball-bearing factories of Changyang Valley, located fifty miles southeast of Suichuan and two hundred ten miles due west of the seaport of Wenchow on the eastern coast of China.

Bordering the factories at the far end of the valley was a moderate-sized village, and bordering the village were many moderate-sized rice paddies and soybean fields which provided subsistence and a meager living for those residents of Changyang who did not work in the factories.

Two steady workers in one of those modest rice paddies were the children Pong-yu, eight, and Ying-yu, seven, daughters of a poor farmer who kept a small but comfortable hut on the outskirts of the community. In addition to the farmer and the girls, this hut was inhabited by a fat but comforting wife and mother, a crippled duck named Cherry Blossom Rose, and a cow without a name who provided cream and milk daily. It was a simple life for all concerned, and Pong-yu and Ying-yu reflected the uncomplicated nature of their surroundings.

So it was one day, as they walked playfully along the

cart trail leading to their hut, that their thoughts (after many hours of tedious labor) were of pure things, such as flowers, fresh milk, a spring rain which had left a pleasant fragrance in the air, the cleanliness of their hut and their injured duck, Cherry Blossom Rose.

The small praying temple positioned a few yards off the trail was the last thing on Ying-yu's mind as the sisters skipped so playfully homeward. Only at the insistence of Pong-yu, the more sensitive of the two, did they stop at all. It was Pong-yu's intention to say a brief prayer to Buddha, asking that Cherry Blossom Rose's damaged foot, which had been run over by a military motorcar during mock maneuvers, be restored to normal.

"Yes, my child," replied Buddha, coming to life just long enough to bend His head forward slightly in acknowledgment. Then he assumed His stony countenance once again and, for the moment, said no more.

At first Pong-yu thought nothing about it—a direct answer to a direct request seemed logical enough. Then, when she considered some of the remarks of her father, the impact of what had happened began to set in. She looked carefully at Buddha, noticing that He looked no different than usual. Ying-yu made a comment that indicated she was frightened.

"Do not be frightened, my child," soothed Buddha. This time his arms moved slightly, then returned almost immediately to their rigid poistion. "You have nothing to fear." Pong-yu wasn't certain if Buddha's lips moved or not, but she did know she was no longer frightened. Nor, apparently, was Ying-yu, who continued to pray in her accustomed fashion.

Finally, after a prolonged silence, Pong-yu remarked: "We are not frightened."

"That is good," said Buddha. This time He picked at His nostrils. "There is something I want you to tell your father."

"He is working in the fields," replied Pong-yu.

"This is something you can tell him later, after dark."

"I will tell him," promised Pong-yu.

"After dark," added Ying-yu.

"Tell your father," said Buddha, still picking at His nose,

2

"that a miraculous thing will occur in two days. This miraculous thing will occur in the very place you now are kneeling. It will happen everywhere in this peaceful valley of Changyang. Everyone who lives in the valley must come to watch this miraculous thing. You must tell your father this thing, so that all who live in this peaceful valley of Changyang will come and witness for themselves."

"What is this miraculous thing?" asked Pong-yu.

"It is an answer to your prayer, child."

This sounded good to Pong-yu, the oldest of the two children, but she nevertheless frowned. "My father . . . he will find it hard to believe . . ."

"Do not worry, child," reassured Buddha, removing a dirt-covered finger from His nostril and placing His arms in their original positions. "When you tell your father, he will know you speak the truth."

"Then," said Pong-yu, "I will tell him."

"That is good, child," said Buddha, but then He would say no more, not even at the urging of Ying-yu. Pong-yu was forced to tell her to hush up. "Buddha has said all He is going to say," she told her sister, and they continued along the old cart trail, for by now it was beginning to grow dark.

When night fell, and the cow had been milked, and Cherry Blossom's Rose's dangling webbed foot had been wrapped in a holy cloth, and a sacred song of the Thousand Mountains had been chanted on the duck's behalf, Pong-yu approached her father. Ying-yu held back apprehensively in the shadows of the small room. She had witnessed the wrath of her father when he confronted a falsehood, and she lacked the courage of Pong-yu, even though she knew it was true Buddha had spoken and picked His nostrils.

"Father," said Pong-yu, as reverently as she knew how, "Buddha in the small temple along the old cart trail spoke to Ying-yu, and then He spoke to me." Her father lifted his head, started to reply, and then stopped. Even Pong-yu's mother, a woman quick to reprimand her children, failed to speak, for she too was staring at her daughter. The knitting in her lap was momentarily forgotten.

Both parents gazed at the small circular band of light

3

which had suddenly appeared above Pong-yu's head. The yellowish light within the band intensified and seemed to light up her entire face. When the parents looked into that face, there was no mistaking the truth to be found there.

"Yes," queried Pong-yu's father, waiting anxiously. "What did Buddha say?"

Pong-yu told of the incident. Pong-yu's father carefully folded his newspaper, placed it on the table, and bowed humbly, thanking her. "I will tell the villagers," he stated matter-of-factly.

The halo of yellow light dissolved and Pong-yu's face returned to its former countenance. The purity remained in it even though the halo was gone.

The next day dawned invigoratingly crisp. Pong-yu's Father forsook his rice crops and soybean fields to tell his fellow villagers what his daughters had seen and heard. Each time he repeated the story, even to a stranger, the yellowish halo appeared above his head, dissolving only after the listener had nodded or voiced his understanding. Even beggars and hardened criminals, men whose faces had long ago lost their purity and integrity, were able on this strange day to pass along the information to their associates in begging and thievery. Never was incredulity indicated, nor a word questioned. Each in turn told others of the miraculous thing to come, and so it went throughout the day. By midafternoon the factories closed down, and there were no farmers to be found in the rice paddies or soybean fields. When darkness came, a strange silence settled over the entire valley of Changyang. A mood of expectancy prevailed.

Then it was Sunday, the day of the promised miracle. All enterprise ground to a halt. There was money to be earned, transactions to be completed, and connivery to be practiced, but on this day everyone's interest was centered in the small praying temple a few yards off the old cart trail. The factories of war remained closed, as did the shops and restaurants which comprised the valley's only commercial zone.

The temple had become the center of Changyang Valley.

From that nucleus sprang a 360-degree circle of humanity—nearly six thousand prople were jammed against each other for a closer scrutiny of Buddha, to witness firsthand that which had been promised.

Pong-yu, Ying-yu, and their father and mother had been the first to take their positions the night before, and in no way was this questioned by the others. It was Pong-yu who had been honored by Buddha, and it was therefore her right, and the right of her family, to sit directly in front of Him.

They waited.

And waited.

By one o'clock nothing had happened, and the first signs of restlessness rippled through the crowd.

At 1:30, the yellowish halos appeared above the heads at Pong-yu and Ying-yu.

At 1:32, as a hush of silence was maintained by the multitudes, Buddha stretched His arms, yawned, picked at His nostrils and lowered His head.

"Boo," he proclaimed.

At that moment, those at the farthest edges of the crowd heard the roar of jet engines. At the southern end of the valley, a squadron of sixteen U.S. fighter planes approached at 400 miles an hour. The artillery pieces located at the southern approaches were, like every other mechanical object in Changyang Valley, unmanned, but even if the gunners had been in their positions they could never have deflected their muzzles to fire at such a low altitude. The squadron was broken up into four wings, each four minutes apart, with four planes in each wing. Six 200-gallon cannisters hung umbilically beneath each fighter plane, and at the command of the wing leader twenty-four cannisters were released simultaneously.

The main targets, strategically, were the ammunition and ball-bearing factories, and the American pilots were completely unaware of the huge congregation around the modest shrine. The planes had been traveling too fast for the pilots to see the milling thousands—even after the cannisters had been released.

The technique employed was skip-bombing, the cannisters being released far ahead of the target so the momentum would carry the fiery destruction onward, obliterating everything within the swathe of fire.

5

The napalm cannisters exploded in a parallel line approximately one hundred yards from the shrine, which was instantly enveloped in a 1500-degree heat. Each cannister destroyed an area as large as a football field.

Buddha was scorched the black of eternity. While those closest to the impact points were literally burned to a crisp by the skin-clinging gelatinous fire, those farther back were merely charred to death, with some identifying factors (such as teeth) left behind. Total engulfment was the fate of Pong-yu and the members of her family, who had all been gazing wonderingly at Buddha at the instant of the blast.

The thousands not swept up by the rolling fireball spread in all directions. Of those not fast enough to run (such as the very young and the very elderly) hundreds were trampled to death. As this stampede gained momentum the second wave of U.S. fighter planes began their approach.

With smoke and fire obscuring the approach to the target, the wing commander, as oblivious as his predecessor to the throngs below, gave the command that unloaded an additional twenty-four cannisters "on target."

The resulting fireball enveloped the ammunition works, gutted the ball-bearing factory, and destroyed at least a thousand more lives—many had unwittingly fled in the direction of the war plants. The ammunition stockpiled inside added to the catastrophic result, laying waste to the village and human life.

The ignition systems of the cannisters drove finely divided particles of white phosphorus into the gelatinous substance—particles which burned instantly on contact with oxygen. The phosphorus also produced a dense white smoke, which added to the hellish confusion for those who had survived the first two attacks.

Then a meteorological phenomenon occurred. The raging fires and their skyrocketing temperatures created a vicious draft which sucked away the air. The sucking, in turn, created a high-velocity wind. Changyang Valley became an inferno.

Two minutes remained before the third wave of U.S. fighter planes would appear over the valley, but the holocaust of horror was already at its zenith. The idea of further destruction was unimaginable. For the moment there was only the already-existing purgatory of those who fled in abject terror, seeking a place of safety when no such place existed.

There is a theory that four seconds pass between the enveloping of the body by napalm and the instant of death. It is theorized that the body nerves undergo an ultimate shock which, when transferred to the brain, causes instantaneous madness. Thus, napalm means fire, insanity, then death.

Napalm produces several kinds of casualties, and there were hundreds of every kind scattered on the ground in the moments that remained before the arrival of the third wave.

There were those severely or moderately burned. There were those who had been suffocated—carbon monoxide poisoning—in the airless pockets left by the sucking windstorm. White phosphorus burns scarred countless victims. The wounds smouldered, incessantly eating away at the flesh. Some bodies, with minor burns covering only ten percent of the flesh, were already in the process of dying of kidney failure.

Due to its highly adhesive quality, and prolonged burning time, the napalm left third-degree burns on all those who had been on the periphery of the blasts. Coagulation of muscle, fat, and other deep tissue was in rapid progress. Older people, at least those who had not been trampled in the initial stampede, lay dead—not from severe burns but from cardiovascular collapse.

One man had choked on his own saliva and died without a single indication of a burn or anoxia poisoning. Respiratory failure, shock, fluid loss, and sepsis were other causes of death, or death to come. Those children suffering from anemia wouldn't stand a chance of surviving.

By now several hundred members of the crowd had managed, by sheer panic and an instinct for self-preservation, to reach a series of small, natural caves running along the foothills on the northern side of Changyang Valley. These caves had been heavily fortified during the Chinese Civil War in 1948 but the revolution had moved to climactic victories in other areas. In later years the caves had been turned into playgrounds for the children, or rendezvous points for furtive lovers. Some of these caves were deeply embedded in the hillsides, and the terrorized citizens packed themselves within, thinking they had escaped the holocaust. But there was no hiding place.

The third wave of U.S. fighter planes came equipped with napalm of a different type. While the first two wings had carried standard napalm (that is, pure 100 percent octane combined with a gelatin consisting of the aluminum soaps of cocoanut acids, naphthenic acid, and oleic acid), these planes carried an improved form called Napalm-B, a combination of gasoline, polystyrene and benzene which resulted in a cloudy white, jellylike substance. In essence, it achieved the same result as standard napalm but, thanks to its unique gelatin formation, accomplished it a little more quickly.

So the third wave came, and the cannisters were released, and more of Changyang Valley was consumed in roaring flames. Considerably more. The thousands of casualties caused by the first two fireballs were snuffed out by the third, and thousands of new casualties were created.

The survivors still on their feet assumed the characteristics of a herd of cattle, moving together toward those minute areas of the valley still left untouched, turning left and right, right and left, swirling, wheeling, churning, pivoting, circling, rolling, reversing, swarming, angling, and, in those numerous cases of utter confusion resulting in a loss of direction, retracing their steps back into the raging fires.

Those who did not take refuge in the already-crowded caves sought shelter in the village proper, hiding in cellars or going directly to their own homes, preferring to die in familiar surroundings. The main body of the firestorm burned toward the north, toward the caves, and for a moment the village enjoyed a respite.

Meanwhile, the people in the caves watched as the napalm burned its way nearer, sucking up oxygen in one hundred percent quantities. With a high-velocity wind blowing the toxic gases directly into the caves, there was no chance for survival. What was thought to be a natural protection turned into a deathtrap. Hot wind and radiant heat swept through the carbon monoxide interiors, causing the

8

corpses to become dehydrated immediately. During the fire bombings of World War II, in Hamburg and Dresden, the Germans called this the *Bombenbrand-schrumpfleichen*—"incendiary-bomb-shrunken bodies."

The hot winds continued to blow and the bodies continued to shrink, the carbon monoxide concentration in the collapsed lungs climbing as high as 95 percent.

The fourth and final wave of U.S. fighter planes delivered the *coup de grâce* to the ammunition factory—a load of bombs, discharged at low altitude, leveled the plant to rubble. Some of the pilots, seeing that the destruction of the factories was now complete, turned on the nearby village. What the fire-bombing had missed, the explosives now flattened with a certain punctuation of finality. Those who had sought refuge in their own houses now remained there, dead eyes staring at familiar settings.

The fires continued to burn for the night and half the next day. On the field, as if by some miracle, not a single Chinese resident of the valley suffered. All the bodies lay stiffened in sometimes-peaceful, sometimes-grotesque positions. Some faces were black cinder ovals, others were horribly blistered. Some faces had no visible fire damage at all. Three bodies had bullet holes in their foreheads—these men had been cool-headed enough to shoot themselves.

In the rubble of the hut where Pong-yu had once dwelled, there was a movement.

Out of a shattered cage, its bottom lined with the latest edition of the *Peking People's Newspaper*, waddled a mallard duck named Cherry Blossom Rose, quacking for some kind of recognition.

Cherry Blossom Rose moved forward steadily, toward the front yard where it was accustomed to playing, kicking off the sacred bandage which enwrapped its webbed foot.

The once-mangled foot of Cherry Blossom Rose was mangled no more. Pong-yu's prayer had been answered.

2
Squad C-323 Closes Fast

The scent of Chinese hung as heavy as jasmine, but not nearly as sweet, as Squad C-323 continued its infiltration. The spoor was not to be found on the earth—a slight updraft had seen to that—and King Kong's osmatic process recorded a reek. It was like suddenly being isolated in the midst of a garlic and onion patch. His stomach tightened and grumbling acidically, threatened to turn over, but the musky malodor was dispelled by a gust of wind. He felt he could breathe again.

The Squad continued as staunchly as possible, through portions of the lingering fetid residue, but King Kong could see there was a certain lagging of their step. When you went up against the foulest smell of all, Man, your heart could hardly be entirely in your work.

But he had chosen his approach with caution and not comfort in mind, first by sniffing the air (before it had become so contaminated near the rice flat), then by holding up one finger to check wind direction. As far as being detected (except by aerial observation), it was a foolproof approach.

With the top of the hummock only yards away, he signaled the Squad to stop by thumping his foot twice.

They waited as Bonzo dutifully crept through the grass, refusing to brush away a swarm of flies which whipped around his face and droned across the surface of his neck for fear his flailing arms might be outlined against the edge of the hilltop. Bonzo returned a few moments later, and King Kong knew by the simple nod of his head that their pursuit was nearing an end.

With another thump of King Kong's foot, positions were taken, attack formation. Kong, flushed with anticipation at the same time he was semi-nauseous from the climb and the smell, remained dead center along the perimeter. His unblinking eyes peered over the top of the grass.

To his immediate right was his second in command, Konga, who as usual showed no expression and no reaction to the situation—mainly due to his anosmatic condition, brought about by a defect at birth. Being incapable of smell might be considered a handicap to some, but Konga had proved his worth in obedience and full dedication. Because these commodities were too often lacking in the others, Konga was worth ten sharp-noses any day.

Next to Konga, seemingly ensconced in a bed of grass, but actually ready to leap from it at a moment's thump, rested Sergeant Joe Young. The most rebellious of the lot, and therefore the most unpredictable, his expression was an eternal scowl, which King Kong sometimes found unnerving, but it was a scowl that had frozen the marrow of many men and simplified the Squad's task. His body was covered with splotches of mud and so was his foodpack. As usual, Sergeant Joe Young had been careless during the ascent.

To Kong's immediate left was Son, who kept pounding his long, thin fingers against the lower part of his face for no apparent reason—at least to Kong. But then understanding one's own offspring has always been an impossible task, and Kong thought instead about how he had sired Son with considerably more foot-stomping and flea-picking than he had ever experienced before—or since.

Bonzo, the fifth and final member of Squad C-323, noiselessly took in deep gulps of air as, with his left hand, he picked tics and lice from his armpit. Whatever he found he popped into his mouth and enjoyed as if they were delicacies. It was good not to waste even the smallest morsel, as the foodpacks were never as filled as King Kong would like them to be.

It was now time for King Kong to move forward slowly, just far enough to see the targets. He hunched low in the grass, as the figures below moved in a strange ritualistic fashion. A multicolored object was being attached to a pole in the center of a clearing, and a single file of men raised their weapons to fire at something in the air, although even King Kong could see there was nothing in the air above them. There was nothing unusual about a senseless act. It was similar to many actions he had observed men perform. After a while, King Kong simply forgot about certain inconsistencies, and concentrated intently on the job at hand, as he had been trained.

King Kong moved back surreptitiously, dragging his long arms along the ground as he went. He took his place once again in the attack formation.

Then he thumped his foot three times.

The time for flea-picking and shit-rolling was over.

3
The Lull Before
The Onslaught of C-323

Lieutenant Commander Ju-Chao, assistant to the Commander-in-Chief of the 320th Field Army of the Chinese People's Liberation Army; bearer of the Military Hero's Decoration for his heroism on Pork Chop Hill in 1953; recipient of the Commemoration Badge of the Chinese Communist Republic; author of *Fulfillment of the Role of the Average Soldier During the Coming War Against Imperialism* (1961) and its sequel *The Dragon's Fire Upon the Footpath of the Invaders* (1975); co-author of the 1949 Chinese Republic film release *Victory of the Chinese People* (subtitled *How the Hordes of Chiang Kai-shek Withered Under the Resistance of the Common Farmer*); graduate of the East China Military Political Academy in Nanking; instructor for three years at the famed Whampoa Military Academy; a survivor of the historic "Long March" in 1936; one of the "waders of the Yangtze" during the Second Field Army's Liberation of Tibet in the freezing winter of 1949–50; associate member of the Revolutionary Military Council, Central People's Committee and now-defunct Central Committee; designer of a three-mile section of the Trans-Siberian Highway; attendee of the National Conference of Militia Cadres in Peking in

13

1950; alleged utterer of the now-famous expression "If you have ammunition and want to practice, shoot at either the enemy or stray peasants"; a firm believer in the importance of maneuver and deception (he still carried a copy of *The General Principles of Army Group Tactics,* published September 1947, by Lin Piao's Manchurian Democratic Combine Army Headquarters, to prove it); and father of three children whom he had not seen for thirty years, began to feel a creaking in his bones.

While he firmly believed in the strategist Sun Tzu, and had faithfully read his *Art of War,* which emphasized the simple axiom that "all warfare is based on deception," Lieutenant Commander Ju-Chao had never quite managed to deceive himself about his old age.

He avoided peering into mirrors as much as he could, although this made shaving difficult, especially since the order from Peking had drifted down that hereafter any field officer caught using an electric razor would be shot on the spot as a traitor. So, he had returned to using the hoary straight razor he had carried with him since the crossing of the Yangtze under the command of General Liu Po-cheng with the Central Plains Liberation Army. His years had not been helped by the nearly fatal liver fluke which he had suffered after unintentionally swallowing several mouthfuls of polluted water off Shanghai during the one and only time the Chinese Army had attempted amphibious maneuvers. (His refurbished LST, confiscated from the Nationalists in 1947, had sprung a leak in midoperation and went down with all but himself and three hands.) Nor had he been helped by the athlete's foot he had developed during the campaigns in South China (doctors had said it had something to do with the change of climate, but all he knew for certain was that his once-hardened feet, the result of years of steady marching and regimentation, had softened like melted butter and turned spongy from the fungus).

Ju-Chao patted his copy of *The General Principles of Army Group Tactics,* shifted around the cloth sling he wore draped over one shoulder and under the other (the sling contained rice ration, chopsticks, a cleaning cloth and a few meager toilet items: rancid toothbrush, tooth

14

powder, a tube of cream for chapped lips and several old laundry stubs), and snapped his special detachment to attention.

The Lieutenant Commander, feeling tired after the short hike over the hummock, and wearied by the thought of growing older, signaled the banner bearers. They trotted quickly from the ranks, each holding a corner of the swallow-tailed flag which bore the acreage of red in which rested the single star that had come to represent a population of more millions than could be counted.

In the middle of the clearing, they attached the flag to the pole set into a thin concrete square. Beneath this marker were the remains of Cheng Lu, his compatriot on the Long March in 1936 who had become one of the leading battle commanders in the Korean War. He had been buried here at his own personal request on the day an American bullet had claimed him. Ju-Chao could not help but think of him as a friend and battlefield associate, and for a moment felt maudlin about the fact that Cheng Lu had been buried in the exact spot where the Long March had begun. Mao Tse-tung had decreed that a flag be raised over the burial site on each anniversary of his death. Each year, without fail, Ju-Chao had commanded the detachment which conducted commemorative services. Over the years, Cheng Lu's loyal followers and family had died, until now there was only Ju-Chao and a handful of indifferent men to raise the flag and fire a salvo in Cheng Lu's memory.

With a harsh, hoarse cough he cleared his larynx, tried to control the croupous breathing resulting from the uphill climb, and launched into the words he knew by heart, and which he recited every year with the same emotional inflections:

"People's Republic. I like the sound of the words. They mean that the People of Liberated China can live for the Party, talk for the Party, die for the Party—knowing they are living, talking, and dying with honor. Go or come, buy or sell, be drunk or sober, however they choose, as long as it's in keeping with Party policy and doesn't infringe on the rights of others and if those rights are infringed upon, then those who misuse the power to buy or sell, go or come, be

15

drunk or sober, should be deprived of those rights for the good of all. Republic is one of those words which makes me tight in the uvula ... the same intense feeling a man gets when his baby has his first erection, or picks up his first scale-model T-34 tank or reaches out to rip the robe off a lovely peasant woman who has not yet turned wrinkly from toil in the fields and the back-stooping harvesting of rice crops, or gets drunk on Kaoliang with his entire platoon and staggers back to the barracks in darkness, not being able to see in that darkness, but through instinct and self-control finding the way nevertheless. Some words give you a feeling that makes your heart as warm as a tea kettle, or as full as a foodpack should be but never is. Republic is one of those words that puts a lump right in your ..."

It was at that moment Squad C-323 began its attack, and Lieutenant Commander Ju-Chao, of the 320th Field Army of the Chinese People's Liberation Army, was never to get the opportunity to finish his glowing tribute to Cheng Lu, who had mouldered away to nothingness too long ago for even the worms to remember.

4

The Hairy Onslaught
vs. The Ochre Horde

Private Ling Lu, of the People's Liberation Army, was the soldier standing nearest to the hillside, and therefore was first to catch a sign of movement from the corner of his eye. It was the kind of movement a signalman makes from the bridge of a ship with flags; somehow Ling Lu knew that such a movement was not apropos of a barren hillside. Years of obedient training had taught him never to shift his focus while standing at attention (especially during a solemn ceremony dedicated to the dead), but he chanced a split-second infringement to squint toward the hillside. As he did so, he was reminded that a sidewise glance implied sinister intentions, and he remembered an ancient saying: "When the eye looks askance, the heart is askew."

By then it was too late to react.

The hairy arm which moved to strike him was strangely out of proportion for a human arm—that is, the forearm was exceptionally longer than the upper arm, and the fingers, too beefy to be human, were long and slender, ending in dark brown nails. The arm moved toward Ling Lu. Now that he had broken ranks in a disgraceful fashion by turning his entire body to the right, he saw a pair of equally hairy feet swinging toward him at an incredible speed. He was sloe-eyed with fear.

What was so startling about the feet were the great toes—large, strong, opposable, and webbed. Ling Lu had only a split second more to see the distinguishing features of his attacker. Face: white, with frecklelike pigmented spots; protuberant lips revealing a prognathous jaw and conspicuous teeth; nostrils opening downward; large expressive brown eyes; sparse short white hairs, beard-like on the lower part of the face. Body: stout, heavy, covered with coarse dark hair.

This is what Ling Lu saw before the feet crunched two ribs in his chest and the dark brown fingernails began to sink into his face, penetrating the skin by at least a quarter of an inch.

The attacker went to work on Ling Lu in a thoroughly proficient fashion, and from the bottom worked over the ochre uniform and the 135 pounds of flesh within it. The small field cap was torn to shreds and discarded. The other hand gouged out Ling Lu's left eye, broke his nose, smashed fifteen out of twenty-four remaining teeth, ripped open the agape lips and with one fingernail succeeded in slicing open the ammunition belt which draped Ling Lu's body. The cloth sling (worn in lieu of a pack) was similarly ripped open, and its contents of rice ration, chopsticks, and one drying chicken breast bone fell to the ground. The fingernails now clawed open the fatigue jacket, exposing bare skin, which was also clawed open. The rice bowl with matching cloth cover fell away, rolling toward the next man in the formation, who was just beginning to turn his head to see what was happening. The goatskin belt that held Ling Lu's filthy trousers in place was yanked through its loops in a single motion, and the pants fell around his rope-sole slippers and wrapped leggings.

While the attacker's bare feet pounded on Ling Lu's chest, crushing assorted internal organs and doing considerable damage to the large intestine, his hands went to work on the midsection, slapping the area of the groin repeatedly. By now Ling Lu was experiencing such strong pain he felt nothing extra special about the repeated slapping. The cartilage in Ling Lu's left knee was shattered

18

with a single blow (which could have been called "lighter" than some of the previous blows). There was a cracking sound somewhere below the knee in the region of the tibia.

Before Ling Lu went down, the final insult he endured was a playful stomping of his toes by the feet of the attacker. All ten digits were broken. As he settled into what seemed to him a slow-motion spiral, Ling Lu's last glimpse of his attacker centered on the ring of its anal region, surrounded by a tuft of long, closely set white hairs, and touched with flecks of feces. Those flecks glistened as the attacker angled so that they reflected the sunlight.

That is what happened during the last five seconds of Ling Lu's life. There had been time for only one coherent thought: *Cha-Chi*. Evil Spirits.

As Ling Lu dropped, his formerly sloe-eyes now strangely exophthalmic (for they were hanging at a right angle to their sockets), Lieutenant Commander Ju-Chao evaluated the situation. He realized he was doomed and wasted no time in sprinting toward the flagpole. The formation of men was already a confusion of ragged ochre uniforms becoming more ragged and human bodies being ripped from pate to toe and flailing, bashing arms and legs of brown, black, and red.

It was the hairiest onslaught Ju-Chao had ever seen.

It is difficult to know what oftentimes enables men to perform the impossible. How a ninety-pound mother can lift a thousand-pound car when it is pinning her screaming little daughter beneath ... or how wounded men can scramble up mountainsides or steep slopes, without the aid of anything but the will to stay alive.

Or how, at this very moment, Ju-Chao scrambled up that pole, even though there was nothing on its gleaming, well-polished and rounded surface to which he could cling. Yet scramble he did, higher and higher, while below, the hairy onslaught made mincemeat of the detachment.

King Kong and Son of Kong, in the middle of the foray, flung aside crushed caps, slashed ammo slings, gashed foodsacks, and fingers torn from their sockets. It had taken Squad C-323 less than thirty seconds to dispose of the rifle-carrying detachment, and not a single shot had been fired, nor had a voice been lifted in warning or anger.

Already Bonzo had turned his attention on the flagpole. He stood at its base, looking puzzled at its shiny surface, and felt it with all his fingers, as if touch might provide him with an answer. King Kong and Son of Kong joined him and also stared at the pole. High above, where the flag flapped against his face when the wind was just right, Ju-Chao clung desperately, knowing that if he started to slide he would have no way of stopping himself from riding the pole like a fireman all the way to the ground—where a fate worse than death awaited him. Perhaps it was this thought that enabled him to cling with arms and legs as he had never clung before, and maintain his grip.

Squad C-323 had been trained to hit and run, and had been rehearsed in all phases of (1) blitzkrieg, (2) dragonnade, (3) incursion (which was related to the dragonnade in its rapidity and devastation), (4) irruption, (5) onslaught (in which they had just partaken), (6) razzia, (7) sortie, (8) thrust and (9) running amok in a controlled manner. But Squad C-323 was not prepared for the waiting that often went with stalemated actions or trench warfare, nor did it have the patience for a siege that might take hours to complete. Therefore, King Kong, satisfied with having wiped out the rifle detachment, if not its commanding officer, gave the signal for the Squad to retire into the hills. This difficult decision left in King Kong's mouth a severely bad taste. He was not used to permitting survivors to get away so easily (there he was buttocks staring down at them, only yards away; yet there was no inhuman way to climb that pole), and he swore a vendetta against this officer, studying the features of his face carefully before retiring with the others into the tall grass.

After night fell, and he was certain that the attackers would not return, Ju-Chao decided to slide to the ground.

But he could not.

No matter how hard he tried, he could force neither legs nor arms to move. They had become rigidly locked into position. A stronger force than he could muster would be needed to remove him from the pole. Thus he waited until the middle of the morning before a patrol, curious to find out why Ju-Chao and his special detachment had not returned on schedule to the bivouac area, arrived at Cheng Lu's burial site.

With the help of a ten-foot ladder (which entailed two more hours of waiting), Ju-Chao was finally brought to the ground, but not before the combined strength of two men had unwrapped each arm and leg from the slick flagpole.

As he stood on the ground, humiliated to the quick as only a Chinese military officer can be, he vowed a personal vendetta against the attacker he knew to be their leader. Even in as large a republic as China he would, one day, be certain to cross paths with him. Ju-Chao cursed and inwardly wept over the loss of his men and repeatedly swore vengeance. . . .

5

New Pentagon Experiment
Reveals Roving Death Squad
Fiercest of Killers;
Chinese Cry "Uncle"

(*The following is reprinted, with permission of the publisher, from the news review section of This Earth magazine of the* San Francisco Enterprise.)

by Joel Downie Demorest

Over the years it has been given many names: Chimpansee, Anthropopithecus, Simia, Hylanthropus, Chimpanza, Pseudanthropos, Engeco, Tschego, Pan, Troglodytes, Mimetes, Theranthropus, Pongo, Palaeopithecus, Satyrus.

Last week a new name was added: Killeranthropus.

For it finally became a commonly accepted fact that the chimpanzee is the fiercest killer on the face of the earth. Yet it took this simple, inarguable fact many years to emerge from a morass of wrong turnings, misconceptions, false imagery, and out-and-out lying.

Anthropologists who originally studied the various species of chimpanzees at the turn of the century can hardly be held to blame, since their findings gave warning that the chimp was a natural-born fighter, capable of inflicting grievous wounds so quickly as to induce shock with injury.

William T. Hornaday, writing in *Minds and Manners of Wild Animals* in 1922, observed certain unusual temperamental and dispositional characters of the captive chimpanzee: "Except when quite young, the chimpanzee is either nervous or hysterical. After six years of age it is irritable and difficult to manage. After seven years ... it is rough, domineering, and dangerous. The male is given to shouting, yelling, shrieking, and roaring, and when quite angry rages like a demon. I know of no wild animal that is more dangerous per pound than a male chimpanzee over eight years of age ... when they reach maturity, grow big of arm and shoulder, and masterfully strong, they quickly become conscious of their strength. It is then that performing chimpanzees become unruly, fly into sudden fits of temper, their back hair bristles up, they stamp violently, and sometimes leap into a terrorized orchestra."

PAPER BAG BASH

Robert M. Yerkes, professor of psychobiology at Yale University, wrote in 1929 that "it is a well-authenticated fact that the chimpanzee resents being laughed at and is occasionally observed to retaliate or take revenge against men or other animals who laugh at it." Yerkes goes on to record an incident in which a chimpanzee, after being given an empty paper bag which it expected to contain food, promptly bashed the individual proffering the sack.

Professor Wilhelm van Strenberg of the Heidelberg Institute summed up his observations of chimpanzees over a two-year period by remarking, as he sold his only specimen to the Stuttgart Zoo, "You can keep the little sonofabitch with my blessings. The hairy monster has bitten me on the thumb for the last time." Even more succinct is John R. Roddenberry, who was heard to exclaim, on exiting from a cage with blood pouring from lacerations and a scalp wound that required seven stitches, "Chimpanzees are little s——ts."

PUTTING THE BITE ON

Despite these early warnings of anthropologists, and ample evidence that the average chimpanzee could be turned into an unbeatable killer, the pseudo-domestic nature of the animal led many to believe if better suited for zoos, sideshows and other innocuous enterprises.

Exploited were the superficial aspects of the chimp: its cuteness; its ability to ape the actions of humans when well-trained; its expressions of love. Thus began the dormant period—when the true nature of the chimpanzee, whether of the white-faced, black-faced, or bald-faced species, became lost to mankind.

The false image of the chimp was reinforced greatly in the 1920s with the full realization of motion pictures and their use of "cute" chimps as film stars. Many a human actor came to know the true personality of these beasts when they ran amok, or nipped or clawed a human arm or leg. But so as not to spoil the illusion of film, these performers only contributed to the conspiracy of silence.

BACK TO THE JUNGLE

The advent of talking pictures by the 1930s only intensified the cuteness of the chimpanzee, enabling him to chatter and squeak and reply to human questions with an animalistic voice. "Isn't that cute?" became the general moviegoer's opinion.

Jungle films became a popular showcase for the chimp—Tarzan's constant companion was Cheetah. When long-time Tarzan Johnny Weissmuller retired from the role, he soon reappeared as Jungle Jim (1948–54), with Cheetah renamed Kimba, who played with loaded revolvers, pith helmets, and the snouts of crocodiles. If Kimba had turned one of those pistols on Weissmuller, things might have started happening quicker.

Comedies also became a common genre in which to find the chimpanzee. Howard Hawks's *Monkey Business* (1952) starred a chimp who accidentally mixed a formula that restored youthful attitudes and postures to tiring

24

bodies. The Bonzo series from Universal-International depicted the alleged home life of the chimp. It was cardboard caricature, to say the least, to see Bonzo running away from Ronald Reagen, apparently because he felt the home situation too taxing.

TICKS, LICE, FLEAS

In 1971–72, when it appeared television was finally presenting situation comedies which reflected the more pertinent problems of American life (e.g., "Way Out With the Winstons," "Up America!") there emerged a tremendous setback: "The Chump and the Chimp," which depicted, in humdrum fashion, a chimp residing in the home of an absentminded geologist.

The sit com never even attempted to reveal the coprophagous nature or documented habits of the chimp, eschewing such timely themes as toilet training, the throwing of waste products when the toilet training failed (which it always does), lousy table manners, the ticks, lice, and fleas which frequent the hairy body, obscene gestures to passersby, and the out-and-out bashing of humans. So while humans were finally being presented in a truer light in such fare as "All in the Family," the chimp was being mollified and falsified more than ever before.

CARNIVAL BREECH

If any one man can be praised for undoing the damage of the media, he is Noah B. Pugilistian, creator of Noah's Nuances & Nuisances (later changed to Noah and the Mark). This was a carnival act touring with Amusements and Pastimes Unlimited. Originally Pugilistian operated a thirty-two animal exhibit, which included a stubborn chimp who adamantly refused, one memorable night, to climb into his cage. One of the "marks" hinted, in somewhat broad terms, that Noah didn't know his job, and volunteered to put "that brown bastard" into the cage for him. But . . . in a

25

matter of seconds, the chimp made mincemeat of the mark. The clothing was ripped from his body, his face and arms were clawed and his head was pounded numerous times against the ground. Noah immediately sensed the gallery was loving the "performance," and this gave birth to the commercialization of Noah and the Mark. Over the next few years, Noah refined wrestling between humans and chimps, and became so knowledgeable that anthropologists often sought his opinions.

"MONKEY SUIT"

Other carnivals followed "the monkey suit" by introducing similar acts into their attractions. One entrepreneur, a Portuguese carnie named Anthony Pinsaretta, refined the details by adding pompous European pageantry and exotic costuming. This, coupled with his charm, good wit, and aristocratic manners, led to his act being presented on a national network special, "The Sideshows of America," which dealt with the bizarre and the extraordinary aspects of America's portable boardwalks.

In no time, Pinsaretta was spotlighted on a summer variety series à la Ed Sullivan. It was a natural step to the late-night talk shows, where millions now saw the true side of the species. First reaction was the cancellation of a Saturday morning children's TV series which showcased chimps in the roles of secret agents. The network claimed it no longer could cast chimps in anything but believable character parts. No sooner had this news appeared in *Variety* when one of the major networks declared it was reviving a science-fiction series in which English-speaking chimpanzees, gorillas, orangutans, and other anthropoids portrayed ferocious inhabitants of a futuristic society. This revival was an astounding success at the box office.

TRANSFORMATION

Almost overnight, the image of the chimp was altered. With the public now exposed to new concepts, it became apparent the animal could never again be regarded as a harmless household pet.

To provide a suitable framework of violence and mayhem for the true nature of the chimp, several films were released; *Legs Chimp, Bullets, Babes, and Bananas, Aping* and *The Wild Simba Bunch.* One TV series featured a masked hero who subdued villains with the use of a smog gun; his sidekick was a chimp who employed forms of Oriental self-defense to protect his master.

ANCESTRAL BACKGROUND?

A major problem existed that no amount of training could overcome. Celluloid chimpanzee violence could never be simulated. If an actor wanted a chimp to bite or hit him, he had to endure the dangers of going through with an actual attack. There was no way to fake it, and casualty rates tended to be heavy—almost always among the humans.

Finally, after only three years of super-realistic cinema and TV, the Office of the Surgeon General released a report ("The Effect of Excessive Violence on the Young as Practiced by the Sadistic Chimpanzee") showing how youngsters in the four-to-eight age group were beginning to demonstrate strange characteristics; leg thumping; excreting in the streets; throwing banana peels on the sidewalk, spitting at passersby on street corners, and leaping up and down in public places and on car-infested freeways.

IMAGE GONE SOUR

This new form of violence, according to one anthropologist, was further proof of man's ancestral background, which only now TV was liberating. This was met with stiff opposition from organized religion, which in turn (with the added support of parent-teacher organizations) applied heavy pressure on Hollywood and the major networks to dump their "new ape image" products. Thus ended the

27

period when members of the ape family were accurately depicted in motion pictures and on television.

And the chimp, who endured all this without as much as a whimper, was once again proclaimed a domesticated animal. Strangely enough, TV from this point on eschewed the theme of chimpanzees, with one network president remarking: "Nielsens are down when the little beggars are on." But what was really down was the love of chimp. America, it seemed, had had it with the little hairy ones. You could call a chimp a sonofabitch again without getting punched in the nose.

PENTAGON DESIGNS

Men with brass on their shoulders, laboring secretly behind MP-guarded doors in the Pentagon, had other intentions in mind for the chimpanzee. Operation Brown Coat required a top-secret security clearance, and for a one-year period only three men (in addition to the President) knew of what was about to turn into the strangest military plane of the twentieth century.

One of those three men, General Howard T. Stepmann, recalled recently how the thinking behind Operation Brown Coat first began. "Our commanding officer, a three-star general, who has since passed on to his reward in the Battle of Shanghai, and whose honor I respect enough not to mention his name, was a fanatic TV watcher." This officer, claims Stepmann, spent every spare minute in front of the box.

SATURDAY A.M. CONFUSION

"He especially enjoyed sporting events," recalls Stepmann, "and one morning he saw a duel to the death between two chimps. It was a regular Saturday morning feature, as I recall. Anyway, the General chanced to say to his wife, as one chimp was lambasting the other, 'I bet those creatures would make one helluva fighting platoon.' Replied his wife: 'You've been training men for years who showed as much sense as a pack of chimpanzees. Why don't you try and see if it works.' Well, that's all it took for the General to start thinking seriously about using chimps as soldiers. But with all the hoopla about apes then going on, he allowed the idea to moulder. Finally, when the stinko about chimps quieted down, and those Saturday morning bouts were only history, Lieutenant Colonel Howie Morton and I were brought in as coordinating assistants."

MOJAVE MANEUVERS

The three-man team of Operation Brown Coat had the seemingly simple task of coordinating the housing and training of an experimental platoon of chimpanzees. Colonel Stepmann's first job was to find the chimps, which he did by scouring carnivals, sideshows and the Hollywood Home for Retired Animal Performers. Once the cream of chimphood had been located, it was gathered secretly in a Army camp in the Mojave Desert under Stepmann's command. (Earlier findings had suggested an indigenous campsite in Tanganyika, but it was decided to simulate rough terrain and hazardous conditions foreign to the chimp as part of the training program.)

DOWNWIND

Stepmann recalls that the most difficult problem during this period in the training program was producing sufficient quantities of Oriental smell. "The olfactory nature of the chimpanzee is such that you've got to really lay it on if you expect the animal to respond. This was accomplished only after our staff went through the painstaking task of rounding up a number of Chinese POW's from the Peninsula Campaign and herding them into an enclosure located a short distance from the training grounds. We then forced the POW's to attack the chimps with clubs (made of plastic, to curtail the possibility of injury) while the animals were chained to posts."

RANK RUMORS

After five days every chimp undergoing training would automatically attack a Chinese if he came within smelling range. (Rumors still persist that some Chinese were sacrificed to give the chimps a chance to demonstrate their ferocity under the best of circumstances, but on this point the Pentagon has remained silent.)

One month ago yesterday, the first special detachment of Chimps, designated Squad C-323, was assigned to rove the Middle Yantgze Plain area, seeking out and destroying the enemy.

Within just two weeks, reports began filtering back that C-323 was doing its job only too well. Huge Chinese formations, organized to infiltrate American lines, were found decimated. Their bodies and equipment littered the landscape of war (see the cover of *This Earth* for a look at the devastation, mayhem, destruction, bestiality, and stomach-churning results.)

CHIMPS ARE CHAMPS

And last week, Army Command reported that C-323 had struck fear into the hearts of the entire People's Liberation Army with such demoralizing power that other roving chimp squads were being prepared.

"From here on out," said Field Commander Arthur L. Connolly, Third Battalion, Sixth Regiment, Ninth Battle Group, "those chimps are going to be tearing up everything they can lay their grubby mitts on between here and Peking."

6
Sarge Meditates:
An Introduction

On the old Khing-lu Trail, which lies between Changsha and Nanchung, in the South Yangtze Hills bordering on the northern edge of the Middle Yangtze Plain, there is an old signpost which provides mileages to both Changsha and Nanchung. A few yards from this signpost is an old dried-up, nameless creek, the left bank of which faces onto the Tung-t'ing and P'o-Yang basins.

Resting against the left bank was a soldier, his bloodshot, glazed eyes peering over the ledge of the bank. The eyes were shielded from the burning sun by the shadow of his steel helmet, well-dented and pocked by the shrapnel of war.

Minutes passed. The soldier continued to gaze out across the open fields, searching for a movement other than the wind through high-standing stalks of grass. During this period, only the slits of his eyes showed the slightest sign of movement.

Then the lips of his mouth parted with the speed of a striking cobra and a volley of tobacco juice emerged. This volley traveled unhindered for well over four feet, then splattered into a day-old pile of cow manure.

The man pressed against the river bank was Sarge. If he

had a name it was not known to his men, nor to his commanding officer. As far back as anyone could remember he had been called only Sarge, and nobody wondered about or questioned the appellation. If he had an identification card, he never bothered to show it, and he never spoke specifically about a hometown, a family or wife—if indeed he had any of these things, and it was assumed he did not.

Crisscrossing Sarge's chest was an interwoven network of holsters, each of a different shape and size, each snapped shut. Various kinds of ammunition, some of which the men in his platoon had never seen before, were inserted into the loops of the bandoliers to which the holsters were attached. Strapped to his waist was a standard Army issue .45 pistol. Few of his men had seen Sarge use it, but most knew of the deadly accuracy of his aim.

His uniform was ill-kempt and baggy, and judging from the several layers of dirt and grime one could count through, it had not been cleaned in some time. The fatigue pants and jacket were bespeckled with tears and cuts. Perspiration stains blended in to the shade of the rest of the material. Several dirty, sloppily affixed patches around the knees indicated Sarge was poor with a needle.

While Sarge's eyes were protected from the sun by the shade from the helmet's tip, his face continued to absorb the rays, as it had absorbed them uncomplainingly for years. Call that countenance time-beaten and battle-beaten, yes; as simple a description as weather-beaten would have been an injustice. His chin was grizzled with a tangled mass of reddish hair, and as often as the sun had tried, it had yet to bleach it, or change a single unit of protein. This same reddish hair extended to the interior of his nostrils, from which thin hairs attempted to sprout. The almost bulbous nose made Sarge seem larger than he really was. His lips were puffy and chapped, and were a wet sponge to moisten them, they would continue to look puffy and chapped. Those lips were an unchangeable feature.

But it was Sarge's eyes which remained his distinguishing feature.

To stare into those bloodshot, burning eyes was to stare into the well of warfare. To penetrate into centuries of military campaigns, frontline combat, and two-fisted tales of the battlefield. One who stared long enough saw the toil and the misery and the death that went with the campaigning, and if one went a layer deeper one could also see the humor, whoring and general debauchery that was the soldier's wont between wars.

The color of Sarge's eyes had originally—at birth and soon after—been blue. In his boyhood they had changed to a shade of hazel, and later, at the height of his apprenticeship as a soldier, aged 18, they had become an amber color. In more recent years the amber had given way to a steely gunmetal gray, almost the color of an overcast, somber day, and there was a certain coldness, almost a frigidity, that made you want to shiver if you stared at them for any length of time. There was every indication that the gray was becoming bespeckled with dots of pure black, and it was only a matter of time before those dots floating amidst the irises would take over completely. You could tell that by staring for only a moment.

Sarge's ears protruded from his head at almost ridiculous angles; on the average man such a binotic condition would have produced laughter. In Sarge's case the contours of his steel helmet only lent his heavy head a peculiar symmetry. His tangly hair also helped in this regard. The surface of the ears was heavily calloused and the lobes were flopping masses of flesh. Many sounds had penetrated those eardrums, and what blended together within was the music of warfare. A cacophonous symphony of screams mingled with grunts of pleasure; groans amalgamated with the tearing of gingham material; victory songs mixed with defeat chants; ballads of death commingled with paeans of triumph; indoctrination speeches interspersed with eulogies and graveside benedictions; blasphemy, cursing and profanity fused with profanity, sacrilege, and irreverence.

Sarge's eyes and ears spoke of a history which was neither all pleasure nor all pain, and which was often as immoral as it was moral. He was capable of a rare objectivity on a subject most men found joyously sadistic and demoralizing.

It was three P.M. in the afternoon and Sarge, as he rested his body against the river bank, wondered just what in hell had happened to the two men he had sent to forage

33

for food. His stomach growled to remind him of the purpose of the mission, and he turned impatiently to glance at the other man who also rested against the river bank.

Private E-2 Ernest Youngman met Sarge's stare, but not impudently. A blond-haired youth, not yet twenty-four, Youngman projected only inquisitiveness and uncertainty in the looks he gave Sarge. Being lost behind enemy lines for the first time in his career as a soldier had aroused in him a depression that so far had been expressed by nervous glances and ill-phrased questions, to both of which Sarge had paid not the slightest attention. Sarge had been lost under similar circumstances several times before, and he knew it was only a natural part of the footsoldier's role. One had to anticipate setbacks at any time. That way, one would be continually surprised when things went well. But disaster, and defeat, and the unexpected—they were the expected. This outlook at least left room for moments of genuine joy.

Youngman, however, knew nothing of Sarge's philosophy, and even if Sarge had told it to him, the chances of him understanding it were less than slim. There was, Sarge could see, far too much hope in Youngman's face for a situation which was bound to deteriorate before it improved.

So Sarge treated Youngman as if nothing were out of the ordinary. They could have been surrounded by an entire brigade, and he would have acted no differently.

Metal clashed on metal. Wood on wood.

"Keep those damn rifles quiet, Youngman." Sarge swallowed the saliva in his mouth, hoping it would satisfy the rumbling that continued to course through his stomach.

Youngman was trying desperately to keep a grip on the bundle of firearms which he had been carrying for the past two weeks. In addition to his standard M-31 automatic, which he kept separate from the others by slinging it around his shoulder, Youngman was carrying six other weapons:

1. A Marlin model 336 .44 magnum with a Leupold 4X scope fitted with a Redfield Jr. mount, with a hand-carved stock depicting two elk locked in mating rites combat. This sportsman model had been picked up by Sarge on the

Shegona Flat, forty miles west of Shanghai after the First Battle for the Peaks. It had been dropped by a U.S. lieutenant colonel who had been killed by tiny nailshaped darts which had made impact with at least ten square inches of his body and brought about paralytic death due to shock. It was more than the nervous system could stand. With the weapon, Sarge had retrieved five clips of ammunition.

2. A Model 1891 Argentine/Belgian Mauser, designed for the 7.65-mm. Mauser cartridge, complete with an action stamped "Waffenfabrik Mauser," which meant it was made at the Mauser factory prior to 1939, when the Nazis took over and made them with cast and stamped parts with a careless process of heat treatment. This was therefore a collector's item, and the prize find. Youngman had stumbled across it during the Second Battle for the Peaks, just below the lowest Peak, dropped there by the commander of an Israeli company which had been wiped out to the last man during the first minutes of the battle. There were only a handful of bullets for this rifle, indicating its original owner had carried it for show rather than for practical purposes.

3. A 6.5 Mannlicher-Carcano, the same kind of rifle which had been used in the 1963 assassination of President John F. Kennedy, equipped with a Marlin 3X-9X variable scope and an embroidered sling, inscribed with several foreign words which neither Youngman nor Sarge had yet been able to decipher. It had been dropped by one of the Minutemen Battalions, comprised entirely of volunteers from the Southern States who had been thrown into the breech during the Peninsula Compaign—a maneuver that had resulted in heavy loss of life for both sides, but a triumph for the American Army. With the Mannlicher, Youngman found a large bandolier of ammunition, which made the rifle useful should anything happen to their own weapons. The ammunition consisted of finely split jacket mushrooming slugs: four to six longitudinal saw cuts, each a quarter of an inch long, were made on the sides of the nose, enabling the top of the bullet to separate on impact and mushroom its way forward. Because these bullets could make a hole in a man's chest large enough for an arm to fit through, the 1899 Peace Conference had out-

lawed them. Obviously, a few rules had been overlooked during the ferocity of the Peninsula Campaign.

4. A Russian M-91 7.62 caliber, equipped with nothing more than standard military peepsights and a tattered old sling about to break in at least three places. Sarge was puzzled when he found it on the outskirts of Shanghai in a pulverized village, for the rifle was obsolete by anyone's standards, and ammunition for it hard to come by since World War II. Yet that was why he picked it up—here was a genuine collector's item! The stiffening corpse of its previous owner, a Russian lieutenant from one of the Siberian units which had fought side by side with Sarge's unit, yielded not a single round of ammunition, although Sarge had counted at least fifty empty cases scattered around the body.

5. A Luger Model 1902 carbine 7.65 mm with 11¾ inch barrel, whose receiver markings read: "System Borchardt Patent. Deutsche Waffen—Und Munitionsfabriken Berlin." Those words had sent Sarge into ecstasy, for this was another rare collector's item, produced by DMW prior to being taken over in 1930 by Mauser Werke to supply the Luger to the German Army. Sarge wondered if it was possibly the same kind of Luger Kaiser Wilhelm had found ideal for hunting with his crippled hand. Ammunition on its one-time possessor was plentiful. Youngman had found the weapon because its extra-long barrel had protruded from a pile of debris, and sunlight glinting off its barrel had attracted his eye. Until then, Sarge had carried a Mauser Luger with him. (It had the letter G stamped above the chamber, which meant it had been produced in 1935 in violation of the Versailles Treaty). He now preferred to use the Model 1902 whenever the occasion lent itself to this weapon.

6. A Japanese Model 99 (Arisaka, 1939) 7.7 caliber, with a standard 30-inch barrel. The 180-grain ammunition found with it was not very plentiful, but like the Russian M-91, it was a vintage World War II item. A Bear Cub 4X scope had been knocked loose from the weapon by a mortar blast; its glass was shattered and the mounts bent, and it was discarded by Sarge as worthless. Its original owner had been a brave man, apparently, for several

nese dead surrounded his own corpse, each having been beaten to death by the stock of the Arisaka. The nationality of its owner was unknown, as his face was completely missing.

The six rifles comprised the bunch which Sarge intended to take back with him as souvenirs, and which Youngman had found to be a pain in the ass from the moment he had first found the Argentine/Belgian Mauser. Youngman finally straightened them out so wood did not bang against metal, and returned his attention to the open field before them.

"What do you suppose is keeping those guys, Sarge?" he asked.

"They're wiping their asses," said Sarge. "How do I know what they're doing?"

"What do we do?"

"Stay put. They'll be back."

"What if they don't come back?"

"Then we can figure the bastards got lost again."

"It is a big country," acknowledged Youngman.

"It's these goddamn Chinese valleys," said Sarge. "If you've seen one . . ."

7

Slaker Slacks Off
While Bran Flakes Out

Both Slaker and Bran knew they were overdue, and they
had no difficulty imagining Sarge's growing impatience.
They'd been too long in his platoon.

"It ain't so much because we might be in trouble," said
Bran.

Slaker nodded. "It's his fucking stomach."

"Well," said Bran.

"Well," said Slaker.

They got up and ran.

It was a calculated move, designed to save time, to get
the cans of rations they had discovered in the burned-out
halftrack back to Sarge as quickly as possible. It would
have been safer to wait until dark, or attempt to crawl
through the fields of grass an inch at a time on their bellies,
but Sarge had taught them to do the unexpected, to take
the initiative, and together they had decided even if there
was a Chinese patrol in the area they could be well across
the field before anything might be done to stop them. So,
sucking extra gulps of air into their lungs, they leaped from
a pair of abandoned foxholes and raced through one of the
small valleys of the South Yangtze Hills. It was a risk
lesser men would not have attempted, but they had been

too long under the tutelage of Sarge, and they were willing
to take that risk.

This was unfortunate.

Unknown to Slaker and Bran, Lieutenant Colonel Ju-
Chao had been on patrol in that same area, seeking out
Squad C-323 with a great deal of vengeance in his heart
and stiffness in his bones. Even a rumor at this stage would
have been enough for him to give the command to fire.
The figment of someone's imagination was in immediate
danger of being fired upon.

It was a squad of men more heavily armed than usual,
for Ju-Chao took no chances. He had seen to it that two
men were equipped with a mortar; a box of ammunition
was strapped to the backs of one of the men. All the men
were armed with automatic rifles, and each man had been
given an extra pistol. They were volunteers and understood
their fate should their viligance prove second best. They
had put their affairs in order before leaving. Ju-Chao
delayed the departure of the patrol long enough for each
man to write a fast note to his loved ones.

By three P.M. he ordered the patrol to take a breather
along one of the ridges looking out over the numerous hills
and dales that rolled northward toward the Middle Yangtze
Plain. The mortar team had positioned the weapon, "just in
case," and men with binoculars were sweeping the hillsides
and valleys, on the off chance they just might see something.

The vigilance paid off. Bran and Slaker were sighted
within seconds of their bugging out. Almost in the same
breath, Ju-Chao gave the command to the mortar team,
and the observer had picked his coordinates for the first
shell. That shell was already on its way before Ju-Chao realized that what he had seen was not a pair of animals but
a team of men. Although he realized they were Americans,
and were more than suitable targets, he was nevertheless
gravely disappointed. He had hoped to blast Squad C-323,
not just two men, all over the landscape.

The first shell, having been fired so hastily, blew up a
good fifty yards from Bran and Slaker, and threw up a
shower of grass and dirt, some of which blew into Slaker's
eye, causing him to slow a bit. Bran, on the other hand,

picked up speed, for no sooner had the shell landed than small-arms' fire was coming from the ridge to their right. They'd really jumped into it this time. He heard the whistle of slugs as they streaked past him. In front of him he saw geysers of dirt kicking up. Rather than run into certain death, he fell into the grass and lay there, catching his breath. Slaker immediately fell beside Bran, a bit too stunned to realize a bullet had clipped the sleeve of his fatigue jacket, taking a thin sliver of flesh with it. It hadn't even been deep enough to bleed.

"Our luck's out," gasped Bran, staring at the place where his flesh was missing.

"Bullshit," said Slaker, who never admitted defeat. Even when the patrol had been ambushed, and Hillary and Bronson blown to pieces, and Henderson cut in half by an incendiary shell, he hadn't thought about the possibility of his own death—just the fact that he had concealed himself well enough to avoid exposure to direct fire. And the fact that Sarge was still in one piece. Even though he hated Sarge every time the NCO opened his mouth, or gave an order, he somehow knew that Sarge would always keep him alive. But now Sarge was nowhere in sight, and although he would have refused to admit defeat even if a Chinese trooper was pointing a rifle directly down his throat, Slaker, for the first time in his military life, began to sweat.

Bran, on the other hand, sweated every moment of his military life, and he was sweating profusely now. In a rather bewildered fashion, he asked: "Where the hell are we?"

"What difference does it make?" Slaker was beginning to peer over the tip of the high grass, to see if they could make out anything along the ridge. The enemy fire continued, but apparently the smoke from the mortar blast had obscured them as they fell, and now their position was not known with any degree of accuracy by the gunners, who mowed the grass indiscriminately. Additional mortar shells had dropped into the meadow, but none of them had come close—yet.

"At least then we'd know how far we've got to go," said Bran. "Maybe Sarge'll hear the firing and—"

"If Sarge hears the firing, he knows well enough to stay put. This is our mess, we get outselves out of it."

"It was his stomach."

"Shut up."

"I'd still like to know where we are . . ."

"I'll tell you where we are," said Slaker. "A hair past desolation, and a fraction this side of futility."

Bran tapped Slaker's fieldpack. "We gotta get these rations to Sarge or he's gonna be——"

"We gotta save our own asses right now. Sarge can go dogrobbing for his own damn rations."

"How we gonna do that? How we gonna save our asses?"

"By doing what Sarge told us a thousand times. By keeping 'our young asses' down!"

"It'll take hours to crawl through this stuff."

"You got a better idea?"

"This is one time I say we run for it," said Bran.

Slaker coughed, cleared his throat, and swiped a tick from his forehead. "You saw what happened a few minutes ago when we tried that. They've got this entire field zeroed in."

"Yeah," said Bran, nodding, "and sooner or later one of those bastards is gonna get lucky and spray the shit out of us—or one of those mortar shells is gonna fall right on our heads."

Bran clutched his rifle, got into a kneeling position, and pulled his helmet tightly down onto his head. "Me, I'm gonna make a run for it."

"Now look," said Slaker, "don't you ever see the movies? Everytime some idiot gets up to run, he's the next guy to get killed."

"That's movie bullshit," Bran said indifferently, as he prepared to spring to his feet.

"Jesus Christ. You're really nuts, you know that? Okay, look, do me one favor. Do like Sarge says, 'Keep your young ass down.' " Then Bran was up and running, like only a man who knows it means his life can run.

41

8
The Elevated Asshole:
Scenario #1

FADE IN

1. EXT. FIELD—DAY—DOLLY SHOT—BRAN

   running through the field of grass as if demons were
   pursuing him.

2. EXT. HILLTOP—DAY—TIGHT ANGLE—JUCHAO

   barking orders in Chinese for his men to commence
   fire.

3. WIDE ANGLE—CHINESE SOLDIERS

   as they fire as rapidly as possible.

4. ANOTHER ANGLE—THE MORTAR TEAM

   as one of the men drops a shell into the tube.

5. DOLLY SHOT—BRAN

as all hell erupts behind him. The concussion of the mortar blast stuns him. He staggers, regains his footing, and hurries on. Bullets kick the dust up around him, and clip off stalks of grass. His eyes widen with fright, and Bran drops to the ground, THE CAMERA STOPPING and HOLDING on him.

6. ANOTHER ANGLE—BRAN

trying to hide in the grass, scurrying. But bullets are hitting everywhere around him. He begins to whine like a frightened child, and in trying to burrow his head and shoulders into the ground in the style of an ostrich, he thrusts his buttocks high into the air.

7. TIGHT ANGLE—BRAN'S BUTTOCKS

sticking straight up in the air, offering a superb target.

8. CLOSE SHOT—SLAKER

lying in the grass, reacting;

> SLAKER
> Pull it in, Bran. Pull it in, damn you.

9. ANOTHER ANGLE—BRAN

as a row of slugs chirps across his buttocks, which seems frozen in its lofty position. Pain is etched on his face as Bran screams:

> BRAN
> SSSSSAAAAARRRRRGGGGGEEEEE!!!

> DIRECT CUT TO:

10. EXT. RIVER BANK—DAY—CLOSE UP—SARGE

His face is grim. A cigar is clenched tightly between his teeth. He tips his steel helmet back slightly.

                    SARGE
          I told that boy to keep his young ass
          down.

Disgustedly, Sarge turns AWAY FROM CAMERA and drops OUT OF FRAME.

                                    DIRECT CUT TO:

11. EXT. FIELD—DAY—ANGLE ON SLAKER

as he fires a wild burst of shots at the nearby hillside and rushes toward Bran.

                    SLAKER
     I'm coming, Bran. I'm coming.

12. WIDE ANGLE—CHINESE RIFLEMEN

pouring additional volleys down into the meadow.

13. DOLLY SHOT—SLAKER

racing through the grass, firing sideways at the hillside as he goes.

14. ANOTHER ANGLE—SLAKER

as he approaches the body of Bran. Slaker is hit in midstride. He spins around, collapsing next to Slaker, who is still locked in position, buttocks thrust upward, smoke still drifting up from the row of bullet holes. Slaker pulls himself forward, close enough to throw dirt onto Bran's buttocks. Bullets kick up around both of them, and this time Slaker goes limp for good.

15. TIGHT SHOT—JU-CHAO

satisfied in some ways, disappointed in others.

DIRECT CUT TO:

16. EXT. RIVER BANK—TWO SHOT—SARGE/
YOUNGMAN

YOUNGMAN
I don't think either of those guys is coming
back, Sarge. I think it's just me and you now.

SARGE
I got some Dogface Data for you, Youngman.
Ain't nobody under forty in this theater of
operations who knows how to keep his ass
down—unless he's limping around with an
artificial rump.

YOUNGMAN
I didn't know they made artificial rumps,
Sarge.

SARGE
This is the Corps, Youngman. You lose it, they
replace it. That's progress.

FADE OUT

9

Dogrobbing the Dead

The weapons had changed, and the ways of fighting had changed, but the food ration had not.

The People's Liberation Army had never bothered to revolutionize its thinking about the stomach, assuming that if a man could live on very little during trying times from 1946–53, then there was no reason whatsoever why he couldn't live on that same amount during better times. So it was that the soldier in the People's Liberation Army of China received his traditional two meals a day: 31.2 ounces of rice (in the North, soldiers received millet instead); 1.4 ounces of meat; 10 ounces of vegetables; as much water as needed by the individual; and a small amount of tea, usually equaling two cups per day.

And so it was, as Ju-Chao and his men approached the corpses of Bran and Slaker, that their thoughts were on food. Inevitably, dead Americans yielded a food supply: K-rations, candy bars, chewing gum, etc. And while it would have been considered treason by the commander-in-chief if he knew his men ate the food of the enemy, there was a silent understanding among the men and their field officers that these delicacies from the States could hardly be overlooked. As a precaution Ju-Chao had always been careful to bury the leftover cans and plastic spoons.

One of his men rolled over Bran's corpse with his Manchurian leather shoe. The movement disturbed a clot of blow-flies congregating about a gaping hole in Bran's chest and clinging to the jagged edge of flesh and congealing blood. The flies scattered as the trooper began cleaning out Bran's pockets. What he found he turned over to Ju-Chao immediately: a comb with three broken teeth, a wallet which yielded $7.56, a photograph of a beautiful blonde in a monobikini, a photograph of his brunette wife and two children (one boy, aged four; a girl, aged six), several credit cards that had expired sixteen months earlier, an ID card granting Bran privileges in the Fort Benning, Georgia, PX, and a handful of Chinese coins. Ju-Chao gave the coins to the trooper and pocketed the rest. It would be worth trading with other officers who gathered similar material.

The search for food was rewarded as Slaker's body was stripped, since he had been carrying the fieldpack filled with K-rations taken from the burned-out halftrack. There were six cans in all, and Jo-Chao immediately saw to the dispersal of the food equally among his squad. The combinations consisted of weiners and beans (always a favorite among his men); frankfurters and sauerkraut; Irish stew (featuring new potatoes); Swiss steak in a special wine sauce; Spam, and baked ham with sweet potatoes and pineapple rings. Ju-Chao chose the Swiss steak. When they finished eating, Ju-Chao gave the signal for them to relax for a few more minutes, and after posting guards, they sat on the ground. All but Ju-Chao smoked Kool cigarettes found on both American corpses.

One of the men, Yhang-ye, took off his yenan soft slipper and rubbed his foot, giving special attention to a blister which had begun to form at the base of his big toe.

Ju-Chao took special note of the blister, shaking his head. "You men . . . you have the softness of a hog's skin."

"It's the walking," said Yhang-ye, almost apologetically. "It's too much, sir." Yhang-ye had fought for many months with Ju-Chao, and assumed a familiarity that their common exposure to danger had earned him.

"You dunghead," interjected Chi-yung, the sergeant given the can of baked ham with sweet potatoes and pineapple rings. He too had fought long and hard with Ju-Chao and Yhang-ye, and frequently took certain advantage of that fact to speak his mind. "A Chinese soldier must live on his feet."

"Bah," sneered Yhang-ye. "This is the mechanized age. Let the machines do the walking."

"While you sit at the controls on your ass, which is as wide as the Yangtze River."

"There are no blisters in tanks."

"But you can still fry like an egg of the goose," said Chi-yung. He scraped the final chunks of ham from the bottom of the K-ration can. "I've seen it happen to men in the Russian T-34s."

"Obsolete hunks of tin—sardine can material," said Yhang-ye, continuing to rub his foot.

"The more reason to remain on your feet."

Yhang-ye frowned. "What in the name of a turtle's bottom do you know about feet?"

"I know nothing about feet. The thousands of miles I've walked are inconsequential compared to our lieutenant commander. Ju-Chao has seen feet save many lives."

Both men turned their attention to Ju-Chao, who had remained silent since starting the conversation—an habitual practice in the field, since it gave impetus to others to speak, and helped to pass time that might otherwise slip by in silence.

"It used to be," began Ju-Chao, "that if you passed through a certain area of China, and found all the women in that region making slippers in large quantity, then you knew that the People's Liberation Army was in the vicinity. It was the only way, in the olden days, for the Army to stay supplied with enough shoes for its men. Back in the 1940's . . . it was not uncommon to hear, among the men, a poem, which as I recall was entitled 'Love Thy Feet.' "

Chi-yung picked up the conversation at that point, as if to prove to Yhang-ye he was as knowledgeable as Ju-Chao:

"Very useful is a pair of feet;
   Without us you can't do a damn thing.

48

I am glad to learn we're marching again,
For here comes a chance of rendering service.

"In case you get blisters,
Gently pierce and dry them, applying kerosene,
For Heaven's sake, don't peel blisters;
Bathe them when you camp down
And don't forget to give them credit at summing
up time."

"It doesn't even rhyme," criticized Yhang-ye, who seemed to be paying too much attention to his foot.

"We have lost the proclivity for marching," said Ju-Chao, with some remorse in his voice.

"Wait a minute," said Yhang-ye. "A moment ago this son of a dragon's flea said you know of feet which saved lives."

"Gave purpose to life might better describe it," replied Ju-Chao.

Chi-yung threw his K-ration tin to the private who was already in the process of burying them and directed his words specifically at Yhang-ye: "For the unenlightened among us, he is talking about the Long March."

"I was educated in your country," sneered Yhang-ye. "I've read of the Long March."

This time Chi-yung sneered. "You've read it. My ancestors are impressed as far back as the Sung Dynasty. The point is, Yhang-ye, you have never felt it."

"And you have?"

"Through the words of the Lieutenant Commander, yes."

It was like a signal, and all the men turned to look at Ju-Chao, as if asking him to express those feelings once again. Ju-Chao did not need to look up at their faces to know—he could feel their inquisitiveness and their curiosity. He nodded his head, lit his pipe (which he had taken off a dead American during the Shanghai landings of the winter before), crossed his feet and leaned back.

10
Feet of Clay

In the beginning (narrated Ju-Chao) we marched with great pride and spirit, and our feet did not ache. It did not matter if other men—even comrades—fell by the side of the road. We had a strong, unswerving belief in Mao Tse-tung, the Chairman of the Provisional Government of the Soviet Republic, and in the cause of the First Front Red Army, which in those days was 100,000 men strong. This was when we left Kiangsi in October 1934, the place where the body of Cheng Lu now rests. In our hearts we felt the strength of the 10,000 Greeks who, 2300 years before us, had battled from hostile Persia to the Black Sea. Now we marched and fought to prove that the imperialist Chiang Kai-shek and his Nationalist forces, the Kuomintang, could not destroy us and our manifesto—and that behind us stood 200 million people living in eleven provinces waiting to be liberated by the Red Army.

In the words of our great leader, Mao, we were a seeding machine, and soon our seeds would grow leaves, blossom into flowers, bear fruit and yield a harvest of the future. This we sincerely believed in our hearts, and it was a belief that did not wane in those early days, even when we sustained frightening casualties in our running-and-hitting battles with the Nationalists. Neither hunger nor bitter cold prevented us from finding enough faith to march on. Eating the roots of trees only seemed to strengthen our ideals. For twelve months without letup, without respite, the men of the First Front Red Army were under constant observation and bombing—we were surrounded, chased, hindered and intercepted by thousands of Nationalists, who always succeeded in outnumbering us, but never destroying us.

It has been asked since: Has there ever been, in history, a long march like ours? And it has been answered: Never, never. But what they do not write in the pages of history is the waning and dying of hope that took place during those twelve months and during those six thousand miles of marching, and the strange ways that men, even weaker than I, found new hope and courage before the march came to its end.

There are men who march quicker than others, even in the Chinese Army, which thrives on the heels of its feet. I have often said that toes are what won the cause of the Red Army, but that is after the fact. Among those men who marched at a phenomenal rate was Sun Yat, a man of sixty-five, whose hair was as white as the snow which we often shoveled into our mouths when there was no other source of water. He would easily wear out a pair of rubber-soled shoes every few days, but enough bodies littered the sides of the road that he could take his pick of a new pair at will—at least new in the sense they had never encased his feet before. He would then subject them to a new tempo in walking. This Sun Yat, how he did walk. Oftentimes he would strut far ahead of us, and then pause to rest at sundown. I would continue walking, and stop only when I came to Sun Yat. Usually this involved, on my part, an additional two to three hours of walking a day. Which gives you some idea of just how quickly this Sun Yat could travel. It was phenomenal, and other men, some of whom never finished the Long March, wrote *lu shihs,* poems in eight lines, each of seven characters, dedicated to the nimble mobility of Sun Yat.

And thus it is that Sun Yat takes his place among the great who spearheaded the Long March: Mao, Chou En-

51

lai, Chu Teh, P'eng Teh-huai, Yeh Chien-ying, Liu Ya-lou, Lin Piao, Hsiao Hua, Liu Po-ch'eng, Lo Ping-hui, Nieh Jung-chen. Yet it is Sun Yat whom I remember today, while the others, who may have flourished at this time or that afterwards, seem only hazy, shapeless faces to me.

And so we marched onward, forever fighting the Nationalists, our avowed enemies, and dying by the scores, picking up new volunteers along the way—cherub-faced youths who also spouted philosophy and ideals but who did not have the stamina in their untrained bodies to endure the myriad ordeals.

Almost constantly beside me was a boy I had grown up with in my home province, a boy named Cheng Lu, whom you know only too well from your history. But then he was only a boy like myself. His heart and body were as sturdy as mine, and although he bettered me slightly because of his fewer years, he maintained a pace to which I could hold, for we were close friends and even in those days, when your heart was filled with hope and trust in a cause, you still needed a touch of reality, a voice to respond to, a hand to touch as you traded ammunition packs, a face to stare at and ponder over during those cold nights around campfires when we sat in lengthy silence, contemplating the significance of the ordeals that still awaited us.

But after eight months of marching, fighting and going too many times without food and proper water rations, both Cheng Lu and myself grew weary of heart, and we began to voice our dissension and uncertainties about the leadership which seemed to be taking us deeper and deeper into turmoil and hardship. It was after three days of "fast march"—or what averaged out to 120 *li,* or almost thirty-five miles a day—that we approached Kwangtung in an effort to break out of a trap set by Chiang Kai-shek. We met the enemy in brutal combat, and death was at our elbows from dawn to dusk. Only 30,000 of us emerged intact. Cheng Lu and I no longer talked of tomorrow's glory or of the future of the Red Army. Instead, we turned inward seeking a new kind of strength which our youth would not seem to grant us. Neither of us had the necessary political foundation, and our hope wallowed and expired in a morass of confusion.

It was when we reached the great upper reaches of the Yangtze, "the River of Golden Sands," or "the River of Fragrant Teafields," depending on your province, that we sat down on the earth in abject despair and proposed that we bring to an end our contribution to the Long March. But Cheng Lu, whose heart was as bleak as my own, would not entertain the idea of desertion. He who rides a tiger, he said, cannot dismount. And there was truth in that, for to leave behind the comrades of the Long March would not leave behind the memories, nor the truth of what we had done. I think it was I who proposed suicide, by falling into the waters of the Great River. But Cheng Lu, better versed in lore and history than I, reminded me of the poet Li Tai-po, who drowned in the Yangtze in 762 A.D. while in a drunken state. According to Cheng Lu, the poet was attempting to catch the reflection of the moon on the water. Thus, the Yangtze was a sacred shrine to most Chinese, and to desecrate such holy waters was, in the opinion of Cheng Lu, worse than continuing the march. (It was only in later years I came to realize that the story of the bibulous poet was steeped heavier in legend than truth. It is true he had a consistent drinking habit, as was so profusely expressed in "Drinking Alone in the Moonlight," but in actuality he died in bed, of old age, as he wrote the line: "I dance, my shadow goes tumbling about.")

In anger that he was rejecting my every suggestion, I turned on Cheng Lu, accusing him of having the eighty-one scales of the dragon. We were suddenly interrupted by the arrival of Sun Yat, who was examining the feet of a number of men who had died of exhaustion on reaching the shores of the Yangtze. As always, his search was for new shoes, and so we watched him scavenge the dead, although by no means was this practice frowned upon by the First Front Red Army, as scrounging and scavenging were the first orders of survival.

Sun Yat turned to look at us for a moment, and the defeat on our faces must have been so obvious as to make him scowl, then turn away in such a manner as to dishonor us. It was a jarring experience, to see this gallant old man turn away from us that way, and for a while neither of us spoke as we gazed out over the Yangtze. Cheng Lu reached

53

over in the grass and found a cow's tooth, which, of course, is a sign of extreme good fortune. He wanted to give it to me, but I refused to rob him of this fortunate find. Finally, he decided to give me half an interest in the cow's tooth, which I humbly accepted, and we plodded on, expressing our bitter disappointment no further.

Shortly after that incident, we completed a successful crossing of the Yangtze. One of our patrols disguised in Kuomintang uniforms managed to cross to the other side and seize control of a fleet of boats, and our spirits picked up again. But soon after the food and water situation deteriorated, and once again we ate off the dregs of the landscape—from the roots of evergreen trees to the fleas off a dog's back (the fleas were selected and eaten after the dog had been butchered, but before the savory animal had been served up in one of the regiment's giant stewing pots).

If we thought we had experienced total despair before, we now realized, Cheng Lu and I, that what lay ahead made the mileage behind us seem pleasant in comparison. We had, by the last week of August 1935, completed our passage through the Great Snow Mountains of Szechwan and begun the lethal trek, lethal for many of us anyway, through "The Grasslands." This was wilderness as we had never seen before—a barren empty land inhabited only by fierce Mantzu and Tibetan tribesmen, who were experts in the art of ambush, a military phase that, until now, we had mastered over the Nationalists. Not only were these tribesmen superb with ancient rifles and self-honed spears, but they were capable of slipping into our sleeping areas after dark and stabbing and beheading men without making the slightest sound. Then they would vanish back into the darkness, taking with them whatever they could carry . . . in addition to the heads. "The Grasslands" themselves were huge bogs, and it was not uncommon to sink to the ankles in this ungodly, clinging mire. Yellow and black marshes, with deep pools of black mud, claimed as many lives that month as the Nationalists and natives put together. The Red Army's Political Department tried to pass new propaganda among us, booklets and leaflets and pamphlets, but Cheng Lu and I found these useful only for eating, as the pages supplemented our meager, often-nonexistent diet.

As we emerged from the last of these devilish bogs and marshes into country that consisted of what seemed a rarity by then, solid and flat ground, both Cheng Lu and I wanted to collapse . . . which is just what we did. The spirit flowed from our bodies as we lay down, face-up, on the earth, and I think we both felt that we would never be able to take another step.

As I lay there, I felt a presence above me and looked up to find Sun Yat standing over me, looking at my shoes with a curious gleam in his eye. I promptly nudged Cheng Lu with the spirit I thought was gone from my body. We both leaped to our feet and watched Sun Yat as he strutted away from us, marching at a fast speed, as though he were doing the first mile of the Long March and not one of the last.

"He has faith," said Cheng Lu. "Where does he find such faith?"

"He believes in the cause," I replied. "He is old enough to keep his spirits high. It is what General Peng te-Huai has said: 'What we lack in weapons will be balanced by our men's knowledge of what they are fighting for.' He has had the time to think and study and learn and understand, this Sun Yat. While we are so young, and just beginning to think and study and learn and understand, he has lived and seen much, and we have lived and seen little."

"Then," said Cheng Lu, perking up, "we were right not to drown ourselves in the River of Fragrant Teafields. Whatever we feel ourselves, it is nothing. It is insignificant. The *Cha-Chi,* the malign spirits, have tried to blind us. But Sun Yat has shown us the greater meaning. A cause cannot die unless those who believe in it die. A cause lives on, even if we do not, as long as we leave behind others who will believe in our cause. The old man, Sun Yat, has given us the spirit, for he knows he will one day be gone and that he must instill in those he leaves behind the urge to fight on, to breathe the beliefs of the First Front Red Army, and all the Red Armies of future generations."

It was like a flash of inspiration. I had never heard Cheng Lu speak so profoundly before, and, forgive me for saying it, he never spoke as profoundly again, even in his days as one of our better field commanders.

And so we stepped off with new devotion and determination, working our way toward Wayaopao, where the Red Army would establish its new headquarters. That final day, despite our weariness and the fact my feet were sore, Cheng Lu and I removed our leggings and shoes during the final hours of the march and chanted, along with the other survivors of this heroic feat, "March on! March on! March on and on!" following, literally, in the footsteps of Sun Yat, who continued to set his usual pace.

Twenty thousand of us reached North Shensi, and within our ranks was the core of the Party's political and military leadership. It was here we would renew our strength, organize the peasants, and rebuild our depleted ranks. We had frustrated a thousand attempts to stop our march. We had every reason now, Cheng Lu and I, to finish triumphantly, thanks to Sun Yat and the new heights he had inspired us to.

As we reached the base camp, our marching sergeant congratulated us, gave us each a packet of dried watermelon seeds as a feeble attempt at a reward, and patted us on the back with heavy thumps.

"Come on," urged Cheng Lu, "let's go thank the old man, Sun Yat."

We reached the outskirts of the bivouac area, startled to see that Sun Yat was continuing to march over the base of a barren hillside, his tempo unchanged. We shouted at him, but he did not turn to look at us or acknowledge our cries, and soon disappeared from sight.

We were too tired to run after him, and we just stood there for a while, thoroughly puzzled.

Later, while Cheng Lu was washing his leggings in a nearby stream, I went to our marching sergeant, hoping he could explain the strange actions of Sun Yat.

The marching sergeant laughed at me quite broadly. "That old fool? You wonder why he walks away over a hill? I'll tell you, young soldier. Because he doesn't know any better, that's why he walks away over a hill. He is an old, old fool."

I explained Sun Yat's prowess during the Long March,

and the marching sergeant laughed only harder. "That old man went crazy many years ago, long before the March began. He knows nothing of politics. He does not even know what the name Mao Tse-Tung means. He thinks Mao is one of the tiger gods who has gone to do battle with the sky demons. That old man is a complete idiot."

For some reason, I never bothered to tell Cheng Lu what the marching sergeant had said. In years to come, until the time of his death, Cheng Lu would address his men, and use old Sun Yat as an example of loyalty and truth.

11
Ju-Chao Strikes Back

The land mine had apparently been set for anti-personnel purposes, for it exploded instantly under the 250-pound weight of Son of Kong. Because he had been running in a crouching position (swung forward with his weight wholly on his arms), the toes of his right foot had taken the brunt of the blast. The rest of Son of Kong remained untouched by the flying shards.

The place was the old Khing-lu Trail, approximately three miles south of the position Sarge and Youngman occupied. The purpose for Son of Kong being alone was foraging for food. It was an everyday assignment given to him by his father.

Son stared at the place where his toes had been only moments before and began to cry. Since a chimpanzee does not shed tears, it was closer to a cry of distress, punctuated by a long lamenting whine. During the five minutes he remained in that position, Son of Kong did not once whimper.

It was only when he smelled the men approaching that he started to move. He tried to scamper into a drainage ditch which paralleled the Khing-lu Trail, but his enthusiasm and animal instinct exceeded his physical ability. The violent surge of motion was intensified by the pain in his foot, which he was forced to pull along the ground. Son of Kong instinctively knew he would not reach the ditch before the men arrived.

They came quickly, for they must have heard his cries of distress. Son continued to drag himself toward the ditch, then stopped when he realized the men were grouping in front, their weapons trained on him. He stopped thinking about the ditch and turned his attention to the men.

Chi-yung approached Son with a narrow limb from a nearby fallen broussonetia tree, and poked at him. Son ignored the insult, and instinctively braced his body for the attack. When he sprang, the men shrunk away, though they needn't have bothered. Son covered only half the distance he expected, and lay in the middle of the road again, a pitiful sight.

It was then that Ju-Chao stepped forward, taking the limb from the hands of Chi-yung. He spent the next five minutes, his face registering no expression, his complexion strangely ashen, poking Son of Kong, not only on his bleeding foot but on his genitals as well. Unable to help himself, Son urinated on his own injured foot. He experienced an unusual kind of pain, which reminded him of the time he thrust his hand into a blazing fireplace at the age of six months.

Son occasionally lashed out harmlessly at Ju-Chao with his hand, and snarled and exposed his half-rotten teeth, but he must have realized the uselessness of such tactics, because he soon gave up and tried to ignore the prodding stick, even when it struck a delicate area.

Meanwhile, some of Ju-Chao's men, at his order, were sharpening sticks to needle-fine points, chattering eagerly among themselves as they contemplated the singular purpose of the patrol. They also touched on the story of the Long March related by Ju-Chao, and indicated they had all been moved by its content and by the professional way Ju-Chao had delivered it. Nobody was reluctant to show his sensitivity.

When the men were finished sharpening the sticks, Ju-Chao positioned them in a ring around the slowly dying Son of Kong. At the nod of his head, they began probing

Son's body. It was when one of the points penetrated Son's genital sac that he leaped into the air and began to spin around madly, lashing out but never reaching anybody as his body sustained jab after jab. Air was ejected in great gulps through his glottis as Son cried out in agony, making a "Ghak-gho-ga-ha" sound.

It was Ju-Chao who finally delivered the *coup de grâce*. He simply took one of the sharpened sticks (by now well-covered with blood) and shoved it into Son's rectum. Ju-Chao's timing couldn't have been better, for as the last ounce of resistance drained from his body, relaxing all the tensed muscles, Son's bowel tract released its contents, which flowed toward the opening. The stick, however, prevented passage, and the feces remained in his system.

12
A.:
Sarge Pays Tribute

Sarge and Youngman were the first to happen upon the body of Son of Kong as they trudged—with the direction of east their only goal until a more specific destination could be selected—beside the Khing-lu Trail, staying out of its center since they knew it was heavily mined with anti-personnel devices.

By then Ju-Chao and his special squad had gone, and Son of Kong experienced the first throes of rigor mortis.

"Squad C-323," muttered Sarge, under his breath, as he paused to pay momentary tribute to this fallen comrade.

"I thought they were supposed to be the worst killers in the world. He doesn't look so tough."

"Things aren't always what they seem," responded Sarge. "I've seen these boys in action. They're tougher than any man. And more deadly. Hmmm. Judging from that pole sticking out of his ass, and the fact I see no dead Chinks, and the fact a mine has been exploded in the road over there, and the fact the toes on one foot have been blown off, I'd say they cornered him right here after he'd been wounded by the blast and finished him off."

"Jesus," said Youngman, "this ape has been pretty well gouged up. They even cut off his balls."

61

"The Chinks have been cutting off balls for years. It's nothing new."

"I'd say they were pretty agitated."

"Agitated, my ass. They were pissed."

[...] [...] [...] [...] [...] [...] [...]

B.:
King Kong Vows Vengeance

Although there was no way to mistake the signs of death, King Kong nevertheless made several attempts to rouse Son of Kong. It was the nature of the chimpanzee. As he did so, the other members of Squad C-323 leaped and bounded about the area, being sure not to come down upon the surface of the Khing-lu Trail. This was also the nature of the chimpanzee once he saw a blast mark that clearly indicated antipersonnel devices.

King Kong's next step was to begin tearing at the short hair on his head (which, to those who knew him well, meant a mixture of anguish and anger). He then issued a yell of rage. To C-323 this was unique, for despite the many deaths under his command, King Kong had never used this particular cry. It sounded like "Hah-ah-ah-ah-ah-hah-ah-ah," and it had that peculiar quality of being uttered both under his breath and above his breath—a subtle change of pitch that only the chimpanzee ear could detect, and then only under ideal acoustical situations.

This cry was accompanied by additional attempts by King Kong to lift Son of Kong's head and hands, and rolling his body over and over. There was no mistaking the depression, grief and sorrow manifested in the father—nor

63

the whining, moaning, and crying. Yet not quite in the human sense—for there were no tears.

At the end of one hour, the period of grief was over. A slight wind that had originated in the Central Mountain Belt gently stirred up the odors that, during King Kong's mourning, had gone unnoticed.

He paused, sniffed, and analyzed.

The mixture was strange. On the one hand, there was a remarkably familiar smell, which King Kong instantly associated with a flagpole. On the other, there was a smell which was superimposed over the first—a smell of graphite, gunpowder and the metal of weapons. It carried with it the odor of blood and death, but not Son of Kong's death—rather, the death of men, the smell of his Chinese victims. Above all, it was the smell of masculine pride and valor, of military honor and tradition.

The effluvium of the two blended into a single bouquet—it was impossible, even for King Kong's macrosmatic olfaction, to keep them separated.

And that's why he signaled for Squad C-323 to pick up the trail, vowing within his heart, in the subconscious manner of the chimpanzee, to wreak havoc on both forces which had obviously (to him) been responsible for the death of Son of Kong.

13

Résumé of an Unsold Writer

Ernest Youngman was born in the vineyard country of Napa, about 50 miles north of San Francisco. His father was a hardwood floor layer, and Ernest found himself working after school, with little opportunity to play with children his own age in the rural area in which he was raised. But he never resented his father, a quiet, self-made man who knew little else than the profession he had mastered so well. Rather, Ernest grew very close to his father, perhaps closer than most sons. His grades in school were only average, although he did distinguish himself in the journalism class which, once a month, published the high school newspaper. Ernest found that he enjoyed writing, and began composing articles for the campus publications, including the yearbook, on which he worked for two consecutive years.

It was during his early days in high school that he developed an interest in the science-fiction novels found in the school library. He soon began to spend much time browsing in old magazine stores, collecting dog-eared copies of *Weird Tales, Astounding Science Fiction, Famous Fantastic Mysteries* and *Planet Stories*. He became a devourer of Robert Heinlein, Isaac Asimov, and Ray Bradbury. The latter, in fact, made such a strong impression on him at the age of sixteen that for one of his English classes Ernest copied a Bradbury story, word for word, and received an A from the instructor, who went so far as to read the story to his class. Ernest was embarrassed, and suddenly realized the teacher might accidentally stumble across the original and expose him to the others as a fake. The ruse went undetected. To make up for it, he wrote two more stories—one of them a war yarn entitled "Foxhole" and the other, "Shootout," a Western in which two gunmen faced each other down in a deserted cowtown street. Neither story was read aloud to the class, but the instructor praised Ernest and he continued to write.

The stories flowed very quickly from then on. One of his earliest works was about an isolated deer-hunting camp in the wilds of Nevada, where a band of men suddenly found their Sunday afternoon hunt disturbed by a former Army general, who went berserk when the young hero shot a three-point buck the general had his sights on. The general accused the young hero of being a fifth columnist, an infiltrator sent by a foreign power to undermine the traditions and strengths of America, and pursued him with a high-powered rifle. It was an attempt to write a meaningful, contemporary story, but it was mawkish in its sentiment, the characters were stereotypes, and the action strictly for the pages of a pulp magazine. Unfortunately, pulps had not been published for many years. He put the story into a drawer and forgot about it.

Ernest's next attempt was set on an alien planet whose humanoid Federation Master and wife were being stalked by usurpers who had managed to pull off a *coup d'état*. It was a blood-and-thunder yarn, in which blasters zapped back and forth and several of the insurgents were turned to ashes. Ernest lingered a bit too long on the passages describing anatomical destruction, and it turned out to be a gory piece of writing with nothing to recommend it. His "Fruit of Mars," written soon after, concerned a university professor who woke up one morning to find an apple from Mars on his dresser. Since the idea had come to Ernest in a dream, he was never able to provide a climax for the plot. As a result, he became somewhat disillusioned with science-fiction and abandoned it as a literary form, even though he still read an occasional novel.

He then saturated himself in the Western novels of Clarence E. Mulford (on which the Hopalong Cassidy movie series had been rather loosely based) and Frederick Schiller Faust, otherwise known as Max Brand. His first story was about a cavalry scout named Dave McKay who was stranded in Sioux Indian territory without a horse and had to make his way, on foot, through hundreds of miles of treacherous terrain. McKay was riding dispatch for the Seventh Cavalry and carrying an important message for General Custer, commanding him not to ride from Fort Laramie as previously ordered. After an encounter with three leering gun-runners, who all died in violent fashion from McKay's Winchester, he was within sight of the fort when an Indian arrow finished him off. His dispatch case fell into a crevice between two rocks, where it remained for the next hundred years. Ernest called this story, "Against a Nation." His journalism teacher read it and told him to stop wasting his time writing such trash. Write for a particular market, said the teacher, and earn some money.

Which is exactly what Ernest did—earn money. A student from another English class came to him and said he needed a short piece of fiction the following day, and he would pay Ernest ten dollars if he could deliver it. Ernest took the assignment gladly, and for six hours solid wrote a fantastic World War II plot in which a fighter pilot was taking part in the invasion of Tarawa. After shooting down a number of Japanese Zeroes and Zekes, his propeller was destroyed in a midair collision, and he was forced down on the atoll of Betio after it had been secured at great cost by the U.S. Marines. As he stepped from the plane, a bullet fired by the last remaining Japanese soldier on the island struck him down. Ernest was paid his ten dollars on delivery, but the student later came to him, complaining that the teacher had accused him of copying the story out of a book or magazine. The teacher insisted it was too good for a student to produce. Thereafter Ernest thought he was better than he had been giving himself credit for and he returned to his own writing with great excitement.

Writing about World War II had stimulated new interest

in that phase of history in Ernest, and he began to read a great deal of war literature. He first turned his pen to the Cuban Invasion of 1961, and wrote a novel of 150,000 words about an ingenious scheme conceived by Fidel Castro to kidnap and brainwash a select group of American children (including the fourteen-year-old son of the President of the United States). These children, once brainwashed, would become the personal bodyguards of Castro. The main concept was hailed as innovative by his creative writing teacher (he was by now in his first year of junior college in Napa, and under the tutelage of Harold Errickson), but he deemed the handling inept, the characterization incompetent and some of the slam-bam action unbelievable. Discouraged, but refusing to give up, Ernest wrote "Jungle Experience," the story of an American soldier in Vietnam who undergoes a religious experience in a mortar-torn forest near Hue. The characterizations were better, said Errickson, and the action was believable, but the concept just didn't work. Errickson claimed Ernest had neither the background nor the writing ability to make such a difficult theme work within the context of what appeared to be a rousing war story.

Feeling frustrated by his unappreciated attempts at action fiction, Ernest turned inward to examine his own personal experiences. One of his first truc-to-life works was "The Roof," the simple story of how his father had fallen from a roof one day and broken his leg, leaving Ernest in complete charge of the hardwood floor company. Ernest dramatized the trials and tribulations of a young man trying to do the work of an adult. The characters, for a change, were believable. However, there was little action. The dialogue seemed pretentiously "homespun" and the ending was a bit pat, with Ernest finishing the roof shortly before a menacing rain shower. Errickson urged him to submit it to *The Atlantic Monthly,* but it was rejected, as everything he had ever written had been rejected.

He returned to Westerns again. Feeling ambitious, he started a novel *Ruthless,* and a neighbor, who was then learning to play the guitar, composed a ballad for the story, which urged Ernest to continue with it. He broke the ballad down, and placed a stanza at the beginning of each chapter. It began:

> His gun is quick and ruthless,
> His heart is filled with hate;
> But come tomorrow's dawn,
> There'll be a twist in fate.

The novel was packed with action, and several colorful characters—e.g., a sexy rancher's daughter, who is whipped to death by a sadistic gunslinger named Garth; a Mexican laborer, who is forced into murder in order that his wife may have her next baby in a hospital; a tinhorn with ambitions for taking over the largest spread in the state, etc. It seemed cliché-riddled when he finished it, so Ernest threw it into the drawer, refusing to show it to Errickson or any of his close friends.

A period of melancholy ensued, which was not helped by additional rejections received in the mail. One pink slip called his story "slight." He entered into another period of abject depression, and for two months wrote nothing.

Shortly after, he graduated from junior college, said good-bye to Errickson (who urged him heartily to continue his fictional efforts) and moved to San Francisco. Taking a room for thirty dollars a month in the Sunset District (his father had agreed to support him while he was away from home), he began writing again, turning out fiction for every conceivable market. He even wrote short mysteries (the kind with the solutions printed in the back pages of the magazines) for the crossword puzzle market, but he received notices that this was closed and no unsolicited material was needed "at the present time."

He then struck on what he thought was an ingenious idea about a pair of inventors, named Triplett and Smallwood, who were constantly being swindled out of their new gadgets by gentlemen named Bell, Edison, Franklin, and Stanley. They dwelled in a kind of timeless ether, and while there was a certain satiric charm to the idea, it soon grew repetitive and lacked reverberation.

Abandoning comedy and parody, he turned to social relevance: "Just a Matter of Time" was about a copyboy on a large-circulation metropolitan daily who is looking for a story to prove to his city editor he has the makings of a general assignment reporter. He is witness to the horrible death of a little girl under the wheels of a municipal streetcar, but when he returns to the office realizes he hasn't the stomach to write that kind of news and quits his profession. "A Matter of Fire," the story of a young man who, in the fashion of Hemingway's Nick Adams, is exposed to an experience which teaches him some sense of responsibility, flowed from his typewriter effortlessly. "A Car in the Lake" was about a drunken man who drove his recreational camper into the waters of Lake Berryessa, submerging all but the roof. Two boys who witnessed the accident agreed to drive the men to a nearby gas station so he could call for a tow truck. It was a slice-of-life thing with some fascinating characters, but it, and the other two slice-of-life stories, had a certain artificiality that brought only negative responses from editors. So, as he had done so often in the past, Youngman threw his assorted manuscripts into a drawer and tried to forget all the work that had gone into them.

By the time Ernest Youngman was twenty-two, he had sold exactly nothing. But he swore, when war began and he was inducted, that nothing would stop him from writing. During basic training he wrote profiles on his company commander and first sergeant, which were found one morning during a battalion inspection and ripped up in the presence of both the company commander and the first sergeant. Youngman promised, in front of the entire platoon, never again to write about his officers or NCO's. It was an unfortunate method of humiliation which he took weeks to recover from, the idea of rejection in any form filling him with repugnance and insecurity. But he recovered and tried to write a piece for one of the architectural magazines about the construction of the new plasto-barracks. This was turned down as "too drab" by the editors, who were looking for "colorful construction and design, definitely of a nonmilitary nature." The manuscript and rejection notice he dumped into a garbage can early one morning while on his way to report for KP.

But he vowed to himself, "I shall write again."

And that's where his literary career stood when orders came, and he was assigned to the Asian Theater of Operations.

14
Squad C-323 Plans the Kill

King Kong, Sergeant Joe Young, Konga and Bonzo trudged through grass reaching their armpits. Human scents assailed their nostrils relentlessly, continuing to turn their stomachs in a fashion to which they never became accustomed. They pressed on in search of The Man Up the Pole in the tradition they had been programmed with in the Mojave Desert.

They were fifteen minutes from the site of Son of Kong's death when it became apparent to all that The Man Up the Pole and his followers were seeking Squad C-323. The human was chasing the tail, and the tail was chasing the human.

King Kong sent Bonzo to scout, and he was back within minutes. The patrol was well armed, according to Bonzo, who reported The Man Up the Pole's strength by thumping on the ground—once for every rifle, twice for every automatic weapon, three times for every mortar, etc. King Kong had to hear no thumps to know that The Man Up the Pole would be searching with a vengeance, for vengeance was the very thing he himself now felt.

Bonzo, finished thumping, waited for orders.

The others waited for orders.

It was apparent King Kong had to decide: Go after The Man Up the Pole, or return to Command Center.

King Kong made his decision and passed it on to the others by crossing his arms and holding them out in front of his chest. Konga, loyal as ever, turned to move in the direction of The Man Up the Pole, but Sergeant Joe Young made his feelings known by snorting. The sounds he made were of home and safety. King Kong made a reply with sounds that spoke of pursuit and drive. They were louder than Young's. The Sergeant turned suddenly sullen and refused to speak to anyone.

King Kong assigned Bonzo to move ahead of The Man Up the Pole and leave an obvious trail. Try to make it appear the entire squad had passed. This could be achieved in a number of ways:

1. Bonzo was to scatter his offal in several places along the trail.

2. Wherever he slept at night, he was to prepare extra beds, so it would appear the entire squad had spent the night there.

3. Numerous banana peels and other food residue were to be left in obvious places beside the trail.

4. Urination was to be kept to short bursts, so Bonzo could scatter it in several detectable places.

5. In the dead of night, he was to take up a position near the camp of The Man Up the Pole and chatter wildly, keeping everyone awake and their nerves on edge.

6. His pace during the day was to be Quick March, to tire The Man Up the Pole as quickly as possible—this being not a deception but a strategic part of King Kong's plan.

Bonzo acknowledged and moved out. King Kong gave an indication of his pleasure by scratching the nape of his neck as if to say, If there were only more like you . . .

Now King Kong was prepared to implement his plan. Let The Man Up the Pole and his followers wear them-

73

selves out, thinking they were close on the tail of Squad C-323, while he, Sergeant Joe Young and Konga followed leisurely, waiting for the right opportunity to strike.

Then, vengeance would be King Kong's.

15
Fighting the Forces of Evil

A quarter-mile off the Khing-lu Trail, built against the side of a hill, stood the village of Kwang, with a population of 400, one school, three wells, a score of bathhouses, and one main street of shops and restaurants and a single barber. The village had passed from side to side in recent months, but neither force deemed it strategic and therefore no battle had been fought for it. Not a single bomb nor a mortar shell had, by some miracle, fallen, and not a single citizen had been claimed by the cruelties of war.

Whoever wanted it for the moment could have it, and at this particular moment nobody wanted it. Nevertheless, Sarge insisted that he and Youngman approach cautiously, and for fifteen minutes they studied the activity along the main *hutung* of the village through binoculars.

Everything appeared normal. A beggar dressed in unbelievably dirty tatters, his tousled hair sprinkled with straw and his feet wrapped in grimy rags, stood in front of a lapidary shop with a metal cup in hand, asking for alms. An occasional passerby would walk slowly past, studying some of the shop windows, but in no case did anyone enter to barter or to buy. The beggar was having an equally unprofitable afternoon.

"Jesus Christ," said Sarge, studying the doorway to one of the shops. "That goddamn door to that place is really out of plumb. Those bastards must construct without levels."

"They do it that way on purpose, Sarge," replied Youngman, who couldn't possibly see the doorway clearly at this distance.

"What the fuck are you talking about?"

"Evil spirits. They walk in straight lines. So the Chinese build everything crooked to ward off evil spirits."

"Where'd you learn that?"

"Basic. Everybody gets it nowadays. Indoctrination for easier adjustment to alien environmental conditions."

"No shit," said Sarge, casting a sideways glance at Youngman. "What else did those bright boys back there tell you?"

"Everything's backwards."

"You mean everybody's trying to ward off evil spirits . . . ?"

Youngman shook his head. "It's the nature of the people. Think about it, Sarge. They read right to left, and footnotes are placed on *top* of the page. They take off their footgear before entering a room, not their headgear. And they eat dessert before the meal. When in mourning they wear white not black. They place a saucer over a teacup, not under it. They dry after a bath with a wet towel, and their compasses point south not north."

Sarge frowned a little, and chomped harder on his soggy cigar butt. "Did them environmental conditioners tell you how to move in on a village?"

Youngman shrugged. "Search and destroy."

"Anything else?"

Youngman shrugged. "Routine probe and reform."

"So, given this village, how you gonna do it?"

"You mean you're asking for my opinion?"

"Yeah, yeah. I'm asking for your opinion. But don't let it go to your head."

"Well, we could split and move around to those old ruins over there. You come up on the left, me on the right."

"Brilliant, Youngman. Only one thing wrong. We could get ourselves dead doing that."

"How do you figure, Sarge?"

"Those old ruins you're so quick to go around . . ."

"What about'em?"

"Could be a great place for a machine-gun emplacement."

Youngman, feeling a little foolish, stared at the ruins. "I think I see what you mean."

"It's quiet," said Sarge.

"Too quiet," added Youngman. After a moment: "Looks deserted."

"Old ruins like that always look deserted."

"What now?" Youngman was beginning to experience a slight feeling of nervousness—a condition Sarge repeatedly induced with his pessimism. But, Youngman realized, it was that very pessimism which had kept him alive a couple of times. And with some luck that pessimism might keep him alive a while longer—perhaps even for the duration.

"You cover me from here. I'm going to work my way through the grass on this side of the old ruins. When I give you the all-clear signal, come on in. And Youngman . . ."

Youngman looked blankly at Sarge.

"The rifles. Don't forget the rifles this time, Youngman."

Sarge wriggled away into the grass, and within ten seconds Youngman was no longer able to see him. He wasn't even certain of Sarge's approximate position. He was like a worm or a snake, slithering soundlessly away on his belly. In fact, Youngman was still trying to determine Sarge's position when an olive drab streak suddenly appeared next to the concrete foundations of the old ruins. The weapon in Sarge's hands bucked as an entire magazine quickly passed through it. Then he gave Youngman the signal to advance.

Not forgetting the bundle of rifles, Youngman moved somewhat clumsily through the grass and took his place beside Sarge, who was staring down into the ruins. Youngman's gaze followed Sarge's. Together they saw two carcasses, terribly ripped by bullets. The carcasses were a mucky gray in color, with tails that were at least a foot long.

Sarge tipped his helmet back from his forehead. "Take a good gander," he said, still staring downward. "You're looking at them, Youngman. Commie rats."

16
Kwang Hospitality

The old beggar in the smelly clothing was the first to greet Sarge and Youngman, and it was no surprise to either of them that the Chinaman spoke impeccable English. This ability was necessary for men of his ilk when the tide of war ebbed and flowed so readily. "I am a prince, once heir to a dragon throne, now an abandoned character in need of your assistance, oh worthy one." When he saw his pitch was wasted on indifferent ears, he returned his attention to swatting at the gnats in the air with his tin cup.

Youngman was immediately attracted by a shop specializing in fans and, like some youth eager to buy a jaw-breaker in a five-and-ten, studied the displays in the window. One in particular caught his eye. Its frame was made of colored bamboo sandalwood over which an ivory-fabric had been stretched. The background was of gilt—a silver swarm of butterflies and a flock of birds. A more decorative fan, with blue kingfisher feathers and iridescent beetle wings, also caught his eye, and for a moment he considered bartering for it. He was enchanted by the dangling silken cords and pendants of amber and jade.

But at that particular moment, a conjurer had appeared from between two shops, where he had been taking a nap until aroused by Sarge's gunfire. He began producing things from impossible places, and in less than a minute had conjured a bird cage, two live toads, one table lamp, several lighted cigarettes (some of them filter-tipped), a potted palm tree and at least a dozen pieces of rock.

Just as Sarge turned to continue along the street, the conjurer snapped his fingers, jabbered in a dialect that not even Youngman could comprehend, and weaved his hands through the air, as if tracing the shape of an outdoor toilet. Then, out of thin air, or so it seemed, the conjurer produced a thin, rectangular object, covered by a wrapper. There was writing on the wrapper. The conjurer bowed and handed the object to Sarge, who took it warily. Sarge studied the wrapping before turning it over to Youngman.

Youngman recognized it immediately, although he had not seen one since his high school days. "Hershey," said Youngman. "Extra large."

Sarge nodded. "World War II surplus."

It was then Sarge permitted the faint suggestion of a smile to cross his face, and Youngman was startled, for he had never experienced that before. Sarge even gave the conjurer a hearty slap on the back. "You can relax, Youngman. This enemy village is friendly."

Youngman had just started to browse through one of the lapidary shops, examining jade rings, jade bracelets, jade hairpins, jade beads, jade pendants, jade seals, jade images of dogs, jade images of dragons, jade demons, jade gods, jade lions, jade temples, jade trees, jade people, when a commotion caused him to turn. He accidentally knocked several brocade boxes (apple green, white, pinkish gray) to the floor, and although he wanted to stop to pick them up, he feared there was trouble outside.

There was trouble, but not quite the kind Youngman had expected. A group of Chinese peasants had begun to swarm around Sarge, and he looked somewhat bewildered. He was trying to calm them down, but without success. Youngman saw the opportunity to stop not only the confusion but any possible violence to Sarge by firing three fast shots into the air. Instantly, the mob quieted and its anger abated to a whisper.

In Mandarin Chinese, Youngman asked what was wrong.

In Mandarin Chinese, a spokesman for the group, whose anger was instantly rekindled when he began to speak, explained. Youngman listened, then turned to Sarge, ignoring the fact that the spokesman had yet to finish.

"What the hell is all this noise?" Sarge chomped down harder on his cigar.

Youngman shrugged. "He says he's the mayor of this village. Called Kwang."

"Tell Kwang to go play politics somewhere else."

"No, his name isn't Kwang. The village is called Kwang."

"So what did he say?"

"He says the dragons of heaven spit much fire."

Sarge tapped his rifle. "Well, you tell the head politico of this rally there are dragons that spit much lead. And for him to get these people out of here."

"They won't go, Sarge. They're all pissed off."

"About what?" Sarge's impatience was beginning to show.

"According to this guy . . . well, he says there's a slant-eyed bastard in that hut over there."

The mayor turned to face Sarge again, and began jumping up and down, pulling at the bags under his eyes to emphasize Youngman's verbal description. He chattered away again, and Youngman translated. "He says . . . get this, Sarge . . . he says the guy in there is a phony . . . yellow-colored monkey. An Oriental throwback."

"What the fuck . . ."

In unison, Sarge and Youngman turned to stare at the hut in question. From inside, there was a slight stirring sound. Youngman thought he heard the sound of a baby crying.

Sarge started to turn. "Hold it, Sarge," cried Youngman. "What if it's a trap?"

"Now you're starting to catch on, Youngman."

Suddenly they were both soldiers again. Letting the bundle of rifles fall quietly into the doorway of the lapidary shop, Youngman brought his rifle into position (covering the only window in the hut) as Sarge took up a position next to the hut's door.

Nodding at Youngman, Sarge kicked the door back, and disappeared inside. The sound that had been slight only a moment before increased in tempo, and there was no longer any doubt in Youngman's mind. It had been a baby he heard. The cloud of dust kicked up by Sarge's forceful entry quickly dissipated in a mild wind, and Youngman followed him inside. The villagers, apparently satisfied that they had done their civic duty, followed the instructions of the mayor, who ordered them home.

17
Sarge Pays a Social Visit

The mother couldn't have been more than eighteen—a lissome, shapely creature who immediately reminded Youngman of his high school days. She seemed unfazed by unexpected company, and registered no sign of surprise or emotion as Sarge and Youngman quickly gave the hut the once-over. She cradled the infant in her arms, rocking it soothingly back and forth, singing to it about a bird that had turned into a man and become a copier of manuscripts until he lost his job because he also copied all the ink blots from the original papers. He had returned to the heavens as a bird and flown across China happily ever after. At least that was the gist Youngman got.

"She looks legit," said Sarge.

"The mayor out there was talking about a male slant-eyed bastard. Definitely not her."

"Sometimes," decided Sarge, approaching the bundle the mother held, "the biggest surprise comes in the smallest package." Very carefully, as if it might explode in his face, Sarge flipped back a corner of the blanket. An infant's face was revealed—a face that was a singular mixture of Caucasian and Chinese, with the former predominating. Sarge and Youngman stared closely at the infant's features, because there was something strangely familiar about them.

"I swear . . ."

"Just like Smitty, Fourth Platoon."

"Naw," said Sarge, assuredly. "Anderson, Third."

"Could be. Especially with Anderson bugging out all the time. You always said those guys in the Third were sneaky bastards."

Youngman then saw the steel helmet hanging from a peg on the wall. And beneath it, piled on the floor, a pair of fatigues. Government issue. Only a few feet away from a narrow cot on which the mother and baby rested, a trapdoor had been built into the base of the wall. The door was slightly ajar.

Youngman studied the door dubiously. "Could be another trap, Sarge."

"Ain't no such thing as a trap, Youngman. Until someone walks into it."

18

Into the Darkness

Sarge slithered into the yawning hole first. Youngman waited until Sarge's boots disappeared from view, then followed. The last thing he noticed as he started downward was the Chinese mother, continuing to cuddle the baby and ignoring him.

Youngman found himself in a tunnel wide enough for a single body. He inched his way forward and downward at a gradual angle, stopping every few feet to listen. At first, there had only been the almost-inaudible rustling of Sarge somewhere ahead. Then the rustling had stopped, and Youngman could make out a sound. At first faint. Now louder. Youngman attuned his ear.

It was organ music. But then the music stopped, and he heard voices. Dialect. Negroid. A heated exhange . . . he wasn't sure what he was hearing. Then applause—of that he was certain. More organ music, more voices. High-pitched, authoritative, persuasive. Then something quite distinct, less hollow than the voices and music. A metallic ring. Something rolling, something banging. Like a garbage can . . . ? The first set of sounds returned. Again organ music. The word "Oxydol." He heard that word clearly.

What the hell . . . ?

Disoriented for a moment, Youngman stared straight ahead as hard as he could. He could see nothing but ink. He felt lost in the confines of the tunnel, and he began inching his way ahead again, thrusting his buttocks into the air to make faster time. The tunnel was leveling off now, and the sides were widening.

"Get your young ass down!" Sarge's voice came through that darkness like a rifle bullet. Those words seemed to have a force of their own because Youngman instinctively obeyed by flattening out again.

"... and now Oxydol presents Ma Perkins. Well, it's just a few minutes past seven now as Ma walks into the kitchen and goes to the sink for a glass of water. Seated at the table, reading his evening newspaper, is Walter. He looks up at Ma, studies the tired look in her eyes, and puts the paper down ..."

What the hell ... ?

Youngman, despite the growing volume of the sound as he neared its unknown source, could still attune his ear to Sarge's movements. After a few more yards, the tunnel broadened considerably on both sides, and Youngman found himself in a wide pit, with a ceiling stretching a good ten feet above his head, and walls receding away into darkness. He could discern the dimensions because a ribbon-thin shaft of light was pouring through some kind of opening overhead. An opening that appeared to be covered by some huge swinging lid. Now, when he moved, he seemed to be making a great deal of noise. He felt beneath him, and came up with a handful of refuse—papers, moist pieces of wood, empty tin cans, a matching set of chopsticks.

Garbage.

What the hell ... ?

It was then Youngman realized he was at the foot of a garbage pit. Subterranean, but unmistakably a garbage pit. So this was how the Chinese got rid of all their crap ...

And out of the mound of rubbish before him, Youngman saw a form rising up, and sound rose with this grotesque shape.

"... please, Mrs. Perkins, you've got to allow your son

to live his own life. You mustn't stand in the way of hap-
piness for him and Sally . . ."

Shafts of light leaking through the wooden lid above threw streaks across the face of the figure. Youngman could now see he was an Oriental soldier. He threw his weapon to his shoulder, readying fire, his breath stopping for what seemed an eternity. The figure seemed oblivious to his or Sarge's presence, so Youngman held his fire, watching the figure as he fell back on his knees and continued to rummage through the heaps of garbage.

" *. . . Mr. Allyson, I'll have to ask you to leave." " . . .*
I'm not leaving this house, Mrs. Perkins, until I'm assured
you won't interfere in any way with their marriage . . ."

Youngman watched, in almost hypnotic fascination, as a second figure reared up out of the debris and moved toward the first shape. It was like two Gargantuas coming together to do battle. The imagery of a monster film—the clash of the century!

Then Youngman realized it was Sarge, closing in on the first grotesque shape, thrusting his rifle into the man's face.

" *. . . We'll get right back to Ma Perkins and her*
dilemma over the pending marriage, but first, here's a word
from Oxydol."

Finally seeing the rifle only inches from his face, the grotesque shape threw up both arms, and inched forward into a wider shaft of light, and stood exposed. "442! 442!" he barked, or tried to bark. His voice quavered and collapsed. His arms were visibly shaking in the thin streams of light. He held an object in his hand.

Youngman covered the distance to the center of the garbage heap in a few bounds, keeping his rifle trained all the way. "He's covered, Sarge. If the sonofabitch moves, he's finished."

The figure shook his head—and somehow recovered his voice. "No, no! He's got it all wrong, Sarge. I'm 442! 442!"

"Code, Sarge. He's trying to signal his buddies." Youngman brought the muzzle of his rifle closer, and now could see that the man's entire body was quivering—not just his arms.

"Get that rifle out of his face, Youngman, so I can see."

" *. . . a whiter, brighter wash. So remember, from now*

*until January twenty-fourth, you can get one box of Oxydol
free, with every regular purchase . . ."*

Sarge pointed to the object in the figure's hand. "What is
that goddamn thing?"

"Nothing, Sarge, nothing. Just a radio tape. An old soap
opera. That's all. A radio tape."

"Bullshit, Sarge. The guy's an infiltrator. Dressed like
one of our guys. Just like that time outside Shanghai when
we—"

"All right, Youngman, all right."

"I ain't even dressed, Sarge."

"Oughta gun him down right here, Sarge. Just like the
way they shoot our guys."

The figure quavered again. "You guys got me all wrong,
Sarge. He's snafu, Sarge, snafu. I'm on your side. I swear
it."

Sarge grabbed a fistful of the man's T-shirt, pulling him
into eyeball-to-eyeball range. Below his waist, the man was
wearing only BVD's. Sarge yanked the object from his
hand.

" . . . *And now back to Ma and Carter Allyson as they
continue to*—"

Sarge had turned a knob. Thank God—it was one less
conversation to contend with. He tossed the radio back.
"Okay, start talking. What're you doing down here?"

"Scrounging."

"Scrounging?"

"Every outfit has a scrounger."

"A dogrobber, huh?"

"Yeah. For the Colonel."

"Colonel, my ass! You're scrounging for the slut."

"What slut?"

"The slut in the hut."

"Piece of ass never hurt anybody, Sarge."

"Shut up that kind of talk."

"I still say we should shoot him, Sarge."

"We'll shoot him later. Right now, we'll listen to him
talk. . . . All right, what're you doing here?"

"I got separated. From my outfit."

"Yeah, the Tse-tung Elite Guard."

"The what?"

"There's that code again, Sarge."

"The 442nd. I'm as American as you guys. True-blooded American."

In the darkness, Youngman could imagine Sarge's lips curling as he asked: "What kind of rifleman rot are you trying to hand me?"

"Regimental Combat Team. The 442nd."

"Wait a minute, wait a minute, Youngman. 442nd. Hey, I got it now. This guy is a Buddhahead."

"Yeah, yeah, that's right, Sarge. I'm a Buddhahead. Now you're getting it."

"Hey, Youngman, we got ourselves a Buddhahead. How about that?"

"So? All the more reason to shoot him."

"No, no, you don't get it. This guy's legit." Sarge turned to face the figure again. "Hey, I heard they reactivated you guys for the Shanghai ballet. You shoulda said so to begin with. Let's see now, how did that indoctrination pledge go . . . ?" Sarge stared off into space, trying to remember. The figure assumed an at-attention position, and began reciting:

"You have been called back to duty to finish the task your Honorable Ancestors began back in 1937 under the guise of Imperialism, a well-intended but misconceived pogrom of conquest and annihilation. You have been called back to duty to prove to the Ultra-American Free Liberation Front that the Japanese-American is a loyal—"

"Nisei," interjected Youngman. "Now I get it."

"Shut up and let him finish."

"—a loyal, dedicated American first, Japanese second. Ready to prove, with his life if he must, that in no way is he involved in the Oriental Fifth Column Movement to prevent the complete destruction of the Chinese War Machine. You are now a member of the 442nd Regimental Combat Team, which during the Italian campaign of World War II received 3915 individual awards, ten unit citations and 3600 Purple Hearts." The figure went limp again.

"And," added Sarge, "a lot of busted asses. What's your name?"

"Charlie Brown, Private First Class Charlie Brown."

"Well, Private First Class Charlie Brown, suppose you scavenge your tail back to the hut and get your pot and jock. From now on you're with us."

"Where we going, Sarge?"

"You'll find out soon enough, and listen—that girl up there—I don't want you messing around with her."

"I haven't touched her, Sarge. She was in that condition when I found her."

Sarge cocked his head slightly. "Anderson?"

Charlie Brown shook his head. "Smitty, Fourth Platoon."

"I was right," said Youngman, without trying to rub it in.

"Shit," grumbled Sarge. "Getting so you can't tell one GI from another anymore."

There was a noise above them—someone was lifting the wooden grate. Directly overhead stood the conjurer, with a wicker basket in his arms. He turned the basket over, and dumped its contents into the pit.

"Look out!" shouted Youngman.

At least a dozen cobras, weaving sinuous arcs and forming an interlocking pattern, fell hissing through the air. They drifted as if in slow motion, and as they neared the three men, who had all instinctively ducked, throwing their arms above their heads, the snakes began to dissolve into nothingness.

Then the cobras were there no longer.

The conjurer laughed in silence, letting the lid of the garbage trap fall back into place.

"How the hell," asked Youngman, "did he do that?"

Sarge fired a short burst into one of the walls. There was the tinkling of glass—Youngman could see large pieces falling to earth, occasionally throwing off a glint when they passed through the shafts of light.

"Mirrors," said Sarge.

19
A Pleasant Evening in Kwang

That night, while Charlie Brown continued scrounging, Sarge and Youngman, at the recommendation of the mayor, ate in one of the restaurants located on Kwang's commercial row. Youngman ordered the Dinner for One Please: wonton soup, chow mein, sweet and sour pork, noodles, steamed rice, almond breast of chicken (in a special mouth-watering soy sauce), Chow Sub Gum, a seafood mixture, and Sang Gai See, for which this particular restaurant was famed. Sarge simply ordered rice curry and oolong tea. The chef personally stepped out from the kitchen to apologize for the current shortage of black mushrooms, water chestnuts, and the usual hearty supply of pan-fried noodles. It was, of course, the war.

After chow, Sarge and Youngman returned to the hut, where Charlie Brown listened to an episode of *The Fat Man* ("Murder Rents the Flat") and the young mother nursed her baby. Youngman unpacked his small porto-typer, rolled a sheet of paper into it and began writing. He wrote for about half an hour, took out the sheet, and placed it with several others. He tapped the top page.

Sarge, watching Youngman with restrained interest,

looked at the top page. "What the hell is that, Youngman? Your will?"

"Another story, Sarge."

"Shit," said Sarge.

"This time it's a war story."

Sarge's interest perked up. "Well, at least you're writing about something this time. That last love story, 'The Man in My Heart,' was a hunk of pure shit. What's this one about?"

"The Vietnam War."

"No kidding. Let me take a look." Sarge picked up the sheaf of papers.

"Now that was one of the real chickenshit wars."

"How do you mean, Sarge?"

"Chickenshit war, limited war, it means the same. Hitler had the right idea when he fought a war. He went all out. Blew the hell out of everything. He didn't pussyfoot around the Thirty-eighth Parallel. He didn't stop at the Yalu River. No Demilitarized Zones. Vietnam, pure chickenshit. Your story about that?"

"Naw, this is a character study, Sarge."

"Shit," said Sarge. "Maybe I'll read it anyway."

And he curled up.

20

"Crossing" by Ernest Youngman

He walked across the road.

He was glad to be walking again. Too long he had been on his belly, surrounded by death. To reach the road, he had crawled over the bodies of his buddies, his clothes and face covered with blood sloshed from puddles.

While he crawled he knew the rest of the company would be waiting in the ditches across the road. Just before standing he had experienced the jab of pain in his chest again. He wondered why it kept recurring, then promptly forgot about it.

Now he slung his submachine gun, looking for those ditches.

Men appeared out of the ground, and he knew he was safe. "What happened over there?" asked the lieutenant.

"We got hit."

"Where's the rest, Middleton?"

"Dead. Gone." Middleton made an effort to wipe the blood from his face, but he only succeeded in transferring it to his hands. "We got hit."

"Sergeant Grundy?"

"Hit. Hit in the head. He never ..." Middleton shifted his weight from one foot to the other. "They were waiting for us ... with machine guns. We walked right up to them before ..." He shifted his weight again.

"How many Cong you get?" asked one of the new replacements.

"I didn't see anybody," said Middleton. His head had been pressed into a bank of mud. He had thanked that bank of mud a thousand times before he crawled away from it.

Middleton was glad to see so many living, curious faces on this side of the road.

The lieutenant and the green replacement waited for him to finish, but when he said nothing more, the lieutenant nodded understandingly. "We'll pull the company back from here right away." He motioned with his arm.

The evacuation of the company began. And Middleton was pleased. He wanted to return to the living and forget what happened on the other side of the road.

Seven days later the war ended, a truce had been signed after years of negotiations, and Middleton, with the survivors in his company, celebrated in a rear-echelon PX. A truck driver had stolen a dozen crates of beer from somewhere. So the men drank beer, shouting their joy over the armistice.

They talked about the fact there would be no more killing and butchering, and the celebration was very lively by midnight. One of the soldiers threw his helmet into the air. The helmet crashed against the bare head of a nearby sergeant who, a week earlier, had wiped out three Viet Cong machine-gun nests single-handedly. There had already been talk of a citation.

The sergeant sprawled on the ground, a bottle of overturned beer spilling into his straggly hair. He sat up, cursing the helmet thrower and refingering his bottle of overturned beer. He ignored the stream of blood that dripped down his neck onto his fatigues because he was so drunk he couldn't feel anything.

Middleton's head spun—everything moved in a spiraling motion. He had become as drunk as the sergeant. "Now there's a man," roared Middleton, holding up his bottle of beer. "There's a goddamn man. Goddamn man. Drink."

"Drink," roared the men in unison.

"You want a medic?" asked a wide-eyed soldier standing next to the bleeding sergeant.

"He don't need no medic," said Middleton. "Get a medic for those Cong he worked over last week. Now *they* need a medic."

The sergeant became aware, for the first time, of the blood flowing from his head. "I better take it easy," he said, plopping his buttocks on an overturned helmet. "I feel dizzy all of a sudden. I better take it easy."

"Easy?" Middleton laughed. "How the hell can a man like you take it easy?"

"Better not press my luck," said the bleeding sergeant. "I figure I'm out of luck after rushing those Cong last week."

"Ah, come on." Middleton slapped the sergeant on the back. "Don't give me that. A man like you never runs out of luck."

The bleeding sergeant shook his head. "I'll finish this beer and then get some shut-eye."

The men of Middleton's company drank through the night, except the bleeding sergeant, who kept his word and went to bed. Someday they would all forget the war and the death, but tonight they celebrated and talked about sex and America. The men breathed fast and deep. Drunkenly, Middleton watched their rising, falling chests.

When the celebration was over, the Army sent him home to San Francisco, his home before the war. After locating an apartment, he walked through the downtown area, taking in fresh sea air that blew droplets of mist on his stinging red face.

He had no trouble with the printers' union in securing his old job as a linotype operator. During his absence, automation had replaced much of the equipment, and many of the men he had worked with before had either been phased out or retrained to run new machines. It wasn't quite the same atmosphere, but he went to work feeling pretty good about it.

The linotype machine rattled and clattered. Each time Middleton struck a key, the belts whirled and spun along narrow treadmills. The long bars carrying the lead moved constantly about the apparatus like human arms. Rising up, sliding down, lunging across, then beginning the process all over again. He enjoyed watching one wheel in particular. It rotated endlessly, groaning for oil, reflecting the overhead fluorescent light in an eerie fashion. At the end of the day, Middleton was always a little disappointed to see that wheel come to a dying stop. Without that wheel rotating, the room was peculiarly cold, and Middleton felt as if darkness was closing in on him, and would always hurry to get outside. At least the darkness out on the street seemed natural.

On the street, he couldn't get the linotype machine out of his mind. It was like a shapeless celebrator of life, groaning and clacking with its tubes of metal and curving cold steel. The machine lived and died with the flick of a switch and it cooled and warmed and lived and died day after day. There were nights when he dreamed about the linotype machine.

One evening when Middleton was drinking in a Mission Street bar, he became friendly with a young man who bought him a bottle of beer. Middleton, ever since that night of celebration, drank nothing but beer. Middleton told the young man he was a typesetter—"I'm the guy who sets all that crap on page one."

The young man laughed. "Sounds exciting. Me, I'm a clerk myself. I'm—"

Middleton slammed his bottle of beer onto the surface of the bar. "Damn! I knew a clerk once. Vietnam. Hell of a nice kid. Until we started seeing action. Then he started bugging out. Getting all the soft, safe jobs in orderly rooms. I don't think that kid ever did go on a patrol."

"Vietnam. Now there was a bum deal," said the young man.

"Yeah, rough. But anyway, we got to hate this kid's ass royally. You know? Everyone figured him for a bugout. One day a Cong infiltrator, dressed in a GI uniform, came walking into the command post tent. That Cong slit that kid's stomach and scattered his guts all over that tent. Damn kid didn't even have his rifle near him. So I always say that being a clerk is like being dead. You know?

There's no life in it. What kind of life is there in a lot of paper and a lot of filing cabinets?" Middleton paused, aware that the young man was studying him a little strangely. He shrugged it off and continued:

"But now you take a newspaper office, where I work. Now there's something alive and pounding. A damn breathing thing. Listen to that streaking paper on those presses and tell me if your heart doesn't pound faster, mister. After that a man can't be a clerk, no sir." Middleton stared at the young man, questioningly. "What did you do during the war?"

But before the young man could reply, Middleton picked up his bottle of beer and walked to the other end of the bar. It was there he met Rita.

An hour later they were still drinking—Middleton his beer, Rita her martinis on the rocks.

"Rita," said Middleton, realizing that the reflections in the lengthy bar mirror were beginning to ripple, "Rita, tell me about you, Rita."

"I'm just a woman," said Rita. "Just another woman. Not much else to tell."

"You're half of it. You know that."

"Half of what?"

"Half of everything there is. I'm the other half. Because we're all there is, Rita. Male and female. Two sexes. That's all there is."

"What do you do?" asked Rita.

"What do I do?" Middleton was staring at beads of water on the bar. "I do what everybody else does. I live and breathe."

Rita laughed. "You're a character. I think you're a real character."

They drove to Rita's apartment in her Chevrolet. As they sat in the car in front of her apartment building, while Rita was curbing the wheels, a lanky cat, with a lashing tail and yellow eyes, pranced off the far curb and walked into the street.

Middleton watched that cat, which was easily visible in the glare of streetlights. The cat stopped in the center of the street, its tail in constant motion. Middleton knew by a screeching of brakes that a car was coming. It hung fast around the corner, bearing down on the cat.

The cat turned to run as the car wiggled from taking the corner too fast, its tires squealing loudly enough to drown out the squealing of the cat as the front left tire passed over its spinal column. The cat managed to crawl to the curb, but once there stopped moving, its body broken into two portions. The tail hung down into the watery gutter.

"That cat bought it," remarked Middleton.

"None of them make it," said Rita. "Those damn foolish cats are like rabbits. All over the place all the time, getting run over." She urged Middleton to come up for drinks and fun.

"Love to, baby, love to." he replied.

Inside, Middleton prepared the martinis for Rita, but continued to drink beer. Middleton had a hard time matching Rita's intake, so finally he poured the remaining gin down the sink, and threw the bottle into Rita's garbage bag. "I'm getting tired of drinking," he said.

Rita nodded, placing her hands on her hips. "Yeah, me too. So am I."

"Now let's see," said Middleton. "What else could we do?"

Rita beckoned to him with her little finger. "Come here and maybe I'll show you."

"You mean I'll show you—"

He froze where he stood. His heart raced. The pain was stabbing at him again, as it last stabbed at him when he had stood by that road in Vietnam. Only this time it was worse. Much worse. He winced, and clutched at his chest. Rita seemed concerned. He sat down. "I'm sorry," he said, "something . . ." She sat down next to him.

"Are you all right?"

He looked at her, as if thoughts about his health had never before crossed his mind. The pain eased off, and his fingers reached out to unbutton her blouse. Her concern began to turn to desire. His fingers were closing around one of her nipples when the pain struck him again. This time she insisted he lay back on the couch, which he did.

"You'd better take it easy. I had no idea I excited a man this much," said Rita, rebuttoning her blouse.

Middleton didn't like the idea of lying here, when a woman as desirable as Rita stood above him. But she insisted, and covered him with blankets. The pain subsided. It started to return a couple of times, but never reached the acuteness of the initial jabs. Rita went to bed, explaining she would awaken him in the morning before she left for work.

Middleton woke up feeling lousy. Rita came in soon after, and fixed him some coffee. He could still feel something strange in his chest and refused the coffee. After Rita left for work, promising to call him at the newspaper later that day, he called a doctor who had once treated him for a gash in his forehead. He remembered the doctor clearly because he had taken measures to minimize the pain of the stitches. The appointment was set for the next afternoon, because Middleton had made it sound as urgent as he could.

In the evening he met Rita and told her there was still a constant dull ache in his chest and, although she wanted him to come up to her apartment, he left her early, went home and slept without interruption until eight o'clock the next morning.

That afternoon, shortly before his appointment, he went up to the shop foreman, an old friend, and told him about the pains in his chest and the doctor's appointment. The foreman joked with Middleton about wine and women suddenly becoming too much for him after all these years. After all, Middleton was almost forty.

Middleton kidded the foreman right back and slapped him on the arm. "Wait until you see me in action when this pain stops."

The doctor took a series of X rays and told Middleton to return in two days. For the next two nights, Middleton didn't go out with Rita. She called him, but he begged off. He bought a six-pack of beer, and tried to drink one can each night before going to bed, but he didn't really feel like it and ended up pouring the beer down the drain.

On the day he was scheduled to see the doctor, he reported to work on time. The shop foreman told him he was being recycled down to paste-up stereo. His linotype and three others just like it were the last of the hand-set machines to be removed from the printshop. Everything from now on would be automated. And he would be re-trained in some new phase of the operation. There was nothing to worry about. Middleton begged off, explaining he had another doctor's appointment, and although the foreman was less sympathetic this time, gave Middleton the nod.

The doctor didn't look too cheerful when Middleton sat down in front of his desk. The doctor cleared his throat and Middleton watched his huge, bloated stomach rise and fall with each breath. Rise and fall.

"I'm afraid," said the doctor, matter-of-factly, "that you have cancer, Mr. Middleton." Rise and fall.

Middleton didn't say anything.

"Yes," said the doctor.

"What ... what happens now?" The words had almost choked and died in his throat.

The doctor slowly placed his arms behind his back and stared seriously at the linoleum floor. "I'm afraid it's too late to do anything that would be effective. If we had known six months ago ..."

"Six months ago I was fighting a war. When you're fight-ing a war and you feel a pain ..."

"Yes, well, we're working and experimenting all the time for cures to this, you know. One never knows when we'll come up with a drug, or something. I'd like to keep you under constant watch from now on, and I want you to re-port to me at least twice a week. Starting now." Rise and fall.

But Middleton's gaze was no longer focused on the doc-tor; it was focused on the plain-looking, cold linoleum floor. "How long do I have?" God, that was a trite ques-tion. But he didn't know what else to ask.

The doctor frowned. "That's very difficult to say. A good while yet, anyway."

"What's a good while yet, anyway?"

Rise and fall. Rise and fall.

"Well . . . perhaps four or five . . . months."

"That isn't long . . ."

"No, it isn't," said the doctor, reluctantly.

"How many days is that, I wonder."

The doctor looked questioningly at Middleton. "Some."

"Yeah, some."

"Yes, some."

Middleton lifted his eyes to the doctor's now-expressionless face. "This whole thing . . . it doesn't seem real."

"I'm sorry," said the doctor. "I only wish there was some assurance . . . but there isn't. I'd only be lying to you."

"Yeah, sure." Middleton walked down to the street, staring at his shoes most of the time.

He walked the streets the rest of the day and part of the evening. He thought a lot about his childhood, and he thought some about his manhood. Finally, he found himself near the newspaper building, so he went up in the elevator to the composing room and stood next to the empty space where, only a few hours before, his linotype machine had stood.

He listened to the silence.

Rise and fall.

Rise and fall.

For the next week Middleton lived alone and saw no one. He seldom went out of his room, except to buy groceries. He didn't bother to read a paper anymore. He kept his windows closed to shut out the street noises below.

Late in the evening, the phone would ring. He knew it would be Rita. Once there was a knock at his door, and he could hear her voice calling him, but he remained frozen in bed. Strange, he thought, that a girl you spend only a few hours with could care so much. One morning there was another knock on his door, and at first he refused to answer. Then he heard the voice of the landlady and realized the rent was due. He paid her just to keep her from knocking again.

One morning, after a restless night, the phone rang, and he groggily answered it, not realizing what he was doing. It was Rita. They talked for a while. She asked him where he had been.

"Out of town," he replied. "I have a new job out of town. I work days in a real estate office. I'm a clerk. I file papers. And close filing cabinet drawers. Good-bye."

He never heard from Rita again.

He stopped dreaming at night.

Then he stopped counting the days.

He stopped eating. He became thin. Ironically, the pain went away. He almost felt normal again.

Early one morning there was a knock at the door. He opened it, but had to lean against the frame for support. He felt that weak. He wore well-rumpled pajamas and hadn't shaved for ten days. He was quite a sight. "Hiya, doctor," he said.

"Where have you been? I had a hell of a time finding your address. You forgot to leave it with my nurse."

"Right here I've been," said Middleton.

The doctor expressed genuine concern. "Why haven't you come in or phoned me? I said I wanted to see you at least twice a week."

"For what?"

"Observation . . . treatment . . . there are pills I can give you to ease the pain if—"

"The pain doesn't bother me."

"Well, that's something, anyway. Listen, Mr. Middleton, I realize . . . I want you to enter the hospital today. There are some tests I can run . . . X rays . . . there may be more to your case then we know . . . and please bring along your personal items. Now get dressed and we can go down there in my car right this very minute."

"Naw, you go ahead, Doctor. I'll walk down there. I'd rather walk."

"Do you feel up to walking? You're pale."

"Yeah, sure, I'm okay. Look, if I have to go to the hospital, I prefer to walk." Middleton narrowed his eyes on the doctor. "I want to have a look at the streets."

"The hospital's down on Potrero," said the doctor. "It's quite a ways to walk from here."

His voice was firm. "I said I wanted to see the streets."

"I can count on you to show up?" There was some degree of doubt on the doctor's face. For the first time Middleton smiled. That seemed to clinch it for the doctor. "All right, I'll see you in about an hour then."

The doctor went out and Middleton shut the door. He walked back into the bedroom and placed his toilet articles in a small overnight bag. He dressed in slacks, a Hawaiian sportshirt with the name of a beer lettered on it, and sneakers. Comfort may as well be his while he walked. He folded his pajamas carefully, shoved them into the bag. He opened the windows in each room, picked up the overnight bag and walked to the front door.

Opening the door, he stepped into the hallway, making certain the door did not slam behind him. He walked down the hallway. He did not look back.

On the street he ignored honking horns when he crossed a boulevard on a red light. A trucker cursed at him but he kept walking.

He walked only one block and stopped to lean against a lamp post. The San Francisco coolness struck his face and he could feel his face glowing red. He turned his back to the wind and the mist and decided he hadn't really wanted to see the streets after all.

After a few minutes he halted a cab. "Hospital on Potrero," he told the cabbie. The cab traveled a couple of blocks. Middleton said to the driver, "Make it that little coffee shop a block this side of the hospital."

Middleton coughed slightly, but otherwise could feel nothing wrong with his chest. He was still a little dizzy from lack of food. He would remedy that at the coffee shop.

The cab stopped and he got out to stand in front of the coffee shop a block away from the hospital. He paid the driver and stood near the door. "Naw," he said aloud, shaking his head, "I don't want anything to eat."

Middleton walked to the end of the block and stood on the corner.

Middleton thought about the doctor's stomach. Rise and fall.

Middleton thought about the bleeding sergeant in Vietnam. The bleeding sergeant had felt dizzy and sat down. He wondered if the bleeding sergeant was still alive.

Middleton looked at his watch. He knocked a speck of lint from the sleeve of his Hawaiian shirt. He retied his sneakers and looked at his watch again.

He stared at the white hospital. "Well," said Middleton.

He walked across the street.

21
Critique #1

"Shit, Youngman."

"What's wrong, Sarge?"

"This story, that's what's wrong. How the hell do you know what'll happen to a vet? You ever been a vet?"

"I'm still serving my enlistment, Sarge."

"That's what I mean. How the hell can you know?"

"It's fiction, Sarge."

"It's shit, Youngman."

"Don't you see the parallels between the road in Vietnam and the street leading to the hospital? And the—"

"That's got nothing to do with a veteran and what happens to him after a war. Why the hell don't you write something that makes some kind of sense? About something you know."

"Like what?"

"Like maybe this war. You're living it. Now write it."

"Maybe I will."

"Get the feeling of war into it, Youngman. Forget about this 'Crossing' shit. It stinks, Youngman. Really stinks. The whole thing is a bigger hunk of bullcrap than that romance yarn I read last week."

104

"I think you've got something—about writing about the war, I mean. I'll see what I can do, Sarge."

"Now you're starting to talk like a writer."

So, right in front of Sarge, Youngman tore up "Crossing" and began working on his next story. He typed silently for the next three hours. The pages began to stack up. Once, Sarge started to reach for a finished page, but Youngman shook his head. No deal until the story was completely written.

Sarge crossed his legs and lit a fresh cigar. Maybe, he thought, I can make a writer out of this kid yet.

Sarge glanced over at Charlie Brown. The small radio was lying beside him. From it ran a slender cord to his ear. Nobody could hear it, but he was listening to more episodes of "Ma Perkins."

22

The Ear of Charlie Brown

Youngman didn't know it, but he had once been seated in
a movie audience with Charlie Brown, watching a revival
of *The Good, the Bad and the Ugly* and *Once Upon a
Time in the West,* two interpretations of the Old West by
Sergio Leone, a director who had first found fame in Spain
by casting Clint Eastwood as a bounty hunter, quiet of
voice, quick of trigger. They were separated by only four
seats, but neither ever noticed the other. This was in San
Francisco during Youngman's away-from-home period.
For Youngman it had represented a one-time event, attend-
ing this out-of-the way theater on Post Street, between
Buchanan and Webster, near the Japanese Cultural and
Trade Center.

But for Charlie Brown it was home. He had spent his
entire life in this area of the city, with his mother and father who operated one of the Japanese-owned stores on
Post. The hardware business, flanked by grocery and an-
tique stores, had provided a small but comfortable income
for the Browns. Mr. Brown had served gallantly in the
442nd during World War II, and he had often told of his
Italian experiences, but the impressions of war had been di-
luted by time. To Charlie Brown they represented glorified

moments in an otherwise routine existence, hardly to be taken seriously after so many years. His mother was hard-working, although quiet, and had very little to say to her son after his eighth birthday. Charlie Brown took odd jobs to get away from his parents—not because he didn't love them but because he easily grew tired of their company while he worked in the store, and he needed some diversion from their humdrum.

He shined shoes, he was a busboy in a Chinese restaurant in Chinatown (nobody ever seemed to notice he wasn't Chinese), he worked for a short period as a tour guide through a Chinese wax museum (again, nobody questioned his heritage) and he worked during one summer vacation at a radio station in the thirty-eight-story Embarcadero Center Tower amidst glittering electronic gear. His assignment was to keep the floors swept and mopped. The job was menial at best, but he became acquainted with one of the disc jockeys who broadcast a potpourri of material nightly from eight to midnight.

One of these four hours was devoted to Old-Time Radio.

Charlie Brown had never heard of Old-Time Radio before he went to work for the station. He had once heard his parents talking about it, but that had been years ago. One night, as he waited for the DJ to finish so he could clean up the booth, he settled down to hear his first dramatic event . . .

. . . It was called "Inner Sanctum" and it was all about a woman who thought she was the reincarnation of a Salem witch. A creepy-sounding character, by the name of Raymond, made macabre jokes and horrendous puns during the introduction and closing, and something about it caught Charlie Brown's fancy. At least "The Vengeful Corpse" had been a pleasing diversion from his work.

The next night the offering was "Suspense," a dramatic series that, according to the research-minded DJ, had run for twenty years (1942–62) on radio, presenting some of the best mysteries of all time. This particular episode was "August Heat," with Ronald Colman portraying a confused artist who undergoes a fateful encounter in a stonecutter's home. It was brooding and eerie, and for the first time in his life Charlie Brown began to feel a tinge of excitement. Something unusual, something he could neither understand nor define, was happening to him. The next night he could hardly wait for the DJ to get around to playing the tape of "The Mysterious Traveler" and the story "If You Believe" in which an aging scientist creates an artifical form of life which breaks loose and goes on a killing spree.

The next week Charlie Brown bought his own Sony tape machine, and several blank reels of recording tape. At night, after the DJ had closed down, Charlie Brown entered his booth and dubbed off the shows he wanted from the DJ's collection. Within a month he had sixty-nine shows, ranging from additional mysteries ("The Witch's Tale," "The Haunting Hour," "Murder Clinic") to comedy ("Amos 'n Andy," "Fibber McGee and Molly," "Baby Snooks"). During the school months he found his mind wandering away from the lessons onto mystery plots and variety situations. He kept hearing certain memorable sections of dialogue over and over. Then he got the idea of buying a portable cassette machine and transferring the shows to cartridges. Now, on the way to class, between classes and even during classes, he could listen to programs by placing a miniature plug in his ear and the cassette in his pocket. When his teacher asked about the cord running into his ear he merely explained he was losing his hearing in one ear. The teacher never asked about it again. Charlie Brown escaped into this world of high adventure and comedy on a daily basis. It reached the point where he seldom spoke to his parents, which really wasn't much of a change since they seldom spoke to him anyway. Old-Time Radio became the focal point of his life and he realized it would always be this way.

Charlie Brown became especially interested in stories about buried treasure (e.g., Orson Wells "Mercury Theater of the Air" version of Stevenson's *Treasure Island*), for he saw in buried treasure an alleviation for all the frustrations and mundane tasks which ate into his tape-listening. time. A treasure, he believed, would buy him the freedom to travel the world, amassing the largest collection of Old-Time Radio programs in history. Then he could settle down and spend the rest of his life listening.

He slid deeper into his fantasy. After graduation, nothing in his life really changed. He had left the radio station a few months before (he lost interest once the DJ dropped the Old-Time Radio segment) and he began driving a taxicab, since this afforded him many uninterrupted hours each day for listening. His boss finally got wise to the fact he was pulling his rig over into quiet alleyways and side streets so he could listen to radio shows, so he was fired.

Then came the war. Even with the arrival of his induction notice, nothing really changed. With the new midget units now on the market, he could carry the tape in his hip pocket during basic training.

On maneuvers he heard an entire year's worth of "Mr. District Attorney." During rifle practice he heard a series of "Lights Out" by Arch Oboler. During an inspection by the general in charge of his division he listened to an hour-long "Lux Radio Theater" version of *Broken Arrow*. At night, while the other men fell into a near-catatonic sleep, exhausted after a day on the training courses, Charlie Brown listened to three hours of "One Man's Family" or "The Lone Ranger" or "Casey, Crime Photographer." While other men ate chow, or went to the latrine, he listened to "Richard Diamond, Private Detective" with Dick Powell or "Dimension X," savoring the adaptations of Robert Heinlein and other science-fiction writers. On the day he was finally assigned to the 442nd and took his loyalty oath, he heard three "Gunsmoke" shows with William Conrad as Marshal Matt Dillon and four "Adventures of Sam Spade" with Howard Duff. In fact, Duff was just wrapping up "The Bluebeard Caper" when he was handed his diploma, which was supposed to be proof he had passed the rigorous training fields and was now ready for the frontline.

While many of his ethnic brothers had found solace and comfort in being assigned to the 442nd, for they preferred being with their own kind, Charlie Brown had felt no emotion at all. Other men tried to talk to him, but he never seemed to answer coherently, as if his mind were somewhere else. When he spoke it was in a mumble, and eventually the others gave up trying to converse with him.

One afternoon, Charlie Brown was called on to produce a truckload of spare parts for his unit's broken-down halftrack. On reporting to the supply house, the sergeant there told him he didn't have the parts needed. Charlie Brown, rather than waste time scouring the post, stole the parts from the supply sergeant's own halftrack. This earned him title of Chief Purveyor of Anything. In short, he became a scrounger. He quickly learned to enjoy scrounging, for it took him away from field duty and other mundane daily duties, and while he looked for whatever it was someone else wanted, he listened. This pleased Charlie Brown and he did nothing to tarnish his image as a dogrobber. Word leaked up to higher echelons, and soon he purveyed for colonels, lieutenant colonels, and three-star generals. This coincided with the arrival of fifty new "Suspense" episodes and twenty-five "X Minus One" science-fiction episodes. He was in his glory.

He even did some pimping on the side, but his mind was so attuned to the radio shows he wasn't really aware that it was any different than looking for a spare toggle bolt or size 40 cartridge belt. To him, pimping simply provided more free time for listening.

So, PFC Charlie Brown (he had been promptly promoted by his company commander after proving so resourceful) came to be a talented purveyor, although he had yet to do anything that would prove he was a soldier.

During the initial probes by the 442nd into the Poyang Mountains, Charlie Brown's company had been pinned down by enemy mortar fire. This interrupted an episode of "The Whistler" with Jack Webb (the title was "Blue Alibi") just when he was meeting a beautiful femme fatale in a barroom, and Charlie Brown cursed under his breath as his brethren of the 442nd died around him. The company was eighty percent casualties after the Chinese staged an attack, and those who could still manage to move unaided escaped into the fields of grass. Charlie Brown was among them.

Two days later, tired and thirsty and midway through

"The Adventures Of Sherlock Holmes" with Basil Rathbone and Nigel Bruce, Harry Bartell announcing, he came to the village of Kwang, was befriended by the young mother, and fell idly into her spare bed, where he finished the Sherlock Holmes story and began on a lengthy "I Love Adventure" mystery entitled "The Thing That Cried in the Night." The next afternoon Sarge and Youngman found him scrounging, simply out of professional habit, in the garbage dump.

23
The Night of
The Great Truck Heist

Louis Panayiotis Nikopolis pressed against the running board of the Chinese three-quarter-ton truck and held his breath, not daring to make the slightest movement. Even a detectable inhalation of air could prove fatal. Crunching footsteps sounded like cannon blasts—each more thunderous than the last as they drew nearer.

Three feet away, a Chinese sentry paused to light a cigarette, his submachine gun cradled in his arms. The sentry took a deep drag on his cigarette, made a slight wheezing sound, and slowly turned in Louis's direction. The barrel of the weapon was now pointed directly at the Greek's stomach. Every instinct in his body wanted to leap, but he kept his senses and remained motionless, praying the darkness would keep him concealed.

Although the sentry gazed into the vicinity where Louis stood frozen, he apparently saw nothing. After a few more puffs, he flipped away the cigarette. It fell against Louis's pant leg, dropping down into his cuff. At first Louis felt nothing. Then whiffs of smoke rose from the cuff, and

Louis began to feel the first indication of heat. But he didn't dare move.

The sentry still faced the truck. The slightest movement from Louis would be instantly noticed. Louis cursed himself for not having his bayonet out of its sheath, for with one quick movement he had a chance of taking the sentry out. He calculated the odds and decided they were against him: He would require an extra second to get the blade up where he could use it, and that might be all the time the sentry would need to respond first.

Wafts of smoke started to curl upward toward his stomach. Louis could feel a slight discomfort now—a steadily warming sensation. In a few moments, he knew the cuff would catch fire. He waited . . .

The sentry turned in the opposite direction, yawned as if he hadn't slept in days, and strolled away. Silently, Louis reached down to snuff out the cigarette. A slight "whuff" sounded as he closed his fist around the area of the cuff and pounded it flat. He sighed and glanced at his watch, shielding the phosphorescent face.

12:11—four minutes to go before he would steal his first truck.

The Chinese truck he had selected was one of six parked in a convoy off to one side of a narrow, rutted dirt road which ran through a flat, grassless plateau. He had successfully slipped past the outer perimeter guards and had gone from truck to truck, setting an explosive charge in the supply bed of each. He had reached the fifth truck, and had just finished setting the charge, when the sentry had approached.

The timing of the charges had been critical—each was set for the same moment: 12:15. He had given himself fifteen minutes to place charges in five of the trucks and then slip into the lead vehicle, to wait for the combined explosions. In the confusion certain to follow, he would drive right through the Chinese perimeter.

12:11—four minutes remaining to reach the lead vehicle. More than enough . . . He paused as he heard a yawning sound from the rear of the fifth truck. Someone was climbing out. A sentry grabbing a few minutes of

113

shut-eye. And now he was moving toward Louis, picking up his duty where he had left off.

This time the bayonet was in Louis's hand as he waited. The sentry was almost within lunging range when he stopped, and for a split second Louis was certain he was going to give the alarm. But instead he gave out a hum under his breath. There was a "zip" sound. The next thing Louis heard was a familiar streaming sound, and he could feel something wet splattering off his boots and inundating the cuffs of his fatigues. A sound of relief followed, then a lessening of the flow. Finally the downpour stopped altogether. Louis heard the zip sound again.

The rustling sound that Louis made as his body pushed away from the canvas stretched over the truck's inverted U-frame was enough to betray him, but the sentry only uttered the first syllable of the first word of his question before Louis's bayonet slid between his ribs. The sentry fell limply against Louis, who kept one hand over the soldier's mouth as he quickly dragged him to the back of the truck and flipped his body into the bed. He glanced at his watch.

12:12—it had taken him only a minute. He still had three. Three minutes to go exactly twenty yards to reach the lead vehicle.

He worked his way along the side of the fifth truck, crouching near the front wheel to study the truck he planned to heist. It was deserted. The chances of another guard dozing were unlikely ... nobody in sight ... he decided to work his way across the opening.

Louis was five feet out when he heard the laughter. Chinese chatter. He darted back to the fifth truck and hugged the running board. A mechanic, talking to himself, stepped up to the lead truck and turned over the engine. It didn't catch. The mechanic tried again. The whirring was like a death knell to Louis.

The mechanic got out, lifted the hood and, with his flashlight, examined the engine, chattering all the while, only now in anger. The sentry who had passed Louis earlier came up hurriedly and laughed at the mechanic, so the mechanic laughed right back.

Louis listened to the chatter. He didn't know Chinese,

114

but he knew the truck wasn't about to start. His plan to steal a truck was falling apart right before his eyes.

There was still one chance: Move the charge from the fifth truck and place it in the one with the dead engine. Get behind the wheel of the fifth truck and pray the other explosions didn't damage the engine or tires. Then drive out the fifth truck. He prayed that the sentry and mechanic would remain distracted while he made the switch. He looked at his watch again.

Two and a half minutes left.

He picked up the explosive charge from the bed of the fifth truck (some of the blood from the knifed sentry had sloshed onto it) and quickly sized up the lead truck. The two Chinese stood next to the front tire, so he chose the right side for his approach.

He had just reached the tailgate of the lead truck and placed the charge in the bed, when he saw a flashlight beam bobbing along the ground, not far behind him. Another sentry, apparently, was checking each truck carefully.

Louis's first impulse was to duck beneath the truck, but there was the danger of the light accidentally falling on him. No, the interior of the truck was the only sure place. Wedged against the tailgate, Louis was likely to remain unseen even if the sentry were to play his beam over the supplies stacked inside.

Louis climbed in, being careful his boots made no clanging sounds, and pressed himself against the tailgate. His bayonet was ready. The blade, in fact, was only inches from the sentry's throat when he paused to move his light over the crates. Louis felt something pressing against his spine, and realized it was the charge. There was no comfort in the feeling. The footsteps of the guard moved away. He glanced at his watch.

12:13—three voices chattered now as Louis prepared to make his way back to the fifth truck. Were they examining the engine? Was one of them perhaps glancing back along the row of trucks? He had no way of knowing for sure. He would need to leap from the bed and work his way back, hoping they kept their heads turned. He didn't like relying on luck, nor throwing all caution to the wind, but he had

115

no other choice. In less than two minutes, the entire plateau would be an inferno.

Without looking behind him, Louis silently made his way back to the fifth truck. The voices continued to quibble in Chinese.

12:14—the second hand was a third of the way around. Forty seconds to go. Carefully, he turned the handle to the door on the passenger side of the truck. He froze.

It was locked.

Would the door on the other side be locked? His brain seemed to splinter into a thousand pieces. Sheer chaos. The first hint of panic. Out here in the middle of nowhere, on a desolate Chinese plateau, a locked door thwarting him. Somehow he kept his head and made his way around to the other side. He was oblivious to the fact he was exposed to the sentries and mechanic, but luck was still with him: They remained bunched around the left front tire, their attention riveted on the unworkable motor.

Louis tried the door handle.

It opened. He hurried a look at his watch as he slid behind the wheel.

Ten seconds to spare. Jesus, only ten seconds. Six by the time he found the ignition and had his free hand gripped firmly on the steering wheel.

When the explosion came the mechanic was turning to get into the cab. The blast ripped the canvas and drove part of the inverted U-frame steel bar, which had been sheered in several places, into his lungs. The impact picked him off his feet and carried him away into the darkness. The glass in the windows blew outward, and the hood was lifted from its hinges and gracefully arced through the air with all the style of a magic carpet.

At the very instant of the blast, Louis had turned over the engine. It had whirred for the first four seconds, then sputtered. He tried again, pumping on the gas pedal, afraid now of flooding. This time it caught.

Behind him, the gas tanks of the other four vehicles went simultaneously. Debris fell all around him; his own truck rocked under the impact. Something burning thudded atop the canvas of the truck, but rolled off without

116

catching fire. Something made of steel shattered the windshield. Pieces of supply crates banged off the hood.

Assured the engine was warm enough to stand instant acceleration, Louis twisted the steering wheel as far to the right as he could and drove out toward the barren field. Figures scattered in front of him as he sped through the bivouac area. Good—everyone was in utter confusion, as he had guessed they would be.

All five trucks were burning to his satisfaction as he threw a quick glance through the side window. He returned his attention to the open field, which was full of impossible ruts and chuckholes. He was jostled and thrown as he tried to keep the truck due north. That was important. Due north.

One hole was so deep his head was thrown against the roof of the cab, and for a second he saw only blackness. But he immediately regained the wheel, which had started to drift wildly to the left. Looming in the glare of his headlights were three men, Chinese regulars, part of the perimeter defense guard, no doubt. They were directly in his pathway and gave no indication of yielding. Two of them raised their rifles to fire as Louis bore down. Bullets shattered the already damaged windshield and he felt the impact of one slug near his head as it tore through the cab and passed on out the back. He gave the truck an extra burst of speed and slumped down to offer a smaller target.

He felt the unmistakable thunk of a body. A submachine gun slammed against the glass, skidded across the hood and fell from sight as Louis accelerated and careened. The countryside was open ahead, and for a moment he permitted himself to rejoice. He'd done it! He'd stolen his first truck. And destroyed five other vehicles with supplies in the process. And he was past his last obstacle.

Or so he thought . . .

Abruptly, the ground was falling away in front of the truck. He felt the truck begin to angle sharply and he hit the brakes. The truck went into a skid, the back end swaying around to the front. He didn't try to correct the skid because he saw ahead of him an abyss, or a canyon, or a wide gully—something that angled downward so quickly

117

he knew he had every reason to be scared as hell. His only hope now was to come to a stop before . . .

Louis twisted the wheel to the left, hoping to fishtail the back end to the maximum. At least that would bring him out of it with his front pointed away from the drop. The back end continued to wobble and skid, then whipped around sharply as he hit the brake one last time. The truck came to an instantaneous stop. He could feel the rear tires clutching precariously to dirt, but he knew that not all the tires were catching. Maybe sixty-five percent of the tread. The rest . . . he swallowed . . . they must be hanging over the drop-off. He preferred not to look.

Louis broke into a cold sweat. He would have to ease forward delicately, get the rest of those tires on terra firma. The truck inched forward, then threatened to roll back. He hit the brake at the same time he gave the truck more acceleration. He counterbalanced the rollback, but wasn't gaining any momentum. The engine raced and he was locked there for a moment, going neither forward nor backward.

He would have to hit the accelerator hard enough to pull out of it. And he would have to take his foot off the brake in the same instant. Too much of a delay on punching the gas and the truck was certain to roll back over the precipice. Or whatever the hell it was back there.

He hit the gas.

The truck lurched forward. Louis could feel the tires taking complete hold. They spun in the dirt, kicking up clouds of dust, and the truck was moving again, aimed back the way he had come.

As he drove, trying to avoid the worst ruts and holes, Louis realized that the plateau must be dissected by a cliffline of the Che-ling Pass. When he had made his way out of the Tungting Basin and into the mountains earlier that night, he must have worked his way around the cliffline, coming out on the plateau without realizing that a chasm existed between him and the rendezvous point, which he had designated as due north. That simple arbitrary decision had almost cost him his life.

But how far did the cliffline dissect? At what point could

he safely drive off the plateau and swing back north to pick up Reva and Li Ming?

The only safe answer was to swing back onto the dirt road and hope that Reva and Li Ming would have sense enough to know he couldn't reach the rendezvous point and move down to the road. It would be a difficult run for them, but he was certain they could make it.

Louis had hoped to avoid the road—it was too obvious an escape route, and there was always the danger of oncoming traffic cutting him off. But now he chose it out of necessity.

As the tires clung to the deep ruts, and he continued to bang his head on the cab ceiling, he glanced ahead to see that some of the surviving Chinese had rushed headlong down the road, firing blindly into the darkness. Louis swung the truck back onto the road and raced past the militiamen, who were now thoroughly confused to find the truck they were looking for emerging from the darkness behind them.

Louis stayed on the horn, trying to talk in a desperate, staccato fashion. It was the signal they had prearranged, should anything go wrong. Three short beeps, one long beep, three short, one long. Hustle your ass toward that sound. That will be the new pickup point. He pulled over beside a huge boulder to wait, realizing the militia were closing fast, but also realizing that he had to give Reva and Li Ming a single source of sound. If he continued to move, they would be unable to reach him.

The Chinese were three hundred yards away and still closing. Bullets continued to fly, but there hadn't been a hit in over a minute now.

The distance shortened to two hundred yards and Louis knew he couldn't wait beyond another twenty seconds. He hit the horn again, even though he knew it gave the militia a better idea of his location. Three short, one long, three short, one long. Hurry up! Where were those two broads?

A burst of submachine-gun fire kicked up the dust next to the truck. He threw the vehicle into gear and released the emergency brake just as Reva stepped from behind the boulder, dragging Li Ming, who was out of breath, by the

119

arm. Louis flung open the door on the passenger side and they slid in. Li Ming was barely able to move.

"Hurry up, hurry up! Slam that door!"

Bullets whanged off the tailgate and shattered the side-view mirror. Another round ricocheted off the inverted U-frame.

"Why the hell didn't you pick us up?"

"There's a goddamn cliff over there somewhere. I didn't want to end up at the bottom. That's why."

The truck bounced along the road, and the Chinese were soon out of sight.

"I didn't think you could do it, Louis." Reva took a deep breath and placed her hand on Louis's leg, gently rubbing it back and forth. "I was worried about you."

"You okay, Li Ming?"

The Chinese girl fought for breath. Finally she said: "When a master must suffer, so do his subjects."

"She'll be all right," reassured Reva. "All she needs is her wind back."

Li Ming leaned back against the seat, and her breathing returned to normal. "If the profits are great, the risks are just as great."

"Believe me," said Louis, "the profits are going to be great."

"A truck, I can't believe it, Louis. We've got ourselves a truck."

"Yeah, how about that. A goddamn truck."

"How far to the ammo dump?" Reva could not restrain her enthusiasm.

"In this crate? I'd say by late tomorrow. Maybe by dark. I figure we should travel all night, hole up in the morning and look things over. If we can find another road, one the Chinks aren't using, we should be able to make it by dark."

"Bot Bon Jui," said Reva, beaming. "A dream come true." She put her hand back on Louis's leg. "Baby, just how rich do you think we're gonna be?"

"Rolling rich, Reva. Rolling left and right rich."

Li Ming sighed. "Every highway leads to fortune."

The Chinese truck sped through the night.

24
Squad C-323 Gets the Message

Odor had superimposed itself on emotion, and as a result, emotion had been blunted.

By nightfall, King Kong had begun to forget that his son had been killed only a few hours earlier. But the odor ... that strange blend of The Man Up the Pole and graphite, gunpowder and the metal of weapons. It was the memory of that commingling that had taken deeper root. It was the memory of that mixture that motivated him now. The cause for his hatred, ironically, was vanishing: by dawn, or by noon of the next day, he would have no further memory of Son of Kong.

Squad C-323 had taken up bivouac position along a bend in the Kun, a narrow tributary of the Yangtze River, and under the direction of Kong, second in command, had begun *kanga* procedure. Under normal peacetime circumstances *kanga* would translate as "carnival," but here it is translated as "communications contact."

The first step was to secure clay from the banks of the river. This clay was carried by hand, a lump at a time, by Sergeant Joe Young and Bonzo and deposited, while still in a plastic state, into a small area of sonorous earth, two feet wide. There it was pounded down against a bed of peat,

121

which became a resonant cavity capable of intensifying sound. A giant drum, in essence, producing a flat, dead sound but a sound of considerable volume. Under normal circumstances, one would leap up and down on the dry clay in a wild, grotesque manner and utter long, rolling sounds, melodic in their effect. In this case nothing so uncontrolled was permissible. Here careful rhythm and controlled tempo were necessary.

The message went out: thump — thump — thump — thang — whang — whap — thunk — thunk — thump — thunk — bimp!

When the message was finished, the members of Squad C-323 ate chow and waited for the return message. It came as King Kong bit into sliced, well-seasoned pieces of canned foliage of the rare and tender *cunninghamia* fir tree. Konga had just bitten into a palm nut, and Sergeant Joe Young savored the juices of a papaya, floating in guava pulp. Bonzo was being sloppy as usual—half a jar of peaches had spilled onto his open foodsack, drenching an overripe banana.

The message was concise and clear: Return to Battalion Command Group Center. Immediately!

Sergeant Joe Young drank down the last of the guava pulp and threw away the ration can, smacking his lips. Bonzo was tearing open the overripe banana in an effort to save as much of the spilt juice as possible. Konga was just swallowing the last of the palm nuts. As second in command, it was his duty to reply to the message, and he started to stand. King Kong flung a piece of foliage at him and pounded the ground with his free fist.

Another stomping tirade, and Konga got the message. King Kong would send the answer himself.

The commander of Squad C-323 swallowed the remnants of his foliage ration, walked to the drum pit and tapped out a fast reply.

In anyone's language, it was plain and to the point.

Squad C-323 would not be returning to Battalion Command Group Center.

which became a pivotal stage-piece of International ....
....

25

Sarge Forms a Plan

Youngman wrote with a frenzy born out of a determination to succeed as a writer, and out of a sense of desperation which had been induced in him by Sarge's negative reading of "Crossing." He spent the entire morning at his porto-typer. The pages mounted. Sarge pretended he didn't care about what Youngman was doing, but Youngman could tell he was eager to look at this latest yarn. Sarge wanted war—by God, he'd give him war. So much war he'd be sick of it by the last page.

Finally, Youngman took a break as Sarge outlined for him and Charlie Brown their next move. They'd head for the main American line, keeping as inconspicuous as possible. They'd have to go easy on water, since there were no maps of this area, and they might go days without find-ing any water. They set out and went five miles without stopping.

Sarge called a break and they settled into the ruins of an old railroad depot (the tracks had been ripped out by peasant partisans during the Chinese Civil War, and the line had subsequently been abandoned). Sarge watched as Youngman dashed his way through the last pages of his new story. Sarge decided right then and there to read it, to find out if Youngman had been heeding his criticism or was just masturbating himself again.

Sarge took the manuscript and leaned back against an old concrete pillar. He read.

26

"Aceldama" by Ernest Youngman

Machine-gun fire enfilades the torn hillside. The hot red-tipped bits of lead churn endlessly through smoked air and eat into the dirt—geysering clods, whirlpooling dust, thunking with distinct tone into chests and legs and arms, rending flesh to shredded strips and punching organs vital and otherwise with 150 grains of power. Added to this song of bullets is the song of men—screams from twisted mouths which belong to seared bodies thrashing in the earth of the hillside, rolling and falling and staggering.

* * *

"Push on, goddamn it. Move those men up."

"Sir, we're pinned."

"Move them up, I said."

"That machine gun is picking my men off."

"We've got to take the crest."

"What about my men?"

"At all costs. Now move."

"I can't do that, sir."

"Lieutenant, are you refusing to obey an order?"

"I'm not refusing anything. I'm just telling you my men aren't going up that damn hill."

"That's court-martial talk, Lieutenant."

"It's nothing but common sense, based on the urge to live, sir. And anything else is bullshit."

"Fuck, why do I have to get the shitheads . . ."

* * *

The fingers keep the bullets going. They wrap tightly on metal, glued by fear, squeezing the metal, pulling the metal, yanking the metal with furious impulse. All kinds of fingers—long fingers with short fingernails, short fingers with bitten nails, bitten nails on slender fingers, fat fingers with tapering nails—all yanking as spasmodically as their owners' insides.

* * *

"Ammo! Ammo!"

"All right, all right. I'm feeding these fucking belts as fast as I can."

". . . now slide her forward."

"There."

"Nothing happens."

"What?"

"It won't fire."

"Must be jammed. Jesus, hurry up and clear it. Those men are depending on our fire."

"Give me your bayonet."

"Here."

"Slide the handle back."

"Steady . . ."

"Cartridge lodged."

"You got it. It's clear."

"They're charging. Feed me the belts. Feed me."

"There, there. Fire."

"Ammo! Ammo!"

* * *

Below are the bellies—bellies on the left, bellies on the right. There are fat bellies . . . fingers squeeze easy on fat bellies. Skinny, baggy bellies . . . more steadiness in the fingers on these bellies. Empty bellies . . . steady fingers

126

there. Bellies covered with thick layers of hair . . . fingers keep on jerking. Bellies crisscrossed with ammo belts . . . fingers leap quickly, steadily, as though having eyes. Bellies covered by a row of grenades . . . fingers hesitate long there, until smoke and fire tear into the bowels of earth and men and the fingers lurch from the metal with the roar but settle back down almost instantaneously to go on down the row of bellies of fatness, skinniness; bellies of young bodies, middle-aged bodies, old bodies; along bellies full of meat and potatoes, bellies empty from regurgitation, bellies filled with green beans and gravy, bellies with coffee, some with sugar some with cream some just black; bellies with milk made from powder, bellies with eggs made from powder, bellies with nothing but phlegm and yellow fluid from stuffed noses, bellies upside down with fear, bellies without food or fear from lack of appetite and thought; bellies, all of them, for the slashing of a bullet.

* * *

"Medic! Medic!"

"Okay, take it easy. I'm here. Just take it easy."

"He's hit bad."

"Yeah, stomach wound. Real bad."

"It's . . . wide open."

"If it gets to you, don't look at it. There, a shot of morphine. That's all I can do."

"Aren't you gonna patch him up?"

"A wound like that? I can only lay a bandage on it."

"You gotta do more for him. He's my friend, my buddy."

"Don't think about it, pal. Don't let anybody be your buddy today."

"But . . . he's dying."

"Nothing I can do."

* * *

There are the helmets. Helmets are in every position on the hillside. One helmet is tipped on its side so that the chin strap is dangling on the earth just inches from the wearer's outstretched fingers; one helmet is upright on the soil, as though the hillside were its wearer; one helmet is dented at the top from pieces of steel and rests completely upside down, rocking gently with each nearby explosion; one helmet has been separated from its liner and both pieces have fallen atop an armless and legless torso; one helmet rests comfortably in the stagnant water of a shell-hole, one helmet is still on its owner's head, and the owner is face down in the mud so that just a tip of the helmet is coming in contact with the hillside. A helmet here . . . a helmet there . . . a helmet rests on the slope for each and every head that has drooped and fallen to earth.

* * *

"Captain, give me your hand."

"I—I can't move it, Tyler."

"Sir, your hand."

"Numb. Numb all over, Tyler. That last shell—"

"Sir, you've got to get out of the open. Just try to move toward this hole."

"Numb. All over. Can't . . . move."

"Here, pull yourself in on my rifle stock. All you have to do is get a grip on it."

"Can't move."

"Please, Captain. A machine gun is getting our range."

"Numb. My God, I'm so cold."

"Jesus, sir. Move!"

"Too cold to . . . live."

"Sir . . ."

* * *

The discarded weapons show the fury. An automatic rifle rests half-buried on the rim of a foxhole where its firer had to leave it when a bullet ate into his brain, and now the eruptions from grenades have leveled portions of the curving convex hillside onto the stock of the weapon, so that only the dull barrel shows. A rifle rests atop a pair of legs, pointing down the ridge from where it came, no longer a menace to its opponent or its carrier. Another rifle rests beneath a sprawling set of arms and legs, smoke still curling from its hot muzzle. A carbine has been split in
128

half by shrapnel fragments, and the stock portion still rests in limp fingers while the other half has flown up the hillside to settle into a hole that is the grave for two other carbines and one heavy-caliber automatic. In fingers of now-dead authority rests a fully loaded pistol; the pistol still has its safety catch on lock and the safety catch is close to a head that once examined maps and gave orders to charge because of two tiny silver bars that now only clutter the environment.

* * *

"Keep your men down, Sergeant. Have them dig in good and deep. We'll try another push in a minute. As long as those jokers up there don't try a counterattack . . ."

"A massacre. A fucking massacre."

"I know. I've lost all my patrols as well as a platoon. At least."

"Captain Hollister is dead. Still lying out there. Someone should bring him in."

"Not worth the risk of losing another man. Don't worry, Sergeant, he's dead. Worry about the living. How many men're left?"

"Don't know. I'll check."

"Forget it. No use moving around for some sniper's pleasure."

"Cigarette, sir?"

"No. I never smoke."

"This'll be just like the last hill. I won't be able to eat for a week."

"Yeah."

* * *

The canteens show the misery. One canteen is clutched tightly in fingers no longer able to unscrew the lid; the water is fresh and clean but warm and was intended to satisfy dry lips and arid tongue but will never satisfy any lips or tongue. Another canteen rests on its side, a steady drip coming from its neck, down over the silver chain, plinking ceaselessly into the cork inserted in the lid, dripping off the cork in splattering specks that wet silent faces and inanimate hands. One canteen rests in its holder which is still tightly buttoned in place; but it is empty of water, for the water has run out onto the ground through a small round hole in the center of the canteen; on the other side of the canteen in another hole, this one pushing a sharp rim of metal outward; through a webbed belt is a third hole; this hold is shredded with dangling threads of redness from the final hole in a belly of skinniness filled with potatoes and gravy that can see sunlight for the very first time. Another canteen is twisted into jagged, biting edges after being lifted into the air and flung through space and slammed against a rock.

* * *

"Hey, you."

"Me?"

"Yeah, you. Come here."

"What's wrong? I'm a runner and I'm supposed—"

"I don't give a damn who you are. Help me get out of here. A shell knocked these timbers in the bunker in on me. I'm pinned. My leg—it's caught under this beam."

"Jesus, why didn't you call for help?"

"What for? I'm safer down here than out there."

"Yeah, but your leg. It's . . ."

"The hell with my leg. It's no good anymore and there's nothing I can do about it."

"I don't think I can lift this beam by myself."

"Just try. That's all. Just try."

"Hey, it's moving!"

"You can lift it, boy. Go on, you can lift it."

"Yank it back!"

"Oh Jesus. It's out."

"The bone . . . it's sticking out of your knee."

"Get a medic, boy. She's starting to hurt now."

"Yeah, sure."

"Thanks a lot, boy. You're a real pal. Hope to see you again sometime."

* * *

The bodies hold the terror. In every form imaginable, death has leaped out with gashing claws, spilling bodies into muck and slime and dirt to live no more. A young soldier rests on his back, his eyes wide open, his hands lifted before his face as though attempting to come together to form a prayer; the plea that must be on his lips goes unheard by the others around him. An older soldier has his belly webbed between his sticky fingers; the blood is dried and the only movement in his vicinity is his wavy black hair fluttering in the breeze. Another soldier appears to be all right; there are no belly pieces in his hands, nor are his arms and legs torn to shreds; the only fault seems to be of minute size and it is in the back of his head—just a tiny little slit where a sliver of steel has entered. The youngest soldier on the hillside rests on his golden hair, his eyes closed to the blueness above him, his green drab uniform seemingly unfit for a man to risk his life and eventually die in.

* * *

"My mother."

"What'd you say, Ed?"

"My mother. I'm thinking about my mother."

"How the hell can you think about your mother with all this shelling going on?"

"It's real easy. All you gotta do is try."

"Well, I can't do it."

"Mother and those wonderful Sunday meals she used to cook. Mother and her—"

"Duck. Incoming barrage."

". . . Goddamn, that was a real whopper. Almost blew me right out of this fucking hole. Okay, Ed, go on about your mother. I'm listening. . . . Hey, Ed, you all right? . . . Ed . . . Jesus . . . my God . . ."

* * *

"My foot hurts. That damn pig of a mortarman stepped on it when the attack started."

"There's a medic just down the slope."

"No, I'll be all right."

"Sure?"

"Yeah."

"We gave them hell today."

"God, my foot hurts."

"Hey, you've picked up some shrapnel."

"Maybe I'd better see that medic."

"Here, I'll help you down the hill."

"All right."

"Steady."

"Ah!"

"Can you walk?"

"I can barely stand."

"Easy now."

"Wait . . . they're coming back."

"You work the gun. I'll feed it."

"Ammo! Ammo!"

* * *

Sudden roaring, explosions, screams, fingers tighten, bellies appear far below—all kinds of bellies again. Pull, yank, twist, throw, sprawl, heave, bellow, fling; wood against bleak cheeks; encircling fingers onto fragmentary grenades; outstretched boots; *clack* of closing bolts; *pop* of unsnapping buttons; *bang* of steel helmets hitting earth; booted footsteps in gravel, sand, mud, and blood; waving arms; glint of steel; chattering teeth; *click* of safeties; flowing vomit onto the surface of a fieldpack; rending explosions; dirt clods falling; barbed wire against stomachs; fingers coming away from a knee under which a leg dangles like a matchstick; canteen cup bouncing along the slope; the pounding of fleeing feet and rolling bodies.

* * *

"The mortar! The mortar!"

"Shut up, damn you."

"But the mortar . . ."

"Fuck the mortar. We'll never reach it without getting blown to bits."

"But the company is depending on the mortar."

"We'd never reach it alive. Forget it."

People gotta seem alive. They gotta breathe. Maybe you oughta try that."

Youngman felt a sagging sensation. The impulse to rip up pages was returning, but he fought valiantly against it. A writer had to retain his pride at all costs. "But the action . . . you still have to have action, Sarge."

"You gotta have action, Youngman, or you ain't worth a shit as a writer. But give us real people. Not some idiot like that Middleton, or whatever his name was. Give us a guy with a motive. Then you'll have yourself one helluva story and not this crap you keep handing me to read."

"Motives," Youngman thought about that for a while. "You know, I did some research on the Philippine Islands just before they called me in. I was thinking . . . how about this World War II story . . . in the Philippines . . . guerrillas . . . motive . . . yeah . . . Japs . . . I think I got it, Sarge. You've given me a great idea . . . and a story slanted for the market . . . the men's magazine market . . . yeah, yeah . . ."

"I figured you'd latch onto some of my ideas sooner or later, Youngman. You know, I think maybe I'm gonna make a writer out of you yet."

"Yeah, yeah." Youngman got out his porto-typer and went to work. The first few pages flowed without any trouble.

"Kick the shit out of them, Youngman," urged Sarge.

It was then they heard a mortar shell explode and long bursts of automatic rifle fire.

"Chinese," said Sarge, without even raising his head. "About a mile from here."

28
Short Circuiting
The Vidtape Column

The Vidtape Column—two trucks and one jeep—drove right into the trap prepared by Ju-Chao and his patrol, mainly because the point scout in the jeep had been distracted by an old horror movie which, somehow, he had never seen before. The scout had been watching this horror film on a TV set mounted on the windshield of his jeep. He had wandered off the main supply route into enemy territory. Now, unthinking, he drove through the narrow pass without stopping to think it might be an ideal place for an ambush.

A scaly, slimy creature with three eyes embedded in its misshappen head and several protuberances rising like horns from what passed as a forehead had just picked up Abby Dalton and was carrying her in such a manner that her dress slid up above her knees. In those high-heeled shoes of the 1950s, she looked very sexy. And this was what had distracted the jeep scout.

So, the trucks drove right into the mouth of the ambush. Sergeant Chi-yung dropped his arm, the signal for all three vehicles to be hit simultaneously.

A sniper took out the jeep driver, firing but a single shot. It was a foolish death that a fool as big as the scout

136

deserved. The jeep banged up against a hillside and stalled, rolling back a few feet before coming to a full stop. The scaly monster snarled and dropped Abby Dalton, then was blown into glass shards when a fragmentary grenade, dropped onto the front seat, shattered the picture tube.

Meanwhile, a mortar shell had fallen directly on the hood of the first truck. Instantly, the engine was a mass of metal whirling in four directions. The two Americans in the front seat were aflame, never knowing what turned them to cinders. Slivers of steel and engine mounts clunked in the grass surrounding the truck, and for a moment it was a deadly area. Not even Ju-Chao's rifle team, covering that lead truck, was able to keep their heads up as pieces of engine block crashed into bushes near their position.

As the mortar shell was still on a downward arc, two men with automatic weapons had opened up on the second truck. The American on the passenger side tried to get out, but he was stitched from thighs to neck by a burst of lead. His chest was also punctured by several pieces of flying shrapnel from the initial mortar blast. The driver never had a chance to climb out, dying with his hands still clutching the wheel. A machine-gun team in the back of the second truck maneuvered its .50 into play and got off several short, uncontrolled bursts, but the truck had no defensive armor and a few more rounds through the tin sidings silenced the gun. One hand grenade exploded in the interior of the truck, and all fell silent. The lead truck, which had carried no one in the back, continued to burn. The gunners raked the engine of the second truck, rendering it useless.

Sergeant Chi-yung raised his arm, the signal to cease fire.

Ju-Chao had hoped the two vehicles were part of a food supply column, but quickly realized, as he and his men examined the trucks' contents, that it would be fish eggs and rice for tonight. The back of the one undamaged truck was loaded with porto-TV sets, cassettes, miniaturized radios, and several stacks of "Vidtape Listings of the Week." No doubt being transported to the frontline to provide entertainment for the stalemated troops. Ju-Chao ordered his men to bash all the TV screens, pull the wiring in the cassettes and toss the earplugs to the winds. No need allowing Americans to be entertained when they could remain bored.

Seven Americans dead. No losses on his side ... but hardly what you would call a victory. Especially since their diet would have to remain fish eggs and rice. He gave the signal for his men to move out.

They trudged through the grass. "Those men back there," said Sergeant Chi-yung, "they died without a whimper."

"That is unusual," admitted Ju-Chao. "Americans are not known for their great personal sacrifice. Give them the choice to live or die, and they will invariably choose to live."

"That is not the way of the Chinese," joined in Yhang-ye.

"We do die bravely," agreed Chi-yung.

"And for a cause," volunteered Yhang-ye.

"Dragon turds," muttered Ju-Chao.

Chi-yung and Yhang-ye glanced at each other.

Ju-Chao continued: "The Chinese soldier has often died needlessly, wishing he did not have to do so."

Chi-yung spoke up sharply. "Surely you speak of cowards. Of riverbed larva."

Yhang-ye was just as emphatic. "And cowards."

"I speak of common, brave men, not unlike yourselves. Hard-working men, loyal men. Dedicated to a cause. Men whose lives were thrown away like so much refuse."

"Surely," said an incredulous Chi-yung, "no life lost in battle is ever wasted."

"It was not so at Tsining." The sentence was punctuated with a finality that induced, for the next few moments, a profound silence. As they trudged, Chi-yung and Yhang-ye waited silently for Ju-Chao to continue.

Ju-Chao pretended to ignore their silence, but in so doing paid tribute to it. "At Tsining, lives were snuffed out as one might yank blades of grass from lawnfields."

"But surely for a goal—an objective." Chi-yung was determined to have it no other way.

138

Ju-Chao shook his head with some sense of bitterness. "At Tsining, there was no goal—no objective. Tsining was a mistake. True, millions of men died in the gallant struggle against the Kuomintang of Chiang Kai-shek, but they died in battles that had to be fought. Tsining was a battle that should not have been fought."

"Tsining," mumbled Chi-yung, "I remember no such battle."

"It was not recorded," replied Ju-Chao. "It was meaningless, and therefore it was not recorded."

"And you fought in this battle?"

"I commanded a battalion. Eight hundred and fifty-two men in all. Officially, five survived."

Incredulity permeated Chi-yung's voice. "Five!"

"But I was just one commander among many. There were others who suffered as severely as I."

They continued through the grass; word, by now, had passed up and down the column. Ju-Chao was about to begin another narrative.

"The dead," added Ju-Chao, "were many."

It was the prelude statement.

Ju-Chao began his story.

29
Tsining Tapestry

This is not an easy story to relate (narrated Ju-Chao) for in its telling I must describe the deaths of many friends and comrades with whom I fought side by side in the great struggle against Chiang Kai-shek in those bitter years of struggle, 1946–49.

Bloodshed is not an uncommon sight to the average soldier in the People's Liberation Army, for if he has not witnessed the fiercest of fighting on the battlefield first-hand, he has certainly viewed the devastating carnage reaped by the myriad revolutions which have swept China these past fifty years.

We have, in this manner, become a calloused band of men, with a side for sadism that is unsurpassed by any other army, including the Greeks, whom I had the pleasure of slaughtering during the early days of our present struggle for liberation, and found exceptionally bloodthirsty.

I am not a psychiatrist, so therefore I cannot account for our practice of sadism, which incidentally I do not enjoy in the clinical sense—that is, I do not *feel* any great pleasure when I watch men dying in horrible fashion. I feel *nothing*, neither pity nor pleasure, and therein lies my inability to explain. However, we do practice these things. Such as the "Dragon Lantern," a practice whereby the victim's naked body is first slashed with a whip, then kerosene-soaked cotton is stuffed into the openings. This brings forth screams from the victim, but these screams are greatly intensified when the cotton is set afire. The Americans were never able to understand why we bayoneted so many of their wounded and dying during our struggle for liberation in Korea, but, of course, this was for the practical reason that we had not the medical supplies to help these men, and rather than let them suffer we chose to take them quickly out of their misery. Nor do the Americans understand why the "Tapestry Chair"—a basket of glass, thorns, and rusty metal—is so popular currently.

But of these things you already know, and I will linger no longer on them. The point is, we are a hardened band with gritted teeth who are bothered little by emotion. Within our massed formations, clogged by the dust our feet kick up, we tend to lose our individuality, and we sometimes forget that within each man is a network of emotion and experience and history, a network of pain, joy, and anxiety. You must bear this in mind as you hear of the Siege of Tsining, for the suffering was on a scale that even today brings me awake in the dead of night, bathing my face in a cold sweat. Once again my heart thumps uncontrollably from the nightmare I have relived. For what I saw at Tsining surpassed any kind of "Tapestry Chair" or "Dragon Lantern."

I must now disgress momentarily to speak of tactics, particularly that popular maneuver of yesteryear, "the Human Wave," which has since been outlawed by our Chairman, and which is little known among the ranks of the People's Liberation Army except for old-timers such as myself. This was a maneuver that worked well during the Civil War of 1946–49, with the exception of Tsining. Field commanders would send thousands of troops against a single fortified position, knowing that although losses might be considerable, the psychological effect on the enemy would provide an advantageous edge. It worked, of course, until the war of liberation in Korea, where increased American firepower made up for the psychological advantage and resulted in staggering casualties. The commanders could naturally afford the human price tag, for replacements were always plentiful, and military objectives, and not human life, were first and foremost. Much of that kind of thinking has changed, thank goodness, for if you have seen the results of a "human wave" at its devastating worst, you would deem it an act against humanity.

I now come to the Siege of Tsining, which took place in the province of Shantung in July 1947. I do not know, even today, why our leaders chose to attack this city. To my knowledge it offered no tactical advantages; perhaps our leaders felt they needed a victory to increase morale. History does not reveal the motives. Thus, we attacked the city of Tsining. You will find no record of this battle in official Party history, but believe me when I tell you it was a disastrous defeat. We eventually abandoned the attack and wisely moved on to beat the Kuomintang elsewhere.

Tsining is a medieval city, surrounded by a wide, deep moat as well as an ancient wall fifty to sixty feet high and quite thick at its base. Our artillery shells did little damage to this wall in preliminary softening up, although countless barrages were leveled against it. I might add that the wall was heavily fortified by Nationalist troops armed with the latest in American weapons. Their firepower was devastating, to say the least, when brought to bear from trenches dug into the very top of the wall.

For five days the battle raged; and at the end of that time not a single Red soldier had managed to gain access to the wall. For there were fifty to one hundred yards of open terrain which had to be crossed under withering fire. The southeast corner of Tsining's wall was the point of attack, with battalions rushing toward the moat and then swimming their way toward the wall. The Nationalists had only to fire at point-blank range into the moat, and soon the dead were filling the water and stacking up like cordwood along the banks of the moat. However, as the number of dead increased, their stacked bodies began to form a macabre tapestry on which subsequent waves of men could cross, without having to submerge themselves in water.

Men even died in the middle of the moat without getting their feet wet.

It was at the end of the fifth day that my battalion reached the outskirts of Tsining and took up positions on the outer edge of the housing area near the moat. Nationalist artillery had leveled most of these houses, and only smoking rubble and occasional fires remained. I was given the simple order to attack, and I did not question that order, although I immediately made my peace with Buddha and informed my officers and men to do likewise, thinking without a doubt this was to be our final day on earth. With an hour to spare before the attack was scheduled to begin, I approached my regimental commander with the suggestion that I be permitted to leave behind twenty-five of my best riflemen for the purpose of sniping at the wall-top. If an intense fire could keep the automatic rifle fire to a minimum, perhaps there was some chance of a handful of my men reaching the base of the wall. The regimental commander thought this a wise suggestion, and I spent the rest of the hour before the attack instructing my best riflemen to lay out a field of fire so that each man was giving us the full capabilities of his marksmanship.

The attack began, and as it did the Nationalists came out of the depths of the wall trench to take up defensive positions behind thirty-caliber machine guns and M-1 rifles and Browning Automatic Rifles. My snipers went into action immediately, and their first wave of fire took a heavy toll on the defenders, who had not been expecting a carefully planned barrage of bullets. Several of the Nationalists pitched from the wall and thudded atop the bodies of our own dead. Fewer targets were available to the snipers after that but I can say with pride that they continued to fire effectively.

Meanwhile, my men were up and moving. We fired as we ran with the hope that our bullets, even if wild, might keep a Nationalist or two from firing at us. But fire they did, and I could see that even before we had reached the edge of the moat about a third of my men were either dead or wounded, many of them casualties of mortar shells which were being lobbed gently over the wall at close range. Some of the shells landed in the canal, and bodies already lifeless were blown into the air to be murdered a second and third time.

I will never forget the feeling as I ran across the moat. The bodies were stacked so high that at no time did I touch water. Each footstep was implanted in the back or chest or face or arm or leg of a comrade, and the sickening sensation I experienced with each step cannot be described accurately. I did not bother to urge my men on, for I knew they must have felt the way I did, seeing their comrades falling around and under them, and were determined more than ever to take Tsining, as hopeless as it had first seemed. I kept spraying the top of the southeast corner as I ran, knowing that my aim was continually thrown off by the uneven tapestry at my feet. But it was the only outlet by which I could express the horror I experienced as I ran.

I was among the first to reach the wall and glanced hurriedly around, to see how many of my men had made it with me. I quickly estimated that only about a fourth of my men were still standing. The rest had taken their places with the dead and wounded and dying within that horrible moat. There were few bamboo ladders among those who had reached the wall, but fortunately they were shorter than the full height of the wall, so that the Nationalists were not able to push them away as we climbed.

A few of the Nationalists tried to reach down and knock away the ladders, but my snipers made short work of them. Their bodies vaulted down among us, and this was demoralizing in its own unique way, for oftentimes a falling corpse would land squarely on one of my men and put him out of the fight.

I was among the few who managed to scale the ladders and I was quite proud, when I reached the top of the parapet, to find not a single Nationalist soldier there. My snipers had swept the area clear for us to move into. We dropped into the deserted but body-littered trench which ran along the top of the wall and stared down into the city of Tsining—our first sight of the objective we had paid so dearly to see. The Nationalists, not realizing our number had been decimated, had panicked on seeing the ladders

144

and withdrawn about a hundred yards back from the wall. I glanced around to count a maximum of twenty-five men. This was all that remained of my battalion. I did not try to think about that as I directed the handful of survivors to continue offensive action against the Nationalists. Even if the advantage was slight, it was one I intended to exploit to the fullest. We hauled the bamboo ladders up from the outer wall with the intention of using them to lower ourselves into the city to resume the fighting. But rifle fire was too heavy from the Nationalist side and I succeeded only in losing three more brave men. The ladders would have to stay where they were.

I ordered my only remaining scout, Tu-lee, to go back over the wall and tell our regimental commander to send reinforcements to join us before the Nationalists repelled us and resecured the wall. I did not find out until later that Tu-lee was killed by a stray mortar shell as he crossed the moat, and never lived to deliver my directive.

Meanwhile, I was faced with finding a way down from the wall-top trench without exposing my men to the heavy fire that continued to rain on us. This sounds ironic in view of the fact we had just crossed a field bloodied by thousands of our comrades who had willfully exposed themselves to attack, but I was now in command of only fragments of a battalion and needed to take every advantage at my disposal.

Thus it was I noticed the watering trough, which was built near the foot of the wall. One or two Nationalists had fallen into it, and despite their waterlogged bodies, I could see that by careful calculation a man could leap into the water and avoid exposure to gunfire. In this manner I hoped to get my remaining men off the wall and deeper into the city. A problem immediately presented itself: How to keep our firearms dry and in operating condition. We decided to bundle the weapons together, lower them by rope to a safe position behind the watering trough. In the meantime, men were stripping away their fieldpacks and ammunition bandoliers as they prepared for the fifty-foot leap. I must say that the distance seemed greater from a position atop that wall, but not a single man indicated he was afraid to jump, nor did one man hesitate as each was given the command to jump. As soon as a man had safely splashed into the water and climbed out, to take his weapon from the bundle behind the trough, another would duplicate his action. However, after four men jumped, the Nationalists saw our scheme and poured an intense fire at the trough. Machine-gunners even sprayed the air above the water, hoping to bracket a man as he fell. This fire was deadly accurate, and I could soon see that the plan was useless, as those few men who had reached the ground were quickly being picked off. On top of that, our weapons had been bundled and lowered to the ground by rope, leaving a weaponless handful of us on the parapet. (The Nationalists had been very careful to take the weapons of their fallen soldiers when they pulled back from the wall position.)

A glance over the wall, back toward our positions, told me that no further attack from our side was forthcoming. The slight foothold we had so miraculously gained, at such a terrible price, was to be for naught. I think there were tears in my eyes, and hatred in my heart for the blundering of our army commanders, as I turned to tell my men to abandon the attack and return across the moat.

It was then I realized I was alone on the parapet. Increased sniper fire had finished off the two men who had been beside me a moment before. (It should be understood that because of the horrendous din of the battle it was impossible to hear individual rifle shots, or for that matter even distinguish mortar shells from the general chaos of noise.)

It is a frightening experience to find yourself alone, facing a formidable enemy, and it is one I shall never forget. It is as if the human race has been stripped from the face of the earth, and only dragons roam the plains, breathing fire and going unchallenged. For at least an hour I found it impossible to leave the walled position. The Nationalists, for reasons never known to me, failed to try to retake that southeast corner. It is perhaps the only time in Chinese history that one soldier has single-handedly held such a vast position and lived to tell about it.

And so, I remained in the ditch along the top of the wall, wondering why such a military action had been taken against Tsining in the first place. As night finally came, and the Nationalists prepared to reinforce the wall trench, I went back over the wall, down one of the ladders, and started across the canal. I noticed the level of bodies had climbed an additional layer since my initial crossing.

I was thinking about those fallen men when a volley of shots whisked past my ears and I was forced to fall next to the headless torso of what appeared to be the lieutenant of . my second company. Some damn fool in my own lines had seen me coming and thought it to be a Nationalist counterattack. Without giving it another thought, he had opened fire.

I crawled the rest of the way to our lines, for it was impossible to shout over the artillery barrage being laid down by Nationalist guns. I found the soldier who had so brashly fired without orders, and quick-marched him into a field fronting the village.

Calling him to attention, I proceeded, in full view of the battalion which I no longer commanded, to beat him to within an inch of his life.

30
Old Ruins Remembered

"Field Commander!"

Ju-Chao looked up to find one of the mortarmen pointing. Off to their left were the old ruins of a train station—one which Ju-Chao immediately recognized. He had seen it last in 1948, an entire year after Tsining, when elements of the Eighth Route Army had passed through this area on the way to seize and secure the supply depot of *Chun Hsien Ku*. The rails had still been in place then, and supplies were brought up regularly to reinforce the men laying siege to the Nationalist-held weapons supply center. He had spent many hot afternoons here, supervising the unloading of supplies and the loading of the wounded. There was a feeling of coolness and relief which went with the ruins.

"Shall I call a break?" asked Sergeant Chi-yung.

Ju-Chao was tempted. The afternoon was warm and they had marched the entire morning before ambushing the Vidtape Column. It was always nostalgic to return to a place of the past, to remember a day long forgotten by the rest of the world. Besides, the men could use the rest.

On the other hand, there was always the danger of revisiting a place of the past and having certain illusions shattered. Such as the time he went back to the one-room schoolhouse in which he had been educated. He had remembered the flowers outside the window as being tall, reaching into the sky on sturdy stalks. But when he saw them again, the flowers were below his line of vision and the stalks seemed to have the strength of straw. They hadn't even reached the height of his chest. That was one of the ironies of life: Flowers were never as tall as you remembered them. And perhaps old ruins were not as cool and satisfying as he imagined.

On the other hand, he was worried about the trail they had followed. There were telltale signs of four creatures— food residue, excretion, urine stains. Yet there was something strange about the trail. It was too perfect in a way.

"No," said Ju-Chao, "we keep moving."

The patrol moved away from the ruins.

Ju-Chao stepped out and moved to the head of the column. Chi-yung was bending down to examine pawtracks.

"What do you make of it?" asked Ju-Chao.

"Who knows what such creatures think," said Chi-yung uncertainly. "If they think like men, perhaps it is a trap. If they think like animals . . . who can truly predict?"

"Keep moving," urged Ju-Chao, "keep moving."

31
A Tense Moment in the Ruins

Youngman was five pages further along into his latest story when he felt the heavy hand of Sarge on his shoulder.

"People," whispered Sarge.

Youngman scrunched down into the ruins, not daring to move. He could feel Sarge and Charlie Brown moving into position next to him. He realized his porto-typer was still whirring and flicked it off.

"Fishheads," whispered Charlie Brown. "Strung out."

"Like ducks," finished Sarge.

Youngman dared to glance over the crumbling foundation of the depot ruins to see a column of Chinese moving across the open field. The column drew to a stop as one of the soldiers pointed to the ruins. Youngman could sense Sarge tightening. After a moment, the column continued on its way, and Sarge relaxed. Then Youngman saw it. "Hey!" His excitement almost gave him away. Sarge caught Youngman's shoulder as he started to rise, and that hand shoved Youngman back to earth.

"You wanna get us killed?"

"I saw it, Sarge."

"You saw what?"

It was getting hard to whisper.

"The fieldpack. Slaker's fieldpack."

"Slaker . . ."

Charlie Brown, seeing the column moving away, inserted his earplug and began listening to "Secret Missions" ("Tonight: 'Iron Curtain Escape,' based on a true case from the Office of Naval Intelligence as documented by Admiral Ellis M. Zachariah").

Sarge studied the column of Chinese. "By God, you're right, Youngman." Sarge tensed. "That fieldpack's Government Issue."

Charlie Brown was humming the dramatic theme music of "Secret Missions."

"Cover me, Youngman."

"Cover you?"

"Brown, you stay put."

"What're you going to do, Sarge?"

But Sarge had already begun to make his preparations, and felt it unnecessary to answer Youngman. "Give me the 7.65 Luger . . . come on, Youngman . . . the Luger, the Luger . . ."

Youngman pulled the weapon from the bundle's entangled mass of firearms as noiselessly as possible.

Sarge assumed a crouching position. "Synchronize watches."

A fervent spin of the knob.

"Button up."

A fastening of his helmet's chin strap.

"Lock and load."

A working of the 7.65 Luger so a shell was securely in the chamber.

"Over the top!"

A silent scrambling of boots and body.

Sarge was off and moving, hunched low.

"I'll be a sonofabitch," commented Youngman.

Charlie Brown grimaced as a Russian agent ambushed an American CIA undercover man in the streets of Budapest. Then he became bored with the first commercial.

32
One of the Last Great Single-Handed Attacks

With the 7.65 Luger carbine at port, Sarge sprinted into the field, approaching the last man in the patrol column on boots that seemed to glide across the ground without touching it.

Instinctively, Sarge had concentrated his weight into his torso, arms, and neck, shifting it away from his legs in his attempt to move as lightly and as swiftly as possible. He felt as if he were barely touching the earth with legs as weightless as feathers. The effect was startling—the impact of each footfall was minimized, and his approach was almost unnoticed.

Almost—the last man in the column, a private who had volunteered for the patrol because he had known two of the victims of the flag-raising ceremony at Cheng Lu's grave, felt the slightest vibration and turned, more out of curiosity than anything else. Out here in the middle of a huge field, he had never suspected anyone could come so close without first being detected, and he had expected to see a small animal or perhaps discover a mild wind moving the tips of the grassblades.

Instead he saw Sarge, just as he leveled the 7.65 Luger.

The single bullet that Sarge fired, as he continued to approach at eight and a half miles per hour, struck the soldier at the base of his neck. He sank silently into the grass. His life quickly leaked out of him as Sarge jumped over his body to approach the second-to-last man in the column.

The second-to-last man had heard the shot, and was still in the process of unslinging his submachine gun and turning his body when Sarge was less than five feet away. By the time Sarge had pulled the trigger once, the distance was point-blank, the barrel being flush against the militiaman's stomach. The impact of the slug threw him backward, almost as if he had been jerked away by a powerful cable. This enabled Sarge to continue moving in a straight line.

The third-to-last man in the column was Yhang-ye, who, at the moment of the first shot, had been concerned only about the blister which continued to irritate his big toe. Even Ju-Chao's account of the battle of Tsining and its terrible carnage had done nothing to alleviate his own suffering, and the pain of the world still focused on his foot. As he turned, his brain told him in less than a fourth of a second he was going to die. Within another half second Yhang-ye had formulated the beginnings of a prayer. At the end of the second, he was dead, a 7.65 slug buried in his forehead. Like the two men behind him, he pitched forward into the tall grass without a cry, lost to the sight of the others.

The mortarman, burdened by his heavy weapon, should have been easier prey, yet he turned at just the right angle so that the barrel of the mortar stopped Sarge's next bullet. It ricocheted off, leaving a long *wheeeeee* in the air behind it. With Sarge now so close, the mortarman attempted to use the mortar as a battering ram, but its sheer weight prevented this from being an effective defensive movement. Instead, it threw the mortarman off balance and he pitched forward at such an angle as to take Sarge's next bullet squarely between the eyes. A dumfounded expression remained frozen on his face as he continued to sink from Sarge's sight, the falling action uninterrupted by the bullet.

In front of the mortarman were two soldiers carrying a heavy box of ammunition and mortar shells. In unison they dipped toward the ground to set the box down, then rose

153

quickly to face Sarge's unstoppable charge. Both men had their rifles unslung and were almost in position to fire when Sarge, setting the 7.65 on full automatic, sprayed the area with a single sweep, left to right. Both men were stitched across their chests. As the one on the left went down, screaming, the one on the right held his rifle away from his body with both hands, as if offering it to Sarge.

Taking the rifle, Sarge used the butt against the next man, swooping it around his head twice before slamming it against the Chinese trooper. The impact was terrific enough to split open the man's head and spill his brains into the grass.

At this moment, only two men remained in the column: Lieutenant Commander Ju-Chao and Sergeant Chi-yung, with Ju-Chao at its head.

What had accounted for the fact that one man, Sarge, had single-handedly worked his way forward, wiping out trooper after trooper without one shot being fired in return?

Believers in good luck will be disappointed to learn that it was all in how Sarge had initially approached the column. If there is one consistency in the structure of the Chinese patrol, it is its marching formation. From the earliest days of training, the Chinese are fastidiously taught the importance of symmetrical formation. Each man must be "dressed" on the next so that a near-perfect straight line is formed, and this perfection is drilled into each soldier.

In that field of grass, even without a pathway to guide them, the patrol, out of military habit, had formed a quasi-perfect rank. Coming up behind the patrol had been Sarge. Thus only the last man, on turning, could have seen Sarge. (The thought of stepping out of line had never occurred to any of the troopers, as individual initiative was always left in the hands of field commanders and officers.) While surprise may have accounted for fifty percent of Sarge's success, the rest could be attributed to Sarge's understanding of Chinese marching precision. And his keen, cool eye.

Sergeant Chi-yung was the first to get off a shot, but it was a snap shot at best, and missed Sarge by several inches. Seeing that he had reached the front of the column, Sarge threw himself forward, wildly spraying the area in front of him, mainly as an attempt to send the two remaining Chinese rushing for cover. In this case, however, Lady Luck was with him.

Two of the bullets struck Chi-yung in vital organs and he pitched forward, his eyes staring upward at Sarge as if he were reprimanding him.

Now began an incredible duel. It commenced with Sarge in his peculiar prone position in the grass, and Ju-Chao standing a few feet in front of him, submachine gun poised but not firing for the simple reason Ju-Chao could not see Sarge hidden in the tall grass. Nor could Sarge see Ju-Chao, although it is true both men had a general idea of the location of the other, and had the sound of gunfire by which to judge their target.

Ju-Chao opened fire first, his row of slugs chirping away from Sarge instead of toward him. Sarge returned the fire, but his bullets were also poorly directed.

Sarge rolled over, fired again. Miss.

Ju-Chao leaped to his right, returning the fire. Miss.

Sarge rolled.

Ju-Chao jumped. First one way, then the other.

Sarge commenced a roll to the left. Back to the right.

Bullets tore up the soil and grass next to him.

Ricochets whined overhead.

The dance-to-avoid-death continued.

Click.

It was Ju-Chao's submachine gun. The noise of the firing pin falling against nothing was like the noise of an erupting volcano. A thousand hot lights flashed in front of his eyes, and he knew he was finished. A prayer formed very quickly on his lips so he would be ready to meet Buddha head-on.

Sarge sat upright in the grass, leveling the 7.65 Luger.

Click.

At first Sarge couldn't believe it. He looked dumfoundedly at the weapon. The idea of it failing him, in the heat of battle, hadn't occurred to him. Self-preservation had taken over from cool reasoning. That 7.65 Luger had meant life and death, and now it meant something in be-

tween. Reprieve for Ju-Chao from the mouth of death;
fifty-fifty odds for Sarge.

There was also an element of incredulity in it. It had
happened countless times in the movies—a gun clicking
empty. Often, the villain's gun clicking empty and the hero
blithely throwing his own weapon away to finish off his opponent with his fists. Sometimes, both guns clicking empty,
and the opponents squaring off equally. Yet in all the campaigns fought, wars won, revolutions lost, Sarge had never
seen it happen. The odds were ten thousand-to-one at best.
The ever-present Fu Bird of Fate had just shit on Sarge.

33
Scrambled Lead

Who would be the first to reload?

Sarge had been faced with loading weapons in emergencies before. In Korea, members of a "human wave" had raced toward his foxhole on Hill 231 as he unjammed a malfunctioning M-1 rifle, but there had been distance between him and the Chinese and distance had given him that extra iota of time he needed to clear the breach. In Vietnam, he had been literally surrounded by Viet Cong during the Delta Campaign and had lunged from firing position west to firing position south to firing position east to firing position north to keep himself alive, reloading during the few moments it took him to rush from one direction to another. But never had he raced against another individual who was also reloading.

As Ju-Chao fought what seemed an unyielding mechanism, he felt a strange form of tranquility that can only be the outgrowth of the cool, calculated Oriental mind. There was no need to permit fear to interfere with his movements, for if he were slowed by fear it would only lead to his death. He must, therefore, permit only calmness and self-assurance to dictate his movements, and this he accomplished without once bumbling his new clip of ammunition.

Loading the 7.65 Luger under these conditions might have led an inexperienced soldier to panic, to drop his clip, to fumble anything he touched, but Sarge realized that the only way to prevent the panic he felt from gaining control of his fingers was to move slowly. Theoretically, this would put him behind his opponent in terms of time, but, on the other hand, a single slip up would put him behind his opponent for certain. At least this would give him some small advantage. Therefore, Sarge took his time and achieved his loading with cool efficiency.

As did Ju-Chao. He brought up his weapon in the same instant that Sarge brought up his.

But neither fired.

The shot that did resound came from the old ruins. Ju-Chao stiffened as a tiny red splotch (approximately the size of a fifty-cent piece) appeared high on his chest, near his shoulder. He staggered back three steps and bumped into a camphorwood tree. He rested there a moment, supported by the trunk of the tree, staring at Sarge with a vague look of surprise. His weapon fell into the grass at his feet. Ju-Chao began sliding slowly down the trunk of the tree. When his buttocks touched the ground, he rested there, closed his eyes, and went to sleep.

Sarge let the 7.65 Luger hang limply at his side, and turned to face the old ruins. Rifle in hand, Youngman was halfway up.

"You glory-happy sonofabitch," yelled Sarge. Youngman froze in his tracks. "From now on I'll tell you when to be a hero."

34
Chow Among the Dead

The Chinese Trooper Chi-yung, although dying very rapidly from the two bullets which had struck him down, had somehow staggered to his feet. Blood streamed from the gaping wounds in his chest. He stumbled toward Sarge, holding out a blood-covered hand as might a beggar pleading for alms.

"Uhh," said Chi-yung, incapable any longer of articulation. "Uh-huh." He fell to his knees, his eyes still searching Sarge's for some indication of mercy.

But Sarge was only moved enough to place the tip of his boot against Chi-yung's chest and shove him over backwards.

"That's for gunning down our medics," explained Sarge.

Chi-yung had stopped moaning, and now said nothing as Sarge removed Slaker's fieldpack from around his shoulder. He turned as Youngman and Charlie Brown approached him.

"Tell me something, Youngman," said Sarge. "Why is it everybody in this war is goddamn trigger-happy?" Without giving Youngman time to respond, he brought forth a K-ration can from the fieldpack. "Look at this, Youngman, I always did figure Slaker a holdout type. Keeping one can for himself. A great buddy." Sarge began to open the K-ration can. Youngman looked at the corpses of the Chinese patrol in dismay. "All these guys ... single-handed ... how'd you do it, Sarge?"

"I got a hot Leatherneck Flash for you, Youngman. Some day you'll learn it's expected of you to be a hero. Especially when you've been a noncom as long as me. But next time don't go trigger-happy on me just when I'm finishing up a job. *I'll* tell you when to be a hero, Youngman. *I'll* tell you."

Sarge squatted and began to eat. He wrinkled his nose after the first bite, and glanced down at the stiffening corpse of Chi-yung. "Whew. This guy stinks like fish eggs. He must have had a bath in the nearest rice swamp." Sarge took a few more bites, and paused, remembering . . . "Reminds me of a ROK I knew. Korea. Spring of '53. Pork Chop Hill. The last big one before the Panmunjom boys sewed things up. Anyway, this ROK ... ate nothing but fish eggs. Maybe a little rice, a little millet, but mainly fish eggs. Finally, we couldn't stand him any longer so we got him transferred to another company. One night he up and got himself shot."

"Dead?" asked Youngman.

Sarge nodded. "On patrol. Enemy sentry smelled him coming."

"Jesus," remarked Youngman.

Sarge ravenously continued to stuff himself. "Youngman ... you too, Brown. Make sure these guys're all dead. Chinese corpses have a tendency to resurrect themselves just when you ain't looking."

While Sarge ate, Youngman and Charlie Brown rummaged through the bodies. "Hey, here's something, Sarge." Charlie Brown threw an unopened package of prophylactics at Sarge's feet. He examined the package, then threw it back to the ground. "Too bad somebody didn't show these guys how to use these things. Maybe we wouldn't have to kill off so many billions more to win this war."

"You think maybe that's become standard Chinese Field Issue, Sarge?" asked Charlie Brown.

"Probably Korean War surplus," replied Sarge, scraping the bottom of the K-ration can.

Youngman, meanwhile, had paused to stare down at the grass into the face of the man whose brains Sarge had spilled. "Face . . . bashed . . . that's . . ."

Sarge snickered. "You miss the point, Youngman. I'm surprised at you, after reading that 'Aceldama' with four thousand corpses. That bashed-in face, Youngman, that's what war is all about. The more horrible the death, the more successful the war." Sarge took one look at Youngman's greenish complexion and knew more explanation was necessary. "All right, take a Marine Corps memo, Youngman. You get this too, Brown. The purpose of war is the product known as death. The more efficient that death, the more efficient that war, and the closer war comes to reaching its ultimate height. Trouble nowadays is, war's gotten too impersonal. Cold steel, now that's real war."

Something that might be called a faraway gleam came into Sarge's eyes. "Knew some guys once. North Africa. 'Forty-three. Survivors of Kasserine Pass. Germans caught 'em sleeping in their fartsacks and bayoneted them all in the throat. Now that's the way, Youngman. A clean, well-honed piece of steel through the throat. It has feeling, style, class. It has personalized delivery. Man to man."

The faraway gleam grew more luminous as Sarge thought back even further. "That's the way a lot of the boys bought it on Bunker Hill, Youngman. A bayonet right through the throat." Sarge tossed away the K-ration can, and removed his bayonet from its scabbard. He laid the blade in the palm of his hand and stared at it.

"A marvelous device, the bayonet. Like I said, the most personalized weapon conceived by man. A bullet you have to fire, a grenade you have to throw. An artillery shell, you can't even see the guy you're firing it at. But the bayonet. Ah. Did you know it was named after a town, Youngman? . . . Yeah, Bayonne, France. How about that? Leave it to a Frenchman to give it to you in the right place. At first they used these straight, double-edged blades. A foot long, with wooden handles. They'd shove them into the muzzle of a musket and use them as a polearm. But that was a bitch. If you shoved it into the barrel too hard, you couldn't get the bastard out to fire your musket. And if you didn't shove hard enough, it'd fall out. So the Frenchmen got wise and invented the socket bayonet. Bet you assholes didn't know the original switchblade was a bayonet ... Yeah, it was rigged so it folded back on the barrel. You just hit a switch or something and out it'd come. Pig stickers supreme."

"Ohhhh ..." Ju-Chao stirred slightly, and blinked open one eye. Sarge stared down into the open eye, and belched. "Ohhhh ..."

This time Youngman heard the groan and turned, as did Charlie Brown.

"Hey," said Sarge. "We got a live one. A regular vaudeville entertainer. Telling jokes, tap-dancing ... Hey, Youngman. You got dependents?"

"Yeah ..."

"They're gonna be sorry dependents if you keep missing guys like this. When I tell you to make sure a guy's dead, be damn sure you do what I tell you. ... Well, go on. See what he wants."

Youngman leaned down to examine Ju-Chao more closely: ear against heart. "Still ticking." Hands into Ju-Chao's pockets. "Here, Sarge." He handed Sarge one cigar. Hands on bloody shoulder. "He's a real bleeder, Sarge."

Sarge examined the cigar. "They don't make a Havana stogie like they used to."

As Youngman applied a first-aid packet against the wound in Ju-Chao's chest, just below the shoulder, Sarge bit off the end of the cigar and shoved it into his mouth. He felt his fatigue pockets for a match, found it, glanced around for a suitable place to strike it. Ju-Chao's cheek being the nearest surface, he struck the match there. Nothing happened. Ju-Chao groaned and twisted, turning the other cheek. Sarge tried again. This time the match took hold. Sarge lit his cigar. He took a deep drag, while Ju-Chao gasped out some short, staccato phrases, but in a voice barely above a whisper. Youngman leaned closer to listen.

Sarge puffed. "You been to the Language Academy, Youngman. Start translating."

"Rambling, Sarge. He's rambling. Probably delirious. Wait a minute . . . maybe . . . no, it's Mandarin gibberish."

"Hey Sarge," asked Charlie Brown, losing interest in rummaging through the pockets of the dead, "what we gonna do with this wounded guy? Looks like an officer."

Sarge thought for a few moments. "We had a prisoner once. Guadalcanal. Autumn of '42, only there wasn't no autumn—just swamps and mosquitos and lots of cruddy, slimy Japs. Some of the boys got boxed out on 3.2 beer and painted a huge green bull's-eye on the Nip's chest. You know something? Not one guy could lay an M-1 slug dead center into that Nip. Hit all around it, but not one slug dead center. And these were supposed to be some of the best shots in the whole fucking division."

"*Sui . . . sui . . . sui . . .*" gasped Ju-Chao, a little louder then before.

"Huh? What'd he say?"

"Hey Sarge," said Charlie Brown. "I think he wants a smoke."

"Hey, Chink, you want a smoke?" Sarge shoved the cigar into Ju-Chao's mouth. The Chinese officer shook his head frantically, trying to throw the cigar clear of his lips. Ju-Chao grimaced with the pain that accompanied the movement. Sarge retrieved the cigar from the grass. "Hey, these things don't come with Government Issue." He turned to Youngman and Charlie Brown. "That's gratitude. Learn about your enemy, both of you. He's deceitful . . . he's treacherous . . . he's smelly."

"Maybe," suggested Youngman, "he's worth a weekend pass. Battle Command's been looking for a POW."

"Naw, they knock off more guys *behind* the lines than *in* them," said Sarge. The faraway gleam started to return. "Knew a guy named Fuller once. Spent a whole year in the line fighting his way with the Big Red One all the way from France to Czechoslovakia. He was there when they fired the last shot of the war. But that's another story. So he got sent home. Fall of '45, he's two miles from his hometown when he gets hit by a Model-T Ford. Dead on

163

arrival. Now he's one guy who shoulda stayed in the front-line, even after the war. A helluva lot safer, that's for sure."

Youngman suggested they question the wounded officer.

"What's he going to tell us?" countered Sarge. "Where he hides his fish eggs? Where he stockpiles his rice supply? Where to find the best Chinese lay within a fifty-mile radius?"

Ju-Chao moaned again.

"Maybe he wants his prophylactics back, Sarge," said Charlie Brown.

"Maybe we oughta move him into the shade, Sarge. Least it'll keep that wound from smelling."

"Main thing for us to worry about," advised Sarge, "is finding our lines again. Gonna need water soon. In a minute he can stink all he wants and it won't matter, because we won't be here to capture the fragrance."

Youngman looked stunned. "We can't leave him here." Flat, declarative.

"Why not?" Sarge was just as flat, just as declarative.

"But he's—"

The faraway gleam. "Knew a guy who thought like you, Youngman. Corregidor. 'Forty-two. The joint's crawling with Nips. Carried a wounded buddy ten miles on his back to the tunnel aid station. Ten miles, Youngman. Do you know how far that is when you've got a guy over your shoulders? Really something what this guy did. Only trouble was, the guy he was carrying all that time was dead. All that work and effort. For nothing. And that's you, Youngman. You want to sweat a lot. And for what?"

"Sui . . . sui . . . sui . . ." mumbled Ju-Chao.

Youngman pressed his ear close to Ju-Chao's mouth. The Chinese continued to mumble. Youngman straightened up. "Water. He's asking for wat . . . no, he's talking about water. About a water hole."

"Where?" Suddenly, Sarge was interested.

"Not far from here. Near an old deserted ammo dump."

"How far is not far?"

Youngman spoke in Chinese, listened. "Nearer than farther. A couple of miles maybe. Says he can find Buddha there."

"Buddha?"

Youngman spoke, listened. "Says he fought there against Chiang Kai-shek in 1948. A great battle. A terrible battle. A million souls delivered to Buddha. Found strength there as a youth ... now he wants to find the strength to die there. Die at *Chun Hsien Ku,* the House of Guns."

"Can he take us to this joint, this ammo dump, this *Chun* whatever?"

Youngman put the question to Ju-Chao, listened. "He says this ammo dump is a place so holy, it is one of the few places on earth that can be seen from the moon. He says if we promise to take him there to die, he'll guide us."

"Promise? He wants a promise? Tell him on my scout's honor."

Youngman did so. The reply: "He wants you to cross your heart, Sarge." Youngman shrugged. "American custom."

"Hey, I don't believe this," said Charlie Brown.

"Shut up," said Sarge, crossing his heart. "If a half-dead guy, a guy who almost beat me to the draw at that, can lead us to some water, whatta we care about American custom . . . ?"

"Hey," chimed in Charlie Brown, "ask him if he knows where we can get some girls. Tell him that's American custom, too."

Sarge ignored Charlie Brown. "Tell him it's a deal, Youngman. We get the water, he gets Buddha."

"Hey Sarge," said Charlie Brown, "we oughta get out of here. The blowflies are settling in."

Youngman attempted to carry Ju-Chao over his shoulder, but collapsed under the weight. He attempted it a second time, more concerned with succeeding than he was with Ju-Chao's cries of pain, but again the weight was too much for him. As Youngman wiped the perspiration from his brow, Sarge leaned over and, with one arm, threw the wounded soldier over his shoulder. "I'll tell you when to be a hero, Youngman."

Sarge stepped off, and instinctively Youngman started to

follow. Sarge stopped and turned. "The rifles, Youngman, the rifles."

Youngman raced back to retrieve the bundle of rifles he had left in the old ruins, not certain if he felt stupid because he had to carry the rifles to begin with, or because he had faltered once again in his responsibilities.

35
Scrounging is
The Name of the Game

Charlie Brown was the first to see a copy of "Vidtape Listings of the Week" blowing across the ground, and he pointed it out to Sarge. When Sarge saw four copies of "Vidtape Listings of the Week" blowing across the ground, he decided something was wrong. "That Chink fire we heard back at the ruins came from this way. I think we're about to see the results."

When they reached the ambushed trucks, Charlie Brown began to scrounge through the vehicle equipped with the knocked-out .50 machine gun. Beneath one of the bullet-riddled GI corpses he found an undamaged vidpack. Excitedly, he hurried back to the others. "Hey Sarge, what's the date on that publication?"

Sarge picked up one of the half-torn magazines lying at his feet. "This week's."

"Hang on to it. I've found something."

"Somebody in there alive?"

"You find some food?"

"Naw, naw. I got me a vidpack."

"No shit?"

"Let's see it."

"Hang onto that schedule, Sarge. Maybe there's something we want to see."

"Let's see that schedule."

"Uhhh," groaned Ju-Chao, who would have asked Sarge to put him down if he could have articulated that idea beyond a painful grunt.

Charlie Brown placed the vidpack on the ground, and they stood around it.

"Is she working?" asked Youngman.

"Listen." Charlie Brown hit a switch.

"Hey, look at that."

"We got ourselves an airplane picture."

"Fighter planes, World War II–style. Jesus. Those things look outdated as hell."

"They did the job in their time," said Sarge. " 'Specially the ME-109."

Tat-tat-tat-tat.

"Check the listing. What's the title?"

"Let's see ... this must be it ... *Flying Leathernecks,* 1951. John Wayne, Robert Ryan, Janis Carter, Arthur Franz. United States Marine Corps pilots in the Pacific campaign during the crucible of World War II come up against a strict disciplinarian officer who shows little remorse for his lost men and who sparks bitterness within a fellow officer who finally realizes the weight of command following the graphic destruction of several Japanese squadrons. Howard Hughes production incorporates authentic combat aerial footage with maudlin love plot, most of which has been excised for AFVS showing. Four stars for patriotism; two and a half stars for combat effectiveness."

36

Vidtape Listings of the Week:
An Excerpt

"In keeping with the Military Entertainment Proviso Act of 1977, the Armed Forces Video Service presents programming for servicemen in combat zones which has been deemed suitable by the Committee of Motion Picture Clearances, acting under the jurisdiction of the Unitheme Communications Division. All programming has been screened and selected under the strict conditions of Unitheme, which stresses that men in theaters of combat must be given entertainment that (1) activates those instincts which inspire patriotism and devotion on the field of battle and (2) incites those basic, oft-submerged drives that encourage men to inflict severe casualties on enemy forces without regard for moral issues or instincts normally considered "civilized." Any films or teleplays which do not have some strong influence on these drives are excluded from any and all showings on any outlet of the AFVS, and any such showings are illegal and punishable under the regulations of Unitheme, Section 5-10, dated 4 Aug 78."

CHANNEL "A"

6 A.M.

THE SANDS OF IWO JIMA (1949). Hard-hitting combat footage as John "Duke" Wayne, the greatest screen hero of them all, hits the beachheads of Tarawa and Iwo in this blazing tribute to the "semper fidelis" boys of World War II. Furious hand-to-hand combat and massive frontal assaults make this one of the best. Brief romantic interlude between campaigns has been excised for more intense AFVS viewing. This'll wake you up and get you charging.

8 A.M.

BLOOD AND GUTS (1971). No-holds-barred Samurai warrior epic from Japan, featuring one of the wildest Samurai "swingers" of all time. He slashes left and right, leaving a trail of corpses as he fights the forces of evil, thinking nothing of severing six heads, five arms and at least one horse in any day's dueling.

9:30 A.M.

THE STEEL HELMET (1950). One of the toughest war pictures ever made, by one of the toughest directors who ever lived, Sammy Ful-

170

CHANNEL "B"

6 A.M.

THE BLOOD OF NOSTRADAMUS (1964). His thirst unquenchable, his fangs perpetually dripping with gore, a notorious wetback vampire and other cloaked entities of evil flap through the night in search of victims into which they can sink their incisors and draw off life-giving blood. These hideous creatures of the night are abominations of the undead, putrescent in odor and boggling to the eyes of mortal men. Dripping good stuff.

7:30 A.M.

MARK OF THE DEVIL (1972). This one will make you forget your GI Blues. Remember those grand days of the Inquisition, when witch hunters scoured the countryside in search of those consorting with the Devil? Well, see all the documented action here: how girls are beaten and mutilated, probed with sharp-pointed instruments, etc. Best graphic scene shows young maiden having her tongue ripped from her mouth—complete with flowing blood. Herbert Lom chews up not only the victims but the scenery. Roler. Sergeant Zack (played by the grizzled Gene Evans) survives a Chinese massacre and leads a squad of Americans to establish an observation post. Best remembered for its tough combat characters and the scene in which an enraged Zack blasts a Commie POW without mercy, you'll want to kill too after seeing what happens to fine American men in combat. Nothing phony about this one. It'll hit your guts.

11:30 A.M.

SAHARA (1943) Humphrey Bogart's Sergeant Joe Gunn is one of the great cinema heroes of World War II, and his tank, Lulu Belle, an unforgettable piece of war machinery as the pair fight their way across the Libyan Desert. The waterhole siege is a pip of a battle, with Miklos Rosza's music accentuating the tension of combat and always evoking a mood of the hot burning sands. Entire platoons have been known to attack after seeing this effort.

1 P.M.

THE DYING HORDES (1986). Made shortly before the present conflict, this documentary was shot on

mantic interludes have been condensed to insure torture scenes at more frequent intervals.

9:30 A.M.

FRANKENSTEIN MUST BE DESTROYED (1970). That horrendous doctor of questionable credentials is at it again, picking up an arm here, a leg there, a torso now, a brain then, as he pieces together more monstrous corpses in the name of science. Close-up work of glass-encased anatomy and brain exceptionally well done.

11:30 A.M.

NIGHTMARE IN BLOOD (1976). Two madmen carve up some of the most beautiful women in Hollywood in this horror item which opened a new wave of permissiveness when first released. Huge butcher knives, cleavers and executioners' axes are shown chopping and hewing their way into creamy Caucasian flesh. The blood used was a new concoction which reached a new height in screen realism. The famous "bedroom mutilation" scene has been refilmed in slow motion, allowing the viewer to savor the numerous details.

171

the plains of Mongolia and clearly shows what happens to Orientals who thought they could overthrow their Russian leaders. Cameras linger on the frozen corpses which litter a battlefield, proving that the Oriental hordes are not the menace you might think. There's nothing that builds spirit and fighting energy better than seeing the enemy dead at your feet.

3 P.M.

THE FIGHTING AMERICAN (1978). A critic once counted the number of Japanese soldiers killed in this World War II drama by a masked avenger armed with .45 pistols and a homemade machine gun. The count was 547. Each man, by the way, is shown in some detail, so that not a single death is wasted.

1 P.M.

PROGRAMMED TO KILL (1975). They were mindless robots, wired with vengeful circuitry and programmed to kill, kill, kill, these stalking human monstrosities which shambled through the night to mutilate, bash, crash, smash and make hash of hapless humans. The simulated broken bodies are the best special effects work ever done for a film in this genre.

3 P.M.

THE HULKING HORROR (1974). Drooling, warped hunks of quasi-human flesh, babbling verbal grotesqueries, their eyes flaming with animalistic lust, seek out pure white throats in their eternal quest to bring death to the race of men that has artificially conceived them.

4 P.M.

FROM THE BOWELS OF THE EARTH (1973). A mountainous dinosaur rises from forgotten depths, wipes the dust of a thousand years from its eyes, and attacks Tokyo, destroying entire fleets of Volkswagens with a single swish of its tail. Buildings topple, and thousands of Orientals are shown being trampled to death.

37
The Legend of *Bot Bon Jui*

By the possible grace of Buddha, Sarge had decided to stop and rest, and placed Ju-Chao on the ground. Ju-Chao attempted to make a groaning sound but found his windpipe clogged by something rough and dry—possibly postnasal drip. He tried to clear his throat, and in so doing came out of a hazy, semiconscious state to become aware, for the first time, of the inner conditions of his mouth.

To begin with, his tongue was a nuisance. Because the interior of his mouth had taken on such a dryness, it stuck against the roof of his mouth and the linings of his cheeks. It felt swollen several times its normal size—like some giant adder which had crawled through a gap in his teeth and then puffed up in protest. He attempted to flick his tongue away from any contact, and for a brief moment enjoyed a respite as his tongue hovered in midair. But then it crashed once again against the dry interior, and froze there, as might a piece of dry ice. His concentration on his tongue, however, had cleared away the clogging in his throat and he was able to groan for the first time since being put down.

Ju-Chao now became aware of the terrible taste in his mouth. There were distinguishable traces of rancid coffee, acrid tobacco, sour vomit, and an overall vinegary tincture that almost made him choke. Suddenly, he realized he had not thought about his thirst—he had been concentrating on its effects. Now there grew a craving for water. He imagined that this craving was spreading throughout his system like a cancerous growth, and he tried to stop that growth by closing off his mind, but the condition of his mouth wouldn't let his mind completely forget, and he had to be content to let it grow.

Water ... wells ... rivers ... streams ... cool, mountainous ... clean ... it was the Devil putting those thoughts into his head. He could not bring up any saliva. Moisture was something he could only remember, not experience. Lakes ... ponds ... pools ... like a flash it went through his mind: Man was not as free as he imagined. He was bound by an umbilical cord to the oases of the world. Self-sufficiency meant nothing if the world went dry. He strained to remember the flavor of water. It had no color, no odor. Yet wasn't there a certain smell to a droplet? Didn't dew have a piquancy of its own? Didn't the beads of sweat on a frosted mug have a velvetiness? For the life of him, he couldn't remember. His senses reeled under the impact of vacant, odorless, tasteless imagery. The most delicate commodity in the world had no identity. A divinity lost forever ...

Ju-Chao opened his eyes. He saw the three of them. Sarge he immediately recognized as the man he had dueled with. Youngman—a face that had spoken to him out of a pain-riddled haze. And the third—strange to see an Oriental face in an American uniform. That didn't make any sense. Perhaps it was his blurry vision.

Then he saw it. The canteen.

Only a foot and a half from his face.

Sarge had placed in on the ground, then turned to look in another direction. The others were looking away, too, so no one saw Ju-Chao inch out a feeble hand.

"*Sui*," he whispered. But no one heard him.

As his arm inched, his body inched.

"*Sui*," he whispered.

The canteen became blurry.

174

It turned into a flower, blown gently by the wind.

"*Sui*," he whispered.

An inch more. God, what effort.

The flower dissolved into a pot of gold. It glimmered and shimmered.

The distance shortened another inch. The pot of gold wavered. Ju-Chao blinked.

"*Bot Bon Jui*," he said, not in a whisper, but a loud voice.

Charlie Brown whirled, jumping alert as might a man who has just had 20,000 volts of electricity jacked into his body.

"*Bot Bon Jui*," repeated Ju-Chao. Too late. The pot of gold was gone, but the canteen was back.

Ju-Chao's fingers were closing over the canteen when Charlie Brown's foot unintentionally knocked it over. The water poured into the ground and was evaporated in a matter of seconds. Seconds longer than it was possible for Ju-Chao to close his fingers around the canteen. But it wouldn't have mattered anyway. Charlie Brown, who hadn't shown this much spunk since Sarge shoved a rifle into his face, grabbed Ju-Chao by the collar and pulled him halfway off the ground.

"*Bot Bon Jui?* Where is *Bot Bon Jui?* You talk. You speak. You tell. Where *Bot Bon Jui?* You reveal, you reveal."

All Ju-Chao could say was "Uh-uh-uh-uh-uh-uh-uh." At least there was nothing clogging his throat any longer.

"All right, all right," said Sarge, laying an arm on Charlie Brown's shoulder. "Let off the fishhead. We still got a deal and we're gonna live up to it. Buddha or bust."

Charlie Brown obeyed, letting Ju-Chao fall back to the earth. Ju-Chao could only scream inwardly. Something was clogging his throat again.

Sarge gave Charlie Brown a peculiar look. "Let's have it, Brown. What's this lingo, this Bout Junk Jew?"

"*Bot Bon Jui*. It's a great Oriental treasure. He's talking about a treasure that's been sought after for decades."

"What is all this bullshit treasure talk, Youngman? You been to them indoctrination schools."

"It's an old legend, Sarge."

"Legend. Scuttlebutt, you mean. Horse pucky."

"There could be something to it, Sarge. Just about every green dogface hitting the line has heard about *Bot Bon Jui.*"

"I ain't never heard of it," said Sarge.

Youngman shrugged. "Generation gap."

"So it's talk. So what?"

"The Chinese are great believers in burying things. You might say they invented buried treasure."

"That's right, that's right. *Bot Bon Jui* was supposed to be part of the booty from the Chinese Civil War."

Youngman carried on the thought: "During the war they used to bury their bank reserves underground or in caves. They felt it was the best way to safeguard their capital. So, whenever a bank had over one thousand ounces of gold or silver, the vice-president would select three men—one of them always a Communist party member. One vice-president had a saying: 'I personally prefer to bury our gold and silver on lonely mountain peaks.' He had another saying about the three men: 'One killed, okay. Two killed, still okay. Three killed, treasure lost.' That's because only those three men knew the place—they didn't tell the vice-president or anybody else. The *Bot Bon Jui* legend states there were two survivors after its burial."

Sarge frowned. "So this Bout Bunk Jew is a lot of gold and silver buried somewhere nearby, huh?"

"Not necessarily gold and silver. Nobody knows for sure what it is."

"So," said Sarge, with a tinge of sarcasm, "all we gotta do is dig up a few thousand square miles of earth."

"Maybe this fishhead knows something," said Charlie Brown. "He was talking about it. I heard him. *Bot Bon Jui.* He must know something."

"Maybe the fishhead does know something, Sarge," acquiesced Youngman. "Maybe we oughta look into it. A treasure's a treasure. Figure it for yourself. Jewels—emeralds, pearls, diamonds. The fortune of ten dynasties. If we could find it, we'd all be rich for life. We sure as hell wouldn't have to fight in this goddamn war any longer."

176

"Now let me give you a quick Corps communiqué, Youngman. You too, Brown. I ain't running no treasure hunt agency. And even if this Bout Junk Jew was layin' at my feet right now, asking, begging to be picked up, I couldn't care less. We're all headed back for the main line. From now on I don't even want to hear the word treasure. You guys think about pussy to keep your minds off it if you have to. But you forget treasure. Is that understood?"

Perhaps the words had been understood, but even Sarge could see that the look of greed which had sprung so suddenly onto Charlie Brown's face was not going to be so easily removed.

38
Convoy

It had been an active day for Louis, Reva and Li Ming. After driving all night and part of the next morning, they had run out of gas on a lonely stretch of road that, according to the maps, went nowhere of importance, which was exactly why Louis had chosen it. After banging his fingers idly on the still warm hood, and pondering what to do, a small motor car, European-made, approached and stopped, since Louis's truck was blocking the single lane and there was no room on either side to pass. The driver honked his horn impatiently a few times, then climbed out. He was an aging Chinese diplomat. With Li Ming translating, he explained that he and his wife were fleeing to Ningtu. Somewhat belatedly, he added, as there had been considerable paperwork to clean up in his office in Chiuchiang, near Lake Poyang, before he could properly leave. Louis, still using Li Ming as translator, explained that he and the ladies were on an important secret mission for the Greek government—trying to negotiate peace with the Peking regime. The aging diplomat and his wife were extremely apologetic for delaying the important spy and immediately offered the entire contents of their gas tank. They would

178

walk the rest of the way to Ningtu, which was not unusual, as the diplomat's ancestors, he explained, had spent most of their lives walking from one end of China to the other. As Louis siphoned off the gas they began walking, taking with them what few belongings they could carry.

"It's a crazy war," remarked Reva.

"He who looks upon misfortune as the inspiration of the gods will not be disappointed by life," said Li Ming.

Twice they were forced off the road by fighter planes streaking overhead, searching for targets. The first time they had gone unnoticed. The second time the U.S. fighter pilot, seeing a lone Chinese truck below, came back for a strafing run. Tracer-tipped .50 machine gun slugs ripped up the dirt roadway, some of them hitting only fifty feet away, but they were nonexplosive shells, and no damage was done.

Twice Reva had to go to the bathroom, and once Louis had stopped to take a crap. For some reason, Li Ming never got out of the cab for anything. And while this puzzled Louis and Reva, neither said a word about it. Something, no doubt, to do with Chinese custom or character.

At three o'clock that afternoon, they reached a four-way intersection. Louis chose the road leading south. They drove for less than a minute when, on rounding a turn, they suddenly found themselves behind another Chinese supply truck. As the newly sighted truck rounded the next bend ahead, Louis hit the brake. As the truck stopped, he shifted into reverse, intending to back all the way to the main intersection and take a different road. But then they heard a noise behind them. "Jesus," cursed Louis. Another Chinese supply truck was moving toward them. Back at the intersection, he realized he had driven into the middle of a Chinese supply column. That meant trucks ahead and trucks behind. No way to go but straight ahead.

He shifted into low and spun gravel in an effort to equalize the distance between the truck ahead and the truck behind. Stopping on a bend when no other trucks were in sight, he threw open the cab door. "Reva, get your tail into the back of the truck. You'll find some helmets and soft caps. Grab some and get back here. Hurry."

Reva was climbing into the bed when Louis realized the truck behind him was almost in sight. Louis lurched ahead. The truck pulled up on his tail and stayed there. It would be impossible for Reva to get back into the cab without being noticed.

Louis sucked in his breath, and Li Ming literally jumped off the seat, when Reva screamed. Louis immediately realized she had discovered the dead sentry back there—he would have to remember to get rid of the corpse.

Louis sucked in his breath again. The truck ahead had slowed down and he could see that one of the tarpaulins stretched across the back had been thrown aside and troops inside were stretching and yawning. If he got any closer they'd be able to see his face. And that would be that. And if they saw Li Ming . . . he tried not to think about that.

His fingers closed around a wrench on the floorboards. He brought the truck almost to a standstill so the vehicle ahead rounded the bend, out of sight.

Beep, beep, beep.

The truck in back was giving him the horn. He moved ahead, just enough to satisfy them, but not fast enough so he would be in sight of the truck ahead. With one upward swing, he brought the wrench against the rear cab window. He handed the wrench to Li Ming. "Break out the rest of the glass."

She studied the wrench and the glass and shrugged. "Destruction can sometimes be the root of salvation." The truck inched along. Beep, beep, beep. Incessantly. Apparently he wasn't moving fast enough to satisfy the driver behind him. He heard gravelly footsteps. Someone from the back truck approached on foot—no doubt to ask what was holding him up. Louis stepped on the gas, leaving the trooper on foot behind, shaking his fist.

Now there was the truck ahead to contend with. Those troops were staring back at him. Any minute now, they'd get wise. They had to. He tried to lower his sun visor, but it broke off in his hand. The thin iron rods which held it in place had been sheered by a bullet. That left nothing to shield his face with. And he couldn't drive any slower, or that trooper was going to reach him on foot.

180

Li Ming finished clearing away the glass. Reva had passed one of the helmets. Li Ming plunked it over her head. "A cap," shouted Louis, "a cap."

With the window gone, Louis could hear Reva searching through the crates. Finally, after what seemed an eternity, she passed a cap through and he slammed it over his head, pulling the brim down as far as it would go. With his body hunched over the wheel, he pulled directly behind the truck and gave a friendly wave to the troops. They waved back, then seemed to lose interest in Louis and the truck.

They stayed in the convoy for almost an hour. When the trucks pulled over, Louis didn't. Several of the drivers gave him funny looks, but he kept on moving, as if he had the authority to do so. It was a bluff that went unchallenged. He drove as fast as he could, to put as many miles as possible between them and the convoy.

"And now," he said to the women, *"Chun Hsien Ku."*

39
Teutonic Meditation

The Old German sat in an open doorway of *Chun Hsien Ku*.

Throughout his body, there was not a single grain of energy that might have made him move at this particular moment.

He was tired, he was cold, he was hungry, but mainly he was tired.

Was it life he was tired of? He thought not.

Was it the slogging he had experienced over the past forty-five years? He thought not.

Was it the killing and the fighting, which he had seen on such a grand scale? He thought not.

Then it dawned in his creaking brain just what it was that bothered him.

He was tired of surviving.

Every battle has its survivors, and that is to be expected. How else will future generations know how terrible a particular battle was unless there is a survivor who can describe all the horrors in graphic detail?

There is nothing shameful about surviving a battle. If you can't get yourself killed by placing your body in the general vicinity of flying shrapnel, hurtling bullets, and the cold steel of bayonets, then there is nothing you can do about it but survive.

Yet, The Old German was tired of surviving.

Why is that? he asked himself, scratching at his buttocks. Perhaps, he decided, after much deliberation, it is the frequency with which I am a survivor.

Three times The Old German had gone into a major battle. And three times he had emerged the sole survivor.

Not one of three or four or five or six survivors ... one of one survivor.

The first time was the most vivid—but then everything about the Russian Front had remained vivid all these years. It had been the Cherkassy Pocket, February 1944, one of the great Russian encirclements of World War II from which the Germans had staged one of the most heroic breakouts in all military history. He was then attached to Panzerjager Battalion 389, which had broken through Russian lines only to reach the icy waters of the Gniloy Tikich, a raging torrent. Coupled with a freezing wind and a temperature of five degrees below zero, the "stream" as it was called in the communiqués proved the undoing of many of the 18,800 men who died in the campaign.

He had reached the bank of the Gniloy Tikich with four other men. While he covered them, sniping at a handful of Russians who felt brave enough to pursue through the freezing cold and snow, they tried to work their way across a crust of ice formed at a bend of the river. But the ice had caved in under their weight, and one by one they had slipped, screaming, into the raging rapids. Advance elements of the Soviet V Guards Tank Corps—i.e., five T-34s—crunched their way through forest and bodies toward the river. He had removed his heavy overcoat, laid it flat across the water and thrown himself on it, using his arms as paddles to fight his way through the current to the opposite bank. There, he searched for other members of his platoon. None were there. He waited, hoping others might cross. None ever did. He had been the last man.

The second time had been during the six-day Arab-Israeli War in June 1967, when he had been serving with the United Arab Republic's Seventh Division for reasons he couldn't even remember now. It must have been good pay; it certainly hadn't been the food. His company had been hit hard by General Ariel Sharon's forces near Bi'r Abu Uwayqilah, and most of the night was spent in retreating. By dawn, only forty men and a handful of trucks remained. As they drove through the Sinai Desert, headed for the safety of Mitla Pass, Israeli planes, which had controlled the skies since the first shot, came down to bomb the hell out of the convoy. He had raced away from the highway and remained behind a sand dune until the strafing and bombing was ended. When he returned, he found no signs of life.

The third time had occurred only ten miles from *Chun Hsien Ku*, twenty-four hours ago. He had been the only member of his U.S.-Germo infantry company to emerge from a Chinese flanking attack. This was thanks to the fact he had banged his head on the treads of an Allied tank at the moment of attack and lay under its protective covering while the Chinese swarmed over the position, slaughtering everyone in sight as they went. When he woke up, an hour later, not a soul was alive. Well, he thought to himself, rubbing his head, I've done it again; I've survived.

Now he sat wondering in the open doorway. Perhaps he always survived because he was German. But no, there had been thousands of his Germanic comrades who had not survived. Such a thought was pure whimsy.

Unfortunately, The Old German believed neither in supernatural powers nor in out-and-out luck. He had never understood politics well, being a fighting man all his life, so it couldn't be that.

So he could not understand why he survived. He only knew that he did, and each time it was a little more painful, and a little more unnerving. One day, hopefully, the law of averages against surviving would work.

Until then, he would endure his humiliation.

40
Chun Hsien Ku

Chun Hsien Ku, the House of Guns, was an ammunition and supply warehouse which had been constructed originally by the Kuomintang in 1946 to supply armies which had moved into surrounding territory. By the time the Eighth Route Army had conquered most of that territory, *Chun Hsien Ku* had been heavily fortified and turned into a command post for one of Chiang Kai-shek's lesser generals, Nim Yung, who unlike many of his counterparts refused to surrender to the Communists without a fight to the death. To achieve this with a certain dramatic flair, Nim Yung had surrounded himself with a loyal cadre of followers, each vowing to die with Nim Yung if it came to that. And it finally came to that. It was the closest thing the Chinese have ever had to a private elite guard, and it was unique to the Kuomintang, which was founded on corruption, thievery, and outright murder. The Eighth Route Army, even though it ultimately had to destroy Nim Yung, honored the general for his strict discipline and the loyalty he engendered in his followers. It was a loyalty that Chiang Kai-shek had sought during his reign, but which continually eluded him. There were rumors that Chiang Kai-shek had cast out Nim Yung, jealous of his high standards of honor and devotion, but no man ever dared ask Nim Yung if this was true.

Though Nim Yung's forces were small, they were well armed and well entrenched, and proved formidable against the Eighth Route Army, which bore the brunt of a fierce three-day battle in 1948, during which Nim Yung's troops were killed in their battle positions. His elite guard stayed with him until the end. The next day *Chun Hsien Ku* was a stripped shell, its ammunition and supplies (direly needed by the Communists) transported north for pending battles that would ultimately oust the Kuomintang.

It had remained deserted until Sarge, Youngman, Charlie Brown, and Ju-Chao paused on its outskirts.

"Quiet," said Sarge, surveying the ammunition depot. It was a massive concrete block, with several rusting gun emplacements on its upper level, and gunports built into it on all four sides. There was a flight of steps leading to this top level, which made it easily accessible. Along two sides of the depot's ground level were concrete protrusions with numerous metal doors built into them. These were the doors which led to a complicated series of passageways and subterranean tunnels. The remnants of war were visible—pocks of shell craters and machine-gun bullets, rusted remains of gun barrels, odd mechanisms. Even in the grass in which they lay, Sarge noticed many empty cartridge cases. Sunken areas in the earth surrounding *Chun Hsien Ku* gave evidence of the heavy mortar and artillery barrages the supply center had withstood. In fact, realized Sarge, they rested in what was once a shell crater.

"Quiet," said Youngman. There was an eerie stillness about this place that made him uneasy.

Even Charlie Brown, who listened to an episode of "True Detective Mystery," shut off his transistor and stared in awed silence at *Chun Hsien Ku*.

Youngman glanced at Sarge. "Well, what do you think?"

Sarge cast a look at Ju-Chao, who lay behind him in the grass, seemingly unconscious. A swarm of flies buzzed around the red-stained bandage on his shoulder. Sarge swatted them away, wrinkling his nose in the same movement.

"I don't trust him. I've known too many of these Chinks

who were out-and-out liars. I've even known chopstick benders who lied in their own personal diaries. And this guy, he looks like the rest of them. Yeah, we could be walking into one helluva big trap."

"Besides," said Charlie Brown, "I don't see the girls he promised."

"What now, Sarge?" asked Youngman. "We got to do something."

"Yeah," agreed Charlie Brown. "We can't stay cut off much longer like this, Sarge."

Sarge curled his lower lip. "I got hot douche bag news for you guys. You're *both* cut off. You're impotent, sterile, frigid, castrated, emasculated, dickless and without balls. So relax and enjoy being cut off. Brown, you stay here with the fortune cookie franchiser. Youngman, you come with me. We'll check this joint out. That water's gotta be around here somewhere." Rapping Youngman twice on the helmet, he moved out. The private followed closely behind.

When they were gone, Ju-Chao opened his eyes. He wanted to spit the cotton out of his mouth, but he couldn't spit. He could barely open his mouth, and when he did, all he could think of was what he saw.

Chun Hsien Ku.

He was dreaming, of course. He blinked. Reopened his eyes.

Chun Hsien Ku.

So, it was true. He had thought it all a dream about the three men who were to take him to *Chun Hsien Ku* where he would make peace with Buddha.

And there was one of those three men, the one with slanted eyes in the uniform of the Americans. The face was like a mirrored image, as he might have looked himself thirty-five years ago and as *Chun Hsien Ku* still looked the day he last saw it. That fateful day when he, Tsai and Wu-sheng had found it.

Bot Bon Jui.

"*Bot Bon Jui*," he said, instinctively.

It was all Charlie Brown had to hear. "*Bot Bon Jui?*" he asked frantically. "Damn you, where is *Bot Bon Jui*? You tell, you tell. Charlie Brown friend."

"*Bot Bon Jui.*" Ju-Chao pointed at the ammunition

187

dump. Then he slumped forward, on his face, unconscious.

Charlie Brown stared at *Chun Hsien Ku*, the House of Guns, and he smiled slightly.

Meanwhile, Sarge and Youngman had reached the upper level of the supply depot and had found several scattered bones. Sarge picked up an ulna and a coccyx, realized they were human and not animal, and threw them down. Youngman was checking out one of the rusting gun emplacements when he found an old fieldcap. He showed it to Sarge. "That Chinese officer was telling the truth, Sarge. There was a battle here, all right. A long time ago. And you can sure tell the Chinese fought it. They never were good at burying their dead. Something about their spirits being free to roam the universe."

"It's the old teahouse in the sky legend, Youngman. Every country's got one."

"Maybe that's why the Chinese don't fight at night," speculated Youngman.

Sarge held up one hand, his standard signal for silence. "I hear something." He cocked his head to one side.

"What is it? What do you hear?"

They both listened. Then, faintly, Youngman thought he detected a sound that was almost ethereal. Very far away. Rhythmic. He was reminded of something spiritual. "Spirits," he whispered.

"Hearing spooks again, Youngman? Last time it turned out to be a soul group."

"Restless spirits of the men who fought and died here. There're legends about blood-soaked battlefields still frequented by the souls of the men who fought there. Sarge, I think this place is haunted."

Sarge cocked his head. "If they're ghosts, they're wearing skirts. Hear that?"

This time Youngman cocked his head. And he heard it.

The laughter of women.

The clapping of hands.

The hissing of a snake?

And there were voices, singing voices: "Ouzo ... ouzo ... ouzo."

The refrain rang on.

41
The Man With Steel Teeth

This is the story of Louis Panayiotis Nikopolis. It should begin in the mountains of the Balkan Peninsula, or on one of the islands of the Aegean Sea. It should be set amidst the extensive olive orchards in the Peloponnesus or the Ionian Islands, among the tobacco fields of Macedonia, perhaps even, from a romanticist's point of view, among the Corinthian and Ionic temple ruins of Athens.

Yet Louis Panayiotis Nikopolis is apropos of none of these places. Born and raised in Nebraska, he was the son of Greek parents who had sailed from the old country three years prior to his birth to begin a new life in America. They had settled in the Pierre Shale region (otherwise known as the Badlands) in the county of Sheridan, chiefly because his father, being a fan of Hollywood Westerns dubbed in Greek, had often heard the phrase "badlands" and associated a certain amount of romantic adventure and pioneer spirit to it. Actually the Pierre Shale wasn't badlands at all, since its soil was rich and the slopes and valleys weathered enough to provide good grazing land and abundant crops. With the Pine Ridge and Wild Cat Hills nearby, the Pierre Shale afforded a breathtaking view—another factor which contributed strongly to the Nikopolis family settling where it did.

Since goats were a tradition in Greece, Mr. Nikopolis had bought a large herd his first week on his new spread. Another reason he wanted goats was to provide his large family with fresh milk daily. (In addition to Louis, there were four other brothers and two sisters.)

Louis, from his first memory, had never developed a taste for goat's milk. His father insisted, and he drank it nevertheless. The milk was colorless and had no stronger flavor than cow's milk, but in Louis's mind goats had always had an unpleasant connotation. Mr. Nikopolis hammered it over and over into Louis: goat's milk was naturally homogenous; it had great quantities of albumin and nitrogen; it was more digestible than cow's milk, ad nauseam. It contained more niacin and more thiamine, yes yes yes, and more calcium, phosphorus, iron and copper, yes yes yes. In later years some of these ingredients were proven by scientists to be less than their reputations. By then his father was dead and there was no one left with whom he could argue the point.

Over the years, Louis developed an intense hatred for goats. He found the Toggenburg breed to be especially offensive when downwind. During those early years Louis and his father raised corn, sugar beets, oats, potatoes, beans, and other vegetables. Louis grew to love the smell of the earth in the spring when he plowed. His father, having put everything into the farm, was too poor to buy food, so they raised everything themselves.

Still, he hated the goat's milk more than he loved the earth, and when his older sister married and moved to Fresno, California, Louis was overcome with joy, for his new brother-in-law had invited Mr. Nikopolis to give up the farm and move west to join him in a restaurant enterprise.

Louis settled into his new environment with relish, but this very swiftly dissipated when he was put to washing dishes and bussing tables at the Pig 'n' Stick, a downtown breakfast-lunch-dinner café, which was a half-notch above a glamorous greasy spoon. He stood on Coke boxes to reach the sink, and Seven-Up crates to reach the cash register, which he operated during the less busy hours of business. By the time he was fifteen, Louis was a full-fledged chef. He worked tremendously long, difficult hours, and received no pay for it.

Despite his basic, deep-rooted love for his family, he ran away at the age of twenty and became a chef for the Division of Forestry in the Sierra country. His first military stint was with the U.S. Navy, and in his enlistment papers he avoided any reference to his cooking experience. He actually played dumb in his aptitude tests, answering all questions related to cooking with the wrongest answers in sight. Nevertheless, he became a cook's helper aboard an aircraft carrier, and for the next four years did the very thing, day in and day out, which he abhorred more than anything else.

On his discharge, he returned to Fresno. The Pig 'n' Stick had doubled in size, and although his father had died, his brother-in-law had made it a successful business. He felt a nostalgic twinge when he walked through the kitchen. As he left he experienced the gnawing of a new conflict. While he wanted to hate the restaurant business (and cooking in particular), he had a deep-rooted love for the preparation of food and the business that went with it.

By the time he settled in Fresno he had decided to buy a restaurant. He chose a Greek-style business (he made the down payment with a loan from his brother-in-law) and suddenly realized he knew absolutely nothing about Greek cuisine—or anything Greek. It seemed to him the kind of place a guy named Louis Panayiotis Nikopolis should own. He changed the name from The Athenian to The Balkan Taverna, hoping to avoid any prior reputations he might have to live down, and opened for business one rainy Monday night with a bouzouki band and one genuine Greek cook. The next week he hired an Armenian dancer, a buxom brunette named Sonja Zalian, who taught him all the basic Greek dances: (1) the *Syrto*, the national dance; (2) the *Kalamatiano*, another national dance but with rhythmic differences; (3) the *Hasaposerviko*, the Greek butchers' dance which carried a slight Serbian flavor and had been handed down from the Byzantine Era; and (4) the *Tsamiko*, the dance of the warrior designed to reveal strength, wisdom, and courage.

One evening, after closing time, a few of Louis's friends

stayed behind to toss down a few extra glasses of ouzo, a licorice-flavored distillation from the anise herb. One of them challenged Louis to perform the Dance of the Zebeks. This choreography was first dreamed up centuries before by half-breed Greek-Turks, outcasts until they proved themselves fierce warriors. With arms outstretched (to represent the wings of the eagle), Louis circled one of the dining tables (representing a dangerous snake) while his friends hissed.

It is normal for the dancer to incorporate feats of strength into the Dance of the Zebeks. He can pick up heavy objects, balancing chairs on his head—anything that would outdo the feat performed by the previous dancer. One of the most difficult of these time-honored feats is *Ouzo Zembekiko*, the refined art of picking up a dining table with nothing more than *dondia*—teeth.

As Louis approached the end of his dance, the men began to chide and dare him to pick up the table. Louis had never before attempted *Ouzo Zembekiko*, but he had put away such a large quantity of ouzo that before he realized it, he had squatted down, gripped the corner of the table in his mouth and brought it straight up. To Harry Stamos, a professional bouzouki player, then out of work and hanging around the club for free drinks, this was more than his manhood could bear. To prove to the others that *Ouzo Zembekiko* was just as easily in his grasp, he also picked up a table *dondia*-style and loosened his entire set of teeth. He fled from the Balkan Taverna, never to be seen or heard from again.

It was the start of something big for Louis. Stone sober, he introduced the act the next night and was an immediate sensation. He experimented with *Ouzo Zembekiko* and was delighted by its variations, as were his audiences. The highlight came when he put a topless dancer on the table and picked her up with it. Another favorite was to have Sonja the dancer do the difficult *Founda* on his stomach as he lay on the floor with the table in his teeth. Louis always used the same *trabezi* ("that's uh my table," he would joke with patrons) and the maître d' always seated somebody important there, so they shared in the excitement when Louis, in midact, unexpectedly lifted the table—napery, dishes, purse and all; up away from the guests.

Throughout these performances Louis wore the *foustenala*, the uniform of the *Evzones*, the Greek Royal Guard, whose members once met rigid requirements of physical ability and bravery. This colorful uniform—red for the bloodshed that went with honor and independence, white for purity of heart and spirit, and blue for the freedom of the sea—consisted of a *fousta* (skirt) with *shelahi* (wide belt, *tsarouhi* (white stockings and shoes) and *founda*, a pom-pom atop each shoe. Into the belt he stuffed a short knife known as the *spathi*, designed to add a note of realism.

Soon a talent scout discovered Louis and booked him for a late-night talk show. Louis did his bit with the table and was interviewed briefly by the host. The next week he inked a contract to appear on Broadway in *Nick the Greek*, a musical version of the life of one of the greatest poker players of all time. Louis was to be strictly "ethnic background color," but he intended to make the best of it.

On opening night, the property master placed a newly starched tablecloth on the *trabezi*. When Louis bit into the table he thought it felt peculiar, but proceeded to dance. When it came time for the lead male dancer to stand on the table . . . pandemonium. The boards and the lead dancer dropped away from Louis's mouth as the table literally fell to pieces. He stood for a moment with a single board jutting from his mouth, then turned to the audience and took a bow. Such bravura could only be rewarded with a standing ovation. As Louis repeatedly bowed his acknowledgment of the applause, the lead dancer glared at him through the debris and tried to get off the stage as gracefully as possible. The show ran only a few more performances—then Louis returned to Fresno.

When the war started, Louis was immediately declassified as "U.S. Citizen—Standard Caucasian" and reclassified "Greek-born—Specialized Foreigner" and placed in the Entertainment Branch, BIE, where he underwent orientation and was assigned recycling. During this phase he went through Stereotype School and, upon completion of his examinations, was deemed a suitable subject. That is, he now conformed to the preconceived notions of those he would be entertaining. As for the *Ouzo Zembekiko* act, his *foustenala* was equipped with additional weapons and he underwent a brief training period when he learned to fling the table with his teeth. Stereotype School felt this would enhance his image as the fierce warrior. He was also given poisonous snakes which he encircled as he danced, and which he dramatically sliced in two with his *spathi* at the climax of each performance.

Reva was assigned to BIE to augment his act. She was almost the counterpart to his former dancer Sonja, although she was a little less buxom, had lighter hair, and tended to spend more evenings with Louis after the show was over. She also spent early mornings with Louis. Together they found company in each other which made their humdrum BIE bookings bearable. The attraction was very physical and each promised the other a number of things that each knew the other could never live up to. Louis grew to hate the repetitive BIE junkets. He tried to transfer out, taking Reva with him, but every attempt was thwarted at one command level or another. He was, in their words, too indispensable—the morale of the frontline troops depended on *Ouzo Zembekiko*. Thus he and Reva sank ever deeper into a morass of bitterness and disappointment. There were far greater things waiting for them in the outside world, if only they could find a way to return to it.

Louis and Reva entertained troops during the R & R phase of the First Division's recovery from the terrible Battle of Shanghai. Although they were received as they had never been received before, with five-minute ovations, they were almost oblivious to this recognition. Louis had encountered an old Chinese peasant who, for reasons he never learned, had an intense craving for ouzo. Since Louis always kept a large supply on hand (drinking ouzo was always part of the table-lifting act), he gave the old-timer several bottles in exchange for a number of scrolls and documents which the ancient one said had been given to him by a gentleman he had found dying one afternoon behind a bed of roses. Within minutes of taking possession of these seemingly worthless rolls of parchment, Louis real-

194

ized he might have something valuable. Written across the top of one of the sheets: *"Bot Bon Jui."*

He, too, had heard the legend of *Bot Bon Jui.* After carefully authenticating the geography of a map attached to one of the scrolls, and convincing himself that the whole thing must be genuine (*had* to be genuine), he deserted his outfit, taking Reva with him.

They had moved southward on foot, holing up by day and traveling only by night. In a deserted temple, they paused one morning, only to be discovered by a young Chinese girl, Li Ming, who had come to the temple to pray and ask forgiveness for giving her body repeatedly to men of high military stature.

A friendship was immediately established between the three, for Li Ming could speak English and was searching for a deeper relationship with others. When both Louis and Reva were convinced that her philosophical attitude and her vow never again to be concerned with earthly goods were genuine, they no longer kept the purpose of their journey a secret. By bringing her into the "caper," as Louis preferred to call it, they could rely on Li Ming to serve as interpreter along the way. As soon as this new relationship was established, Li Ming, much to her own surprise, found that she missed men of high military stature and was satisfied, for the time anyway, to give her body to at least one man of low military stature. With Reva as warm as ever, Louis had nothing to kick about.

As they daily traveled further south, Li Ming began to express a renewed interest in earthly goods, and soon a new relationship within the new relationship was settled on. Li Ming would receive fifteen percent of the goods in exchange for her services—whatever they might be. She profusely apologized for the fluctuation of her desires and admitted that her whim to go spiritual was always put asunder sooner or later by the quest for flesh and/or earthly goods.

It was then Louis observed the column of Chinese trucks, pulled off the heist, and drove them all to *Chun Hsien Ku.*

42
The Waterhole Three

Sarge and Youngman took up positions atop a hillock flanking the ammunition depot. They realized that the singing voices had led them to the waterhole Ju-Chao had promised, but this was not what held their attention.

What they now were more interested in was the scene of entertainment below. A dancer clad in a foreign costume circled a bare wooden table, clapping his hands and hissing. Nearby stood a Caucasian and an Oriental woman who clapped and sang. "Ouzo ... ouzo ... ouzo ..." A Chinese truck was parked behind them. Sarge scanned the surrounding area. Was this a trap? Were the three below bait for that trap? If so, why would they leave the truck in plain view? None of it made sense.

Sarge fired at a rock. The bullet ricocheted in the fashion he had hoped—the piece of lead left a nice loud *zing* behind it that sent the dancer down behind the table for protection. The two women remained vulnerable, exposed, waiting in the open. Sarge took special note of them now. One was a well-stacked, hard-bitten broad—statuesque, leggy, whorish. The Oriental girl was lithe of figure, fragile, soft, seemingly out of place in a tight-fitting gown that opened at the front as she walked, revealing juicy legs.

196

Nothing else had happened. The dancer stayed behind the table. The two women remained motionless in the open. The whole affair seemed incongruous. Sarge stood up, silhouetting himself to those below. "Cover me, Youngman. I'm going down."

The gutsy move followed Sarge's basic philosophy: Do the unexpected before the enemy can do the unexpected to you.

As Sarge made his way down the hillside, Louis nonchalantly moved closer to the women.

"When an American comes to a foreigner, it is in the mood of liberation," said Li Ming. "Has this man come to save us?"

"I doubt," replied Reva, "we've got anything he could save now."

"Does this not mean the nest is now overflowing with birds?"

Louis shook his head. "This could work out in our favor if we play our cards right, girls. Just play it cool and everything should be all right. We'll use the Sullivan story."

"Beware," warned Li Ming. "The blind are quick at hearing; the deaf are quick at sight."

"You forget," replied Louis, "there are days to dry your nets and days to cast your nets. Today we cast . . ."

Sarge, still looking suspicious, stepped up to them. His weapon was leveled at their chests. Louis went into action. He threw out his arms, ran forward, jabbering in Greek, as if he were welcoming Sarge as a long-lost brother. Sarge took this affectionate outburst for only a few seconds. "Jesus Christ, man, get a hold on yourself. Pipe down, pipe down, cut that gibberish. The authorized language in this country is English."

Louis stepped back and bowed. "It is like the Phoenix which rises from the ashes of despair to prove that hope is eternal, after all. The sight of you stirs the Grecian blood in my veins and makes me yearn to dance and sing and . . ." Louis leaned forward to kiss Sarge on the cheek, and for a split second, after his lips met the hardened skin, he thought he might have made a fatal mistake. Sarge lurched backward, threatening to fire. Judging from the look in his eyes, Louis realized Sarge wanted to fire. A modicum of civilization had stopped him.

"Ten-shun!"

Louis stiffened and assumed the position of attention, realizing that the part of the fool had just been written out of the play.

"What the hell are you trying to pull? Something funny?"

Louis shook his head. Frantically. "I was only—"

"What's your name?"

"Sergeant Nikopolis. Sergeant Louis Panayiotis Nikopolis."

"Greek . . ."

"I apologize if I've offended you, Sergeant."

"The name's Sarge."

Louis would never make that mistake again. "I was only following Regulation 362, Section IV."

"Regula—hey, what are you, anyway?"

"I'm . . . an entertainer. BIE."

"Brigade of International Entertainers?"

"That's right."

"What's this getup?"

"The *foustenala.* The uniform of the Greek Royal Guard."

"Out here?"

"My standard uniform, Sarge. According to Regulation 362, Section IV, I am conforming to the prescribed concept of the Greek citizen as it exists in the eyes of the American. This image was first introduced to the American public during the early 1960s in a series of films and plays which depicted the average, day-to-day Greek as a fun-loving, zesty type, who loved his wine and was larger than life and who lived life to the very fullest. Who sought to savor the soil and the flesh and the dance and the bottle, who yearned to fulfill lust, love, longing. Women like Melina Mercouri and men like Anthony Quinn who—"

"What're you doing out here . . . with these?" Sarge motioned toward the two women.

Louis might have been a ringmaster, introducing the next act. "This is Reva, my dancer, also of BIE. And this is

198

Li Ming, a beautiful creature assigned to travel with me under special orders."

"I'll bet that ain't all she's under . . . where'd you get that Chink truck?"

"We were on our way to Second Battle Command, Central Unit, when our column was strafed and bombed by enemy fighters. We managed to escape, found that truck over there, and have been traveling steadily for several days in an effort to rejoin our unit."

"Why was the girl, Li Ming, assigned to you?"

"She was needed by General Sullivan."

"The *rear* echelon," contributed Reva. "What he's trying to say, Sarge, is that Li Ming was to be one of the women used by the High Command. Carefully selected to keep the VD rate down. First the general, then the men of his headquarters company."

"It's the General's way of keeping the men healthy," added Louis.

"And unhorny," concluded Reva.

"So," said Sarge, eying all three suspiciously, "here you are, in the heart of Chinese territory, *entertaining* . . . ?"

"Chinese territory . . . BIE camp . . . wherever, a performer has to rehearse . . . keep in shape. Dancing is a strenuous job, Sarge. Miss a day of it and you start to slide."

The crash was so loud everyone instinctively dived for cover. It was the sound of metal against metal, followed by the sound of something rolling across cement. And then a banging noise as whatever it was came to rest. "The ammo dump," said Sarge, leaping to his feet. He handed Louis his .45 pistol. "Come on, you said you wanted exercise . . ."

43
Gold Among the Mold

They found Charlie Brown doing what he did best—scavenging. In a corner of one of the upper-level gun emplacements he had found a garbage can and overturned it, spilling out its contents. As the can rolled its way down the flight of steps, finally coming to rest on the ground, he had begun picking his way through the waste, which happened to be human bones. Vertebrae, spinal columns, fibulas, shinbones, breastbones, tibias, ulnas. Ossicles up the ass, had been Charlie Brown's first thought. There was even one skull with a gaping hole in its cranium. The clatter of Sarge and Louis rushing up the steps gained Charlie Brown's concentration. When Louis saw a pair of Oriental eyes glaring up at him, he was ready to fire the .45, but Sarge waved aside the pistol. "He's 442." Louis lowered the .45.

"Who is this guy?" asked Louis. Charlie Brown returned to rummaging through the heap of bones.

As he scrounged: "Looks like the garbage collector didn't get around to picking up everything. That's the nice thing about a garbage can—it'll hold most anything." Charlie Brown held up the skull so Sarge and Louis could see two gold teeth set in the jaw.

Sarge grimaced. "I thought I told you to babysit the Fishhead."

"He started mumbling something about *Bot Bon Jui*. So, I decided to take a look. I think the POW knows something about this place, Sarge. When he saw it, it was like old home week."

At the mention of *Bot Bon Jui*, Louis stiffened. Somehow, he managed not to blink his eyes, slap the side of his face, say something like "*Madre Mia*" or collapse in a dead faint.

Charlie Brown was examining the two gold teeth, trying to evaluate their worth, when Sarge grabbed him by the collar and pulled him to his feet. They stood eyeball-to-eyeball. "Knew a guy like you, Brown. Guam. 'Forty-two. All he could see, all day long, were flashing emeralds, sparkling diamonds, shimmering opals. One day, he saw something flash in front of the company's position. He figures it's gotta be some valuable piece of rock God put there just so he could pick it up and get rich. So he decides to take a closer gander. You know what it was he saw, Brown? The sun off a Nip's helmet. And pretty soon there was something new shining on the ground . . . this guy's blood glistening."

Charlie Brown stared at Sarge with no change of expression.

"Now I've told you, Brown. Forget this Bout Junk Jew. And next time I tell you to do something, you'd better damn well do it."

Charlie Brown, carrying the skull with the two gold teeth, quickly moved across the open field toward the impression where Ju-Chao lay. Youngman ran up, panting for breath. "What happened, Sarge?"

"I'll tell you when to be a hero, Youngman."

"I'd better round up our girls." Louis turned and moved off.

"Who is that guy?" asked Youngman.

Sarge patted Youngman twice on the cheek. "He's movies for tonight."

44
Veterans' Reunion

The Old German was still seated in the open doorway of *Chun Hsien Ku,* where, in a contemplative mood, he had plopped several hours before. He had not moved from that position, although he had reached around to his back pocket at one point for his tobacco pouch. This movement shifted his buttocks a few inches.

The Old German had heard the voices of angry men, but they were not the voices of the enemy, and he realized, with what might approximate a sinking heart, that he would soon be reabsorbed into the ranks of the massive land army. That meant new situations, and new situations always meant the possibility of once again emerging a sole survivor. Therefore, he was not eager to make his presence known. He chose to remain seated. And silent.

Now, with the completion of his ritual of emptying, cleaning, filling, lighting and tamping his pipe, he sat in the open doorway and meditated—despite a creaking and groaning brain—about his past life and about the beautiful sunset. He wondered if all the men who hadn't survived his battles would have really wanted to survive if they had been given a choice. He had known many men on the Russian Front who had, after months of unbelievable hardships, given up wanting to live. On the other hand, some of those men had screamed for mercy before they were blasted apart by Russian submachine guns. So it was a matter that might take hours to ponder. This would help him pass the time. The Old German felt very relaxed.

He saw no reason to get up when Sarge and Youngman approached him slowly, weapons raised.

"I thought I saw a wisp of smoke," said Youngman.

"*Danke schon*," said The Old German.

"*Guten abend*," replied Sarge, nodding.

"Ach, so then you know German." His pipe went out again, but The Old German decided not to make any sudden moves to relight it until he had the full trust of these two. "You fought in the campaigns?"

"First Infantry Division. Big Red One. *Kaput Reich*. We used to process you guys for POW compounds. You guys were coming out of our ears." Sarge made a movement with his arm, and a gesture with his fingers; his feelings were clear.

"The First . . . yes. We fought the First during those last days in Czechoslovakia. Perhaps we've met . . ."

"Over a rifle sight we've met."

The Old German sighed. "I had great respect for the First. A tough outfit. I would not like to have to fight the First again."

"An old man like you shouldn't have to fight at all."

The Old German sighed. "I had great respect for the young anymore yourself, Sergeant."

"Sarge," corrected Sarge. "Panzer?"

The Old German shook his head. "*Gross Deutschland. Siebzehntes Bataillon.* One of the best of units."

"Yeah, I remember. The Ruskies chewed up a lot of you guys at Belgorod."

"The beginning of the end," said The Old German, remembering it all suddenly, as if it had happened only an hour before. "There was a certain regiment. Made up entirely of *Hitlerjugend* Hitler Youth . . . boys not over eighteen. Their first time in the line. Six thousand killed in less than a week. It was the day of the butcher, but not the day of the youth."

"Well," said Sarge, "it's all ancient history now. You can read about it in the manuals. How not to fight a war."

"It was a gallant effort," said The Old German, proudly.

"But the cause was wrong." Sarge spat into the grass at The Old German's feet.

"Perhaps . . ."

Sarge gave the Old German a curious glance. "You with one of those European re-up outfits?"

The Old German nodded. "There was a unit of Wehrmacht, Schulzstaffel and Gestapo people . . ." The Old German relighted his pipe now that it was obvious they were all good friends. "Composed entirely of Germans over sixty. I thought it only fitting to join. There seemed nothing better to do at the time."

"Yeah," acknowledged Sarge, "you Germans always seem to find time for a war."

"I might say the same for you Americans." The Old German puffed on his pipe, once again feeling a certain contentment. "As I recall, you *did* start this one."

"This is one we're going to finish," Youngman said.

"Ach." The Old German stretched and yawned. "We used to say the same thing on the Russian Front. Of course, we weren't taking into account the fact Hitler was a poor strategist once he overextended himself and began choking up under pressure. Or that the enemy, by 1943, was numerically superior. We lived on zeal in those days."

"No such thing anymore. Hasn't been any zeal in the world since Vietnam."

"Yes, that war did do something to zeal."

"How the hell did you come to be sitting in this open doorway?" asked Sarge.

The Old German told of the ambush, and how he had escaped death. But he did not tell of the other times he had survived. No use burdening comrades with his stories. Even for those who enjoyed a good exciting war story, there was a certain repetitiveness about his experiences. They merely bored the listener and added to his own weariness.

"And so now you're just sitting here . . ."

"Just sitting here," echoed The Old German.

"May as well get off your ancient ass and come over and

join us for chow. It's a ragtag outfit, but at least you'll eat. In the morning we'll all head back for our lines."

"Yeah," added Youngman, "stragglers should stick together."

The Old German cleared his throat. "I am not a straggler," he said. "I am a survivor."

45
Squad C-323's
Moment of Indecision

The bodies of several enemies strewn lifeless in the grass was a pleasurable sight for Squad C-323. Sergeant Joe Young and Konga passed from corpse to corpse, snarling, pawing and occasionally ripping off a sleeve or a trouser leg. King Kong did not discourage this, for it was good that the squad members stay in constant practice—whether the quarry be living or dead. And, while they occupied themselves among the corpses, King Kong mulled over a problem.

It was a problem of smell.

The smell of graphite, gunpowder, and the metal of weapons was overpowering around each of the bodies, and this told him that the individual he associated with masculine pride and valor, with military honor and tradition, had been responsible for each enemy losing its life force. But how could this be—that the quarry he now sought was also killing enemies? This contradiction greatly troubled him. Should he follow The Man Up the Pole . . . or the odor of graphite, gunpowder and the metal of weapons ... or should he return to the original purpose of his mission? He had forgotten that purpose, but he had not forgotten there was a mission.

But odor continued to predominate over idea. Instinct that had been born into him was certain to win out.

Another thing equally troubled him. The odor of graphite, gunpowder, and the metal of weapons had left this place with the smell of The Man Up the Pole. They were as one.

That could not be. For the odor of graphite, gunpowder, and the metal of weapons had killed the men of The Man Up the Pole.

And yet, there it was for his nose to absorb.

King Kong gave the order to follow the fresh trail, which had branched off to the east.

Sergeant Joe Young was the first dissenter. He thumped and brayed a rasping sound, which expressed the attitude they should continue following the trail Bonzo was leaving, and eventually rejoin Bonzo and return to Battalion Command Group Center.

Konga jumped up and down, thumped his feet, shook his arms. As usual, he was unable to make himself clear; neither King Kong nor Sergeant Joe Young knew what attitude he tried to express.

In frustration, Sergeant Joe Young flung himself on his back and rolled wildly to and fro, shrieking his disapproval.

King Kong leaped on and off his exposed stomach. It had been a simple movement, but one which carried with it the expression of humiliation. Sergeant Joe Young had lost face. He would not be able to look at the others now that his anger had been challenged. When Young shamefully bowed his head, the argument came to an end. He and Konga fell into formation as King Kong indicated the new direction they would now take. East.

46
War Dance

▬▬▬▬▬▬▬▬▬▬▬▬▬▬▬▬▬▬▬▬▬▬▬▬▬▬▬▬▬▬

It was *Tsamiko,* the dance of the warrior. It was a dance
that bespoke courage, it was a dance that told of furious
battles in which men wielded knives for the sole purpose of
cutting the throats of lesser men. It was a dance that her-
alded the wisdom of the Greek people down through the
ages, from days of the Spartan Empire through Alexander
the Great to the overthrow of twentieth-century dictators.
It told of honor, death, and victory. Always it told of victory.

Louis Panayiotis Nikopolis danced it with the spirit of
one who has lived through these glories. His legs assailed
the air as if it were his bitterest enemy. His arms and hands
weaved patterns that made the air itself dance in utter
confusion. He twisted and writhed. Then he leaped atop
the tense stomach of Reva, who lay on the ground. Her
muscles waited to accept the massive weight with the same
kind of dedication with which Louis performed his dance.
His *tsaroush* worked strange, Gene Kelly-like patterns over
the surface of her belly, highlighted by the insertion of the
pom-pom of his shoe into her belly button. It was an action
which always threatened to bring a smile to Reva's lips, but

she always managed to suppress that smile, knowing it would destroy the illusion Louis had so vigorously created.

Louis leaped from Reva's stomach and began his *Ouzo Zembekiko,* lowering the table at one point so Reva could climb on top. He began twirling then, and the upper level of the ammunition depot became nothing more than an elongated blur, broken by the sharp yellowish red of the campfire each time he circled past it. The faces of his audience—Sarge, Youngman, Charlie Brown, and The Old German—were lost in the semidarkness. He whirled as Li Ming emerged from the shadows of one of the gun emplacements (that had been Louis's idea—good, he thought, for dramatic effect) and walked toward the campfire. Once there, she became fully illuminated—a tall, lithe figure enwrapped in an angelic white gown.

Her dance was the direct antithesis of Louis's. While he was fury, she was gentleness incarnate. He was anger; she was love refined. He was steel warrior; she was fair maiden. He was conqueror; she was protector.

Hers was the dance of *Yangko.*

It has been said that the *Yangko* is a beautiful sight to behold. It uplifts the spirit; it enlightens the soul. Foreigners have attempted to imitate it without success. Danced by the feet of aliens, it is a spiritless, awkward performance, soon abandoned in absolute frustration. It is a dance only to be found in the feet of the Chinese. Li Ming's flowered slippers demonstrated that art as her dainty but assured movements told of legends and liberations. It revived Confucianism, Madame Chiang Kai-shek, and all the phases of the Chinese Revolution. Yet while these were oftentimes bitter things to the Chinese, in the *Yangko* they were never expressed bitterly. They were told with sincerity and honesty, with great compassion for the corrupt landlords, and with pity for the firing squads of Chiang-Kai-shek, and with pity for the victims of those firing squads. Gracefulness was alive in every inch of Li Ming's body as she leaned forward to dance another phase of history—the invasion of her homeland by the conquering army from the West. These were brave warriors, said her hands. Yet they know not what they do, said her feet. And we will one day have pity for them as we stand over their defeated bodies, said her eyes. There was wisdom in every crook of her elbow and there was philosophical understanding in every bend of her knees and there was compassion in the air as her hands weaved sinuously above her head. Even for her lifelong enemies, there was understanding and sympathy.

It was akin to watching the spirit of man as Li Ming came together with Louis. As they danced side by side, incongruous styles meshed to tell a complete, unabridged history. The warlike nature of man, the purity and sweetness of life. One encircled to liberate the other; one hovered clawlike and threatened to exterminate the other, yet each held its own ground. Neither seemed to dominate the other. It was the way of life.

And so the dance came to an end. All that was left of the struggle was perspiration and heaving bodies and a lingering hint of compassion in the eyes of Li Ming. The three dancers hurried down the steps and disappeared into a side door.

To Sarge, the dance was a flurry of activity that had momentarily taken his mind off how he was going to get this ragtag outfit back to the main lines.

To Youngman, it had been an interruption in the middle of a tense scene in "Mindanao Marauders." As he watched the dancers, however, he began to take some notes, realizing he might one day incorporate such an unusual dance into a story.

To Charlie Brown, it was visual accompaniment to an episode of "The Eddie Cantor Show" in which announcer Harry Von Zell had quit Cantor after winning $10,000 in a horse race, only to learn the horse had been disqualified. As the dancers worked their way back and forth before Charlie Brown, he divided his thoughts between (1) the possibilities of Von Zell getting his old job back and (2) the possibility that the half-dead Chink knew the whereabouts of *Bot Bon Jui*.

To The Old German, it had been a nostalgic reminder of his days with the Hitler Youth, when he had gone on week-long field marches with his *Jungvolk* detachment, hiking through Alpine meadows and singing victory songs ("forward, forward, sound the fanfares, forward, forward,

210

youth knows no dangers"). Too bad those good times couldn't have lasted a little bit longer. The Old German watched the dancers and remembered. When he felt a tear forming in the corner of one eye, he fluttered his lashes quickly and blinked it out of existence.

47
A Reading

Youngman immediately returned to "Mindanao Marauders," heading into the climactic scenes. He felt great as line after line flowed from the porto-typer. It was as if the story had taken over from him, and he was merely the servant to a great happening in his subconscious.

Charlie Brown snapped on the vidpack and watched *Fixed Bayonets*, unexpurgated.

The Old German recalled greater glories, and sighed.

Ju-Chao had not had his bandage changed since Youngman applied the original compress to his wound. He thought he could feel maggots crawling around the surface of his shoulder, and his throat screamed for water.

Sarge watched Youngman work over his porto-typer. "You know something, Youngman?"

Youngman paused reluctantly in midsentence. He tried not to appear annoyed as he looked into Sarge's face. He was surprised to see something that might have resembled envy.

"I'm a writer myself," said Sarge casually.

"No shit? You never told me that."

"Hell, yes. The battle of Iwo Jima."

"You fought at Iwo?"

The Old German cocked his head.

"I fought the battle, and I wrote about it." Sarge reached into the deepest lining of his breast pocket. "Fought with the Fifth Amphibious Corps. Went ashore with the first wave. I was in one of the last units to be relieved. Costliest battle for the Corps in 168 years of fighting." Finding nothing in his breast pocket, Sarge explored the pockets of his fatigues. "All those historians, they wrote about the big picture, but they never got the little picture because they never came around to talking to guys like me." Sarge finally pulled out a bundle of stationery that threatened to crumble in his fingers. He gingerly unfolded the packet. Some flakes of paper fluttered to the ground.

"Looks like you've been carrying that for a long while," remarked Youngman.

"Longer than you'd believe, Youngman." He finished unfolding the pages and placed it on the ground carefully. As Sarge beamed his pocketflash across the pages, Youngman saw the writing was smudged in places, but still legible. The handwriting was tiny, as if Sarge had been trying to squeeze as many words as possible onto each page.

"Want to hear it?" Sarge asked.

"I would like to hear it, yes," said The Old German.

"Good ahead, Sarge."

"Yeah, sure, Sarge. Read it."

"It was written to my mother," said Sarge. He began to read:

Foot of Suribachi
23 Feb 45

Dear Mom:

Your Son really had it crammed to him this time, Mom. & the Corps was using every deception in the book. The weather was great when we came on deck—clear with one helluva refreshing mist after all that time spent in the hold. When the Corps feeds you steak & eggs, you know your chances of becoming another name on a white cross in an endless row of white crosses are better than excellent. The Navy pounded the hell out of this piece of Pacific real estate, & it's not coded Hot Rock for nothing. In less than 30 minutes the sailor boys poured 8000 rounds onto the island, & for a while some of the boys thought it was going to sink. Mom, this is the kind of crap the Hollywood writers will use in the movies when they get around to showing how we took these islands, so if you ever hear some kid in the movies saying something like that, you'll know Your Son was there to hear it. Like always, they crammed us into LVT (A)'s & we went through the Line of Departure, Lock & Load procedures. Just before 9 A.M. the barrage lifted & the boats started in. One of the squad leaders started to say something, but Your Son told him "I'll kill the first sonofabitch that says 'this is it.'" & so he shut up. Mom, if you read about anyone taking credit for saying that, you know he's a damn liar. Your Son said it.

Well, we went toward Beach Red One, Your Son feeling like he's never felt before. We were up against a tough outfit, Major Tatsumi's 311th Independent Infantry Battalion. A slough of tough little bastards, who weren't going to throw their lives away in a Banzai attack. Not this time. This wasn't going to be Guam or Guadalcanal. No, Mom, this one was going to be different. Your Son could sense it as the boats went in, with that bastard of a volcano rising to our left, its top hidden by clouds. & those sandy barren terraces rising in front of us. The whole place looked bare and deserted, & that's what scared the hell out of us, because we knew at least 20,000 Japs were crawling all over the place, dug in like rats. One of the guys called it "a fat porkchop sizzling in a skillet." If you ever hear that one, you know Your Son didn't say it, but he was there when it was said.

Well, we hit about one minute to nine, & right away Your Son can see there are problems. The LVTs, which are carrying 75-mm. howitzers and plenty of machine guns, can't even make it up the first terrace, which Your Son estimates to be ten, fifteen feet high. Nothing but loose sand. A lot of them turn around &

go back out into the surf to shell the island from there, but that isn't giving us the frontal support we'd counted on. Meanwhile, we're scrambling like crazy up this terrace, & getting nowhere fast with a good 50 pounds of equipment strapped to our backs. You didn't climb. You swam. So far hardly any shooting. Not even any mortars. & that scared Your Son more than anything else, because Your Son knew that sooner or later all hell had to break loose. It did.

That's when the guys started dying. Small-arms' fire coming from Mt. Suribachi & from the flat terrain beyond the terraces. Only it's not so flat. It's honeycombed with spidertraps, pillboxes, machine-gun nests, you name it, the Japs have dug it. Dug it deep. Constant bombing & barrages haven't helped all that much. Now that the Japs've let us swarm onto their little island, they're providing a warm reception. Your Son swears, Mom, some guy said, "The Corps lying to me. The natives on this island ain't friendly." You know Your Son didn't say it, but . . .

You won't believe this, Mom, but Your Son plopped down next to this guy lying on the edge of a shellhole, & talked to him for a good 30 seconds before Your Son realized the guy was dead. He had his M-1 propped up in firing position, the butt resting against his shoulder. His eyes were open & he was aiming at the slopes of Suribachi. Everything about him was alive & animated. Only trouble was, there was this hole in his helmet. Right above the eyes. & then Your Son saw this narrow trickle of blood start to creep down his forehead. Your Son felt pretty uncomfortable after that. & things didn't exactly pick up a little later when Your Son crossed through what had once been a minefield. Your Son says once because a platoon of guys had run through it, & what was left of them was scattered all over the field. Including one boot with a foot still inside it, smoking. Somehow Your Son kept the squad moving, & we were at least glad to be the hell off that beach because now the Japs on the northern part of the island were leveling everything they had on us. Every inch of the place must have been zeroed in. Just being on that beach made you an automatic target.

About 11 A.M. we heard the news about John Baselone. By now you know all about that, I'm sure, him being a Medal of Honor winner & all that. Well, Your Son don't know how they told it in the newspapers—probably some crap about dying valiantly trying to Storm 500 Nips in a king-size pillbox—but Your Son knows for a fact he died like a lot of other guys here, anonymously. Old Manila John, the hero of Guadalcanal, was leading his machine-gun section past the southern end of the airfield when a mortar blast knocked off him & four other guys. Somebody said they'd seen a tattoo on one of his arms—"Death Before Dishonor." Sounds like a piece of shit to Your Son, but Your Son wasn't there, so he can't say for sure.

Well, Mom, Your Son could go on like this about everything that happened that day & the next but by now Your Son guesses you get the idea this Iwo gig is one rough mother, & it ain't gonna be over in no ten days like some of those big-shit generals are predicting.

We swung over toward Suribachi on Wednesday & got the Big Order. Clean out that mother hump so the boys attacking to the north won't get fired on from above. & this is the story Your Son's gotta tell you about because you won't find it written up anywhere else in the books, ever. This is something only Your Son experienced. Remember that, Mom. Only Your Son. & Bumblefoot Jonesy.

Thursday morning our platoon was given the order to clean up a series of bunkers & pillboxes dug into the side of the mountain. We started with 75-mm. half-tracks & some 37-mm. guns, but it still boiled down to the flamethrowers and demolition teams burning out each enemy emplacement, & each rifleman individually advancing yard by yard. Same old shit, right?

We must have progressed a good 200 years up the lava slopes when it looked like things had changed a little to the good. The Jap fire suddenly ceased so the platoon swarmed upward. The company commander, seeing our gain, decided to send up a halftrack filled with several giant water containers. We needed it, because a lot of the guys were dropping from heat prostration & fatigue. You Son swears the temperature, what with the heat generated by the flamethrowers, must have been 105. We'd just gained another 100 yards when Your Son began to smell it. A trap. You ever stop to think a trap has a smell to it, Mom? You know what Your Son means—you can sense something in the air—something that's about to happen. & it sure as hell did.

The Japs had been leading us on, sucking us into a breach in the lines. Then, when they had us where they wanted us, they opened up. The platoon was finished, chewed up in a matter of minutes. About 30 Nips came out of their ratholes in a spirited counterattack; that's what did us in. We stopped the attack, but died doing it. As a fighting unit, we didn't exist any longer.

Your Son was trying to get the men in his platoon back together, but they were getting knocked off too fast for him to do any good. Finally it was just Your Son & Jonesy. Bumblefoot Jonesy, the biggest mess in the squad, & he was to survive while a lot of better men didn't. But then that's war—that's something you learn to live with after a few campaigns like Iwo. Ten yards from us is the burning halftrack with the water cans, hit on the treads by a mortar shell, or maybe a mine. Its driver & gunner are dead, & the gun is shattered. It offers the best cover on that particular stretch of slope, so we heer for it. Your Son notices right away the water cans are still okay. Not a single puncture from shrapnel, which has got to be something of a miracle. We hunch down in that damn smoking halftrack, & for the moment the war passes on down to the leathernecks below us, who're really pinned down by a sudden burst of fire which seems to be coming from right next to us.

Then Your Son sees it. Buried up against the slope

of the mountain is an old Nip tank, covered with several layers of dirt, but a lot of that dirt has been knocked aside by near-misses. Your Son & Bumblefoot Jonesy can see the muzzle of its cannon, & even the muzzle of a light-caliber machine gun which is raising hell with the boys below—killing some of them. Some slugs started slamming against the halftrack & Your Son realized he was being fired upon by his own men, who by now are concerned with getting that tank. Now it's one thing to be fired on by the enemy ... that's to be expected ... but when your own men start doing it, it leaves a very bad taste in the mouth. Your Son guesses he got very mad at that moment. But Your Son & Bumblefoot Jonesy are in one helluva fix, because neither has any ammo left, and their supply of grenades was expended in repelling the Jap attack. So we dodged our own lead in a burning halftrack, with that Jap tank stuck away in the mountain not more than eight feet away, blasting the U.S. Marines to bits. Your Son looked at those water cans, & at some hose coiled up on the floor of the halftrack, & Your Son began to remember how he used to flush rats out of their holes. And Japs are rats. Well, Bumblefoot Jonesy was hunched down on the floor, quivering like crazy, because he figures he's had it. This is it. That kind of crap. Your Son shook him out of it, though, & had him tear the lids off all the water cans. Then Your Son took the hose, & dropped one end into a can of water. Uncoiling some slack, Your Son leaped over the side of the halftrack & crawled to within a few inches of the machine-gun slit. Now that may sound easy, but believe me, Mom, it was a bitch because our boys below were still laying down an intensive fire. That tank was a big target, & there was Your Son, crawling around its front like some kind of curious gopher. Your Son tries not to think about that as he siphons water into the hose, then shoves the open end against the firing slit. The machine-gun fires occasional bursts, but the gunner doesn't seem to be aware of what's happening. Fortunately for us. Your Son hurries back to the halftrack,

& you can thank your Lucky Stars or whatever that Your Son wasn't hit by one of his own guys.

So for the next 10 or 15 minutes we're streaming water into that Nip hulk as fast as it'll pour through the hose. We've pumped maybe 75 or 80 gallons when Your Son suddenly realizes that sooner or later those Japs are going to get wet feet & maybe plan on coming out of there. How to arrange for a surprise reception? Especially with an occasional M-1 slug ricocheting off the tank's hide, which curtails the idea of climbing up onto the hatch & waiting for a little yellow head to pop out. Suddenly it dawn on Your Son that the halftrack being the nearest object to the tank might be the first place a half-drowned Jap might head for. That's the way it seemed at the time, so Your Son & Bumblefoot Jonesy crouched in the halftrack & waited. By God, it took just about all the water we had. We were on our last can, & Your Son had pretty well decided it was a bust when the machine gun and cannon both stopped firing almost simultaneously. & we could hear the chatter of Nipponese coming from inside the tank. Within seconds the hatch popped open & there was that little yellow head Your Son was telling you about. A fast glance & he riveted on the halftrack & Your Son knew he'd been right. It never has been hard to outthink a Jap, especially under battlefield conditions. That sonofabitch of a tank commander or whatever was headed straight for us, & as he came over the side, Jonesy & Your Son went into action, just as we'd rehearsed it a couple of times. We slammed the open end of the water can against the Jap, aiming it so it fit right over the top of his head. That Jap commander or whatever let out a yell, but it ended up just an echo, buried somewhere in that water can. We left him kicking & squirming & picked up another water can & aimed it, & waited. The next Jap out of the tank must have been up to his neck in water, because his uniform was soaked, & he made some funny gurgling noises that reminded Your Son of some of those rats we used to drown down in the cellar. This Jap also headed for the halftrack, & damned if we didn't have the chance to repeat the routine. In our haste we'd picked up a water can still half-filled & when we got that Jap wedged into the opening we just put the can down upright & let him kick his feet in the air. He started to gurgle again. Your Son guesses that can was filled with more water than he realized, because after a few moments that Jap stopped kicking, his legs went limp & we didn't hear any more gurgling sounds.

Well, that finished that tank & in minutes the Leathernecks were swarming around us & moving on to take the top of Suribachi. A little while later, when Your Son & Bumblefoot Jonesy are coming down the slope, they meet three guys trudging up. By then word had filtered down that the mountain had been taken. You'd think the mountain had taken us, the way we looked. Anyway, all three of these guys are carrying cameras. One of them tells me he's a Marine Corps photographer & he's going up with an AP photographer—they've heard there's going to be a flag-raising or something in the upper lip of the crater—& he's going to take this AP photographer, Rosenthal something, up to the top. The third guy, he's got a movie camera, & he's eager to shoot some live-action stuff in color. So off they went, & Your Son never saw any of them again, but if you see any pictures of a flag-raising, or something like that, you'll know Your Son wasn't there, but he knew the men who were.

So now, Mom, Your Son is in a foxhole somewhere at the foot of Suribachi with Bumblefoot Jonesy curled up next to him, snoring. We've already agreed not to tell anybody about the tank incident. Like Your Son said, this is one action that'll never make the history books, But . . . if Jonesy should ever blab about what happened, he's got a big mouth & a tendency to run off when he's smashed, & word filters back to you, remember that whoever's telling the story isn't as big a damn liar as he might seem.

With love,
Your Son.

"Hey," said Youngman, when Sarge had finished, "I'd like to know one thing."

"Which is?" Sarge carefully folded the letter and slid it back into its cherished position in his pocket.

"You went to the trouble to write all that . . . how come you never went to the trouble to mail that letter to your mother?"

Sarge looked incredulously at Youngman.

"Mother?" he roared. "Hell, I've never had a mother in my life."

48
A Plot is Revealed

After racing down the steps of the ammo depot, Louis, Reva, and Li Ming had entered one of the small supply rooms which had been converted into a dressing room/sleeping quarters. They stood for a moment and caught their breath. Louis wiped his face with a towel, realizing how sweaty he had become during the dance with Li Ming.

"I think they loved us," he said proudly.

"Is that all you can think about, Louie? We got problems."

"We got an audience now," stressed Louis. "Haven't had an audience for two weeks."

"I'm crying all over my personal tour contract." Reva started to wiggle out of her dancing gown. She paused in midwiggle: "You're the brains behind the outfit, Louie. What now, Lover Boy?" She continued wiggling and threw the gown onto the damp, moldy floor. With her hands on her hips and with her lips pouting, she turned to face Louis. She was wearing only her bra, panties, and black hose.

"You should relax, Reva. Don't you recognize a budding genius when you see one?"

222

"No, but I know a blooming idiot when I see one."

"Look," said Louis, a tinge of frustration entering his voice, "everything is working out fine."

"Oh yeah, sure." More pouting. "The place is crawling with souvenir hunters and you insist everything is hunky dory."

"Reva, either you're hot or you're cold. And right now, you are very very cold."

"I could try to disprove that."

Louis slapped one of Reva's probing hands. "Stay on the subject, Reva. How many times do I have to tell you. Stay on the subject."

"All right, all right." Reva slipped into a tight-fitting, scarlet minidress, which was deeply scooped out at the top. Her breasts fought the weak material, but the material managed to win, for the time being. She pulled the thin dress down over her bikini panties and turned to look at Louis, who had lapsed momentarily into what would appear to be deep thought.

Louis snapped his fingers. "Remember when Li Ming asked if those guys were gonna save us?" As a token of appreciation, Louis rapped Li Ming somewhat vigorously on her buttocks. "Well, they are going to save us. They're gonna save us a lotta time and sweat. And we're gonna take full advantage of it."

"What about that fishhead?"

"The POW? He's all shot to hell. No problem."

"The Jap, Charlie Brown, he said that POW knew something about *Bot Bon Jui*."

"Now you're beginning to get the picture, Reva."

"So you want the Jap to nose around?"

"Exactly. Let him nose around all he wants." Louis paused to remove a microminidress from a suitcase and throw it to Li Ming. "Here, honey. Climb into this thing. You've got work to do tonight."

As Li Ming undressed, Louis continued: "I want that slant-eyed bastard to dig into this place. All we have to do is keep an eye on him—and the POW. Sooner or later, one of them is bound to tell us what we need to know."

Reva squirmed. "I don't know. It's risky."

"Fighting all those other sperm cells to reach the womb

223

was risky too. But you made it, didn't you? Here, look at this."

Li Ming had climbed into the micromini, but Louis shook his head with disapproval. "The panties have to go, baby. Like I said, I got action for you, and I don't want anything hindering that action." Without a word, Li Ming slipped out of her panties. She tugged at the micromini, but even at maximum length the dress left almost nothing to the imagination. But that's the way Louis liked it.

From his duffel bag Louis pulled a scroll of paper which he quickly unfurled and placed upon his sleeping bag. "I've seen it before," said Reva, "we've all seen it before. So what's new?"

"Let's look at it from an architectural point of view, Reva. This old joint is honeycombed with corridors and subterranean warehouse areas. Its purpose was to supply and feed an army when Chiang Kai-shek built it. There are literally scores of passageways that eventually branch from the main exits. Scores more of other passageways which branch off from those. It could take years to check them all out, and we don't have that kind of time. All we have to know is which outer door leads to *Bot Bon Jui*. Once we know that, we narrow the odds real fast, and *Bot Bon Jui* will be ours ..."

"A blessing," Li Ming said, "often comes in the form of trouble."

"And we've been blessed," replied Louis.

"All right," acquiesced Reva, "let's say the POW Chink and the Nisei fathead lead us to the stuff. Where does that leave the rest of those bananaheads—Sarge, the young Hemingway, that old fart with the hobnail boots and bad breath?"

"They're our muscle. After that, they can fertilize rice paddles for all I care."

"Are not the most honorable of men tempted by the treasures of the earth?" questioned Li Ming.

"Most men, but not Sarge. He's loyal only to his cause. He'll only be interested in rejoining his unit. He won't have the time to bother with us after we've used him and the others."

"I'm still bothered by one thing." Reva looked at Louis

and then Li Ming, so there was no doubt about the sincerity of her question. "Isn't it a pretty funny coincidence? I mean, we come here with the map looking for *Bot Bon Jui* and these other guys—they end up here just when we need them."

Louis frowned. "I hadn't quite looked at it that way. It is strange. Especially that POW. The old legend goes there was a survivor or two. I wonder . . ."

"The weariest dragon will mount to Heaven sooner or later," philosophized Li Ming. "Why then should not man stumble across good fortune?"

"Yeah, I guess life is full of coincidences," said Louis. "Which reminds me of a coincidence coming up. Li Ming, I want you, purely coincidentally, to bump into some of those jokers out there. Maybe you can pick up something."

"Yeah," laughed Reva, "the clap."

Li Ming bowed and left.

Louis turned to Reva. "You too, honey. Mingle."

49

Services Rendered

When Sarge put away his letter Youngman saw a white packet of news clippings fall from Sarge's pocket. Judging from the dog-eared condition of the paper, it had been wedged—like the Iwo Jima letter—for a long period of time in the lining of Sarge's pocket. Sarge was talking to Li Ming when Youngman reached for it. Rather than interrupt their conversation, he shoved the packet inside his fatigue pocket. He would return it to Sarge later.

Soon Youngman was typing again on "Mindanao Marauders," and the light tap-tap-tap-tap of the keys drowned out the weakened moan of Ju-Chao when he rolled over to a more comfortable position.

Sarge's eyes swept the figure of Li Ming, drinking in the micromini and all that went with it. He drank, then shook his head. "That's not your standard uniform."

Li Ming looked appreciatively at Sarge. "Women of a certain height must wear clothes of a certain length." Li Ming lowered her head slightly, staring at Sarge's combat boots. "It is dress for special occasions. Such as this one."

"You been servicing the General's Staff long?"

It was not easy for Li Ming to lie, but somehow she overcame twenty-five years of traditional upbringing and

226

righteousness. "A thousand subjects, a thousand methods. It is my wish to one day escape from all this; to ply a more honorable trade. But that is one day that is not this day."

"Look," said Sarge, "I have a favor I'd like to ask of you. A favor ... well, I think it's the kind of favor a girl like you would understand."

"Without experience one gains no wisdom. What is this favor you ask? There are many you may ask, and there are many I may satisfy."

"No, no, this isn't for me. This is for another."

"He who seeks a favor for a friend is mightier than a friend who seeks a favor only for himself. Who is this other?"

Sarge nodded in the direction of Youngman.

Li Ming studied him for a moment. "While the boy is small, you can see the man."

Sarge walked back to join Youngman. "Okay, pack up the porto-typer for the time being, Youngman. You pull guard tonight. I want you to take the top of the hill overlooking the waterhole. That'll give you a clear view of anything moving toward this position."

Youngman scrambled for his rifle. "Right, Sarge."

"And Youngman, keep your eyes and ears open—for once." Sarge winked at Li Ming.

The next movement she made was subtle; Sarge didn't even see it, but it caught Youngman's eye, for which it had been intended. Had it been a blink of her eye? Had it been a slight movement of her head? Had it been the delicate twisting of an ankle? Not even Youngman knew, but a movement, refined to ultimate subtlety, had been made. Youngman looked at Li Ming. Li Ming looked at Youngman. The two vanished from the flickering light of the fire.

Sarge was hardly aware of Reva emerging from the supply room, hardly aware of the slinky way in which she approached him, hardly aware of the way she pressed her entire body against his. He should have felt hot breath near the base of his neck. He should have sensed the rutting look she gave him. All he thought about was that electricity between Li Ming and Youngman. He had never experienced anything like it before.

"You must be very lonely after all these weeks in the
227

line," whispered Reva, passionately, unmistakably inviting Sarge into the sensuous secrets her syllables and phrasing promised.

"If you'll just let me . . ."

"Excuse me," interrupted Sarge, who had been scarcely aware of her invitation, "excuse me . . ." Without even turning to look at her, without even seeing the figure which promised so much from beneath the skimpy material that covered it, Sarge turned and walked away, shuffling his deck of cards absentmindedly.

Reva shrugged off the outright rejection as a peculiar quirk of one man, and turned her attention to Charlie Brown, who was seated near the campfire, watching the vidpack. *Fixed Bayonets* was ending, so he switched on his transistor.

"*. . . operator? Operator, get me WHitehall 7800. And hurry. This is a matter of life and death. . . . Oh please, hurry.*"

"Excuse me, soldier."

"Charlie Brown."

"Charlie Brown. It must be lonely out here . . ."

"*. . . what do you mean there's no answer? Someone has got to be there. You don't understand. There's this man who's going to kill someone and . . .*"

"*. . . after spending so many weeks in the line you must be ready for . . .*"

"*. . . you incompetent woman. Can't you do anything I ask you? I said I wanted WHitehall 7800. My God, someone's out in the hallway. Don't you understand? There's this man. I overheard him talking on my phone. He's going to murder somebody . . .*"

Reva leaned forward so that the swollen tip of her breast fell against Charlie Brown's jacket. He stared enthralled at his transistor.

"Surely a strong man like yourself . . ."

"*. . . My God, I understand now, operator. That man, he's going to murder me. Not somebody else. And he's out in the hallway. You've got to do something . . .*"

"Jesus," said Charlie Brown. Even Reva paused to listen to the next line.

"*. . . he's coming toward me. He's got a knife. He . . .*"
228

Reva withdrew her breast. "Oh shit," she said and walked away.

She noticed The Old German, who leaned back next to the fire, puffing his pipe. Her approach was no different, and she was delighted to finally find a reception. "Pray, sit down, little thing."

Reva touched his arm gently. "I was just thinking, after all the weeks you've spent here in the line . . ."

"Ach, it has been a lonely time."

Reva smiled and placed her hand on The Old German's stained tunic. He took her hand into his and squeezed it.

"It gives one plenty of time to sit and think, I'll tell you that much. Gives you time to sit and think. That it does."

Reva attempted to slide her hand along the tunic, but The Old German held fast and wouldn't let go. He stared into the fire. "I was just recalling those days at Orgenburg—did you know that was where they had one of the largest SS training schools? Near Brunswick. I can still remember the day we arrived . . ."

Reva attempted to remove her hand, but The Old German's grip was unbreakable. He stared downward into the fire, as if oblivious to her withdrawal. Her hand felt as though it were in a vise. Jesus, thought Reva, what have I gotten into this time?

". . . stood in front of us, and I can still recall most of his words to this day. Not every word, mind you. But the meat of it I remember. He was a mean bastard, that one, but he was a colonel we were ultimately proud of. He died on the Russian Front with the rest of the men. But he was tough, and we were frightened of him that day—of that you can be certain. He addressed us . . . 'Welcome men. As special volunteers of this unit, you of the Hitler Youth have graduated to act out your destiny for Greater Germany. You have volunteered for the SS, so you have already begun to show your faith. Iron discipline, blind obedience—these are the first things you must learn.' "

Reva slipped her free hand around the neck of The Old German. She toyed with his Adam's apple, then began to work her fingers down beneath his tunic, encountering a tangle of matted hair through which it was impossible to maneuver.

" '. . . and you must feel pride in everything you achieve. One day you will belong to a unit that will have won the respect, and the dread, of the entire world. You will be the elite representatives of the Aryan race. But anything that is worthwhile must be paid for in blood.' "

Reva withdrew her roaming hand, but no sooner had it emerged from the tunic than The Old German clutched it also. He held fast both her hands. " '. . . and that blood must be yours. Each day in the years that lie ahead, you may be called upon to earn the privilege of staying alive. You will be youths like the world has never seen before. You will be invincible in your loyalty to the Führer. In your eyes there will be the gleam of pride, independence, the gleam of the beast of prey. You will be a violent, dominating, brutal youth, from which the world will shrink away . . .' "

The Old German was remembering faster and faster now, and more clearly, and his grip on Reva had taken on the grip of death. Reva did not fight it, but froze, and listened.

". . . the colonel, he was the first, with his beautiful rhetoric, which so instilled in us the spirit to destroy, to conquer. Then there was the major. Yes, the major, who stood before us a few months later, after the ordeal of training was over. Did you know that we were forced to put hand grenades atop our helmets and then pull the pins? If we didn't stand motionlessly at attention, the grenade might fall at our feet. Several of my comrades died that way. Then there were the tanks. We were forced to dig narrow foxholes over which the tanks could pass. They couldn't be too big, or the treads would sink into them and squash us like ripe bananas. And it still had to be strong enough so the sides would not collapse and bury us alive beneath. More comrades lost. And then the Alsatian dogs. Kept in cages for days without food, then released. Each of us had to stop that dog, before the dog stopped us. But of course, I must sound foolish to you. I've been trained too long to allow sentiment for fallen comrades to make me melancholy." The Old German paused, as he tried to retrace forgotten thoughts. "Oh yes, the Major with his beautiful rhetoric. Graduating class of '39, or was it '40? Funny
230

how you forget something important like that, and yet you can remember all the words. Richter was his name. Perhaps von Richter." The Old German cleared his throat, and spoke in a loud, more authoritative tone. "I swear to you, Adolf Hitler, my leader, fidelity and courage. I promise you, and all those whom you choose to command obedience unto death, so help me God." The Old German stared into Reva's eyes for the first time. "When we had all spoken the oath, the major turned to us and said: 'You have sworn your oath of fidelity. You have pledged your existence body and soul to Der Führer. You are now SS. Remember your motto: *Meine Ehre Heisst Treue*. My honor is loyalty." ' "

The Old German released Reva's left hand, but kept her right tightly gripped in his. He drew a bayonet from a worn scabbard around his webbed belt, and held it up for Reva to see. Reva sucked in her breath and brought her free hand around to her side.

"See this knife? Right here, inscribed in the hilt. *Meine Ehre Heisst Treue*. I still carry it." He stared down into the flames: " 'You must now prove to your superiors that each of you is a living, breathing organism for National Socialism, helping to achieve its eventual liberation from inferior breeding and from those who would destroy us." The Old German fell strangely silent. He resheathed his knife, and released Reva's other hand, which had gone to sleep. She hit the palm against her side.

The Old German continued to stare into the fire and resumed puffing on his pipe.

Reva, for the first time in her professional career, retired gracefully.

If Louis wanted information, he could damn well get it himself.

50
A Campaign Relived

Sarge had been right: the hill overlooking the water hole afforded a view in all directions and was the best spot for posting a sentry. Youngman ensconced himself against a pile of rocks, facing toward the hills which fronted *Chun Hsien Ku*. If there was to be any danger, it would materialize from that direction. He took the bundle of newsprint from his jacket and opened it.

It was part of a Sunday newspaper magazine supplement. The pages were old, and torn badly at the folds, so Youngman spread them open carefully.

Youngman read with the aid of his pocketlight:

THE REDCOATS ARE COMING!

THE ECHOES OF A REVOLUTION
STILL RING AFRESH
IN THE EARS OF A
TWENTIETH CENTURY WARRIOR

By Marion Z. Rivers

(EDITOR'S NOTE: In its Wednesday final edition, the *Times-Post* carried a short account about a soldier stationed at nearby Fort Lewis, Wash., who claimed to be a survivor of the battle of Bunker Hill in 1775. Since this famous clash took place more than 200 years ago, a certain tongue-in-cheek attitude was assumed by the reporter. This attitude was seemingly reinforced by the fact this "survivor" had just busted up the biggest barroom in downtown Seattle. Five civilians and two commissioned officers were put in the hospital. Arresting officers claimed the NCO was in a considerable state of inebriation when he made his claim on history prior to the arrival of military police. In keeping with its policy to never look a gift story in the mouth, and to give subjects a chance to present their side of a story under more favorable circumstances, the *Times-Post* presents an interview with this "survivor"—a sergeant whose name we have agreed not to reveal here.)

The rumble of tanks, the barrage of artillery, the "rat-tat-tat" of air-cooled machine guns, the dull *blumm* of the atomic bazooka—these are the sounds of the contemporary soldier hears, whether he is being trained on the infiltration course or is actually fighting for his country on far-flung battlefields.

But in the ears of one man—a noncommissioned officer who says he has served in the military as far back as he can remember—there are additional sounds: the echoing *ka-rump* of a light six-pounder; the *ka-rang* of a 5½-inch howitzer, the bark of muskets and long rifles; the regulated cadence of red-coated British troops marching abreast to their deaths.

And there is a vision of Breed's Hill, the battle-scarred terrain of Charlestown Peninsula where, on 16 June 1775, a fierce struggle, now known as the Battle of Bunker Hill, became an historic moment of the American Revolution.

It was here that men under the command of Colonel William Prescott held off a superior force of British troops, inflicting devastating losses before a lack of ammunition and a spirited British bayonet charge by the men of Major General William Howe swept the hill clean of Yankees.

233

That noncommissioned officer, who asks to be identified only as "Sarge," claims to be one of the men who fought there. Those who immediately sneer at his claim should first hear his story and then pass judgment.

Sarge is a solidly built dogface (it is difficult to estimate his age due to his crusty and grizzled appearance) who is currently in charge of an infantry unit undergoing intensive training at Fort Lewis. He bears the scars of at least three wars and commands, with his confidence and military demeanor, a great sense of authority.

During our interview he spoke slowly, deliberately, and often frankly. He never faltered in telling his story. We were impressed by the fact that occasionally we were caught up in the grip of his narrative, and felt as if we were right on the field of battle with this unusual individual. (We hope the printed word carries the same impact.)

The basic facts told here are verified by history. As for the rest, the reader will have to decide for himself.

At first, Sarge was entirely against speaking to us. "I was drunk when one of your newshounds saw me in that bar, and I did too much talking—bad habit of mine when I've had too many. Forget the whole thing."

However, on being pressed for a detailed account, Sarge finally relented, indicating a touch of the military raconteur's ego. "All right, you want to hear the story, I'll tell it to you. I don't care if you believe it or not. But if you want to get the facts straight, straighter than you'll find in the history books, here it is . . ."

Offering us a long black cigar, which we kindly refused, Sarge propped himself against the treads of a Sherman tank, lit a cigar for himself, spread his combat boots before him and began.

"We blew those British bastards to hell that day. We shattered every European fighting tradition. Howe, and those other generals of his, Clinton and Borgoyne, thought they knew how to wage a campaign, but they didn't know s——t. Major f——k ups, that's what they were. Wanna know why? They were gentlemen who thought they could fight a war for independence like some kind of traditional duel. Field of honor, that kind of bullroar. Strictly gentlemen.

"They lined up their men in bright red coats, loaded them down with knapsacks, greatcoats and a lot of other bogging s——t and marched them into the sights of our muskets.

"Splat!

"Well, it was on Breed's Hill that the British finally got the idea that with superior firepower, you could get your a——s chewed up pretty fast trying to act like a dandy."

We interrupted to ask why the Battle of Bunker Hill, if it had been fought on Breed's Hill, had been misnamed.

"Not even the history books ever got that straight. Rum, that's the reason. First you gotta understand Charlestown Peninsula. It's got three hills on it: Morton's, which we never defended, Breed's and Bunker. Now Bunker Hill was the highest hunk of real estate and gave us the best view of what was happening. That's where we shoulda fought the battle. But instead, Prescott and some of his reconnoitering boys marched us over to Breed's where this chief engineer, Colonel Gridley I think it was, laid out the fortifications. We lost a great advantage there. It put us within heavy cannon range of Boston, but who the f——k would want to waste cannonballs in that direction?

"I arrived that midnight with 200 Connecticut troopers under Captain Knowlton and we started to dig the redoubt and breastworks. This engineer, Gridley, he was getting pretty heated up and was constantly shoving the map in Prescott's face, trying to tell him we were on the wrong hill.

"Well, Prescott must have been hitting the rum reserve we'd brought up on mules to maintain the spirits of the men, because he staggered around, slobbered and talked in general like his mouth was full of s——t. Finally he told Gridley and his aide to shove off—that he was in command and what he said went. Gridley told Prescott right back to go f——k off, but kept right on entrenching. So that's why the battle of Bunker Hill was fought on Breed's Hill.

"We dug all that night. By morning, Colonel Bridges and Lieutenant Colonel Brickett had reinforced us with special detachments. A detachment of militia in those days wasn't what you probably think it is. Just a bunch of strays and ragtags, hodgepodge. From Massachusetts, from New

235

Hampshire, Rhode Island, Connecticut; farmers, merchants, yankee doodle upstarts; no uniforms. A mixture of good men and the dregs.

"I was assigned to join Prescott's 300-man regiment which took up defensive positions along the breastworks, and in and around the stone wall.

"Now I've got to tell you a little about that stone wall. It extended from the rear of the redoubt down to the shores of the Mystic River. The history books call it the rail fence, and you can damn well be sure it kept that battle from being a British victory right from the start. Only open land sloped up to that fence, and it served as an obstruction to anyone advancing and a shelter for us to fire from."

Sarge paused long enough to relight his cigar, shift his weight around so he was more comfortable, and continued.

"By early afternoon on the 16th, 1750 Britishers had landed at Morton's Point to push us off the neck of land and kill our chances of bombarding Boston, which we couldn't have done very well anyway. Nowadays, 1750 wouldn't be much of an attack force. A dozen quad-.50s and a few artillery pieces could handle a bunch that size with no sweat.

"But back then, 1750 men, that was formidable. Crack troops, men from the 52nd Regiment of Foot, 17th Light Dragoons, the Ten Elder Company of Grenadiers, the Second Battalion of Marines. Gentlemen they were too, marching abreast right up to our positions. Now in those days officers expected their men to go into battle fully equipped, so each limey in the formation was loaded down with a hundred-pound fieldpack. Called heavy marching order. And each limey was expected to march upright at attention. Up the steep slope they came, burdened down like you wouldn't believe, but trying not to show it. British stiff upper lip and all that rot.

"A lot of people today think the Kentucky rifle was used by all those dead-eyes on Breed's, but it was slow loading and it didn't have a stud for a bayonet. What most of us were using was the 'Brown Bessy,' otherwise known as .75 caliber long land musket with a 46-inch barrel. The walnut stocks were unpainted and the barrels had been browned to prevent rust or glare in bright sunlight. The loading procedure required five steps: half-cock firelock, handle cartridge, draw rammer, ram home the cartridge, return rammer. Now, that may sound like a lot, but it got so even a recruit could load and fire fifteen times in less than four minutes. The 'Brown Bessy' is what gave us our firepower.

"Me, I was in a forward position just beyond the stone wall with three men. One of them was from Charlestown, who had come up in the middle of the night to cover the battle for his paper. Right away I could see this reporter, this Boynton, that he was hard of hearing. He was always cocking his head to one side, and shaking his head as if to clear his ears. Got so I was shouting at the top of my lungs everytime I spoke to him because he'd ask me to repeat it. Then he'd scribble down whatever it was that had been said. He asked a lot of the men their names and in general tried to get a feeling of what was going on.

"Another man with me was named John Tillotson, who had come in under the command of General Israel Putnam. We called him Till for short and he was one helluva marksman—the kind who could pick off a squirrel chewing on a litchi nut at a hundred yards.

"Then we had this German baker named Thweitz, who had also come in with Putnam. Thweitz was a bundle of hell, that man, maybe he had some Prussian blood in him, I'll never know.

"But that sonofab——hing Thweitz was hitting the rum ration harder than Prescott. When he arrived early that morning he was singing one German ditty after another, doling out loaves of bread which he'd brought with him, freshly baked, so he said, but it tasted to me like it was at least fifteen days old.

"The sonofab——h got into the position with us, and it was then I could see his canteen was filled with rum—siphoned off, no doubt, from the regimental kegs brought up by mule. Well, Thweitz kept singing his songs and snortin' from his canteen, and finally he passed out. Since it was apparent he couldn't've fired a straight musketball anyway, nobody bothered to wake him up.

"About two o'clock, the bastards came at us. Firepower wasn't very accurate in those days, even if you weren't cross-eyed, but on Breed's Hill even a blind man couldn't miss. All you had to do was point your musket in the general direction of the attack.

"We were so heavily bunched up along the defense line that when we opened fire, the slaughter was something you wouldn't particularly want to see—the bodies were heaped in front of our rifles, two, three deep. The 52nd was bled white. Grenadiers, nothing left but garbage.

"When you get a volley like that, you've got yourself one helluva roar. Enough to wake the dead, only in this case it awakened that baker I told you about, Thweitz. He leaped up and threw his musket so high in the air it came down and beaned the regimental commander's aide—put him out for the rest of the fight. I guess Thweitz was so crazy drunk, and so confused coming out of a dead sleep, he must have thought the world was ending. Because before I could do anything about it, he'd jumped out of the breastworks and made fire-ass toward the British lines. He disappeared into the gunsmoke, leaping over the sprawling bodies of the grenadiers. So we wrote him off. There was still a war to fight and a battle to win.

"They pulled back fast and we made a quick check of the line, with General Putnam right there assisting. Because the British had fired as they advanced, we had quite a few casualties—mostly head wounds. The wounded were pulled back to the redoubt and we waited for the next attack. Which wasn't very long in coming.

"Down below we could see the limeys instinctively throwing away anything that weighed them down. This time they'd come light as feathers, and would save their musketballs until they actually reached our forward positions.

"We beat them back a second time, but by then we were running low on ammo. On third charge, the b——ds came with firelocks secured and with bayonets in pig-sticking position. Some of the boys decided to clear out right then. A wild shot from here or there knocked off a few figures in the advancing columns, but the majority kept right on coming, building momentum and breaking into a run as they drew near our forward positions.

"Off to my right, I could see two Englishmen advancing with their bayonets pressed against the back of one of our
238

men, using him as a shield. Not very gentlemanly, but these were two blokes who were finally getting the right idea about how to fight a war.

"The men positioned on both sides of us were the first to catch the bayonets, and they were wiped out to the last man in fierce hand-to-hand combat. Let me say that when it comes to close quarters, nobody beats the British at lunges and jabs. I could see some of the boys getting it in the neck. They kept going for the neck, and those boys of ours kept screaming, and pretty soon they didn't scream anymore.

"Some of the fellas ran back to the redoubt to fight from there, and still the British came. They had the bloodlust now, and nothing could stop them.

"Damned if the smoke didn't clear good enough for me to make out that prisoner I told you about, the one being used as a shield. It was Thweitz, his eyes still bloodshot, his mouth still open in surprise. Those two Britishers were prodding him right toward us.

"About then, General Putnam, who was running along the line, trying to rally the men, dropped into our position just as Tillotson raised his 'Brown Bessy' to fire at Thweitz, so he could then get the two b——ds behind him.

" 'Jesus Christ,' shouted Putnam, over the roar of battle. 'Don't shoot, Till. You can see Thweitz on the rise.'

"Boynton, who had been writing down just about every word said that day, stopped scribbling long enough to pop up from the depths of the breastworks. 'What did he say?' By then, Putnam was off and running, trying to jazz up some of the boys who were headed for the redoubts or parts beyond I told him. Boynton continued his scribbling, still cocking his ear to one side, and looking very pleased with the whole thing. I think Boynton said 'marvelous' or some such thing, and then I forgot about him for a while.

"Tillotson was felled moments later by a musketball which knocked him in the back of the head. I guess it was fired by one of our own men in haste. Anyway, he never moved after that. Those two Britishers kept prodding Thweitz toward us, and finally I gave the fool a good kick in the stomach, which doubled him over and gave me a good look at the two behind him.

"I dropped them both—one with a slash of my bayonet, the other with a chop to the jaw with the butt of my musket. Thweitz tried to straighten up, but lost his balance and tumbled down the hill. I never saw him again. I grabbed Boynton, who was still scribbling notes, and pulled him out of the hole. I'll say this for the little guy—he didn't seem a bit fazed about what was happening. He kept trying to write as we ran, and he kept trying to get the names of the men, even their addresses, as we reached the redoubt. That guy could concentrate like nobody I've met since.

"Even in the relative safety of the redoubt we knew we'd lost the battle. Pigot's men had moved across the Charlestown Road and were attacking from the other flank, cutting down anyone who now tried to reach the fortifications. I could see nothing was going to stop those redcoats now, so I had Boynton and some other men help me gather cannonballs from our out-of-action 18-pounder.

"We began rolling them down the slope, and by the time they reached the British they'd built up considerable momentum.

"What was nice about those cannonballs was, after knocking down one man, they'd continue on down and crash into the British reserves. Most of them ended up covered with blood in the Mystic River. You could see a lot of redcoats hopping up and down, clutching at crushed feet.

"Colonel Stark and Putnam began ordering us to throw rocks we'd stockpiled in the redoubt, once the cannonballs were gone. Putnam came to me and said 'Sarge, I want you to get the journalist Boynton off this hill to safety. He may be the only man able to record a true account of what we did here today.'

"I was young and headstrong in those days—hell, for that matter I'm still headstrong—and I tried to tell Putnam I wanted to stay on that hill and fight. Something about seeing our guys get bayoneted in the throat ... I don't know ... anyway, I argued with Putnam. Told him I was bound to stay. Even called him a sonofab——h, but I don't think he really heard me, or he could see I didn't really mean it. But Putnam was determined to get Boynton off Breed's, so I gave in. We pulled out and worked our way off the hill, eventually getting the hell off the Charlestown Neck. Behind us were 140 dead and 270 wounded on our side; 226 dead and 828 wounded in the British ranks. Not impressive casualty figures by today's standards—but back then pretty fierce considering the battle lasted only an hour or so.

"Charlestown proper had been shelled and burned earlier that day by the British, so I turned Boynton over to a supply column that was moving north, away from the flight.

"Before he left, Boynton excitedly read over the notes he'd taken during the battle. I was pretty tired, and I fell asleep half-way through ... well, I guess I don't have to tell you the misquotation that resulted from Boynton's subsequent war dispatches.

"Years later, after the Revolution was over, I bumped into Boynton in a public bathhouse. In Boston. He must have been in his forties by then; he looked blankly at me, cocked his head to one side in that special style of his, and looked like he was trying to force something out of his ear. I spoke to him, but he never replied. The keeper of the bathhouse said Boynton had been stone deaf for years. And that was the last I ever saw of him."

As he finished his narrative, Sarge spat once and ground out the soggy stump of his cigar. We asked him about his beliefs in reincarnation.

He shook his head and curled his upper lip. "Bulls——t. I've read some of those stories, and they're all hogwash. I can't explain how I know this story. I just know I lived through it, and every damn word is true. Just don't ask me to explain it."

(EDITOR'S NOTE: Research into the Battle of Bunker Hill reveals there was a correspondent named Thomas Boynton, famed throughout the war for independence for his detailed battlefield reports. Boynton was killed at the age of 46 in downtown Boston when he walked in front of a fast-moving baker's cart despite repeated warnings from passersby of the cart's swift approach. The driver was named Thweitz.)

51
Inspection

"So this is your idea of guard duty . . ."

Youngman sprang to his feet at the sound of Sarge's condemning voice. He had been so caught up in the flow of the article he had forgotten where he was, where he had placed his rifle and, above all else, what his purpose atop the hill had been. By the time he got to his feet, Sarge had yanked the newspaper article from his hands.

"Where'd you get that?"

"It . . . it fell out of your pocket, Sarge. You were talking to that Chinese girl, so I decided to give it back to you later. Then, while I was standing here, I decided . . ." The rest was self-explanatory.

Sarge stared at Youngman, then seemed to relax a little. "Well, what'd you think?"

"The story? It was . . ." He realized he was at an absolute loss for words. He shifted his weight from foot to foot. "Well, Sarge, it was . . . weird."

"Every word of it is true."

"Man, that's—"

"Every goddamn word. I can't explain it, Youngman. But it happened to me. It's all up here." He tapped his temple. "I don't know how it got there. But it's there. Just like with those guys in North Africa who got caught in their fartsacks by the Krauts. I wasn't there, and I didn't see it, but I felt it, Youngman. Right here, in the throat. I felt every lunge of those German bayonets. I can still feel them if I think about it hard enough. All I have to do is think. Like Bunker Hill. All I have to do is think about that place, and it's all there. The whole thing, like a painting." Sarge carefully folded the newspaper article and placed it back in his pocket.

Then Sarge stiffened again, and Youngman decided he'd better stiffen too—to absorb the inevitable chewing out.

The chewing out didn't come; Sarge called Youngman to attention.

He began an inspection of Youngman—the buttons on his pockets, the adjustment of his ammo belt, the condition of his rifle, the laces of his combat boots, the contents of his first-aid packet. It continued in absolute silence for another minute. Then Sarge peered intently into Youngman's face. It was the closest eyeball-to-eyeball contact Youngman had ever had with Sarge.

"Your eyes all right, Youngman?" The concern in Sarge's voice tried to ring with conviction, but Youngman suspected it was a bit strained.

"Sure, Sarge. They're okay."

"Lemme see." Sarge pressed ever closer; all Youngman could see were two glazed, bloodshot eyes staring into his with the intensity of a hypnotist. "They look blurry to me, Youngman."

"Blur—"

"Bloodshot. You need something to stimulate them. You need a pickup, Youngman. I think I know what you need." Sarge removed the packet of playing cards from his pocket, taking off the rubber band holding them together. The corners of the cards were dog-eared; each card showed signs of considerable use—wrinkles and creases. He began to show the cards one at a time to Youngman. Sarge was slow, letting Youngman stare at each one. "Take your time, Youngman, take your time."

Youngman's eyes grew larger at the sight of one card. "Where'd you get these, Sarge?"

Sarge ruffled through the deck. "I got a Semper Fidelis

White Paper for you, Youngman. After you've been in the Corps as long as I have, this stuff becomes Standard Regulation Issue." He raised the deck again. "This one's upside down." He straightened the card.

"It didn't matter," said Youngman. "Either way, it works."

Sarge showed the rest of the deck to Youngman and resumed his eyeball-to-eyeball position.

"Hey," said Sarge, optimistically. "That's better. More color. Fewer bloodshot veins. A gleam, Youngman. I see a gleam that wasn't there before." Sarge nudged Youngman, almost knocking him off balance. "Gives you ideas, stuff like that, here in the Chinese moonlight—right, Youngman?"

"There's no moon, Sarge."

"Don't give me that shit. With young guys like you, there's always a moon some goddamn place. You just don't always see it. But it's there, Youngman. Ain't it?"

"Yeah, I guess so, Sarge."

"Awright. I gotta check the outer perimeter. Make sure some creepy Chinks don't slip over one of those hills out there while you were straining your eyes on newsprint. See you, Youngman, see you ..." Sarge patted Youngman twice on the cheek, sharply. It was hard enough to sting his face, but Youngman still felt fortunate. There hadn't been one of Sarge's royal chewing outs. And that was a good fortune he would have to dwell on for a while.

Sarge Takes a Position

Out of sight of Youngman, Sarge doubled around the side of the hill and took up a position from where he could watch Youngman on the hilltop. He removed the packet of cards from his pocket and spread them on the ground in front of him. He began to examine the cards, occasionally throwing a glance at Youngman, and grew impatient.

B.:
Charlie Brown
Makes a Proposition

Ju-Chao was sure it was water, but he was not so sure he would ever taste it. He had gone the entire day without a drop, and his mouth was so parched he could barely pull his lips apart. They felt like they were glued together, and he was afraid he might pull the skin from them if he were to open them suddenly. His body yearned for the water, and his mind screamed for the water.

Charlie Brown had poured the water into his canteen cup and was holding it just out of Ju-Chao's reach. "*Bot Bon Jui . . .*"

Ju-Chao inched forward as Charlie Brown inched backward.

"Where *Bot Bon Jui*? You tell, you tell."

It was then Ju-Chao got smart. Instead of worrying about the water, he decided to concentrate on what the strange slant-eyed American said. Feebly, he scratched something in the dirt with his index finger. To make certain the strange American got the idea, Ju-Chao placed a knob toward one side of the rectangular shape. Though a tiny circle, it was enough. Charlie Brown nodded his head eagerly. "Door? Door? You show, you show." Charlie Brown removed a piece of scraggly paper from his pocket and placed it on the ground along with the stub of an ancient pencil. "You show here. You draw . . . picture, picture."

With painstaking effort Ju-Chao scrawled with numb fingers across the paper. Charlie Brown, his eyes ablaze with what Ju-Chao recognized as undiluted greed, clutched the paper and stared at it. What he saw was a series of shaky, childlike lines. They managed to form the crude outline of a door surrounding several Chinese symbols.

A door. *The* door. Leading to the treasure.

Charlie Brown's heart leaped. Somewhere below was *Bot Bon Jui*. He, only he, Charlie Brown, knew of its whereabouts. He whirled to face *Chun Hsien Ku* and, abruptly, the world melted away, and reality was gone. It was replaced by a dream in which there was nothing but him and a fortune of sparkling gems—nothing but *Bot Bon Jui*. Not even a wounded man at his feet, reaching desperately for a canteen cup filled with precious water, which, as he moved, was knocked over by Charlie Brown. He never knew he had knocked it over because he was running—running to search for the door, running to greater riches and greater glory, running for *Bot Bon Jui*.

Ju-Chao moaned. He moved. It was a pitiful effort to reach a single drop of the spilled water. By the time his fingers reached the spot, the dry earth had absorbed the moisture down to the last drop. Ju-Chao lay there, not believing what was happening. He began to chant a song of death, but he had a feeling that with his luck death was still some distance away.

As he continued to chant he was unaware of the presence of Louis, who emerged from the shadows of *Chun Hsein Ku* to stand next to the Chinese officer. Louis stared down at the outline of the door which Ju-Chao had drawn and with his foot rubbed the drawing out of existence and smoothed out the earth. Ju-Chao was still unaware of him.

Louis moved off in the direction Charlie Brown had taken. Now Ju-Chao became aware of his presence. It came in the instant Louis's boots unintentionally crushed Ju-Chao's outstretched fingers.

Ju-Chao shifted from a chant of death to a chant of despair.

C.:
Youngman Takes a
Position of his Own

It was a slow, gentle strip. Sarge could see every movement Li Ming made from his hiding place on the side of the hill.

Youngman, although puzzled, drank in every movement. It wasn't every night on guard duty that a beautiful Oriental girl stepped out of the bushes and began to undress seductively, drawing closer each time she removed a garment. Nor was it every night that a young woman's eyes locked on yours and refused to let go, and pleaded with you to come to her, to hold her, to kiss her, to love her body ...

By the time Li Ming was down to her wistful bra, Sarge had reached a new level of excitement. He occasionally beat his fists on the ground, and shuffled the cards and placed them on the ground in fresh order. It was all he could do to restrain himself.

Li Ming, in what appeared to be a miniaturized dance, crossed the remaining distance to Youngman and began unbuttoning his shirt. He eagerly slid out of it as her fingers dropped to undo his belt buckle and creeped over the top edge of his shorts to disapear inside.

That, in itself, was too much for Sarge.

It was like one of the barrages on Iwo—a hundred

248

mortar shells descending on a single coordinate, tearing at the earth and trying to tear at human flesh; a million pieces of shrapnel all screaming and burning their way through the concussed air; hot, slicing pieces of shrapnel; a roar of whirling metal and churning earth that drowned out every other sound; a roar that left a ringing residue and a burning sensation that ran downward from the ears, through the torso, into the legs. It was the torrents of war as only Sarge could have experienced them. His body tightened, then relaxed.

He lifted his head off the ground and smiled.

It had been a good barrage.

Sarge glanced toward the top of the hill. Li Ming was nude now, and Youngman's fatigue trousers were falling away. He was certain Youngman had the right idea, as his hands fumbled amateurishly over the surface of Li Ming's body. She began to return Youngman's kisses. In his eagerness, Youngman pressed harder against Li Ming. Judging from Li Ming's expression of surprise, he achieved some success. On target, thought Sarge, as he shuffled the dog-eared cards again and spread them on the ground.

Li Ming lost her balance, but she never lost Youngman. As she started to fall back, she pulled him with her. They went down the hill together, each clinging to the other.

Roll her over again, Youngman. Again . . . and again . . .

When they reached the base of the hill, Youngman and Li Ming lay together. He stared down at her, she up at him. There was an expression on Li Ming's face that Youngman knew she had never worn before.

She spoke with reverence. "It . . . it has never happened to me . . ."

Youngman smiled. "Me either."

". . . in midroll."

Youngman's face dropped. "It's never happened to me before, period."

"And that," said Sarge, "is why you're a man now, Youngman."

Sarge towered above them. Grinning broadly, a man with a look of devilish accomplishment, he tossed his head and threw his hands to his hips. "You did good, Youngman, real good." A hand shot down to strike Youngman solidly on his buttocks. More laughter. "I told you to keep that young ass down, didn't I, Youngman?"

Youngman stared upward at Sarge. For that brief moment he saw something he had never noticed before. "You rigged this . . ."

"And none too soon, Youngman. Nothing like a little tumble in the grass to make a man fit." Sarge's smile and good nature fell away. After all, there was a war still to be won. "Now all you have to be is a hero, Youngman. Then maybe we'll make a soldier out of you yet."

"You gonna rig that too, Sarge? Me being a hero?"

Sarge pointed a finger at Youngman that seemed to accuse. "I'll tell you when to be a hero, Youngman." He stalked away.

Youngman looked at Li Ming, who had not moved since Sarge's unexpected appearance. "Why'd you do it?" The gently put question had only a vague trace of recrimination.

"As a favor."

"To Sarge?"

"I owe him nothing."

"Why then?"

"As a favor. A favor can mean different things to different people."

"As a favor to me?"

"Perhaps. Do you see it as a favor?"

"I . . . I should be mad."

"Why be angered by pleasure?"

"Yeah . . . yeah . . ."

The pleasure she spoke of was in the fingertips which caressed his forehead. He felt another of her pleasures stirring against his groin and began to kiss her again, more passionately than before.

The hell with Sarge. A man couldn't spend all his time fighting a war.

53
The Lovers
and Other Fragments

Reva was pissed. Royally pissed.

One by one the men around the campfire had left. And now she was alone with Ju-Chao, who groaned and caught Reva's attention.

She had that old feeling of needing a man—like right now.

She sat down next to Ju-Chao, who said "*Sui . . . sui.*"

Reva knew nothing of the Chinese language. Until now, men like Ju-Chao had been wormeaters. Fishheads. Chinks.

On the other hand, Reva had always been good at rationalizing a situation. Make it work for you when you could. Tell the situation to buzz off when it didn't. Right now, that Chink, wound and all, could be made to work.

She sat down next to Ju-Chao and took one of his feeble hands into hers. She squeezed that hand warmly. "You must be very lonely by now, having spent so much time in the—"

"Uhhh . . . uhhhhhhh . . ." Ju-Chao's hand tightened as he attempted to pull it free. He glanced upward and saw the passion and lust and the wantonness and the seduction in Reva's eyes.

She had no intention of stopping now. Ju-Chao knew

that. He struggled. In his condition it was a complete waste of time. Reva slid the upper half of Ju-Chao across her lap. He had given up struggling in favor of groaning with pain in the faint hope that some element of humanitarianism would find its way into the situation, but Reva remained oblivious to his pain, and seemed only aware of her own unsatisfied longings.

Reva paraded her fingers across his feverish brow. "Reva will take care of you, brave soldier of the Chinese Army. Reva knows how to care for the needs of the soldier of any nation." She unfastened the buttons of his bloodstained blouse, completely ignoring the blackish-colored bandage. By now, she was concerned with only one thing. "Brave soldier, love me . . . love your Reva."

She pinned Ju-Chao against the ground as she pressed the full length of her body against his. Her actions were passionate, frenzied, but Ju-Chao enjoyed none of it. If anything, every muscle in his body ached, and every nerve screamed with acute pain. Blood pressure rose and fell. His wound throbbed. The maggots were back, but they had swarmed from the gangrene-tainted bandage and were racing over his entire body.

Death, Ju-Chao realized, was still far away. His chant of despair had been helpful, as he no longer felt despair. However, it had been replaced by abject depression. Depression had led to the only remaining outlet: insight penetrating enough to let him see the comedy.

In his own plight, even in his own dying, Ju-Chao saw the ultimate irony, the Divine Comedy, and he laughed.

Reva did not hear him laugh. She remained lost in a frenetic quest for pleasure, to satisfy a body engulfed by desire. That made the irony and the comedy greater to Ju-Chao. He continued to laugh, until he choked on his own saliva, and fell silent. He groaned. In gulping air as he laughed, he developed a mild case of colic.

* * *

Charlie Brown had examined all the doors on the western side of *Chun Hsien Ku* without finding one which matched the drawing on the scrap of paper. Each door
252

held an individual array of symbols and Chinese characteristics, which made the search a slow one. In his eagerness, Charlie Brown became frustrated. He sat down once, realizing he was so excited his hands were shaking. He calmed down, told himself to remain cool, and walked to the eastern side.

His hands began to shake again when he flashed his penlight on the first door he came to. The symbol was as Ju-Chao had drawn it. What appeared to be a giant bird hovered above a row of objects. The objects were a mystery.

This was it—the door to *Bot Bon Jut.*

Without further thought, Charlie Brown entered.

* * *

As the door closed behind Charlie Brown, Louis walked up to the door and made a note of the giant bird and the strange row of objects.

54
Still Yet
Another Plot Revealed

"What the hell have you two been up to?"

"Like you wanted. Talking to those jokers."

"Talking? Isn't that a little offbeat for you, Reva?"

"All right, so I kept the dialogue to a minimum."

"And found out what?"

"That these guys are a real bunch of creeps who seem to know very little about anything, including treasure."

"And you, Li Ming?"

"A dry finger cannot take up salt without first seeking moisture."

"And you found that moisture?"

"Of a certain kind."

"What'd you hear?"

"What one hears is doubtful; what one sees with one's own eyes is certain."

"All right, so what did you see?"

"I saw a boy become a man, and I saw a man become a boy."

"Goddamn, while you both've been farting around, I've been finding out things."

"What things?"

254

"They're of a nonsexual nature, so I doubt if you'd understand."

"Try me."

"That Charlie Brown has found it. The door leading below. That POW Chink did know, after all."

"The Chink . . . I'll be damned. I had that guy under my finger all evening long, and he never said a word. How do you like that?"

"As a spy, you're the shits, Reva. The royal, pure shits."

"If you're so damn smart, how about telling us what you plan to do about it."

"Tomorrow me and the other fellas are going to take a subterranean hike."

"What about us?"

"I want you to drive the truck around to the eastern side and park it close to the first door. There's the outline of a giant bird on it."

"You mean we may have it tomorrow?"

"Not may—will!"

"When fortune is good, you rule over the devils. But when fortune is bad, they rule over you."

"Meaning?"

"Consider the past and ye shall know the future. I have given much thought to this treasure, this *Bot Bon Jui*. I think it should be left where it is."

"Why do you think that?"

"Yeah, what's the big secret?"

"Deeds done in secret are seen by the spirits as a flash of fire, and therefore I know of no secrets. But I had a vision, in which I saw evil things, and several signs of death. These are the things sure to befall us if we quest for treasure."

"Are you backing out on us?"

"To leave a ship in the middle of the river is to desert one's own soul. I only warn you, so when misfortune falls, it will not be a complete surprise. I will stay."

"You'd better stay. I've got plans for all of us when we get out of here tomorrow. Now I want you all to grab some shut-eye. Be ready for a big day tomorrow . . . Goddamn it, Reva, keep your hands to yourself."

55

Squad C-323
Settles for the Night

The rebellion came at dusk.

King Kong had slid into the V-crotch of a eucalyptus tree and deposited his knapsack in the center of the bed of grass, leaves, and dried branches which Konga had woven together. Konga was still in the process of bending more twigs into position: While he sat on those already bent or half-broken, his arms stretched out to grasp and bend more twigs. Eventually these crisscrossed twigs fit together and, with other branches wedged between them, formed their shelter for the night.

Sergeant Joe Young bounded up the tree in three leaps, dumping his knapsack on top of King Kong's. Its contents spilled messily. Joe Young chittered uncontrollably. It was the closest thing to insubordination he could approximate. His slender fingers formed fists and the supra-orbital ridges of his forehead wriggled and leaped. His bare feet thumped so hard against the bed of grass that one foot crashed through it. Konga was obviously angered, but chose to remain silent and typically lethargic. While Sergeant Joe Young extracted his foot through the ragged opening, King Kong made clear his attitude toward insubordination. This he achieved by slapping the somewhat distracted NCO on

256

his concave crown. As the sergeant's fingers flew to the top of his head, in an effort to ward off any subsequent attacks, King Kong loosened one of the freshly bent twigs and let it spring back, smacking the sergeant across his protuberant lips. Konga remained his retiring self, but watched with interest every move being made. Although it was difficult for Konga to understand the full ramifications of the argument, he knew it had something to do with Sergeant Young wanting to return to base—an idea directly opposed to King Kong's wish to continue after their quarry. King Kong had made it more than clear they would continue in the morning, moving at double-march speed to complete their mission, hopefully before another sun set. Then, and only then, would they return to base. End of thumping. And end of rebellion.

Sergeant Joe Young curled up to sleep, but even Konga could sense he had not been completely satisfied by King Kong's thumping and passionate pounding of his chest. His agitation was keen; he refused to eat any supper while King Kong and Konga enjoyed dried grasshoppers, pickled spiders, rat tails in vinegar, banana bread, and rations of cod liver oil. For dessert they munched on raw peanuts and cashews. King Kong appeared troubled because the sergeant would not eat, but attributed this to childish and immature behavior. He would check his future sergeants with greater care.

56

Mindanao Marauders
by Bart Hoffman (U.S. Army-Ret.)
(As Told to Ernest Youngman)

Sariol darted across the road, crouching as he ran, and took a position in the ditch beside me, training his light Japanese Nambus machine gun so he could easily sweep the narrow highway cutting through the dense jungle. At first glance I thought he was frightened, but a closer look told me he was shaking because he was so filled with hate.

He couldn't wait for the Japanese truck convoy, which we could now hear moving toward us, to come into sight. I gave him a light pat on the shoulder and returned my attention to the ambush.

The boys had done a good job of preparing both sides of the road for an effective crossfire, but then my men were the fiercest and most feared fighters in the world: Moros.

Warriors who, centuries before, carried nothing more than barongs, krises and camilanes into battle against the Spanish, the Moros were now a well-armed band of guerrillas, striking fear and death into the Japanese forces of occupied Mindanao. Killing came natural to them. Centuries of warfare etched this talent into the violent Moro nature. But it was Johnny McLean and I who had molded these warriors into a tight-knit, cooperative team of battle-seasoned soldiers. We taught them the importance of command, of hit-and-run tactics, and we'd instructed them in the use of firearms. Yet, no matter how good they became at firing Springfields or 45s, they were still best with their own lethal weapons. Many a Jap departed to his honorable ancestors with a Moro lance pinning him to a tree like a limp doll. A Moro could walk up behind a Jap in broad daylight and stick a kris into his belly without making the slightest sound.

Me, I'm Bart Hoffman, U.S. Army. McLean and I were the only survivors of a special detachment protecting a small radio tower on the outskirts of the port city of Zamboanga. After a lucky Jap shell had killed the rest of our men, we'd vanished into the steaming jungles of the island, refusing to spend the rest of the war in a prison camp. Now there was a new kind of monkey in Zamboanga.

The Moros—slain, imprisoned, beaten, tortured, and spit upon by the conquering occupation forces—had also shrunk away into the impenetrable, shadowy jungles, where few Japs dared to follow. It was in these dark, unexplored regions where we joined forces with the natives to avenge our losses.

We began with small raiding parties, hitting the Japs where they least expected it, then retreating back into the sanctuary of the jungles. After we permitted a few Japanese to survive our raids, so that they might tell their officers of the ferocity with which we fought, a large reward was offered for our capture.

Things had gone well for about a year, and we prayed for the day when U.S. forces would liberate the Philippines. The Japanese, still inept in the ways of the Moros and inexperienced with jungle warfare on their terms, had suffered heavy losses under guns and knives, and soon the Japanese soldier became fearful of wandering out from the cities and posts scattered on the island without a heavy guard in tow.

Things toughened up. A new Japanese commander, Major Higoshita, took command of Mindanao's forces and he became obsessed with our capture, doubling the reward set by his predecessor. He laid a number of unsuccessful traps and, according to our scouts, was always on hand to witness our defeat should it come about. But we remained

259

one step ahead of Higoshita, which forced him to take drastic measures. Twice he wiped out entire Moro villages when suspects refused to supply information as to our whereabouts. And then Higoshita had a special jungle-fighting unit shipped from one of the South Pacific islands—for the sole purpose of wiping us out.

After a while I, too, became obsessed—with seeing Higoshita in my gunsights. I had seen those villages he had wiped out, sparing neither woman or child. He had become a butcher whom I could not erase from my mind, who haunted me with equal terror when I was awake or asleep.

Now, as we lay in the ditch beside the road, I thought of all the sweat and blood that had gone into this ambush. In a small clearing on the edge of the jungle was a tiny Japanese outpost. We had hit the bivouac area so many times that the detachment of troops garrisoned there had been diminished to the size of a haggard platoon. Sooner or later, we knew, the Japanese would transport a fresh company in from Zamboanga. Our waiting had finally paid off.

We had placed a mine in the road to stop the lead truck. Some of the Moros were in the trees that sprawled over the road, ready to fire down on anything that passed.

I glanced again at Sariol, realizing he was about to experience his first taste of combat. Two months before, the Japs had entered his village, Tawi-Tawi, and wiped out his entire family in a massacre personally supervised by Major Higoshita. His fourteen-year-old sister was raped, then slashed across the stomach. His father, an old man, was shot down by a drunken officer while Higoshita stood by, gloating and watching, laughing each time the old man gave a death kick. And while three Japs held Sariol in check, his mother had been decapitated by a Samurai sword—wielded by none other than Higoshita.

Managing to escape the next day, Sariol had immediately joined our band, demanding a chance to kill Japs. Both McLean and I took a liking to the boy, and we spent some time showing him a trick or two. I gave him the Nambus and he practiced with it every day. Until now I hadn't let him loose with the weapon lest his loathing for Japs get the better of him and ruin our entire operation.

260

Sariol spent hours sharpening his kris, the short, wavy dagger that almost all Moros carry. This piece of devilish steel is no doubt the deadliest weapon conceived by man. A kris can produce unhealable wounds in hand-to-hand fighting. During one raid I saw a Moro sever a Jap in half with two quick blows of a kris.

I hoped that Sariol would get his revenge. Finishing off Japs had become our job, and every dead Jap meant one less defender when MacArthur returned to the Islands.

Sariol kept looking down the sights of his Nambus, squeezing the trigger. Each time the weapon clicked, he would grin slightly, but it was an evil grin. And with ammunition bandoliers crisscrossing his body, he took on an unearthly appearance.

McLean ducked across the road. "Both sides are covered," he reported. "Sali says there's four trucks. Loaded down with troops."

"The machine gun?" I asked. McLean pointed to the high slope behind us, densely covered with jungle. "That baby'll sweep this entire stretch of road."

I slapped McLean on the knee. "Now get your freight across the road before the Nips show up."

McLean returned the slap, recrossed the road and vanished into the ditch.

"I hope," swore Sariol, "that one truck stops here so I can spit in the driver's face and then streak it with the blood from his belly." His English was fractured but I got the point.

He wanted to kill Japs.

The trucks came. Their roar increased to such a pitch I thought they were going to pass right over us. The first truck slipped by. I felt relieved—the waiting was over at last. The thing I noticed as the vehicle passed was the huge machine gun mounted on the cab and the sober-faced Jap gripping the handles.

As the third truck was about to pass us, the lead truck hit the mine. The screeching of brakes was ear-shattering as I scooted to the lip of the ditch, my Thompson tight against my shoulder. I began my gun four feet ahead of the truck. I held it steady until the truck ran into the stream of

261

fire. The roar of my gun had caused Sariol to fire his Nambus harmlessly across the road.

My bullets shattered the windows of the cab and then hit the two Japs inside. One Nip had leaped from the back of the truck, but the instant his feet hit the ground his body jerked and smashed against the vehicle's tailgate, a burst of bullets slapping his chest into a pulpy mess.

"Spray that truck," I shouted. "Spray that truck to hell." I watched my bullets move accurately along the canvas of the truck. Screams came from within. "Spray the other side," I yelled across the road. McLean and others opened fire and cut the canvas to shreds. I gave the canvas another burst as bullets from the other side of the road sang over my head.

I glanced at Sariol. The crazy kid was still spraying the Nips in the front compartment. I shook him savagely and he looked into my face with burning eyes. "Swing it," I ordered. "The next truck. Swing it." I jumped back to the bottom of the ditch and Sariol followed. As I ran I sprayed the windows of the next truck. A flock of Japs poured out the back; a hail of bullets from a Moro in an overhead tree dropped most of them.

A grenade hit the truck as Sariol and I started up out of the ditch. The concussion threw us into the mucky ditch bottom. Bodies flopped in the road. With our faces streaked with mud and our mouths filled with grit, we got up in the next second and moved up. Ahead, bursts of gunfire crisscrossed the road. I saw one of the Moros in a tree buy it when he leaned out too far to get off a better shot. He doubled up and fell gracefully from his high limb into a blazing truck.

Then I saw the Nip who had fired the shot. When he saw me coming up out of the ditch his mouth fell open in surprise. I put a burst of slugs through his head and motioned Sariol into the road. He started to follow me but stumbled and fell, his Nambus going off and spraying the sides of the ditch. "It's Sali," he cried, "I tripped over Sali. Look at his head."

"There isn't any head," I told him.

Nips were still pouring out of the lead truck. I caught a glimpse of McLean as he climbed across the front of that truck, heading for the huge machine gun mounted there. Jandi, a Moro who had fought the two bitter years with us, stepped in front of me to stop a Jap bayonet. I emptied the remainder of my clip into the responsible soldier. Another Nip came around the side of the truck, his clothes on fire. His mouth was open, but the hammering of Sariol's Nambus drowned out the terrifying shriek and the Jap's body jumped off the ground. It crashed against the truck's bumper, then spun around and thumped to the ground. It disappeared into the ditch, leaving a trail of smoke behind it. Burning flesh seared my nostrils.

As Sariol and other Moros appeared in the road one Jap came crawling out from beneath a pile of bodies, his face half-crushed and his legs dangling behind him like matchsticks. Sariol walked over some bodies and placed the muzzle of his gun against the Jap's head. He scattered the man's brains all over the road.

McLean, by this time, had reached the mounted machine gun and had gotten off a few short bursts. Which wrapped it up. Not a Jap was left standing. The four trucks were burning and shattered. The road was littered with torn pieces of human flesh and twisted bodies.

The last thing I remember before it happened was McLean standing behind the machine gun, a look of victory on his face. Then the entire jungle seemed to explode in a volley of leaden death. The sharp zang of bullets forced everyone to flatten out behind the burning trucks. We lay breathless, unable to stick up our heads for fear of stopping one of hundreds of slugs whistling around us. Somehow the Japanese had overtaken the machine-gun crew we had stationed on the hillside. Now the Nips had turned the weapon on us and were firing right down our throats. A dozen Moros spun around and died in the road. Sariol stuck close to me, spraying the treetops to our rear.

McLean shouted orders and swung the heavy-caliber gun toward the hillside. But before he could get the gun working some slugs thumped against the cab and he spun around, sprawling over the side.

I started to reach for McLean's hand when I got a good look at his blank staring eyes and bloody face. I dropped back to the ground as a volley of slugs tore into McLean's corpse.

I lay staring up at McLean. Until that moment, killing Japs had been a job. Now it took on new meaning; now I knew for certain how Sariol felt when he saw his family slaughtered before his very eyes. Killing suddenly meant something new to me.

The next time I pulled the trigger of my Thompson it must have been with the same furious yanking that Sariol had demonstrated; it must have been with the same cold, piercing gaze I had seen in the boy's eyes.

The Jap fire continued. While we had been focusing our attention on the truck convoy, the Japanese, under Higoshita's command, had cleverly placed a cordon around us, sacrificing their trucks and men so they could take us in one fell swoop.

Every tree came alive with sniper fire; every bush concealed a Jap taking a careful bead on us. Not even the Moros, who had been born in the jungles and knew every inch of Mindanao terrain, could hope to escape the murderous volley that plunged us into the mud.

Grenades came rolling out of the jungle, turning some of the Moros into nothing more than slivers of human flesh. The surviving natives leaped into the ditch to escape the gunfire.

Three bullets tore my clothing. One shot kicked up so close to Sariol that mud spattered into his eyes. We had been more fortunate than the others. The flaming truck we crouched behind offered more protection than the shallow ditch into which the Japs were deflecting most of their fire. But shortly grenades came bouncing onto the road. I motioned to Sariol to head for the ditch. Somehow we managed to roll through the bullets and fragments. We fell into the muddy bottom of the ditch and paused to gather our wits and form some plan of action. The only Moros around us were dead. The Jap fire, fortunately, had moved up the ditch to where a handful of natives were still resisting. But I knew it would only be moments before the Japs would advance, bayoneting the living as well as the dead.

I pointed to a wooded area not far in front of us. We would have to cross a clearing to reach it. Sariol showed no signs of fear; he just nodded. We both knew it was our only chance—the Japs weren't going to leave any survivors.

Even before I realized it, Sariol was moving across that open clearing. I've never seen anyone who had as much guts as that Moro. Maybe the boy didn't know the feeling of fear. He moved across that clearing like a gazelle, firing his Nambus all the way. The machine-gun and rifle fire kicked up the mud around his feet, but he made it safely to cover.

I tried next, barely rolling behind the nearest *narra* tree when the machine gun let up on Sariol and swung over to pick me off. The bullets slammed into the tree trunk. Wood splinters flew over my head. I rolled through the hemp grass toward Sariol. The boy was still firing his weapon. The barrel was red hot when I reached him, and a heap of cartridges lay at his feet. I flattened the Moro out, telling him to hold his fire.

We waited a few moments; the firing had stopped. Through strands of hemp grass, we watched as the Nips walked among the flaming trucks. And we watched as they bayoneted the bodies of the Moros. Some of them were alive. An occasional scream split the air. Sariol clenched his fists, held his Nambus menacingly, and started to get up. It took all my strength to hold him, and then he continued to wiggle and squirm to break free. "You fool," I whispered, "if you go out there now they'll just gun you down. The only way to keep killing Japs is to stay alive." He stopped struggling after that.

When I saw them bayonet McLean's body it was my turn to want to leap up and kill Japs. I started to rise, but stopped myself in time. I was thankful Sariol had been incited first; my own words had stopped me from such a stupid act.

Some of the Nips were headed across the clearing in our direction. Sariol set his machine gun on the ground and opened fire, but after getting off a short burst his Nambus clicked. I had plenty of clips left so I signaled Sariol to duck and began firing.

As the Japs went down, Sariol stood up, yelling and waving his kris. "Run like hell," I told him. "Run like you've never run before." We started to turn when I heard a twig snap. My blood froze; Sariol swung around with a growling cry. That unexpected shout stopped the Jap officer standing behind us for a split second. That split second was all I needed. The Samurai sword lifted above the officer's head never descended. The stock of my Thompson struck his forehead. Sariol immediately fell on the Jap, plunging his kris into his heart. I grabbed the Moro by the arm. Already the Japs were advancing rapidly across the clearing.

We tore off through the field of hemp grass and *narra* trees. In the next few minutes we must have raced through the densest part of the Mindanao jungle.

As I leaped over a log my foot landed directly in the center of a huge outstretched cobra. Sariol swung his kris and the snake's head rolled off into the grass. We stopped for a moment, gasping for breath. I realized we were running senselessly, out of self-preservation. Our bodies were covered with welt marks where vines and sharp limbs had scratched us.

"We're going back," I told Sariol. He didn't question the order. I guess he sensed what I was thinking. We turned and started back. "Higoshita," I said. He nodded but said nothing, trudging beside me.

I didn't have to tell Sariol where we were going. I guess he sensed that too. By the time we reached the machine-gun emplacement on the hillside overlooking the stretch of road where we had ambushed the Nip trucks, the crew was just preparing to take the gun apart and join their comrades below. I riddled them with slugs; then we rolled their carcasses down the hill.

Sariol loaded the .30 while I leveled the barrel on the Japs milling below. Some had heard the shots and were starting up the hill toward us. They died on that slope, every one of them. When I couldn't see anything moving, I stopped firing.

We immediately moved out of the gun emplacement by carefully working our way through the brush and trees.

What happened next happened so quickly it is hard to remember every detail or the thoughts that rushed through my head with the initial shock. As we rounded a small clump of trees, we came face-to-face with a high-ranking Japanese officer and his gun-carrying aide. Even though I had never seen him before, I knew instantly it was Higoshita. Sunlight glinted off his pompous chest of medals, and there was a perpetual sneer of evil on the Jap's face, even before he had time to react to our sudden meeting. The four of us were frozen for a split second, Higoshita's eyes widening with simultaneous hatred and surprise. His aide mumbled something in Japanese and brought forward his weapon. So close were they to us that I had only to extend my hand to deflect the rifle barrel to the ground. A single slug tore the grass at my feet as my other hand shot out and caught the aide by the throat. I squeezed with strength I never knew I could manage.

A glance out of the corner of my eye told me Sariol had leaped toward Higoshita, memories of the village massacre no doubt fresh in his mind. The Japanese officer must have also remembered Sariol, for fear replaced the hatred in his face. Both men grunted and fell to the ground, rolling behind the clump of trees.

The aide was not a solidly built man. I felt life flowing quickly from his body. He choked and grunted, managed to fire another harmless shot near my boot, then began quivering all over. A sickly blue color flushed the skin of his face. I continued to squeeze ever harder until I heard a sharp snap. His weapon thudded to the ground and I released my grip. His corpse fell straight past me, the livid-blue face taking the full brunt of the fall.

I rushed into the trees, looking frantically for Sariol. The Japanese officer had managed to pin down the Moro lad and was seated atop him, delivering karate chops to his undefended neck. Sariol still fought back, pounding the Jap with his bare fingers and screaming curses of hate.

Higoshita must have heard me running through the grass, for in the next instant he picked up the boy and, with one arm around his neck, held him fast against his well-decorated uniform. I couldn't fire for fear of hitting Sariol, so I stood there helplessly, catching my breath.

With a grunt Hiboshita flung Sariol's body directly at me, and began reaching for the .32-caliber pistol in his holster. I couldn't fire without hitting Sariol and he knocked against me, forcing my Thompson off to one side. "Hit the deck," I yelled, for I could see that Higoshita had cleared leather.

As I sprawled in the grass, Sariol regained his footing and stood upright, uttering one final curse at Higoshita. The Jap pistol barked three times and I could see Sariol stiffen, with three tiny red marks appearing on his chest. By exposing himself and drawing Higoshita's fire, Sariol had given me the time I needed. Higoshita turned his pistol on me in time to catch the full load of my Thompson slugs. I didn't stop firing until the clip was finished. Then I inserted a fresh one and continued to fire, working the gun up one side and down the other, lingering whenever I came to the head or belly. By the time I was out of ammo, Higoshita was mush.

I made it a special point to see that Sariol was buried on the outskirts of his village, next to a common grave which contained the bodies of his family. In a way, Sariol was lucky. No longer would he have to seek revenge; no longer would his eyes burn with hate. McLean's death had created a passion that Sariol's death now kindled. Once again my emotions for killing were extinguished. Once again I could return to my job of killing without sensitivity attached to it.

Of the original sixty-two who were involved in the Jap truck ambush, only eleven others managed to survive the trap. They came wandering into our base camp the next day.

The fight was gone from us.

Three weeks later, on March 10, 1945, the Army landed at Zamboanga, with the 41st Infantry Division pushing the Japs back into the jungle.

But we didn't bother to go down into the city. We stayed in our camp and slept, trying to forget. When American trucks passed on a road nearby, we got up and went down to watch the convoy moving toward the frontlines.

I hitched a ride with a young PFC who was heading down toward the sea. "What outfit you in, Mac?" he asked, eying my clothing.

I threw my Thompson into the grass as the jeep sped along. "No outfit, Mac," I replied. "I just retired."

57
Critique #3

"What do you think, Sarge?"

"Who's this Bart Hoffman you wrote this story with?"

"He's a guy I invented, Sarge. This is supposed to be one of those 'as told to' stories for the men's magazines. They do it all the time."

"That's being pretentious and phony again, Youngman. I thought I told you to watch stuff like that."

"What about the story, Sarge?"

"You gotta neat way of wiping out Japs, Youngman, I'll say that much. I liked that whole business. I could see those Nip cruds flopping in the mud. And I could see that Moro, Sariol what's his name, plunging that wiggly kris of his into every Jap that came along. But I don't know . . ."

"What didn't you like?"

"No characterizations, Youngman. I thought I told you about characterizations."

"It's an action story, Sarge. It doesn't need characterization."

"Bullshit. Every story needs characterization, Youngman. Without it, you got nothing but a bunch of people selling bananas."

"But there's motive. For Sariol and for Hoffman."

"Killing Japs? Shit, that's not motive. That's supposed to be their job. They're supposed to be professionals, right? I'm sorry, Youngman, but this yarn doesn't make it either. As much as I liked the killing scenes, and that bit where Hoffman's turning Higoshita to mush, it boils down to a big hunk of shit, just like 'Crossing' and 'Aceldama.' "

"Jesus Christ fuck almighty," screeched Youngman. He picked up the manuscript of 'Mindanao Marauders' and attempted to rip it in half. The pages were too bulky. Sarge took the first few pages off the top and tore them for Youngman, while Youngman tugged at the remaining pages. They both scattered the pieces among the rocks of the hilltop. The same fate befell the manuscript of "Aceldama."

"Sooner or later," said Sarge, wiping off his hands, "you've got to stop writing shit, Youngman. You've just got to stop writing shit."

58
Dawn's Early Light

Li Ming came up the hill quickly, out of breath but unstoppable. Youngman, who had scanned the nearby hills for any sign of movement, went part of the way down the slope to save her the trouble of coming all the way to the top. "There's an old proverb," he said. "One in a hurry often lacks the breath of wisdom."

Li Ming bowed to that one. "And he who does not get the message in time often misses the reward."

"What's wrong?"

"A bird has flown its nest. And Sarge wishes you back."

"Which bird?"

"He cannot find the one with the plug in his ear."

"Charlie Brown? . . . What's he upset about? Good riddance, I say."

"Nevertheless," and Li Ming bowed humbly again out of sheer habit, "he wishes you to search for this missing bird."

Youngman slung his rifle and started down the hill with Li Ming, carrying his porto-typer in a lackadaisical fashion. "What's going to happen to you?" he asked.

Li Ming shrugged. "A home away from home is better than no home at all. I go with Louis—and Reva."

"To please the General and his staff? Or to please Louie?"

She shrugged again. "A road can lead in numerous directions. If I am called upon to please the General and his staff, or to please Louie, then I will follow that road."

It was incomprehensible to Youngman. "Why'd you get mixed up with something like this?"

"Did I not bring you pleasure last night?"

"Well, yes . . ."

"Then I am capable of bringing pleasure to many men."

It was a fatalism Youngman knew he would never fathom. When they reached the bottom of the hill, he put the porto-typer down and faced Li Ming. He kissed her long and hard. She gave her entire mouth to him, and for a moment their tongues met in midair, and Youngman experienced another new sensation. He pulled back and studied her for a moment and felt sorry that after today he might never see her again. Not if Sarge got them back to the main line and Louis and Li Ming and Reva went their separate way, searching out the General and his staff.

"I guess I better start looking for Charlie Brown." As he moved away, she soared with him even though she did not move from her spot. She, too, had experienced a sense of sorrow. It boded ill, and Li Ming was frightened.

* * *

"No sign of him, Sarge."

"You checked out this whole area?"

"The whole area. No trail, nothing."

"Shit." Sarge turned to look at the sun, as it broke over the hills. Louis came yawning and stretching out of the converted supply room. "Did I hear you say someone was missing?" Louis scratched at his *foustenala*, as if it had suddenly been invaded by fleas.

"The nutty Nisei."

"The Jap?"

"The fishhead," corrected Sarge. "He took a powder last night."

Louis looked closely at Sarge. "Or so it would appear."

"What're you getting at, Show Biz?" asked Sarge.

"*Bot Bon Jui.* Or have you forgotten Mr. Brown's actions here yesterday?"

"I haven't forgotten anything. What about Bout Bunk Junk?"

"Well, Charlie and I were having a little talk last night. He made it clear he would stop at nothing to find it."

"So?"

"Which brings us around to your prize package there." Louis pointed to Ju-Chao, who was still lying at the foot of the steps of the ammunition depot. "Charlie suspected the POW knew something about this place—something that dated back to the days when a fierce battle was fought here, and a treasure buried somewhere nearby. Now it seems that last night Mr. Brown had a little chat with our friendly POW."

Sarge cocked his head. "I thought you were supposed to play the fool at all times, Show Biz. Regulation 362 . . ."

"Even a Greek can step out of character, Sarge."

"Since you seem to have all the ideas in this outfit, Greco, what would you suggest?"

"I don't think Charlie Brown took a powder."

"You don't say."

"I think our chopstick bender over there told Mr. Brown where to find *Bot Bon Jui.*"

"Keep talking, Show Biz."

"I guess Mr. Brown to be somewhere very close—right under our feet in the old subterranean passages of the ammo dump."

"That's all very ingenious, Show Biz. What do you base it on?"

"One little thing, Sarge. It's right under your nose." Louis walked over to the wall of the ammunition depot, where a pile of equipment was heaped. "This is Brown's gear. And this is his radio outfit . . . here." Louis held up the unit for all to see. "Now I ask you, have you ever known Mr. Brown to go very far without his radio outfit?"

Sarge looked at Youngman. Youngman looked at Sarge.

"Very interesting," said The Old German, who appeared at the top of the steps and cradled his Schmeisser. He came down the steps slowly. "After the war, in Germany, there were men who believed the stories about Hitler dumping his booty into the waters of Toplitzee, the deepest and most inaccessible lake in the Austrian Alps. These men spent their lives, often losing them in the process, searching for this so-called treasure." The Old German reached the bottom of the steps and stood next to Louis. "In 1958, they fished out fifty million pounds sterling. There is often truth connected to legend."

"If this wasn't a war," swore Sarge, "I'd leave him down there to rot. But I'm responsible for that sonofabitch."

"You can count on my help," said Louis.

"And maybe help yourself to some Bout Bunk Junk in the process?"

Louis shrugged. "A man can be curious."

"And my help," said The Old German, slinging his Schmeisser.

"Looks like we all got a little of the mole people in us," replied Sarge.

"Wait a minute," piped up Youngman. "How do we know exactly where he went? I mean, there's a slew of doors leading below."

"Spread out," said Sarge. "Check all those doors. If Charlie Brown went through one of them, there should be some sign. Nobody's been around this place for years."

As Sarge, Youngman and The Old German began the search, Louis turned to Reva. When the others were out of earshot:

"You know what to do, baby."

Reva put her hands on Louis's waist. "Will it take long, honey?"

"How the hell do I know? You just be ready and waiting when we come up."

"And when the flower has been plucked from its stalk?" asked Li Ming with a slight bowing motion.

"Then we haul ass out of here."

"And the others?" It was Li Ming again, bowing again.

"Fuck the others. We'll be on easy street from here on out."

"Hey!" It was the voice of Youngman, excited, unrestrained. "Over here. I've found something."

What he had found was an open door.

"That was closed last night," remarked Sarge.

274

"That must be it," said Louis, coming up behind Sarge and The Old German. "The door to *Bot Bon Jui*."

They peered into the dark passageway. Barely discernible, and leading downward, was a flight of stairs. Something scampered across the top step.

"Joint must be crawling with rats," said Louis.

"More rats than you know," said Sarge.

The Old German stared into the gloominess. "This reminds me of the underground bunkers at Normandy."

Sarge looked at The Old German. "You fought at Normandy?"

"For a short while. They transferred us from the Eastern Front to reinforce one of the forward positions about two weeks prior to invasion."

"I was with the Big Red One. Omaha Beach."

"Our position," said The Old German, "was at Omaha Beach." He chuckled. "We shot up the first wave of boats pretty good."

Sarge took a step toward The Old German. "I was in that first wave of boats. The bloodiest goddamn ..." The Old German looked blandly at Sarge. Sarge returned his attention to the passageway. "All right, let's get moving. Everyone stay close together."

"Everyone got their flashes?" asked Youngman.

Heads nodded. They entered the passageway.

59

Descent

When Reva was certain they were gone, she drove the truck over to the door and shut off the engine. Ennui set in as she sat in the cab of the truck. She yawned. She scratched. She glanced over at Ju-Chao. She felt she needed a diversion. Her fingers itched, but she restrained that itch, and kept her hands on the steering wheel.

Ju-Chao, who lay near the steps, had spent a restless night. He had awakened with a dull ache in his throat, though he was not thirsty. His mind was suddenly clear and sharp and he remembered the night before, when he had drawn the outline of the door on the scrap of paper. The memories of that door—what had happened before and behind it—flooded back to him. Pain was gone; thirst vanished. Only images remained. They danced through his brain and were as stark as reality . . .

They had fought their way across the open ground, advancing a few yards at a time, dropping behind whatever cover was available and firing upon the gun emplacements and sniper holes which fronted Chun Hsien Ku. Casualties were heavy, but somehow Ju-Chao's unit had made headway. The first day it was measured only in yards, but by the second day the mortar teams had zeroed in on the advance positions and destroyed many of the machine-gun and cannon emplacements, and the advance was measured by tenths of a mile.

Ju-Chao himself had taken a slight wound in his right leg, but this had been quickly bandaged and forgotten. On the third day, the advance was measured not in yards or miles but in stubborn bravery. With Ju-Chao on that third and final day of the battle for Chun Hsien Ku were Sergeant Tsai and a private, Wu-Sheng. Most of the others in his unit had been killed or wounded by the time the Chinese forces had moved within three hundred yards of the ammunition depot, which bristled with guns and defenders.

Despite the casualties, Ju-Chao pressed on, motioning his men forward as soon as resistance was eliminated, signaling them to dig in again when they reached the next line of fortifications.

A few more grenade bursts and a carefully-laid-down mortar barrage paved the way directly to Chun Hsien Ku. By the afternoon the depot had been well pounded by artillery and was suitably softened for the attack.

As Ju-Chao signaled his men to close on the fortress in a final sweeping attack, he realized that the figures of men were suddenly visible throughout the depot. His men found themselves being met out in the open by a counterattacking force—the final defenders of Chun Hsien Ku; the personal bodyguards of Nim Yung, who had vowed to protect their general with the last ounce of breath within their gallant bodies. These were fanatical Nationalists, unlike any Ju-Chao had ever encountered before. The hand-to-hand fighting was fierce beyond belief, even for the hardened likes of Ju-Chao and his men.

Ju-Chao saw several of his best fighters go down under bayonet lunges. Several more were beaten to death with bare fists. He knew the only way he could possibly win this fight was through sheer overpowering odds, which is how he won it. For each of the bodyguards killed, Ju-Chao counted three or four of his men being cut down by the vicious bayonet and pummeling attack. His forces came again and again. Gradually there were fewer and fewer of

277

Nim Yung's loyal men. Groups of five or six attacked a single defender, with three of them being forced to hold the fighting madman while the other three plunged their knives into the body. Even then, the soldier might resist as he died, kicking and squirming as he dropped helplessly into the grass where his blood flowed from slashed veins.

Ju-Chao, Tsai and Wu-Sheng fought their way toward the heart of Nim Yung's stronghold, carried herdlike by the forward momentum of the charging troops behind them. If one stopped, death by trampling resulted. When they reached the steps leading to the upper level of the ammunition depot several of Ju-Chao's men were killed by a burst of submachine-gun fire from the southern corner of the depot. Tsai stopped a bullet in his shoulder, flung away his rifle, and fought on with his pistol. His wounded arm hung limply at his side.

Wu-Sheng pointed excitedly. "There! There he is!" Tsai and Ju-Chao heard him, but the rest of the troops swarmed past them, charging up the steps to clean out the gun emplacements which were still blasting at the rear elements. It was a bloody, furious moment, and the steps were soon littered with bodies. Ju-Chao barely realized what was happening. He only saw the figure of General Nim Yung, firing a submachine-gun, cutting down another large swarm of men. There was no mistaking it was Nim Yung. He was ringed with personal bodyguards, number-one boys ready to sacrifice their lives in his behalf. One of those bodyguards opened a huge door which, Ju-Chao reasoned, led beneath the depot. There was the outline of a giant bird on the door, and words which described the legend of this bird.

"Tzo, tzo," shouted Ju-Chao to Tsai and Wu-Sheng. The three turned and moved swiftly toward the door as it was closed by a huge, brawny bodyguard.

"The door," cried Tsai. "Don't let it close." Ju-Chao was nearest, but he knew there wasn't time to fire. His only hope was to reach through the narrow space remaining and throw the soldier off balance.

Ju-Chao lunged and his body wedged between the steel frame and the massive door. Caught there, he stared into the face of the straining enemy trooper. Ju-Chao pressed

278

*with all his might and felt his body slipping out of the vise-
like grasp. His full weight fell against the bodyguard,
knocking him to the floor. The door groaned open as Tsai
and Wu-Sheng entered. "Close it," demanded Ju-Chao.
Tsai, his wounded arm still hanging at his side, left that
chore to Wu-Sheng as he hurried around in back of the
bodyguard, who was attempting to rise to his feet. Tsai
plunged his knife into the soldier's throat and violently
twisted it. The Nationalist gurgled once and died at Tsai's
feet. Ju-Chao, meanwhile, helped Wu-Sheng secure the
door.*

"Listen."

They listened.

Far away footsteps moved downward.

"Nim Yung."

"He's getting away."

"I don't think so," said Ju-Chao.

*"He would be a fool not to have an escape tunnel." Tsai
wiped his knife on his trouser leg.*

*In silence Tsai and Wu-Sheng tried to grow acquainted
with Ju-Chao's wisdom.*

*"He's trained his men to fight to the death," explained
Ju-Chao. "Would he himself do the contrary?"*

*"If he did," realized Tsai, "he would lose the faith of
those who respected him—friend or foe."*

*"Therefore, the only weapon General Nim Yung has left
to him is death." Ju-Chao stared into the darkness, as the
sound of the footsteps became fainter. "Death will leave
him the hero he would want to be."*

"A martyr pig," sneered Wu-Sheng.

"A martyr nonetheless," added Ju-Chao. "Come on."

They started down the stairs.

Sarge, Youngman, Louis, and The Old German reached
the bottom of the stairs, and found themselves in a nar-
rower corridor, which smelled of dankness and decay.
Sarge flashed his penlight over the concrete floor. The tiny
circle of yellowish light focused on the vague outline of a
footprint. "Someone's been along here."

"GI boot," said The Old German, squinting. "Three,
four hours ago."

"Looks like I was right." Louis tried not to sound too pompous.

Sarge sniffed. "I smell something."

"Yes, there is something." The Old German's nose did not move.

"What is it, Sarge?" Youngman sounded a bit nervous.

"I smell ..." There was a lengthy pause as Sarge contemplated.

"I can't make it out," said The Old German. His nose had still not moved.

"You wouldn't, being a krauthead. That's fish eggs and rice."

"What's that mean?" asked Louis.

"It's the odor a Chinese bellyrobber leaves behind him after he leaves a Chink chowhall. I'd say there's a Chinese restaurant around here somewhere."

"Come on; let's keep moving."

They proceeded along the corridor.

At the bottom of the stairs Ju-Chao felt the presence of someone ahead of them. Without a word, he placed a hand on the shoulder of Wu-Sheng, who in turn placed a hand on the wounded arm of Tsai. Without realizing it, Tsai let out a cry which sliced through the stillness of the corridor. Slugs ricocheted off the concrete walls and whined softly away on new pathways. Before another round was fired the three instinctively pressed against the floor, their faces tight against the cold cement. Another volley passed harmlessly over them. Ju-Chao returned the fire, sweeping the entire length and width of the corridor, hoping to leave not an inch of space untouched. The singing of bullets dominated for a few seconds. There was another sound—a body slumping against a wall. They moved along the corridor again, coming to an L-junction. From an open doorway near the bend, a pair of feet protruded at erratic angles to each other. It was the corpse of Nim Yung's number-one bodyguard. That meant only Nim Yung was left. They hurried on ...

Near a bend in the corridor, Sarge and the others paused near an open doorway and stared at the outstretched legs

280

of a skeleton, covered only by the mildew-riddled remnants of a pair of ochre-colored pants. Bullet pockmarks in the open door and wall indicated the cause of the soldier's death.

The Old German knelt beside the skeleton. ".30-caliber slugs . . . probably M-1 . . . American . . . thirty-five, thirty-six years ago."

Sarge flashed his penlight around the walls of the room. He whistled.

"Hey, look at that," said Louis.

"Looks like a supply room," said Youngman.

Sarge's penlight played over many sacks of rice and countless crates filled with canned foods.

"The Chinaman's equivalent of the K-ration," remarked Louis.

"These crates haven't been here more than two, three weeks," The Old German said.

"This place isn't as abandoned as it looks." Sarge's penlight played over many more cartons of nonperishable goods. "I'd say the fishheads are using this for a food warehouse."

"Why do you suppose a body's there?" asked Louis.

"Who knows?" replied Sarge. "Could have been a casualty of the big one here in '48."

"The Chinese," contributed Youngman, "are funny about their dead. Maybe they left him here to ward off evil spirits."

"Whatever the reason," and Louis couldn't help but shiver when he said it, "he sure gives the place style."

They moved on, following the trail of footprints left by Charlie Brown.

Ju-Chao, Tsai, and Wu-Sheng went down two more flights and were about to tackle the fourth when they heard a noise from a tiny room at the far end of the corridor.

It was the sound of someone praying.

The tone in the praying voice hinted of death, and Ju-Chao knew they had come to the end of their search for Nim Yung. They reverently stood away from the door for the next two minutes. It was their way of paying homage to an enemy they had never lost their respect for. At least General Nim Yung was a soldier who believed in his cause and had remained incorruptible, which was more than could be said for most of Chang Kai-shek's field commanders. Nim Yung had known the meaning of the word honor, and that was something every member of the Eight Route Army understood and respected.

The voice stopped. The short silence that followed seemed prolonged, perhaps because the three of them were so tense.

A shot rang out, and the tension left their bodies. There was the familiar sound of a falling body.

They entered the room at the far end of the corridor and found a rivulet of blood sluggishly leaking through the fresh hole in General Nim Yung's temple—and found Bot Bon Jui.

For the next few minutes they silently examined the treasure. It was a moment reserved for individual discovery and exhilaration. All three realized it was a moment they would probably never have the chance to live again, so they made the most of it. Tsai did a quick-tempoed dance around the treasure. Wu-Sheng voiced his excitement in a song composed as he went along. Ju-Chao, however, had already begun to feel the hollowness of the discovery, of the victory in taking Chun Hsien Ku, and he lapsed into a peculiar form of melancholia, in which his inner feelings were the antithesis of his smile and his clapping hands.

When the ritual of discovery was over, Tsai immediately began to move part of Bot Bon Jui toward the door. He expressed the idea of taking the treasure and burying it elsewhere, as was Chinese tradition. The three of them would give such an act tradition; three individuals always buried a treasure. Wu-Sheng agreed. One did not.

Ju-Chao ordered Tsai to remove his hands from the treasure. Tsai and Wu-Sheng turned to look questioningly at Ju-Chao. "The war is moving away from this place after today," explained Ju-Chao, "and soon Chun Hsien Ku will be forgotten."

"And what has that to do with us?" Tsai asked with irritation. Ju-Chao attributed most of that to his shoulder
282

wound, which he noticed was bleeding quite badly by now.

"We will move with the war. We will move away from this place, and we will forget about this room."

Wu-Sheng screamed, "But such a fortune . . ."

Ju-Chao nodded. "And a sacred one. Don't forget that."

Tsai sneered. "There is nothing sacred anywhere. There is only what you can take for yourself. I say we take Bot Bon Jui!"

Ju-Chao could not agree. "A far greater fortune awaits us up there. A new free land, a government that will provide us our daily needs, families that need to be raised, crops that need to be fertilized and grown, cities which must be rebuilt." He put his hand on a portion of the treasure. "This will only stand in our way, corrupt us, lead us to consider the kind of values which we have fought so long and hard to put asunder."

If Ju-Chao had not been a high-ranking officer in the People's Liberation Army, Tsai and Wu-Sheng might have easily turned on him and murdered without conscience. They knew of his experience of the Long March, they knew he was a survivor of Tsining, and they had felt the strength of his convictions long before this day. Even greed could not completely suppress their feelings for Ju-Chao.

The argument continued for ten minues. Each time Tsai or Wu-Sheng voiced an objection, it was with far less conviction. After so much death and mayhem, perhaps it was a relief to find someone who expressed a feeling for humanity and life.

At last, they agreed to move the treasure to the lowest underground level, where it would remain, untouched and unreported. Each vowed to the other never to return to the site. The rest of the afternoon they transferred the treasure to the deepest confines of the ammunition depot. They were carrying the body of Nim Yung back to the surface when they met the first of the mopping-up squads coming down. Ju-Chao ordered the squad back topside, claiming he and his two men had already checked out the subterranean chambers and found nothing. None of the subordinate officers had questioned his order. Bot Bon Jui remained in its hiding place.

They had just reached the last level of the ammunition depot when they heard the sound of a nail being pried from a board. There was also the sound of something rolling across a cement floor. "Sound familiar?" asked Sarge.

Louis recognized it. "The most unforgettable scavenger I know."

They moved cautiously toward the sound. Because there was only a single room at the far end of the corridor, the source was no mystery.

Sarge snapped on his penlight and flashed it across the interior of that room as Charlie Brown's face popped, dead center, up into the beam. His foolish-looking face was flooded with greed. He froze there as the others entered the room and flashed their lights across its interior.

Charlie Brown stood in the center of the room. Surrounding him were eight casks. In Charlie Brown's hand was a prybar, which he had been using to lift the lid from a cask.

Contemptuously, Louis grabbed the prybar from Charlie Brown's hands and flung it to the floor. The crashing, echoing sound broke the ice. At once, everyone flowed with eager steps toward Charlie Brown and the casks.

"Hold it," Sarge ordered. He let the barrel of his rifle play carelessly around the chamber. "Nobody touches these barrels."

They all stopped within inches of the casks and obeyed Sarge with their hands but not their eyes.

Louis's anger was unmistakable. "Idiot!" He kicked the prybar and it rolled across the floor, coming to rest against a cask.

Sarge grabbed Charlie Brown by the front of his shirt. "I warned you about this, Brown. I told you to think dogface, or don't think. They oughta put you up against a wall just for laughs."

The greed on Charlie Brown's face did not disappear. "None of us have to think dogface anymore, Sarge. You can turn in your gear to the nearest Army surplus store and all the regulations that go with it. You can think rich, Sarge. Think *Bot Bon Jui*." To Youngman: "Don't you know what's in these things? You've got a whole life ahead

284

of you being rich. Rich! Do you know what that means?" To The Old German: "No more fighting wars. No more stomping around and getting shot up." To Louis: "No more making a fool of yourself in front of a bunch of drunken idiots." To the nearest cask: "Rubies, emeralds, diamonds, opals, jade, rose quartz, rhinestones, aquamarine, sapphires, topaz, turquoise. Name it. In these barrels are the treasures of a thousand dynasties."

"The treasure of one dynasty, to be exact. The Han Dynasty of Emperor Wu-ti, 140 A.D.–87 B.C."

All turned to face the speaker in incredulous surprise.

Louis was ringed with their stares.

Laughing in the next breath, he suddenly turned his venom on Charlie Brown. "You teriyaki chump. You're like a thousand other guys who've heard that *Bot Bon Jui* story and twisted and perverted it until it's lost its true meaning."

"I want to see for myself what's in those—" Sarge didn't get one step before Louis leveled his weapon. "Hold it right there, Sarge." The muzzle remained steady on Sarge. "Everyone, drop your hardware on the deck. Come on, drop it." For the next few moments, weapons clattered over the floor. Louis motioned at Sarge. "The pistols, too."

Sarge turned toward Louis so there would be no mistake about the expression on his face. It was an expression of defiance and with it was the connotation that whatever he was about to say, he meant. "One thing I've never done for any man. That's unload these holsters. And I ain't about to do it for you."

Louis returned the defiant stare for a moment, then grew impatient. "All right, all right. Forget the goddamn holsters. Just keep your hands where I can see them." Everyone looked at Louis now and waited for his next move. It came quickly.

"You, Charlie Brown. Over there with krautface and young Hemingway. Hurry up. Sarge, don't you move— even an eyelash."

Sarge was alone, next to one of the casks. Louis dipped down carefully and retrieved the prybar. He handed it to Sarge. "Now, pry open that lid the rest of the way—very gently, Sarge, ever so gently."

Sarge obeyed. The boards came away effortlessly.

He stared down into the cask. There was a smooth, mirrorlike, opaque surface a few inches below the top edge.

He touched it and felt cool, soothing liquid.

"What the fuck is—?"

He put his fingers to his lips and tasted. Louis smiled. Puzzlement spread across Sarge's face. *"Bot Bon Jui.* The Eight Treasures of the Grape," said Louis.

Charlie Brown's face seemed to fall all the way to the cement floor. "Treasures of the what?"

"Grape, you fucking idiot," said Sarge. "Wine. Goddamn it, wine."

"Wine? What the hell are you talking about?"

Louis laughed. He considered the look on Charlie Brown's face, and the way Youngman's jaw was dropping, and the way The Old German rubbed his bearded jaw.

Charlie Brown was counting the casks—all eight of them. "You mean I been chasing my ass. *Bot Bon Jui* is nothing but some lousy wine that I'll end up peeing all over an eggplant?"

Louis's laughter was instantly replaced by anger. "Goddamn idiot! You spend all your time searching for *Bot Bon Jui* when you don't even know what the words mean. You're so damn typically American to get involved when you don't even know what it is you're involved in, so fucking typical it hurts my ass to think about it."

"But they kept saying *Bot Bon Jui* was a treasure—a treasure!"

Louis snickered. "There're many types of treasures. You, and others like you, make it mean what you want it to mean. So you waste your time on dreams, like the absolute fool that you are. You don't bother to translate."

"You should have been on top of that translation, Youngman," Sarge said. "You been to all them schools."

"Must be one of the dialects I don't know, Sarge. Jesus, they've got a million dialects."

"The Eight Treasures of the Grape," muttered Charlie Brown.

"Yeah," smiled Louis, "the most precious liquid in all the Orient. These eight barrels will take me, Reva, and Li Ming out of this hellhole."

Youngman stepped forward, although a reminder of Louis's cradled weapon froze him there. "Li Ming . . . she . . . she's yours? Not the General's?"

"Li Ming belongs to no one, but she's chosen to play my game, kid, so I guess that makes her mine. You got the hots for her?"

"Wait a minute," said Sarge. "What makes these barrels of wine so fucking valuable?"

"This," said Louis, tapping the open cask, "is known as the Wine of Immortality."

"Chinese folk tale," said The Old German. "Even in Germany we have heard of such legends."

"You mean this stuff is supposed to keep you alive if you drink it?" Youngman had a hard time believing any of this.

"Naw, don't be an idiot, kid. It's supposed to prepare you—open up your psyche so you're never afraid of anything, supposed to show you your true inner meaning—crap like that. After drinking this, you're supposed to be able to face life with full understanding."

"Or so goes the legend," added The Old German.

Louis continued: "This wine was produced from a rare hybrid grape which combined the superior flavors of eight different grapes—thus its name. The secret of growing the grape has been lost but it was known to contain a strange drug. A mind-expanding drug."

"Acid?" asked Youngman. "Hallucinogen?"

Louis nodded. "According to the legend, it imbued one with the Spirit of Immortality. A poet named Li Po experimented with it, but he warned others not to tamper with it. I guess he couldn't stand a kick in the head like his opium-smoking pals, so he turned the eight casks over to his emperor. Wu-ti, being a deadhead, let it set. The casks were handed down, dynasty to dynasty. When civil war broke out in 1946, the wine became part of a large booty claimed by Chiang Kai-shek and hidden here by one of his generals, Nim Yung."

"How the hell did you get into all this?" asked Sarge.

"With a map given to me by an old man, who in turn got it from an ex-soldier named Wu-Sheng, one of three men who found the treasure here but kept its whereabouts secret until the day he died."

Youngman snapped his fingers. "I get it. The wounded POW—he was also one of the three. And it was him who tipped off Charlie Brown to the exact location. All shot up like that, he gave away the secret."

There was grudging admiration in Sarge's voice: "Real cute, Louis, I've got to hand it to you. Playing everybody against each other."

"One thing wrong," interjected Youngman. "I've never heard of any black market for wine."

"Ach," said The Old German, "you should have been in Germany in 1946."

"How about that, Louie?" asked Sarge. "Who, besides the Chinese—and they're hardly in a position to bargain with you—would want this Wine of Immortality?"

"Yeah," agreed Youngman. "Wine's wine."

Louis was offended by that generalization. "Not from the Greek point of view, kid. If there's one thing the Greek truly loves, it's wine. Regulation 362, Section IV." Louis, although he kept his weapon well trained, stiffened into the at-attention position and recited: "One of the keys to the stereotyped portrayal of the Greek is his love for wine, which gives full vent to any remaining repressions. While it is true this facet is a cliché in the eyes of the Western nations, it is also true that this love for wine touches closest to the absolute nature of the Nationalist Greek. Greek is wine, and wine is Greek." Louis unstiffened and smiled again. "But wine in Greece, Sarge, has become a lost art over the past couple of centuries. Have you tried any lately? It's the shits. You can't drink ninety percent of the stuff bottled. They keep adding resin from the Aleppo pine, so it'll last longer, but man, does it do something to the taste. Now, all I have to do is introduce this brand to the Greeks and they'll go apeshit wanting more."

"Eight barrels ain't gonna last you long," predicted Sarge.

"Chemistry, Sarge. That's how I work this deal. We analyze the contents, and start raising that hybrid grape. Vineyard after vineyard, and those Greek bastards will be clamoring for more. There'll be a hue and cry for the Grape of Immortality, and only I will know how to grow it. Pretty soon the rest of the world will want to lay its hands on this, and the recipe will be all mine."

"You are one of the new madmen," declared The Old German. "I welcome you into the fold of insanity, where so many before you have wallowed in conquest and commercial exploitation."

"Cut the horseshit, krauthead, and start moving those barrels topside. I didn't get all of you down here to pass the time of day. Get moving!"

Grumbling and cursing, the men at gunpoint went to work.

60
Topside Turmoil

When they came into daylight again, they were beat. Moving the eight barrels up the many flights of stairs had drained most of their energy. Even Louis was finally forced to help Sarge and Charlie Brown up the last flight of steps, bearing most of the weight of the cask.

Youngman had brought up everybody's firearms in a single bundle, and he fell exhausted near the truck, unable to help The Old German move the eighth and final cask into loading position.

From where he still lay on the ground, Ju-Chao could see the eight casks. He no longer felt pain, thirst or misery.

He felt pride: pride in knowing he had been near death's door before he spoke of *Bot Bon Jui*. Then he had spoken in utter delirium.

He was proud of Tsai, who had certainly never spoken a word about the treasure, because he was dead in a week from his shoulder wound. Gangrene and a lack of immediate medical care had seen to that.

Wu-Sheng had also moved away from *Chun Hsien Ku* with the determination to start a new life, untainted by thoughts of *Bot Bon Jui*. He had returned to farming, but he had a deep-rooted love for *Kaoliang* and other spirited beverages, and this had led him on a long downhill road to poverty and indifference. Over the years, Wu-Sheng's loosened tongue spoke of *Bot Bon Jui*, and soon a legend grew—a legend which was known among the People's Liberation Army and the Americans. Whenever Ju-Chao heard some vague reference to the treasure, he silently cursed Wu-Sheng for his weaknesses. Still, Wu-Sheng never returned to the ammunition depot, nor did he reveal the treasure's hiding place. He had heard of Wu-Sheng's death only weeks ago and had felt relief and sorrow. It had been the alcohol, and not the Wu-Sheng he had known during the civil war, which had blabbered.

Ju-Chao felt nationalistic pride; new strength surged through his body.

He eyed the pile of weapons Youngman had dropped in a heap near the foot of the steps. One submachine gun was loaded and ready to fire.

He inched his way toward the weapons.

* * *

Sarge's strength returned, and he got up off the ground. "Smart, Louie. Real smart, using us to do all your dirty work. But I got a new Corps Communiqué for you, Louie. You're one fucking deserter I'm gonna see gets the firing squad."

"You go ahead and send the firing squad after my ass, Sarge. I'd like to see a handful of jokers try to find me in this country. There's plenty of space for me to get lost in. But you gotta admit, Sarge, I'm probably the smartest damn deserter you've ever seen. I got me wheels, I got me the eight kegs of treasure . . . I got me this . . ." Louis pulled Reva to his side. She had stood for the past five minutes, running her fingers over each of the casks as if she were about to make love to them. "A deserter who bides his time with all the pleasures . . . Li Ming . . ." Louis snapped his fingers, but Li Ming, who stood near Youngman, did not respond.

"Li Ming?" Louis was just a little bit surprised.

Without answering, Li Ming went to Youngman's side, taking one of his hands in hers. Youngman glanced at

Louis. "She belongs to no one, Louis. You said so yourself, remember?"

"Fortunes of war, Louis," added Sarge.

Louis shrugged indifferently. "Have it your own way, Li Ming. At least you didn't cop out on me before I had the goods."

Li Ming bowed her head in humiliation as Youngman slid an arm around her shoulder. "You're not going with him. That's what counts."

Louis motioned toward the casks. "I'm gonna enjoy what I do have."

Louis started to walk toward the nearest cask when the submachine gun opened fire. For a moment his body jerked rhythmically to the staccato burst of gunfire. Bullets ripped and tore into the barrels. Gouts of rich, heavy black fluid chugged through the holes.

Instinctively, everyone dove for cover at the first sound of the burst. Sarge pulled Youngman with him. As the private fell forward, his steel helmet flew off his head and rolled toward the casks. It came to a stop beneath one of them. A stream of wine, flowing through one of the bullet holes, quickly filled the helmet to overflowing.

Li Ming was carried earthward by Youngman's forward momentum. The Old German was the fastest. He clung to the earth with a dexterity and professionalism that made his body appear to melt into the soil. Charlie Brown and Reva also hit the dirt hard and quickly, and they kept their heads pressed downward, too afraid to cast an upward glance.

Louis did not respond in typical military fashion. He remained on his feet. Staring at the casks, he apparently was unable to believe what he saw. Only his head turned as the submachine-gun fire shifted from the first barrel to the second, from the second to the third, from the third to the fourth, and so on down the line. The rich, irreplaceable fluid drenched the ground and formed pools at Louis's feet. The pools quickly evaporated as the dry earth drank its fill of the Wine of Immortality. If anything did not need such wine, Louis's mind screamed, it was the earth. The earth would be here for millenniums more, while he, a mere mortal, would walk the earth but for a handful of years.

The irony of it overwhelmed him. He could do nothing but stand motionless and stare at the swiftly emptying casks.

As slugs chirped into the eighth barrel, Ju-Chao felt the click of the hammer striking an empty chamber—the magazine had held out long enough. *Bot Bon Jui* was destroyed. The weapon slid through his fingers; while pride bore strength, it did not provide sustaining strength.

Ju-Chao was starting to pitch forward when Sarge lifted him to his feet by clutching the front of his blouse. For an instant, Sarge gazed into Ju-Chao's pain-riddled, albeit satisfied, face. Sarge wanted to speak but he could find no adequate words. Ju-Chao pushed his head forward, so Sarge could hear him gasp: "U . . . C . . . L . . . A . . ." Ju-Chao lapsed into unconsciousness.

As Ju-Chao hung limply in Sarge's arms, Reva hurried across the clearing. She struck Sarge sharply across the face. "You leave him alone. He never hurt you. You leave him alone." Sarge released his grip to let the limp body fall into Reva's comforting arms. Cradling his head in her lap, she mothered him and cooed to him.

Sarge turned to see Louis bearing down on Youngman. He swung both arms and knocked Youngman to the ground. "Real smart, you fucking punk kid. Leaving an arsenal within reach of that wormeater." Louis might have continued to pummel Youngman had Sarge not intervened.

Louis never knew what hit him, but when he recovered less than a half-minute later, he saw Sarge standing over him and quickly deduced what had happened. Sarge glared down at him. "You ever heard of poetic justice, Louie?"

Louis sat up and rubbed his jaw, his stomach, his ribs, his knees. Had a steamroller passed over him? "What the hell're you talking—?" Suddenly, it was clear. "Yeah, yeah, poetic justice. I can hear him laughing now."

"Who's laughing?"

"The poet. The poet is laughing. Li Po. Poetic justice . . . listen to him laugh."

And Louis laughed.

He had never laughed like that before, and it quickly caught the attention of everyone.

A chortle . . . a titter . . . a chuckle . . . a roar . . . a howl

. . . Louis swiftly ran the full range of the human guffaw. He was splitting his head. He was laughing his guts out.

It was contagious.

Because, abruptly, the others laughed as well. It was a way of beguiling the present, and giving hope to the future. It was a way of seeing the folly of what was happening, of sharing in the discovery of hilarity as a means of warding off the threat of death. It was a laughter of hysteria and mirth, of cackling and tittering, of convulsion and titillation.

Not even Sarge could restrain himself as the social phenomenon of group laughter swept across *Chun Hsien Ku*.

Ju-Chao, whose wound throbbed again, regained consciousness and joined in the spirit of the laughter. The language barrier did not intervene, the punchline was universal. The infectious howls clutched at his fancy and grabbed his comedic inclination. He was so wracked with laughter that his legs kicked the ground.

After five full minutes Louis recomposed himself. The others followed suit. As his merriment died, so did theirs. There was a period of silence as they pondered what had happened and wondered how they had found humor in anything at *Chun Hsien Ku*. The grimness gradually returned.

"I don't understand it. What the hell was all that about?" asked Louis.

Li Ming answered. "It is customary for soldiers-of-fortune or for men of the battlefield to laugh when irony intervenes. We live in a land where irony is always at work."

Louis looked at Reva, who was coddling Ju-Chao. "I don't think I like this irony. It's playing tricks on me." Angrily, he struck his fist against one of the casks. A few remaining drops of wine sloshed through a bullet hole near the bottom.

"Hey, look at this!"

Youngman's helmet overflowed with wine. Careful not to spill its contents as he showed it to the others, he said, "My helmet caught some of the wine."

Louis perked up. "Careful with that, kid. Maybe we gotta enough there to analyze . . ."

"It is a sign," said Li Ming, staring down into the wine.

"What kind of sign, Li Ming?" asked Youngman.

"A sign of the Eight Treasures of the Grape. We have been granted the privilege to drink the Eight Treasures of the Grape. It is the way of Buddha to tell us He is not angry for spilling His treasure."

"Angry? At us? Hell, we didn't spill it. One of His own boys did." Louis reached for the helmet. "Give it to me, kid. You don't wanna drink that. We might create that hybrid grape yet."

"You keep your hands off that helmet," threatened Sarge. "After all the trouble you've put us through, we're all gonna try a sampling of this Wine of Immortality." Sarge turned to look at Li Ming. "Buddha ain't mad, huh?"

She shook her head. "It is Buddha's way of preparing us."

"Preparing us for what?"

"Death."

"Hey, I'm not so thirsty," said Charlie Brown.

"That is one thing most of us cannot avoid. Most of us," The Old German spoke to Charlie Brown. "It is inevitable—usually."

Li Ming continued: "For he who drinks the Wine of Immortality will go before the spirit of Meng-po, who rules over the Hall of Oblivion. And Meng-po will prepare you for the next life after he has shown you the inner truth of your soul."

"Folk tale," countered Louis.

"A legend is not always folk tale," The Old German said sagaciously. "Always there is a glimmer of truth behind it. I should think the legend of *Bot Bon Jui* would have taught you that."

"Some guys never learn," added Sarge.

Youngman offered the helmet to Louis. "Go ahead, Louie. You wanted *Bot Bon Jui* so badly. Drink."

"Profit down by gullet." Louis stared into the wine and drank. Youngman passed the helmet to Li Ming, who also drank and passed the helmet to Sarge, who drank; and Youngman, and Charlie Brown, and The Old German. Only Reva refused to drink. She rocked Ju-Chao and hummed a lullaby to him.

When he was finished, The Old German handed the helmet back to Youngman. He plopped it on his head. Narrow purple rivulets streaked down the sides of his face.

The Old German smacked his lips. "Salty taste. I think your chin strap was sweaty when it fell into the wine."

"Christ, I didn't taste anything."

"Yeah, it did seem flat."

"Maybe it lost its kick a few dynasties back."

"If you sat around in a barrel for a few thousand years, you might not have much to offer."

"Something this legendary oughta have some sting."

"It is said that that which has the sharpest kick does not always have the sharpest bite."

"Maybe Greek wine is better than I gave it credit."

"Shove your Greek wine."

"Well, I sure as hell didn't see that Meng-po character anywhere."

"Someone's gotta watch the hall."

Li Ming redirected the conversation. "It is also customary for soldiers-of-fortune, for men of the battlefield, to speak of what is going to happen to them next."

"Yeah," agreed Sarge, belching from the wine, "Corps tradition after a campaign. We all light up, lean back and talk."

So they all took comfortable positions near the steps of the ammunition depot, lit cigarettes, and leaned back.

Suddenly, the cigarettes fell out of their mouths and rolled to the ground. No word was spoken; each individual seemed oblivious to the others and stared straight ahead, as if in a hypnotic state.

A glazy film appeared over their eyes. They were in *Chun Hsien Ku,* but they were not in *Chun Hsien Ku.*

The Eight Treasures of the Grape was taking effect.

The part of them not at *Chun Hsien Ku* moved along a corridor. A swirling mist permeated the corridor and it permeated their essence, introducing a chill in each of them as cold as an Arctic wind. They moved onward without fear toward something waiting at the end of the corridor. Their destiny awaited them as they neared the end of the corridor and passed into a wider chamber.

They had entered the Hall of Oblivion.

61
Into the Hall of Oblivion

I.

When Sarge entered the Hall of Oblivion and stood before Meng-po, he spit in his eye.

The interview was at an end . . .

SNIPER'S DREAM

. . . July 2, 1863, had dawned hot and still. The quiet had not lasted for long—Meade's artillery had seen to that. The heat intensified as the day lengthened, until several of the men began complaining to Sarge. It was unusual to hear any bellyaching among snipers—they were generally a quiet bunch, who tended to shy away from the regular troops—but Sarge chalked it up to the heat and ignored them. Their orders finally came around noon from Longstreet's headquarters, as the special detachment of sharpshooters to which he was assigned was finishing a lunch of beans and hardtack.

The effects of the heat began to show on the men as soon as they moved out, and Sarge was angry that his men hadn't been provided with extra canteens. The dust they kicked up choked several of the men. It was like parading through a vacuum. Yet the men kept on moving, this time without bellyaching. When there was killing to be done, they moved harmoniously and efficiently.

Within an hour they reached Plum Rum Creek, which ran on a southerly course through the battleground south of the town of Gettysburg, Pennsylvania.

Sarge knew that whoever controlled the two knobs rising before them—called Big Round Top and Little Round Top—would have complete command of the battle, but already he saw tiny specks moving around near the top, and realized the Yankees had beaten him to the draw. He had to give General Meade credit—he was the fifth man to command the Army of the Potomac in less than a year, and he was proving more formidable than his predecessors with each day of battle. Longstreet's plan had been for the sniper detachment to dig in and hold the peaks, but now they would have to pick off the bastards up there with an intensive sniper barrage, securing the Round Tops later. What the Confederacy lacked in numbers it would make up for in the quality of its marksmen.

Lieutenant Griffith signaled for the pack mules to be unloaded. The twenty-six-pound Whitworth rifles were distributed one to every two men, with fifty rounds for each team. Sarge selected young Hogen as his reloader, as he worked with a calm efficiency that few of the others had demonstrated under fire.

"Sarge," said Lieutenant Griffith, "I want you to lead these men across the creek to those rocks. That'll make the range about two thousand yards to the Round Tops. Dig in good and deep before you open fire. If they direct any artillery down on us, I want my men protected."

"We've got a good day, sir," responded Sarge. "In about an hour the sun will be behind us, which means we'll be shadowed and they'll be illuminated. It's dry, which means our gunpowder won't be affected, and there's no wind to speak of. Means little correction will be necessary."

It took the detachment about thirty minutes to dig in. The lieutenant waited with the mules, scanning the peaks with his binoculars. At his side he kept one Whitworth, with a twenty-power telescope, and one reloader. It was traditional that he fire the first shot of all fusillades poured forth by his detachment.

When the men were all in position, Sarge and Hogen came back across Plum Rum Creek and joined the lieutenant.

"Everything's ready, sir."

Griffith viewed Little Round Top. "Something's going on up there ... I can't quite ... wait a minute. Yes, that's an artillery observer, I'm sure. He's signaling ... I think ... we've been spotted."

"We'd better get across the creek, sir, just in case they decide to send a few balls our way."

With Sarge and Hogen sharing the weight of the lieutenant's Whitworth, they stepped into Plum Rum Creek. Lieutenant Griffith and his reloader were just ahead of them, and had but a few feet to go before reaching the bank, when the first cannonball fell.

* * *

There was a sensation of wetness throughout his body as Sarge regained consciousness to find himself lying in the center of Plum Rum Creek. There was a ringing in his ears and pains in the muscles of his neck. A terrible headache left his temples throbbing. He had the feeling as he got to his feet that he was drunk. His vision was blurred and the creek seemed to rotate in a continuous circle. Nausea afflicted the pit of his stomach, and it was a while before he could take a step.

The body of Hogen, who still gripped the Whitworth rifle, was next to him. Fortunately it had fallen across his chest and remained out of the shallow water. A mark along Hogen's throat told Sarge at a glance it had been slit end to end by a shard of metal.

A different kind of wetness attracted Sarge's attention. His fingers leaped to his forehead; when he brought them away they were covered with blood. He too had been struck by a fragment, but luck was on his side, not Hogen's.

Some of his dizziness dissipated and he became aware of the battle once again. Additional shells had landed near the

299

creek and smoke completely obscured the surrounding terrain. The headless body of Lieutenant Griffith lay up on the bank. Next to him was the body of his reloader. Sarge thought he saw something with a rebel officer's fieldcap on it lying between two boulders near the water's edge, but he gave his attention to prying the Whitworth loose from Hogen's fingers. With thick gouts of smoke whirling around the banks of the creek, Sarge moved toward Griffith's obscenely positioned body. He suddenly realized he had no ammunition for the Whitworth and paused near the officer's corpse to remove a leather pouch of ammunition from his belt. Thrusting the pouch into his breast pocket, he worked his way through the smoke, moving the approximate distance to where he believed the sharpshooters to be dug in. There were familiar-looking rocks, but no sign of any of the men. He then realized that the smoke had blotted out all sign of the Round Tops. He would have to wait for it to clear before getting a good shot. He couldn't understand why none of the men were nearby—apparently the smoke was thicker than he realized, and they were dug in further ahead.

He decided to use the lull to load the Whitworth. He first poured in the powder, doing this with the precision that came after countless hours of firing and seeing bullets fall short or overshoot the target. He would require maximum effect, so he gave it all the powder the Whitworth would stand without blowing up in his face. Using the rifle's iron ramrod, he tamped the bullet down against the powder.

A giddiness overcame him again. To the back of his head, he applied a handkerchief, hoping it would staunch the flow of blood. The ringing was still in his ears. He tried to concentrate on the rifle to forget his own problems.

Under ideal conditions, the Whitworth rifle was used with a lengthy four-legged bench with built-in devices affording greater elevation. But here, in the roughest of terrain, Sarge would have to make use of natural support—a rock or a branch, something to absorb the twenty-six pounds of weight and give him one-hundred-percent steadiness on target. He adjusted the tubelike telescope to a range of two thousand yards, and waited.

The smoke began to clear. For the first time since the blast, he began to see again. None of the surrounding rocks seemed familiar, but more than one artillery barrage had altered a well-known landscape into chaos. He decided that a nearby flat rock would give him the support he needed, and he placed the heavy weapon across it. Pushing the stock to the ground, he realized he would never get the pitch he needed to snipe against the Round Tops, so he began scooping away the dirt where the butt fell. He continued to dig out the hole to increase his elevation. Finally, he had a hole large enough for not only the rifle butt but his own forearm as well.

The smoke continued to clear, and he saw a slope of rock. That would be Little Round Top. He elevated the Whitworth slowly, checking the slope through the telescope as he went, playing over every inch of terrain before moving on.

Near what he guessed to be the top, he saw the first figure. Even with the magnification, he distinguished very little about the man, but there was enough bulk to provide a target.

Sarge scrunched down behind the Whitworth, took a deep breath, and squeezed the trigger.

The rifle jerked effortlessly in his hands, then settled back into its former position. Through the scope, Sarge saw the man throwing up his arms in dismay and pitching headfirst over a boulder and down the slope. With his naked eye he watched the figure fall the rest of the way.

So much for that one.

He scanned the slope after he had reloaded. His second target was higher up. The second figure offered considerably more challenge, as he was crouched behind a pimple on the slope; only his head was visible. Sarge settled the crosshairs on that head, and squeezed.

The figure dropped out of sight, and for a moment Sarge feared he had missed. Then, in a corner of the telescopic sight, he caught a glimpse of something falling and saw that it was a body rolling toward the edge. Again, with his naked eye, he watched the figure falling earthward.

So much for that one.

For the next thirty minutes, Sarge kept a careful count—eight in all: eight bullets, eight corpses.

While searching for his ninth target he began to have the feeling that something was wrong.

The first thing that bothered him: he was the only man firing. What had happened to the rest of the sniper detachment? They should be firing directly in front of him, for there were ample targets scuttling around the slopes. This was the kind of day every sniper worth his weight in cartridges waited for and talked about. It was a sniper's dream. No wind, no dampness, no sun—

Sarge threw a hurried glance upward at the sun, aware now that it had been shining down on him for the past thirty minutes.

In front of him.

Not behind him.

He felt the nausea in his stomach again. The bitter taste of bile was in his mouth.

He tried to get his thoughts straight. He had seen Lieutenant Griffith's body on the bank, and he had instinctively assumed it was the same bank the officer had been headed toward when the first shell fell. But what if . . . what if the blast had thrown the lieutenant and his reloader backward, so their bodies landed on the opposite bank?

But wasn't that Little Rock Top in front of him? Didn't it . . .?

He plastered his eye against the telescopic sight and elevated the muzzle of the Whitworth until it reached the top of the peak. A flag flapped there. Sarge stared at it a full twenty seconds before he made out the design on it.

Stars and bars.

He knew then for certain he was looking at Observation Hill, a position his unit had dug into the previous evening, because next to Big Round Top and Little Round Top it was the highest piece of real estate surrounding Gettysburg.

Sarge kicked and beat at the Whitworth rifle until the telescopic sight fell off. Then he banged the barrel against a rock until it bent. He flung the rifle into a brushpatch and turned and started walking back toward Plum Rum Creek where, on the opposite bank, he knew he would find his de-

302

tachment of snipers dug in and firing in the direction God had intended.

II.

There was no need for Meng-po to speak to Youngman. He simply handed the private a typewriter, turned, and left.

WRITER'S DILEMMA

Youngman sat behind his typewriter, somewhere in the center of the swirling mist. The sheet of paper in the roller was as blank as his mind. He felt like an unsharpened pencil. He placed his fingers on the keys and typed:

Come on, wake up!

Instantly Youngman felt refreshed. To limber up his fingers, he typed:

The quick brown dog jumped over the lazy red fox.

A movement was caught by the corner of his eye. It was a brown dog, acting very quickly as it leaped over the back of a red-colored fox which acted lazily.

The animals scampered away into the mist when they were almost stepped on by a heavy combat boot. It took Youngman a moment to realize it was Major Higoshita, cradling a Nambus machine gun in his arms. Higoshita was snarling, as Youngman had imagined him snarling during the climactic scene in "Mindanao Marauders," and he gave every indication of firing at Youngman. Youngman's first instinct was to dive for cover, but he realized there was no protection, only the density of the mist, and what lay beyond it was as great an uncertainty as Higoshita. He considered throwing the typewriter, but that seemed rather dumb on second thought. Perhaps, however, the typewriter was a weapon in a different sense. He typed furiously:

Higoshita turned to face the other direction.

Higoshita turned to face the other direction. Youngman continued typing:

A stray .30 bullet struck Higoshita in the eye.

Higoshita collapsed with blood streaming down his face, although Youngman had failed to hear a shot. So, the typewriter was a weapon, after all . . .

He was going to need a weapon. Higoshita had only been the first. For those men and women he had created, even though they had never appeared in print, were coming to get him. Tired of wandering aimlessly somewhere between imagination and publication, they were ready to turn on their own God. Youngman had created them, but had failed to give them their proper place in literature, whether it be magazines, books, movies. Youngman had only brought them halfway to life, and now they roamed without purpose, trapped forever between illusion and reality.

Youngman shook his head and called himself a fool for thinking such thoughts. Yet somehow he knew it was the truth. Truth as only it could exist in the Hall of Oblivion.

Middleton was next. He wore a fatigue shirt and cartridge belt, but his head was covered with a slightly squashed fedora. His feet were covered with plaid house slippers. He wore pajamas. Caught, Youngman realized, between the world of the military and the civilian. While he stalked toward Youngman, Middleton coughed up phlegm and blood, which he disgustedly spit out into the swirling fog. "You bastard, Youngman," croaked Middleton. "You've let me live all this while with this thing in my chest. Now you're going to feel a pain in your chest." Youngman typed:

Middleton felt his heart burst.

Which is precisely what Middleton felt within a split second of Youngman's completing the word "burst." Middleton clutched his chest, opened his mouth to scream (but was unable to utter a sound) and fell face foward, his eyes staring at Youngman's boots.

Now others came out of the fog.

There was the Moro named Sariol . . . and another Moro . . . Jesus, what was his name? Hell, it didn't matter. He didn't have to remember names. Hell, he hadn't known the names of the dog and the fox, and they'd blinked into existence. He typed:

Sariol and the other Moro vanished into thin air.

They did.

But there were others.

Dave McKay, Army scout for General George Armstrong Custer, looked far meaner than Youngman had ever envisioned him. Grizzled beard; rotting, blackened teeth; a buckskin jacket laced with rawhide and spotted with blood. He carried a Winchester '76 over his shoulder. The instant he laid eyes on Youngman he unshouldered the rifle and prepared to fire. While he unshouldered, Youngman typed:

A dozen arrows struck McKay's body.

The arrows came out of nowhere, striking with their distinctive sound into McKay's chest, throat, stomach and legs. McKay pitched over backward, but by then Youngman's attention was riveted elsewhere.

Former General Parker Percell, the right-wing hunter who went mad in "Generation of Thunder."

Simpson, the helicopter pilot of "Over the Delta."

Eg Tak, the multilimbed extraterrestrial life form of "Gazza II," who led the *coup d'état* against the human race.

Terrence O'Hara, the World War II pilot who had been the last Marine to die on Tarawa.

Russell Simpson, the hero of "The Roof," who had been so gentle and hard-working; here he still had a hammer in his hand, only now the claws were turned so if Simpson had the opportunity to swing the tool, the claws would sink into Youngman's forehead.

Mendoza, the guitarist of "Ruthless," the sentimental greaser who had watched his wife die because he could not find a doctor. Revenge was unmistakable in that man's eyes. Death to the gringo.

There were too many others. Men of action and violence and death whom Youngman could no longer remember, neither by name nor by story. They encircled him now. Every remembered one was killed off with a frenzied line of prose, but two others took his place.

They came closer, each holding his specialty weapon. There were rifles, pistols, swords, knives, grenades, every conceivable weapon of destruction. Youngman asked himself which would be worst. Sarge had placed great emphasis on the bayonet, but cold steel had never appealed to him. In fact, none of the weapons had any particular appeal to him. He kept attempting to type, but his fingers were getting scrambled on the keys. He looked at his last line:

The private detective fell over frad.

Wrong, all wrong. He noticed that the private detective kept right on coming, although his feet kept striking against a strange ball of fur. He couldn't recall ever creating a "frad," but whatever it was, it lay at the private detective's feet.

When the bayonets and rifles and pistols were only inches from his body, Youngman realized there was only one way to escape death by any weapon. His typing was quick. When he finished, the sound of typing died with him.

Youngman ceased to exist.

III.

When Charlie Brown entered the Hall of Oblivion, he had expected, if anything, a pleasant welcome. Perhaps even a flourishing fanfare. The only thing that greeted him, however, was the scowl Meng-po wore.

"It has been said you are a warrior. At least, it has been said you wear the uniform of war and carry the weapons of war." It was a harsh voice, it was a soft voice. It was angry, glad, and indifferent. It carried a certain melody at the same time it fell flat.

"The 442nd," responded Charlie Brown, with the kind of eager tone one takes when one attempts to please another. "It's a traditional Nisei unit."

"And yet," resumed Meng-po, as if Charlie Brown had never spoken, "it has been also said you do not show the spirit for war."

"I'm here, fighting for my country." Charlie Brown put a little more defensiveness into his voice than he had intended, but was glad he had done so—perhaps it would be better, under the circumstances, to show some degree of aggression.

"In body, yes. That cannot be argued. It is the spirit which we are more concerned with, here in the Hall of Oblivion. You seem to know nothing of true tradition, the code of Bushido, the fearlessness of the Samurai warrior, the Imperial Rescript to Soldiers and Sailors, the arts of karate and kung-fu. You call yourself Japanese, and Japanese does indeed saunter through your veins, but it does not boil as it should. This thing called Nisei . . . I think it has made another kind of man out of you. One in love with meaningless sounds and images, sounds and images which seem to have no heritage, no roots in culture. It is necessary for us here to stamp out this misguidance, and give your spirit new purpose, new direction, new inspiration. It is time to teach you the meaning of Japanese honor and devotion to duty. It is time to cleanse your blood and have you take your place among your genuine brothers."

Although there had been no malice, only authority, in Meng-po's voice, Charlie Brown still felt a degree of humiliation and bowed his head—an act completely alien to him. A greenish fog swirled around him, and his fingers closed around a long thin piece of metal . . .

HERITAGE

. . . Charlie Brown pulled back on the stick and the four-bladed propeller chewed into a cloud's interior as the Shiden pushed its nose through a cumulus formation. The aircraft broke through the top of the cloud and Charlie Brown leveled off to find himself flying with four other Shidens. He noticed the wing commander, Kahushi, pointing below and he looked through the cracked Plexiglas of the cockpit to see a squadron of other planes flying on a parallel course far below them.

He realized, without knowing why, that their best chance now was to remain above those planes and hope they weren't detected until they reached their target. In a way Charlie Brown was annoyed because he could still see Meng-po's reprimanding face before him, and he would have liked to have done something to show that he wasn't spiritless. He remained in formation, also realizing that to

307

follow orders was the most important role of the soldier Such a thought had never crossed his mind before, but then he had never entered the Hall of Oblivion before.

Charlie Brown tossed a wave to Kahushi, who chose to keep his attention riveted on the section of sky ahead. Charlie Brown tried to remember the briefing; none of the details would come to him. For that matter, he had no idea where he was, or why. Had he fallen asleep when the flight plan was being laid out on the blackboard? How had he gotten into the plane? And how long had it been since he stood before Meng-po? Well, no matter. The flight commander, Kahushi, would give him the sign of attack when the time came . . . attack against what and whom?

For the next few minutes Charlie Brown busily checked altimeter, wind velocity, and other gauges, and kept his proper position in the formation. The shape of the stick still felt alien to his fingers, and yet whenever the squadron shifted position, he instinctively knew what to do.

It was only when he saw Kahushi motioning frantically toward the sea below that Charlie Brown tensed. Through occasional thin patches of clouds dispersed by a strong wind, he could see naval vessels in the process of turning. A whitish arc trailed behind each.

The other formations joined them. A batch of Hayabusa II's took up flying position off his left wing, while one Suisei dive bomber and an Akatombo stationed themselves to his right, on the other side of Kahushi's Shiden.

He rubbed his eyes when he saw the Akatombo, a crude Army primary trainer in which raw flying cadets were trained, and the buck-toothed boy who sat in its cockpit Charlie Brown estimated he was no older than fifteen. The flying chart balanced on his knee clattered to the floor of the cockpit.

Kahushi pushed open his cockpit, and the wind whipped a length of white scarf wrapped around his neck. All the other fliers followed suit, as did Charlie Brown, who until this moment had not been aware of the white scarf around his neck. As it billowed behind him in the wind, he thought of the pilots of World War I and how scarves had been a major ingredient in their wardrobe.

In the flash of a second, he realized this was tradition of another sort.

Hachimaki.

The sacred scarf which symbolized but one thing.

Kamikaze!

As the other aircraft dipped to attack the U.S. warships below, Charlie Brown heard his mind screaming. It told him to turn the Shiden around and fly away from the streams of tracers and airbursts which filled the sky before and below him. Instead, his hand pushed the stick down and he felt the Shiden begin to descend.

He picked his target—a heavy cruiser. Charlie Brown wanted to feel fear, for ahead he discerned the clusters of airbursts thrown up by the twin 40-mm. guns, and knew he would be flying through that maelstrom of shrapnel in only a few more seconds. He felt only a deep-rooted sense of loyalty.

Charlie Brown went into a deep vertical dive. He was only five hundred yards from the warship when he realized he had found his true heritage.

IV.

TWILIGHT OF THE PAGAN GODS

As a member of the SS, and as one of the two thousand men SS Oberführer Mohnke had handpicked to defend the Chancellery, The Young German had vowed to fight to the death. When a 152-mm. shell from a self-propelled Russian gun blew Sergeant Kleinz into several well-shredded pieces, he made another vow to himself: to stop any additional killing as quickly as possible.

The Young German stared at the smoking hand which lay in a bed of tulips, then at the rhododendrons and lilacs, which had been in a state of burgeoning before booted feet and falling fragments had crushed them and the serenity of the Tiergarten. Yes, the time had come to do something.

The Young German checked his Schmeisser, assuring himself it was loaded, and hurried past the Zoological

Garden, inhabited now only by carcasses and shattered cages. Yes, the time had come to do something.

The time had come to put an end to the man responsible for the *Götterdämmerung* which was befalling Berlin, and which had befallen The Young German and millions of his comrades on the Eastern Front.

He would murder Adolf Hitler in his *Führerbunker*. Only then would the Russian assault be stopped. Only then would the German people stop dying in the streets and alleys of Berlin, or drowning in the sewers of the River Spree, or hiding like rats in cellars or subways. Only then would Berlin stop burning.

Through the half-demolished grove of trees marking the end of the two-and-a-half-mile long urban park, The Young German made out the complex of buildings which had once been the heart of Europe but which were now gutted tombs—Göring's State Opera House, the Imperial Cathedral, the Kaiser's Old Palace, the Reichstag, the Propaganda Ministry, the many ministries of other nations, none of which had been spared by the American bombers months ago, and which had been gutted and bombed again by the Russians pressing in from the east. The Young German was interested in only one burned-out hulk: the Reich Chancellery.

Earlier, on a warm day in the spring of 1941, as he enjoyed his last hours of leave in Berlin before shipping out with the Gross Deutschland, Siebzehntes Bataillon for the Russian Front, he had spent the afternoon in the Kurfuerstendamm, enjoying its theaters, restaurants and sidewalk cafés before moving on to the zoo and the Tiergarten. He had decided then it was one of the most beautifully landscaped areas he had ever seen. He had strolled leisurely past the Reich Chancellery, amazed at the number of staff cars that constantly pulled up to, and away from, the main entrance.

Now the landscape was drastically altered. Now a constant stream of artillery shells fell in and around Wilhelmstrasse. There were no fellow strollers, and men hung from trees and lamp posts and corpses sprawled forgotten in gutters. Buildings had become hollow mausoleums, their paneless windows like questioning, frightened

310

eyes. Anyone seen leaving an area of action became suspect, at once, in the eyes of the SS officers under Mohnke's command, and once under suspicion they were escorted to the nearest point which could serve as a yardarm. It was, therefore, not advisable to be caught alone, without authorization. Still, The Young German kept moving, feeling that his mission far surpassed any personal danger.

He paused near a lamp post, from which a Wehrmacht private was hanging. The Young German guessed the soldier to be eighteen years of age—all the more reason, he decided, to reach the *Führerbunker* before one more hour of this accursed war passed.

He was in luck. A heavy barrage of mortar and artillery shells, fired almost in unison, began to fall on the antiaircraft batteries and mobile guns SS Oberführer Mohnke had positioned along Charlottenburger Chaussée, which marked the eastern boundary of the Tiergarten.

The Young German watched as the gun crews dived for their foxholes and bunkers. For the next minute anyway they were certain to remain there, waiting for the barrage to lift. In those few moments he might hurry across Voss Strass and emerge on Wilhelmstrasse. Once there, he would have the protection of the gutted buildings. There was the danger of stray shells falling in his vicinity, but at the moment no one in Berlin was safe from that.

He sprinted the distance to Voss, and was about to cross when he heard the sound of a plane over the din of the Russian barrage. It was a low-flying Stormovik, its wing machine guns blazing as the pilot veered slightly to bring The Young German into his line of fire.

Rows of explosions, chirping off the street, sped toward him. The Young German, realizing he was caught in the open, flung himself onto the surface of the street. The shells flew past him, missing by mere inches. He threw a curse at the disappearing Stormovik and again directed his attention on the Reich Chancellery.

The barrage on Charlottenburger Chaussée had lifted, and The Young German watched as the remnants of a flak battery scurried back to their gun emplacements. A small cluster of tanks chugged to life and clanked up the street, moving toward Russian positions. Mohnke's way of showing his disdain was to send a few men and equipment to the attack. Let the Russkies think German might to be as strong as ever.

A staff car sped along Wilhelmstrasse, stopping in front of the Reich Chancellery long enough for an officer to get out. As the car sped away, the officer hurried past crumbling columns of granite and porphyry. The Young German noticed that, ironically, some of the giant crystal chandeliers which hung beneath the main entrance were undamaged. No pieces of shrapnel pierced the swastika flag which drooped from a masthead. On one of the walls, someone had scrawled in black paint: "Every German will defend his capital! The Red Hordes will be stopped!"

The Young German followed the officer through the ruins until he came to a quadrangular opening—the Chancellery Garden. Two SS men, wearing form-fitting black uniforms, well-polished black boots and black armbands inscribed in silver with the letters A.H., stood guard with submachine guns near a boxlike concrete enclosure. The Young German saw steps leading downward within the enclosure. This was it—the underground bunker.

When a squadron of Russian fighter planes streaked overhead to strafe and rocket the flak batteries along Charlottenburger Chaussée, he decided to act.

Both guards stiffened as he fired. Their bodies danced with the impact of bullets. One pitched headfirst into a flowerbed and lay still. The other clutched his chest, turned to give The Young German a blank stare, and crumbled at the head of the stairs. He dragged both corpses into a nearby bomb crater, threw their weapons in after them, and started down the stairs.

It was fifty feet to the landing. The Young German found himself in a corridor twenty feet long by ten feet wide and lined with numerous paintings (they looked Italian—perhaps gifts from Benito Mussolini) and several benches and chairs, upholstered in fine leather. The empty corridor was not quiet.

From behind two huge oak-paneled doors straight ahead of the steps came an unmistakable voice: "... losses can never be too high; they sow the seeds of future greatness, just as the men of Stalingrad had but one duty to Germany—to be dead . . ." The familiar voice raged on in a tirade. Someone, obviously, was being reprimanded—perhaps it was the officer he followed through the ruins of the Chancellery.

The Young German carefully considered his next action. He could spray the oak doors, but there was no way of knowing if those on the other side would be in his line of fire. There was also the possibility the doors were so thick a bullet would not penetrate all the way. He couldn't stand in the corridor much longer. Someone would be bound to pass sooner or later. Footsteps came from the other side of the oak doors. The voice of rage grew louder as it approached the doors.

The Young German threw himself at the giant tapestry which hung near the stairway—no doubt used to close it off when Der Führer so wished it. He pressed himself against the wall, realizing there hadn't been a second to spare. He dared to glance out past the edge of the tapestry and saw two figures standing in the corridor. One of them was the officer he had followed. The other The Young German knew to be Adolf Hitler, even though his features were lost in the dimness of the corridor.

"*Das Schweinehund*! Everyone is betraying me. To have Göring turn against the Reich was one thing . . . but Himmler. That he should do this to me . . . to me! He is to be shot. On sight! I will shoot anyone who even mentions the word peace. Now go, General, find him. And make certain you photograph the pig after he's dead. I want proof that my orders are being carried out to the letter. . . . That he should do this to me . . . to me!"

The oaken doors slammed shut. The General turned immediately and started up the stairway. The Young German stepped out from behind the tapestry and walked to the doors. He pressed his ear against one of the panels. Silence. His fingers closed around one of the knobs. It turned effortlessly in his fingers.

The Young German shoved open the door, stepped inside, and closed it behind him. He whirled and leveled his Schmeisser.

Hitler was standing beside an elongated table on which several maps were scattered. So, this was his *Lagebe-*

sprechungs-Zimmer, his Situation-Conference Room, where recently so many earth-shaking decisions had been made. But Hitler was not, at the moment, studying maps, nor was he reevaluating old strategies. He was staring down at a series of photographs. In each, a man in military trousers and tunic, stripped of all epaulettes, was hanging by a meathook inserted through the back of the neck. A strand of wire was looped around the neck of each victim and knotted into place. He was muttering, almost under his breath: ". . . my generals, your reward for July twentieth . . ." He then turned to look at The Young German for the first time, but there was no surprise, not even a hint of fear, in his eyes. "So," he said with a shrug, "I have been betrayed at last by Himmler, the man to whom I would have entrusted my soul. He offered to surrender my forces—*my forces*—to the Western powers . . . what do you want, soldier?"

The Young German leveled his submachine gun at his Führer's stomach. He did not have to say why he was here. Hitler could now see the reason in his eyes.

"Who authorized you to enter?" Hitler turned to face The Young German. The barrel of the Schmeisser faltered for the first time in The Young German's military career. It was not quite the sight The Young German had expected. He had remembered the newsreels and the photographs, taken on the day of Nazi triumphs, on the day of conquest, when the great leader was at the peak of his power.

But now . . . if there was any magnetism in the dull, blue-gray eyes, it had long since been covered over by a film of exhaustion. The face was fat and puffy, and the complexion had taken on an ungodly yellowish tinge. His head hung to one side, as if it had a kink in it. When Der Führer moved, his body retained a permanent stoop. He shuffled, rather than walked toward The Young German. His entire body seemed to be perpetually shaken by a tremor, and he was forced to hold his left hand with his right. When he released it, the hand instantly leapt away in an arc. His knees quavered, as his voice had quavered. His black trousers and gray coat had lost their press.

On the Russian Front, The Young German had seen too

many pathetic sights not to respond to this one with a deep-rooted sense of sympathy.

"So," said Hitler, "I am finally betrayed, not only by Göring and Himmler, but by the common soldier. Stabbed in the back by the very man to whom I gave a cause."

A barrage of blockbusters struck the Chancellery, and the impact was felt within the deepest chambers of the *Führerbunker*. Sulphur, smoke and chalk dust drifted down from the ceiling. Instinctively, The Young German and Hitler fell to their knees. A streak of chalk appeared on Hitler's face, and for a moment he looked like a grown child who had gotten dirty while playing in a field.

In unison they rose slowly. A fresh tremor swept through Hitler; The Young German feared he would fall forward on his face, and almost made a movement to help him. But it wasn't necessary. Bracing himself with one hand on the conference table, Hitler managed to pull himself to his feet. One hand brushed past the holster at his side, and for a moment his attention was riveted on the 7.65-mm. Walther pistol it encased. Then Hitler snapped his heels together and assumed a rigid, at-attention position. His body no longer trembling, he stared directly into the eyes of The Young German. "Very well," he said softly, "you may go ahead and fire."

But The Young German did not fire. Out in the Tiergarten, when Sergeant Kleinz had been blown to pieces, he could have fired. But now he could not. Why is that? he asked himself.

Hitler waited.

The Young German searched his brain for the answer. Was it because Hitler had been his hero when he was a youth? Admittedly, The Young German had held him in reverence, even up to that moment on the Russian Front when he had found himself crossing the freezing waters of the Gniloy Tikich. It was only after returning to Germany, and seeing the desolation and holocaust war had wrought in his own land and to his own people, that The Young German had grown to despise Hitler. Why, now, with the moment at hand to bring an end to it all, did he hesitate?

As if in answer to that question, Hitler turned to face the table again. "So, you cannot fire."

The Young German was silent.

"Perhaps I understand why, but you do not." He began to unstack other piles of photographs, placing them in rows across the mahogany table. Cautiously, The Young German edged his way toward the table and, in carefully abbreviated glances, looked at the photos.

At first he thought he was seeing battlefield carnage pictures. Then he realized that all the bodies in the pictures were naked. Terribly emaciated, they were stacked like cordwood. The Young German dared to take longer glances when he realized Hitler truly wanted him to see these photographs, and that it wasn't some kind of trick.

Hitler tapped one photograph. "Belsen."

He tapped another. "Auschwitz."

And another. "Buchenwald."

The young German, despite the fact he had seen incredible mass carnage on the Eastern Front during the past three years, felt a sickness grow within him. These were not men. These were women and children, civilians, scrawny, pathetic human beings with looks on their faces he had never seen in all his combat experience.

Hitler patiently waited for him to absorb the content of the photos, then clicked his heels together, as if demanding attention.

"It is for this . . ." fingers tap tap tap on the photographs . . . "and much more, that you have fought these long years."

The Young German swallowed to clear his throat. "Four years," he said.

Hitler nodded, pleased. "Four years. Then you've fought right from the start. Perhaps you were Hitler Youth?"

The Young German nodded.

"Well then," said Hitler, "don't you see?"

"See what?"

"You're one of my children."

"Bilge."

"I've created you."

"More bilge."

"I've made you what you are."

"You've made me—"

"You're like a son to me."

"You're—"

"I am your father."

Silence. The Young German stared at the old man before him, and the barrel of the Schmeisser wavered for a second time.

"If it were not true, you would have fired long ago, but you hesitated. Deep within, you know what I say is true. I've made you the man that you are. I've made all of you into men who can take great pride in the accomplishments of National Socialism. The brave men of the Sixth Army Corps at Stalingrad are among the examples I honor the most. Without me to set the example, to construct the mold, they would have all died cowards instead of martyrs."

The Young German said nothing, for he was staring at the photographs spread across the surface of the table.

"Who," asked Hitler, "do you suppose performed these deeds?" Fingers tap tap tap on the photographs. "Who else but young men such as yourself. My men. My sons. . . . Now that you realize what you truly are . . ." Hitler walked to the far end of the room. At the foot of a map of Berlin, he pressed a button.

The Young German was still looking at the photographs when an orderly entered. "See that this young soldier is escorted back to the street," ordered Hitler. "He has the rest of the war to fight." Der Führer clicked his heels but the boots barely struck together. It was a grotesque parody. His right hand shot away from the left in its customary arc. His knees began to knock again.

With the orderly gripping his arm, The Young German was led toward the oaken doors. He paused to stare at Hitler one last time. There was a look of satisfaction on Der Führer's face. For perhaps the last time, thought The Young German, Hitler had given inspiration to one of his men.

The Young German fought valiantly for the next two days, and had just killed a trio of Russian commissars in hand-to-hand combat when he received word of Hitler's death. He put down his Schmeisser.

V.

"I have given myself," confessed Li Ming.

"You have given yourself without honor," replied Meng-po. His words thundered through the Hall of Oblivion.

Li Ming bowed her head, not so much out of shame as tradition.

"You will go forth and give yourself again." Meng-po pointed. Li Ming turned to face the fog that swirled and clutched at her thin ankles . . .

SERVICE FOR FOUR

. . . Li Ming found herself flat on her back. The four men stood stark naked around her, just as she was stark naked. Once she might have felt a twinge of unease, even embarrassment, to be in such a condition before strangers, but she had passed beyond such modesty long ago.

Now she did what was expected of her and arched her buttocks to take one of the men into her vagina. He humped her without any noticeable delay, finding an even tempo and maintaining it. She did her best to match his movements, which was not always easy under the circumstances. With each hand she reached up to encompass her palm around a stiffening penis. She began pushing the palms of her hands back and forth over the blood-flushed surfaces, seeking a tempo that matched the humping of the first man.

The fourth man stood over her, lowering his genitals toward her mouth. She automatically complied by widening her lips and accepting him. His angle was a bit precarious due to the fact he bumped into some of the other men, but somehow Li Ming managed. This was her line of work, and it was what she did best. She tongued the penis in her mouth between intervals of sucking, maintaining the tempo of her buttocks and the tempo of her palms.

The sperm came at once, drenching her from all directions. It dribbled from the corners of her mouth. It flew from the penises which her palms still grasped. One burst struck her squarely in the eye, the other blasted into her hair and neck. The humping man sighed and sperm flowed into her vagina. Some of it crept out and fell on the ground.

"I have given myself," confessed Li Ming.

"And you will give yourself again," came the booming voice of Meng-po. . . .

. . . Li Ming pulled herself up and glanced around. She lay on the sandy earth, still nude, surrounded by a clump of bushes half-obscured by the swirling fog. From faraway, she heard the sounds of war. No one was in sight. Machine-gun fire sounded, closer this time. Yells of men, voices moved in her direction. Li Ming wanted to get up off the ground, but couldn't. As hard as she tried, she couldn't move any of her limbs.

The cries of the men came nearer. Now they were just beyond the fringes of the fog. Then they were within the fog and among the bushes. Then . . .

The four men stepped out of the fog. They were bearded. Their eyes blazed with a cloudy red that spoke of utter desperation, and their uniforms hung on their scarecrow bodies with a peculiar drooping effect. They stared at the naked body of Li Ming, but the hunger in their eyes was not the hunger of lust.

"Jesus," said the tallest man, who must have been their leader, "do you have anything to eat?"

Another man stepped forward. His eyes were sunken, hollow. Wrinkled skin clung to his bony arms. "We . . . we haven't had anything in three days. They've been after us. Chasing us. Nothing in this godforsaken land to eat. Anywhere."

"Surely," said the third man, "you've got something."

The fourth man was equally desperate. "If you're hiding anything from us . . ."

Li Ming turned slightly, so that her supple breasts jiggled. It was a reminder to them that, indeed, she hid nothing.

"Oftentimes," she said, "the food of wisdom exceeds the food of the earth. I have nothing here. Only myself."

319

The fourth man sat down and wept.

"Jesus," said the tallest man, "we can't go on like this. If we don't find something soon, we'll all go crazy."

The second man sat down and wept with the fourth man.

The third man eyed Li Ming curiously and stepped forward. "Perhaps . . ." His eyes roved over the ample flesh of her body. He said no more.

The inflection in his voice had been understood by the tallest man. He eyed Li Ming curiously. "Perhaps . . ." He, too, said no more.

They contemplated while the second and fourth men wept.

The tallest man, his eyes gaunt from hunger, pulled a knife from its scabbard. "I think," he said slowly and deliberately, "I know where our next meal is coming from."

The heads of the second and fourth men popped up in unison.

The tallest man stepped toward Li Ming.

Li Ming squirmed and stretched her legs out before her. She leaned her weight back onto her arms and gave the four approaching men a seductive stare. She knew now why Meng-po had left her immobile—so she would not flee. She had no such intention, for becoming a meal was, in a philosophical way, quite appropriate in her case. Hadn't men looked upon her in a similar fashion since the day they had discovered her lithe body, and she had discovered her own desires and given as much of that body as she could? Was there not a phrase for one so accommodating and lovely? A phrase men had used over and over, time and again . . .

Eating stuff.

VI.

"They tell me you're a soldier."

"I'm an entertainer. BIE. Haven't fought a day in my life."

"Yet there is something in your blood."

"Nothing's in my blood but that damn wine of yours.

That's why I'm mucking around in this place, isn't it? Because of your goddamn Eight Treasures of the Grape."

"There's more than wine in your blood. There is the seed of the bloodthirsty cutthroat."

"I told you, I've never wielded a knife in my life."

"But others before you have wielded that knife."

"I don't know anything about it."

"You will . . . you will . . ."

CUTTHROATS

Louis Nikopolis and his men had marched halfway across Turkey. The conquering heroes reached a ravaged point of geography between the rail center at Eskishehr and the nationalist capital of Angora before they came face-to-face with Turkish fanaticism and resistance. That was on August 22, 1922.

On August 23, 1922, Louis Nikopolis and his men marched, in rout's disorder, in the opposite direction toward Smyrna, fighting for their lives every inch of the way and burning to the ground every prosperous city, every depressed hamlet, in Western Anatolia. In the process they murdered Turks by the hundreds of thousands.

Where Homer once sang, a chorus of machine guns riddled men to bits. Where the Caesars once gave birth to new empires, mothers were raped and slashed and their newborn and oldborn slaughtered. In the fields where Croesus grew rich, the soil grew richer with the fertilizer of decomposing corpses. The cities, citadels, and palaces created by Alexander the Great were uncreated by the Greeks, who turned them into charred ruins. St. Paul's churches were baptized by fire and christened to rubble. Grecian marble columns, shattered from their moorings by bombs, had been picked up by natives and used as decorations outside the doors of squalid mud huts. A Roman sarcophagus became nothing more than a vat into which goat milk was poured. Chaos and destruction were the new rulers of Turkey.

While a country wallowed in flame, Louis and his men

wallowed in blood. It was a form of wallowing the
seemed to enjoy—at least no one complained about h
profession. It was part of being Greek. The men fro
Crete were towering, dark figures who moved across tl
war-torn landscape with hulking steps. Those fro
Thessaly were calm, slow-moving, and meticulous in the
job of killing. The Macedoniâns were steady and reliabl
The men from Peloponnesus were clever and wily, alwa
suggesting new strategies and methods of murder. The me
from the mountain villages of Epirus were tall and blon
almost Nordic in appearance. *In toto* they were men fro
gray-stone Greek villages and cities whose ancestors ha
fought across Persia and Istanbul, through Berlin and Mo
cow, under the guise of fighting oppression and tyrann
They had transgressed onto Turkish soil to carry on tha
principle.

By early September, they had reached the outskirts c
Smyrna, a city destroyed block by block by the Greek
They were a battered, fleeing force that moved on she
momentum and a hatred for the Turks. The majority of tl
Greek invasion force had been annihilated by the vengef
Turkish army under Kemal's command. In no way had th
deterred Louis and his men from carrying on their origina
purpose: to burn and murder.

In a small clearing outside Smyrna, his sergeant, Ps
choyos, succeeded in rounding up several civilians—me
women, and children. The men were old, the younge
being sixty-two; the women were unarmed, and th
children were young enough to be classified as toddlers c
babes in arm.

Louis considered it an adequate quota for the day (th
total number of civilians was twenty-three) and ordere
his men to get busy. Svergos and Arbousis chose to us
their rifles, but Louis personally preferred the knife. He s
lected one of the old men, pressed him against a crumblin
stone wall and went to work with his *lonkgi,* a bayonet h
had sharpened with the attention he normally devoted t
his straight razor. With the dexterity and expertise tha
come from daily practice and instinct handed down fro
generation to generation, Louis sliced through the ol
322

nan's throat. It was the kind of death only a Turk, young or old, male or female, deserved.

The blade of the *lonkgi* worked its way through the outer layer of skin, piercing the hyoid bone, the thyroid cartilage, the ventricular fold, the vocal fold, the ring of cricoid and the tracheal rings. Part of the steel penetrated deep enough to pierce the arytenoid muscle, the larynx, the ventricle, and the cricoid cartilage. For Louis it was a routine job of throat-cutting, but by the standards of most it would have to be classified a work of art.

Svergos and Arbousis had already finished spraying their quota of Turks with excessive bursts of bullets. The remaining women were carried away behind the crumbling stone wall where some of the privates raped them. Louis stepped behind the wall and ran his fingers across his Adam's apple, giving the verbal order: "K-r-r-k." He was quickly obeyed.

They paused, as darkness fell, in the ruins of a mosque. An artillery barrage plastered the opposite side of Smyrna, illuminating in a pale orange-yellow glow the outlines of half-destroyed buildings. Even though the barrage shifted closer to their position, the men were too weary to worry. Louis selected a place in the center of his men, put his fieldpack in a puffed-up position under his head, and sprawled out, his body aching for sleep. He pulled his *lonkgi* from its sheath and placed his hand across his chest. Should there be any Turk infiltrators, he could defend himself within a split second. His weariness overtook him almost immediately, and Louis Nikopolis slept . . .

"Aera! Aera!"

Louis's men were attacking, fighting their way into the ranks of the Turkish army. The Turks swarmed around them, sometimes aimlessly, sometimes attacking one of his men with snarling eyes. A figure, with bayonet poised, lunged at Louis. Louis sidestepped the advance, realized his *lonkgi* was already locked in his fingers, and slashed upward at the soldier's throat. The Turk gurgled and went down. Others took his place, closing around Louis with the vengeance only a Turk can display so proudly in battle. Louis slashed out again . . . and again . . .

323

As Louis slept, caught somewhere between the attackin Turks and a semiconscious reality, he clutched at h throat, for he imagined a fly, or some insect, had flitte across it. His fingers closed around his Adam's apple. H felt a dampness, and in his dream no longer fought Turk Now he stood in front of a waterfall, but instead of flowin toward him, the water flowed away. Louis felt giddy ar wondered if he wasn't getting light-headed. He felt h throat again. Apparently, some of the foam from the t multuous water splashed onto his neck. He wiped it awa but there was more, which he also wiped away. The foa kept re-forming, so he stopped wiping his neck.

He felt his strength flowing from him and he almo plunged headfirst into the receding waters. He blinked h eyes, watching the water incredulously as it flowed bac over the ledge and disappeared. He fell backward the landing on his side but still able to stare at the sky, whic had grown suddenly dark. Louis decided to close his ey and rest a moment.

When he reopened his eyes, he was lying in the clearin of the demolished mosque. He felt relief. The whole thir had been a nightmare. He noticed his right hand was raise above his face, and he could barely discern the shape the *lonkgi*. Something dripped from the blade onto h chin. After an interval, something else dripped onto h forehead. He counted the next fifteen drops before he d cided to count no longer.

A new darkness descended on him. The stars in the sk spun as if he were aboard a merry-go-round. He started laugh because it was so ironic. His men had said it of hi many times when he swung his *lonkgi,* bringing it dow thrusting it up, swinging it left, lunging it right. It had b come a common phrase in tribute to Louis's skill. He w; the master, the king. He was so damn good . . .

. . . he could do it in his sleep.

62
Reveille

They were still seated on the ground. The cigarettes were burnt to stubs within their fingers and their eyes still stared vacantly into space.

Sarge's features hardened as he came out of his reverie. "Awright, you mothers! On your feet! Fall in!" His harsh voice broke the reveries of the others. They quickly fell to, forming a well-dressed military rank. Li Ming stood rigidly next to Youngman. Sarge slowly paced back and forth before them, gazing into each face with steely fury as he passed it.

"What the hell is going on here? Some kind of Teahouse Syndrome? Sit around and talk, my ass! From now on there's only one thing we care about. That's dogfacing. Belly-crawling. Gut-sticking and bullet-ripping. Chink Stink, that's what we're here to create. We're men ..." Sarge paused before Li Ming "... and women conceived for war. Our mothers and fathers fornicated for only one reason: so we'd exist to kill the enemy. So we could spill his guts on his own doorstep. And anyone who tells you otherwise is full of unmitigated shit."

"*They're coming*!" Reva pointed in the direction of the hills which fronted the ammunition depot.

They headed for the top level of the depot, from where they could observe the slopes.

And the slopes were alive with people—Chinese people. All were headed for *Chun Hsien Ku.*

"Jesus, look at that."

"Swarming . . ."

"Like ants."

"They're coming for us," said Youngman, swallowing.

"The hell!" answered Sarge. "They're coming for something to eat. This is a restaurant, remember?" His eyes narrowed. "That's some congregation we got, boys."

Louis squinted with him. "Looks like a platoon."

Charlie Brown: "That's no platoon. More like a company."

The Old German: "A company? Don't you know a mobilized grenadier battalion when you see it?"

Youngman: "Battalion? That's a regiment."

"Regiment, my ass," finalized Sarge. "That's an entire fucking army. And it's hungry. And in a minute its appetite is gonna change from food to us."

Sarge let out a cry denoting the ultimate satisfaction of the professional soldier.

The men fell in again. Sarge paced rapidly before them again . . . back and forth . . . back and forth . . .

"Men, this is what we've been waiting for. All our training, years of fighting. Now it's going to pay off. This is it. The attack, the assault, the spearhead, the blitzkrieg, the ambush, the bombardment, the sally, the siege, the skirmish, the storm, the strike, the charge, the raid, the dawn surprise, the feint, the foray, the advance, the clash, the combat. It is all these things and more, men. This is the Battle Royal. This is the Big One."

This time, they all let out the cry.

63

Squad C-323, or What's Left of It, Closes to the Attack

Sometime during the night Sergeant Joe Young had deserted. He had taken only his knapsack, leaving behind his few remaining cans of food. The NCO had learned something while under King Kong's command, anyway. Young would have to forage for food along the way (no easy task in country like this), but when they met again, neither would find it in his heart to fight.

So, friendship would be restored and personal wishes fulfilled. It had been clever planning on Young's part.

King Kong and Bonzo ate Young's food to fortify themselves for the arduous march ahead. Belching loudly, they started off at dawn. They clearly smelled the trail Sergeant Joe Young had left, but then he had branched off back toward the main lines, and within five minutes they had lost all traces of his scent. King Kong was forced to urge Bonzo onward, for he could see that even in such a loyal follower there was a degree of hesitation. Seeing a comrade desert, whatever the reason, gave one ideas one might not otherwise ever have.

After a short distance Bonzo's step livened, and he took on his old venturesome spirit. King Kong did not worry anymore about him. Sergeant Young had been forgotten for the moment and they could concentrate on their mission.

They hurried the entire morning, pausing at one point to urinate at a gravesite. By noon, they knew they had almost caught up with the Man Up the Pole—the scent had had little time to dissipate. King Kong immediately realized their troubles were only beginning.

They reached a place where the spoor of the enemy was so strong that Bonzo gagged on his own saliva. Even King Kong had to turn his head in a new direction to avoid the unbearable whiff that seemed to attack every smelling facility in his body.

The number of enemy required to produce such a smell staggered the imagination of King Kong. Bonzo, out of desperation, placed his nose between his feet and rubbed its surface, as if to erase whatever was passing into it. It helped a little, but Bonzo was acting delirious, as if a female in heat stood a few feet away.

Unable to take it any longer, they bounded away from the source of the smell and took up a position on a hilltop. Here the man odor was strong, but at least it did not turn their stomachs so severely. And they could think. And plan.

From their new position, they saw a structure in the center of a field, and in the hills fronting this structure, they saw the enemy. Both of them chittered. They had never even imagined the enemy could exist in such large quantities. King Kong was reminded of the fleas he had often picked off Bonzo. There had always been plenty, but nothing like those hillsides. Humans were worse than fleas. There could be no other explanation.

They heard the unified, five-voice battle cry echoing from the structure. One of the voices carried with it a smell of graphite, gunpowder, and the metal of weapons. Bonzo recognized it as quickly as King Kong.

Both of them pawed the ground. Their bloodlust rose. King Kong chittered the signal to get ready. The structure in the field was their objective.

The moment of revenge was at hand.

64
Attack

They all let out the cry.

The Chinese soldiers pouring down the hillsides which fronted *Chun Hsien Ku* froze in place and stared at the fortification. Each felt a peculiar chill. It was a kind of war cry they had never heard before. It expressed determination, and it promised death in the same ring. The Chinese saw the figures of men standing in the rusted-out emplacements. There were only five, yet those five might as well have been an army, so powerful was the effect of their unified battle cry.

The Chinese paused, pondered, and regrouped. Instead of coming to chow, they now came to battle.

"Lock and load," ordered Sarge.

The Old German did so, then checked his bayonet to make certain its tip was well-honed. "For you, Chinaman," he muttered, " '*Meine Ehre Heisst Treue.*' " Once again he experienced the joy of battle, and he prayed that if anyone was to survive, it would not be him.

Youngman was busy sorting the bundle of rifles and the various ammunition that went with each. Li Ming assisted him. He took time to show her how each weapon was loaded. She watched silently, then turned her attention to the next rifle.

Louis was busy with his *trabezi,* placing a well-starched napery across its top as if he were preparing it for customers. He put the table in one of the gun emplacements and piled rifle ammunition and grenades on its surface. He patted it gently. Reva hurried up to him. "We've got to get out of here, Louie. We'll be killed if we stay." Louis stood upright, as if at attention. On his face was an honorable expression which frightened Reva. She had never seen it on his face before, but it did not slow down her argument. "Please, Louie, we've got to—" She stopped, for she could see by the unwavering determination in his face that he wasn't listening to her.

"Fight with us, Reva," he urged. "Stay and do battle."

Reva threw up her arms and hurried back to the truck and Ju-Chao. Youngman and Li Ming watched her with interest. "It is the way of Buddha," Li Ming said in explanation. "It was destined that you should stand and fight those men who come; it was ordained within the Hall of Oblivion. And, because she was not a guest of Meng-po, it was destined that she should turn and run."

"And you?" asked Youngman. "What's your destiny?"

"By your side. Your fate will be my fate."

"You can reload for me when those brothers of yours start rushing us. Don't think about anything else but reloading."

"My world will become the cartridge and the firing pin, and the bolt, and the sliding mechanism, and the bandolier. There will be nothing else."

Charlie Brown reappeared on the top level of the depot, positioning the vidpack atop one of the walls. He turned it on.

John Wayne appeared, fighting his way through a beleaguered city at the head of a guerrilla column.

"Cap'n, there's an old Nip tank in that grove." ... *"Well, what're you waiting for, Johnson? Blow it to hell out of there."*

Charlie Brown positioned his transistor inside a gun emplacement and turned the volume to maximum.

"Andy, I done told you to quit messin' 'round with that there dress. Give it to me there before ... Oh Andy, now

330

look what I has done. I's gone and spilled that whole bottle of ink all over Sapphire's new dress. Oh, woe's me."

"You is really gonna catch it now, Kingfish."

"We took care of that Nip tank, Cap'n, but scouts report a Jap relief column moving in from the west." . . . *"Well, Johnson, blow that to hell, too."*

Finished with his table, Louis made a few last adjustments to his *Foustenala*. Now he was ready for anything.

"Loaded?" Sarge slammed the mechanism of his M-31.

"Loaded." It was four voices in one.

As one they moved to the edge of the depot wall and saw that the Chinese had regrouped and were now ready to advance.

"For God's sake," cried Reva, desperately. "Let's get out of here, Louie."

Louis beckoned to her. "Come, Reva. Forget all that out there. Join with us and participate in the destiny of the Eight Treasures of the Grape."

Reva backed away slowly, until she bumped into the prostrate form of Ju-Chao. He groaned. "You're crazy," she cried. "Insane. Nuts."

The faraway gleam returned to Sarge's eyes. "Nuts . . . yes, nuts . . . nuts! You tell General von Rundstedt he can't take the Battered Bastards. No matter how many SS turdheads he sends against Bastogne. Half the M-1s in this outfit won't fire until someone pisses on them, but you can't take the Battered Bastards. You tell von Rundstedt the 101st has just begun to set its eagles screaming."

"Got to get away," vowed Reva. "Madhouse . . . got to get away." She heard Ju-Chao moan again, and saw him lying there helplessly, and unintelligibly pleading for water. "At least you'll go with me," she told him. "At least you have sense enough."

It was a struggle, but she finally got Ju-Chao into the back of the truck. Every movement provoked a groan, but when his head settled into a sleeping bag, a look of contentment fell over him; and he went to sleep. Reva ran a soothing hand along his cheeks. She would have to change his bandage, she realized, but first she wanted to put a few miles between her and these madmen.

As she hurried around to the front of the truck, she saw

the Chinese advancing. She couldn't restrain one last plea. "You'll be killed, Louie. Killed for nothing."

Louis turned with the glorious smile still on his face. "In war there is never futility, Reva. I swear to you. There is only honor, glory, and patriotic sacrifice. Come, join us, Reva. Stand beside these brave warriors, these gallant men, these noble knights, these—"

"Fuckers," interjected Reva. "You're all motherfuckers."

She got into the cab of the truck, gunned the engine, and was off in a cloud of dust.

"Women and children are safely gone," said Louis, watching the truck move quickly along the road.

". . . Andy, if Sapphire finds out I done ruined her dress for tonight's dance, I is gonna be mincemeat." . . . "You is already mincemeat in that brain of yours, Kingfish."

"We hold the depot," said The Old German. *"Sieg Heil."*

"Here they come," said Louis.

The Chinese advanced cautiously toward the depot.

"That'll be cannon fodder to feel us out," explained Sarge. "Find out how many guns we have. Check our firepower. Youngman, Li Ming . . . the left flank. Louie, you stick with me. We'll cover the area to the front. Brown, Krauthead, I want you off to the right. To the right." They started to scatter. "And Youngman."

Youngman turned, clutching several of the rifles in an armload.

"Now. Now you're a hero."

"We took care of that relief column, Cap'n, but the boys're shot up pretty bad. We need a rest." . . . "I'll tell 'em when to rest. Now we still got a war to win. So everyone saddles up."

The first shot was fired at one hundred yards and pierced the eye of an eighteen-year-old scout. He crumpled without crying out. Other advance scouts also went down in the first barrage of fire from the depot. The main body of the Chinese platoon broke into a fast run, trying to cover the remaining distance to the wall as quickly as possible. The fire increased. It was a light fire, and an accurate one; every shot seemed to find a target.

"Sighted fishhead—killed same," cried Sarge, seeing his first shot strike home. He carefully aimed and brought

down a second running figure, and a third, and a fourth
. . .

A small body of the advancing Chinese platoon splintered off from the main force and moved toward a grove of trees about fifty yards distant from the depot.

"They're trying to work their way into those trees," shouted Louis. "The bastards want to do some sniping."

"Pick those guys off," Sarge yelled at The Old German and Charlie Brown.

"*Mein Liebling*," cooed The Old German as he patted his Schmeisser. "My little darling." He was quick, he was accurate. Deadly accurate. None of the Chinese reached the grove.

That faraway gleam came into Sarge's eyes again. "The trees . . . they won't take the trees . . . they won't take the woods." Sarge placed his M-31 on the edge of the wall and unfastened one of the holsters on his chest. He drew out an Army-style .45, which had been one of the first ever manufactured. He stood upright on the wall, which would have provided an excellent target for the Chinese had they not been running at top speed to reach the depot. A few tried some snap shots, but they went wide or tore harmlessly at the cement.

"We'll hold the woods," cried Sarge, waving the .45. "There aren't two Germans in existence who could fuck good enough to produce a man capable of taking Belleau Wood. Come on! Come on and try to take the Wood. Try to take the Marne, the Somme, the Fields of Flanders. These are doughboys here, Hun. You can't stop a Devil Dog, you can't beat back a true-blooded American isolationist. You bet, Hun. You've lost your blitz, Fritz. The Yank is here to stay. Johnny Yank is here . . ." His voice trailed off, as though he had suddenly lost his enthusiasm. It was only a momentary pause. He came down off the wall, oblivious to several pieces of lead whizzing through the air. "Yank . . . Johnny Yank . . ." Sarge slid the .45 back into its holster. "I can see them now. Yanks! Yanks tryin' to come over the wall. General Grant's bootlickers. Yankee ying-yangs." Another holster popped open and Sarge slid out a double-action Colt .44. He plinked off three fast shots, knocking down three more Chinese. The last one was knocked backward several feet and died with his feet still kicking pathetically.

"George Kingfish Stevens, what has you done to my dress?" ... *"Sapphire, darlin', I's been wantin' to explain 'bout that. Ya see, me 'n' Andy, we—"*

The voice of George Kingfish Stevens cut off as Charlie Brown inserted the transistor plug into his ear and readjusted the controls for his personal listening pleasure. Ah, that was better. He picked off a running figure. This one so close he could make out the mole on the young man's face. Yes, that was much better sound. Much better. Now the sound filled him, which gave it an intimate quality. The others probably hadn't been listening anyway. So goddamn wrapped up in their shooting. He ducked his head as a grenade blast erupted near the wall.

Charlie Brown almost didn't hear The Old German grunt over the din of battle. The old-timer clutched at his head and staggered around the rusty gun emplacement like a berserk Gestapo officer in "Secret File—World War II" or like one of those pleasant young men in the psychiatric dramas of the 1940s who went crazy and had to be put away in a padded cell.

Charlie Brown took time out from firing to watch The Old German as he plunged over the side of the gun emplacement and fell between two of the empty wine barrels. He then returned his attention to the open field.

"Sarge! Over there!"

A "dead" trooper sprang up and rushed the wall, firing as he ran. Slugs chirped the edge of the parapet. The Chinese soldier wove an erratic pattern through the field, making himself an evasive target which Louis could not hit.

"And we won't be back until it's finished . . . *over there.*"

Sarge's Colt .44 went back into its holster and the .45 was in his hands again. Just in time to blast the running soldier in the head as he reached the wall. The powerful slug made a mess, but the body fell down out of sight before anyone had time to study it. "Drive the Hun bastard all the way back to Berlin, boys. Then Jerry'll think twice before starting another fracas. Let's unite and blitz that Fritz."

"On the wall, Sarge. On the wall."

"Wall . . . the stone . . . wall." Sarge reholstered the .45 and retrieved his six-shooter. He blasted the individual Louis had pointed out to him.

"You lily-livered Northerners. Just try to lay your ornery mitts on the Stars and Bars. Keep them Stars and Bars aflappin', boys. Ain't no whizzin' Minnie balls gonna stop this jinglin' Johnny Reb. Grape cannister shot don't mean nothin' to this hide. Long live Robert E. Lee, Jefferson Davis and General Wallace."

The six-shooter clicked empty.

"Thunderation, Bob. I do declare. I think the Yankees are turning."

Three of the Chinese had turned, the survivors of the first platoon to attack *Chun Hsien Ku.* They were met by a fresh unit of troops pouring toward the depot. This time there could be no doubt of the outcome.

"Cap'n, we got troubles. An entire division of Nips has retaken the town." . . . *"Well, re-retake the town, Johnson, What're you waiting for?"* . . . *"But we're down to only ten men, Cap'n. And they're beat."* . . . *"Nobody's beat until they're dead in my outfit. Now you tell the men to saddle—"*

The bullet struck John Wayne directly between the eyes. He exploded in a shower of broken glass, fractured tubes, and warped wiring. The vidpack crashed to the cement, smoked, and never spoke again.

Cymbals and bugles sounded, inspiring the fresh unit to the attack.

"I do declare, boys, I do think I hear Deguello." The six-shooter was returned to its casement. And out came a .36-caliber percussion single-action revolver, Model 1836. "Deguello, the assassin song of no quarter. It'll be tooth-and-nail from here on, boys."

Sarge then saw the fresh horde moving across the field. Louis and the others picked off the lead troops. Judging from sheer numbers, it was apparent who was going to win this fight. "I do declare again, boys. They're going to rush us. Santa Anna is puttin' everything into this charge. Remember the Alamo!"

Louis fired furiously now, as did the others. The return fire grew more accurate. Slugs chirped endlessly around Sarge. Metal twice ripped through the sleeves of his shirt. A ricochet whined off the wall. The impact chipped the cement and drove pieces into Louis's face. As he wiped the blood away: "There's too many of them, Sarge. Too many of them moving off that damn hill. It's even better than we expected. Too many . . ."

"The Hill," muttered Sarge. "The Hill . . ."

He put away the Model 1836 and yanked out the final pistol on his chest. It was a .50-caliber flintlock dueling pistol, with an octagonal barrel, a saw-handled butt, and a triggerguard spur.

"The Hill . . . of course we can hold the hill. We must hold Breed's Hill. It's the key to Boston Harbor. Indeed, the entire Charlestown Cape must be protected." Sarge began pacing again, holding the ancient pistol above his head. "I realize most of you men are farmers, merchants, Yankee Doodle upstarts—you come from Massachusetts, New Hampshire, Rhode Island, and Connecticut. But we can hold. We *must* hold."

He turned to face the oncoming horde. "Secure firelocks, men, and aim for their waistbands. Don't shoot until you've begun to fight, Gridley, and pass a flask of powder. For he who runs away lives to fight another day but is a coward and a live coward is not a dead hero and war is hell I assure you gentlemen war is hell bear in mind that old soldiers never die they just pass gas praise the Lord and pass the musketballs full speed ahead. This day will go down in history, just as did the Alamo, New Orleans and Chicago. We shall overcome."

The bodies piled up before Youngman's position, for he had the advantage of Li Ming reloading each weapon. That way, he could hurry from weapon to weapon, losing no time between volleys.

Youngman's favorite was the Marlin model 336 .44 magnum, for its 4X scope enabled him to pick off with considerable ease the Chinese rushing directly toward him. He merely had to swing the crosshairs from massive shape to massive shape, squeezing off the trigger gently. Each of the five clips of ammunition found its mark.

The 1891 Mauser with its bolt action was far less effective. He only used it when Li Ming had not managed to load any of the others. The ammunition for the Mauser was soon gone, but Youngman was just as glad.

The 6.5 Mannlicher-Carcano created the most devastating effect on the Chinese, for its mushrooming slugs made terrible wounds. The sight of these wounds caused some of the lesser men to turn and run, while others burrowed against the ground, as if attempting to sink a shaft in the manner of a gopher.

As the Russian M-91 7.62 caliber was without ammunition, that left the Luger Model 7.65 mm. which Youngman reserved for close-in fighting due to the limited range. With this weapon he cut down several Chinese trying to reach the upper level of the depot by pulling themselves up, hand over hand.

Youngman thought he heard Li Ming speak, and turned to glance at her, but she was busy loading his M-31. He returned to his firing. He heard the voice again, this time distinctly.

Youngman turned. "Meng-po! What're you doing here?" He was so startled he dropped his rifle and sat up. The Chinese swept the top level of the depot at that moment with numerous bursts. Youngman lurched under the impact of a slug, but picked up his rifle and cut down the soldiers who rushed him. He was cool and confident, and within ten seconds had the men to his front pinned down again. He continued his heavy firing, making it impossible to rush the position without paying the consequences.

"Pull in the perimeter, men," shouted Sarge. "And remember: *Retreat Hell*. We're just advancing in another direction."

Li Ming picked up the scattered rifles as she helped Youngman toward the center of the depot, closer to Sarge and Louis. Youngman left a trail of blood behind him, but did not decrease his intensive fire. Charlie Brown pulled in from the right, continuously firing and cutting down more Chinese.

Three troopers simultaneously came over the wall. Sarge discharged the .50-caliber flintlock into the face of one,

337

then reached out and grabbed the other two and began choking them to death. He achieved this almost effortlessly using the limp corpses to knock down another trooper approaching the wall.

Charlie Brown sprayed the forward area when a particular line of dialogue caught his attention. The Kingfish's wife, Sapphire, had just discovered that the dress she was wearing was not the one she had purchased earlier that day. She was in the process of blistering the Kingfish with a verbal tirade. These verbal tirades were always a high point in the series, and a feature Charlie Brown always savored. It was only natural he should want to savor this one. It accounted for his momentary inattention, during which a Chinese soldier got to within ten feet of him.

The bullets ate into his body. One nose-dived through the transistor and continued on into a major artery, where deposits of quarter-inch tape and plastic were embedded with the piece of lead. Charlie heard a voice, and looked skyward. "Meng-po! I thought you were watching the Hall." He pitched forward and never moved again.

Louis was out of ammunition. Some of the Chinese swarmed up the steps behind him so he bent down, clutched the corner of the table with his teeth, and stood up, swinging swiftly and knocking down the nearest Chinese soldier. The impact knocked loose his lower teeth. He leaped atop the stomach of the fallen trooper and proceeded to knock the wind out of him with the *Tsamiko*.

More Chinese advanced up the steps and over the wall. Targets everywhere. Louis picked the largest bunch and, leaning back as far as he could, flung himself forward, releasing the table at the same time. This time his upper teeth were knocked loose.

The table flew directly into the men. In a second, Louis was atop them, dancing the *Tsamiko* with wild abandon, rendering senseless each man under his feet. Occasionally he spat a tooth at them.

His *spathi* flashed now, cutting through air and throats.

Men gurgled and died.

Bodies piled up.

Louis continued to wield his knife as part of the *Tsamiko*.

338

Two-step, slash, pirouette. "Ouzo . . . ouzo . . ." He spit teeth.

Trails of blood spurted across his white *fousta*. Two-step, slash, pirouette. The dance continued, uninterrupted, across writhing bodies and motionless corpses. Two-step, slash, slash, pirouette. A clutching hand tore away his *shelahi* and he could feel his skirt falling down around his knees.

Spitting out several teeth, Louis tried to kick free from the skirt. At the same time he slashed out with the knife. It continued to meet flesh and bone and gristle. The skirt tangled around his shoes.

The dancing was over.

Now it was merely a matter of time. How long could Louis keep manipulating the *spathi*? A jumble of arms tried to hold him and break his grip on the blade. The jumble succeeded by sheer brute force. Louis's front was now unprotected and his tangled feet prevented him from kicking away his foes. So he could do nothing when a rifle butt crashed into his chest. He took the impact in a stiffened manner, not flinching, not crying out. The men who held him prevented him from falling, but it was apparent he would not have fallen anyway. He might have spit in the eye of the Chinese wielding the rifle butt had his mouth not been full of floating teeth. The rifle butt came again. Louis gritted his few teeth and said nothing. This time two rifle butts were used simultaneously.

Louis went down. He did not cry out, although huge gouts of tears rolled from his eyes.

The Chinese were all over him then. One stabbed him with his own *spathi*; another strangled Louis with his bare hands; a third broke the bones in his legs with vicious blows from a rifle barrel. Despite his pain and the physical fury which tried to pin him to the ground, Louis was able to pop his head up from the melee of entangled torsos, arms, and legs and shout:

"Meng-po!"

A body fell directly on top of him. The body had a bullet hole through the heart, put there by Youngman, who continued to spray the troops coming up the steps and over the wall.

But Youngman's life was flowing from him . . .

65
The Elevated Asshole:
Scenario #2

FADE IN

1. EXT. AMMO DEPOT—DAY—CLOSE ANGLE—
YOUNGMAN

firing his M-31 furiously.

2. WIDE ANGLE—CHINESE SOLDIERS

dying on the steps, rolling back down to the ground.
The troops continue to swarm out of nowhere, yet
Youngman's fire continues to cut them down.

3. TIGHT ANGLE—YOUNGMAN

as his wound begins to reach fatal stages. He pitches
forward, so that his buttocks are thrust into the air.
Somehow, he manages to keep the M-31 firing.

4. TIGHT ANGLE—SARGE

using the butt of his .45 pistol to subdue Chinese swarming around him. He reacts to Youngman's vulnerable position.

> SARGE
>
> Pull it in, Youngman. Pull it in, damn you.

5. ANOTHER ANGLE—YOUNGMAN

as a row of bullets rakes across the level, spattering the wall and ricocheting loudly. Youngman's buttocks are bracketed. Thin trails of smoke rise from his rump. Li Ming hurries to Youngman's side and smothers the fire.

6. BACK TO SARGE

knocking down more Chinese without really giving the task much of his attention, focusing instead on Youngman's plight.

> SARGE
>
> I told you to keep your young ass down . . .

He goes back to killing Chinese.

FADE OUT

66
One-Man Stand

Li Ming gently placed her fingertips on the burnt buttocks of Youngman. "In death, there is reward. It is the way of Buddha." She, as Youngman had, as Charlie Brown had, as Louis had, looked skyward. "I am ready, Meng-po."

On cue, a gunshot sounded. Li Ming pitched forward and sprawled across the top of Youngman. She did not move again.

Sarge. emptied the .50-caliber flintlock first. Another dead Chinese. He then wielded the .45 without mercy, emptying a fresh clip into as many bodies as he had bullets.

The Model 1836, having already been discharged, was used as a skull-crusher. As the handle was shattered by the blow, Sarge discarded it, braining a private near the top of the steps.

The Colt .44 had two shots left. Two bodies crashed at his feet.

In the confusion that followed, he found the weapons that Youngman had spent so many hours carrying. Although there was no ammunition for any of them, Sarge found them useful.

With the Marlin, he bashed in the head of a nearsighted

lieutenant whose glasses were ground into his eyes with the impact of the swing.

With the 1891 Mauser he doubled over a young private by slamming the butt into his stomach. Then he forced the private to return in the direction from which he came by arcing the Mauser 180 degrees, connecting on the tip of his jaw.

With the 6.5 Mannlicher-Carcano he broke the knees of another private, but at the same time he broke the stock of the weapon. With the two separate pieces he knocked aside two bayoneted rifles and cracked their carriers across their cheeks. One was killed.

With the Russian M-91's long barrel he struck a militiaman in the groin, and succeeded in slashing open the face of another with a single sweep. The M-91 finally was rendered useless when he brained a trooper with it, and the stock separated from the metal.

With the Japanese Arisaka, he slipped the aging sling strap around the neck of a field officer and choked him to death, while with his remaining free hand he ground to pulp the face of a noncommissioned officer. When the strangled soldier slipped to the ground, taking the rifle with him, Sarge quickly searched for more weapons . . .

The last rifle was gone.

The pistols were empty, broken, discarded.

There was always the bayonet—and Sarge used it.

If they had any pride, rationalized Sarge, the enemy soldiers it slashed shouldn't have wanted it any other way. There was nothing like cold steel among real soldiers.

It separated men from boys.

Sarge was proud. These Chinese were dying like men.

They came at him, one after another, trying to dodge his blade, and sink their own, but each time Sarge was the victor. None of them cried out or fled in terror. They came in, took it, and came back for more.

It was a sight to behold. Never had a single bayonet reveled in so much glory, but then it failed him. In dodging a blow, Sarge fell back against the concrete wall. The blade glanced off it and broke off at the hilt.

He shoved the ragged edge into the nearest belly and leaped away.

He was weaponless.

The bayonet-packing Chinese closed in.

Sarge grinned. Hell, this was the way he'd always wanted it: gleaming bayonets.

He looked skyward. "That's it, Meng-po. You've got the right idea now, you sly bastard." He gestured at his jugular vein. He tried to make it stand out by rubbing the skin of his neck. "Right here, boys. No hard feelings. That's where I want it. Just like those boys in '44 in the Bulge. Or on Bunker. Yeah, in the neck. Right . . . here." His Adam's apple burgeoned.

Sarge was backed against the wall now and slowly slid down until his buttocks rested comfortably on the face of a Chinese trooper who had fallen there. He motioned the Chinese to move in closer. "That's my boys . . ."

67

Squad C-323
Makes a Grandstand Play

The only way to reach the structure in the middle of the field was through a huge swarm of humans.

In order to fulfill their objective, they would first have to fight their way through that swarm.

Bonzo and King Kong were eager for action. Their penetration would need to be swift and well-planned. They couldn't stop to linger and tear apart at random. Their choices must definitely be in their pathway. They must clear a way to the structure using the element of surprise.

King Kong thumped.

They were off and loping. Their long, slender arms dragged across the surface of the field.

The first human King Kong came to had paused to reload, and was bent down on one knee, balancing his rifle across that knee. King Kong flew at him feet first from a distance of fifteen feet. When his paws hit, King Kong recognized the cracking sound of bone. He moved on over the top of the human's sagging head.

Bonzo, who had approached at a slightly different angle than King Kong, found himself running in the midst of a rifle squad. At first the men were not aware of him. He appeared to be just another running figure. Then the Chinese running next to Bonzo glanced over and saw him.

Without losing his stride, Bonzo reached out and pounded the top of the soldier's head. The man screamed and fell. The squad kept running, but now the others began to take note of the interloper. A cry of alarm, a cry of fear—it was Bonzo's signal to lash out. The man nearest him fell. Bonzo widened his stride to reach the men ahead of him. These men also fell as Bonzo's arms flailed out and as his feet kicked outright and obliquely. Bonzo maintained his forward momentum. The survivors within the ranks of the rifle squad scattered, several dropping back or running away at diagonals to Bonzo. This simplified his task and left him more time to concentrate on clearing the pathway ahead.

Then Bonzo made his mistake.

In concentrating on his forward movement, he could hardly pause to make certain those he left behind had been rendered completely harmless. This was in direct conflict with Squad C-323 procedure, but King Kong had ordered it.

So, when Bonzo came to a two-man machine-gun crew (which for the last three minutes had been stitching rows of holes across *Chun Hsien Ku*) he leaped on top of the gun, while with his thin, hairy arms he proceeded to pound the heads of the men. Both were knocked senseless by the first blows; both were killed by the second blows. Knowing full well by the heaviness of the blows and the sagging condition of both humans that he had put both subjects away, Bonzo loped on, regaining his former stride.

What Bonzo had been incapable of knowing was that the gunner's trigger finger was still tightly wrapped in position, and the machine gun still pumped its pieces of lead. When Bonzo leaped down from the gun, intending to tackle two men running just off to his left, he came down directly into the line of fire. At least six, perhaps seven, slugs whacked him in the backside before he leaped away to avoid the line of fire.

Bonzo lay on the earth and lived for an additional eight seconds. During the first five, he was aware only of a

346

lengthy brown streak which moved unimpeded over the wall of the structure, and during the last three seconds, Bonzo wondered if the screaming he heard came from his own mouth, or that of King Kong's.

68
Valhalla

"That's my boys."

The Chinese soldiers hovered around Sarge, poking their bayonets down toward his face. Sarge could see the first lunge coming and he thrust out his chest proudly to accept the blade, but it didn't come.

Something else came instead. At first only a black streak, then it slowed enough to become a brown streak. It knocked everything aside.

Chinese scrambled, rifles were dropped. The trooper who had almost made the lunge at Sarge now clutched at his head. Huge rivulets of blood poured through the gaps between his fingers. He went away screaming.

The brown streak slowed even more to become a solid mass bending over Sarge. Cupped, hairy fingers plunged for Sarge's face. They worked in and out, back and forth, wriggling like ten worms. The animal stench was overwhelming at this close range. Sarge couldn't see any more as his eyes were ripped from their sockets.

King Kong continued to work over Sarge for the next thirty seconds. The smell of the flagpole was nowhere in evidence, but the smell of graphite, gunpowder and the metal of weapons had reached its zenith. It gagged King

Kong, but he went on working steadily for those thirty seconds.

Meanwhile the Chinese recomposed themselves and realized what had to be done. Several of the troopers who had dared the open field and then the guns and knives of the unique defenders of *Chun Hsien Ku* had fled in abject horror at the sight of King Kong. Others, however, stood their ground.

"Gwwwkkkk." Under the circumstances, it was the only sound Sarge could make.

It approximated the sounds King Kong made a few moments later as the Chinese redirected their bayonets and plunged them, repeatedly, into his coarse hide. The brown eyes became less expressive and eventually lackluster. The protuberant lips, which had been actively forming a sneer, became immobile.

The bayonets lashed out again.

There was the high *i* for fear, the short *o* for warning, the deep *u* for weeping. King Kong sank onto the chest of Sarge and buried his head against Sarge's chin. All the sounds joined together to form a whimper, which grew weaker and weaker . . . and then stopped. The bayonets lashed out again, but by then even the Chinese knew they were wasting their steel.

A profound silence fell over *Chun Hsien Ku*.

69
Escape

Reva kept her foot on the gas pedal, motivated by but one thought: to put as many miles as possible between her and *Chun Hsien Ku* before nightfall. She sped southward, but took occasional sideroads, remembering Louis's theory about sideroads being less traveled.

Her constant fifty-five miles per hour provided for a rough ride. Frequently, she heard Ju-Chao's moaning from the back of the truck, but she did not slow down. He would have to take the bumps and the dips and the hairpin corners until nightfall when she would make it all up to him.

She had only Ju-Chao to thank for her survival. If he had not filled those casks full of holes, she would never have learned Louis's true nature until it was too late. Thanks to Ju-Chao, the fruitlessness of *Bot Bon Jui* had been revealed. She only hoped she would soon forget what had happened back there.

She took a sharp corner, spewing out a cloud of dust behind her. There was a banging sound from the rear—Ju-Chao, no doubt, rolling and hitting the side of the truck. His groanings followed, but she again rejected the thought of slowing down.

Reva suddenly realized she had no idea of where she was headed. It didn't really matter, she told herself over the sound of squealing tires as she took another dangerous turn at fifty-five mph. Anyplace had to be an improvement over *Chun Hsien Ku* and—

She hit the brake.

Ahead of her the road narrowed as it wound its way through a grove of trees. Two huge gnarly stumps edged the road, giving the truck barely enough space to squeeze through. She shifted down and continued to ride the brake as she aimed the truck through the narrow opening.

Abreast of the trees, Reva sensed a kind of motion above—from out of the trees. This sensation of something falling was followed almost immediately by a heavy object which, at first, was nothing more than a streak as it fell through the air and landed, with a dull thump, on the hood of the truck. The impact was so heavy it made a dent near the front.

The next thing Reva knew, a pair of beady, glaring eyes stared at her through the windshield. The black blur suddenly took on a solidity of hairy arms and legs. The creature was breathing so heavily against the glass it left small circular breath clouds, which it promptly ran stubby, hairy fingers through. Even over the churning of the engine, Reva heard the thing grunting.

Reva came out of her initial surprise to find the truck beyond the grove of trees and heading down a wide dirt lane into a valley. She accelerated and began twisting the wheel—first left, then right. The creature slid across the hood but demonstrated great dexterity in maintaining a grip on the smooth surface of the hood of the truck.

The truck careened from one side of the road to the other and continued to drop down into the valley. The creature hung on with a secure grasp of the side-view mirror. Reva rolled down her window and reached around to break its grip, but she felt indefatigable strength there. When the fingers began to seek hers, she hastily withdrew them and rolled the window back up.

The creature now stared directly at her, pressing most of its body against the windshield. She thought the windshield wipers might discourage the filthy beast, whatever it was.

The wipers squished back and forth, but only succeede in scattering the stream of urine which the creature decided to unleash in Reva's direction.

The careening truck reached the valley floor.

To her right, Reva made out the remnants of a village She decided to stay on the main road where she could keep moving.

The truck rolled past the destroyed village and made its way deeper into the valley.

The beast on the hood pressed its nostrils against the windshield and snorted. The hatred in its eyes was unmis takable, and Reva realized she was going to scream.

But she never got the chance.

As her lips parted and her mouth opened, the truck hit a land mine.

70

Sole Survivor—Again

The Old German sat in the open doorway. He had not moved for more than an hour. He had lost his tobacco pouch during his fall over the side of the wall, and he had not bothered to put his pipe in his mouth. The ground was damp, and therefore his buttocks were damp, but it did not bother him.

The lump on the back of his head did bother him. A rock had been kicked up by an exploding grenade, thrown at just the proper angle to strike him on the head and leave him unconscious.

So now he sat in the open doorway, alive.

The sole survivor.

Besides the lump on his skull, something else troubled him. The Old German's brain creaked and groaned, as he tried to remember all the reasons for the tiredness and the despair he felt.

Some of the reasons escaped him, although one did not.

It was that business about survival.

For the fourth time, he had come out of it alive. Once again his comrades, as short-lived as their relationship might have been, were dead.

Why hadn't those Chinese seen him lying there as they

sacked the bodies on the upper level? Why had they gone away without carefully checking the side doors? Sloppy un professionalism ... they just didn't train soldiers as they did in his day.

A younger man, fresh to the vagaries of battle, would have called it luck or providence.

To The Old German, however, it was the foul breath o fate.

He sighed, decided he should try to find his fallen to bacco pouch, then realized the Chinese had probably seized it. He decided to remain where he was. What was the hurry? He would be reassigned to a new unit soon enough The cycle would begin all over again.

Yet, deep down inside, he knew he would persevere.

He was a German.

71

In the Valley of Death

Sergeant Joe Young had dropped from a tree, and now he was blown back into a tree. His carcass was draped carelessly over a thick, stout limb, and from his gaping wounds blood dripped down onto the road below. His hairy arms swayed without purpose, once bright, wide eyes had lost their exuberance.

Reva had stayed with the truck after the blast. Laws of momentum had tried to propel her forward and upward, though she had remained flat against the seat, pinioned into position by an engine piston which had penetrated her chest, the seat, and the cab. Her hands still gripped the steering wheel, as if she were getting ready to take another sharp corner. The last thing she had seen was the beastly face leering at her.

Fragments of twisted metal and jagged pieces of the engine had been thrown as far as one hundred yards in all directions. The ground was also littered with hundreds of Chinese regulation field caps and helmets—and Ju-Chao.

He lay in the ruts of the road, about twenty yards from the burning truck, moaning in a low voice, as if he were afraid he might disturb someone. To his earlier wounds had been added three cracked ribs (the result of his

striking the ground after a graceful arc through the air)
and several third-degree burns, mainly to his knees and elbows. His face was smudged, and his nose broken by the
fall, but the skin had not been scorched.

Ju-Chao opened his eyes.

He found himself staring at an inscription set in a huge
monument stone, which marked the entranceway to a small
shrine. Inside the shrine was a blackened Buddha statue on
a small wooden table. The inscription read:

ON A SUNDAY MORNING, ON THE FIRST DAY OF THE
GREAT WAR, THE PEOPLE OF CHANGYANG VALLEY WERE
WIPED OUT TO THE LAST INDIVIDUAL BY AMERICAN
AIRSHIPS. THEY HAD GATHERED HERE TO PRAY, AND IN
SEEKING PRAYER WERE DENIED THE SALVATION OF
THEIR SOULS IN DEATH BY FIRE. HENCEFORTH, IN THE
HONOR OF THE DEAD, THE ANNIVERSARY OF THIS
TRAGEDY WILL BE COMMEMORATED AS NAPALM SUN-
DAY. MAY THE GOOD PEOPLE OF CHANGYANG VALLEY
BE REMEMBERED FOR THEIR LAST ACT OF RIGHTEOUS-
NESS, BY THEIR FELLOW MAN AND BY BUDDHA.

During the next hour, Ju-Chao read the inscription
many times. It was something for his burning eyes to do,
and something for his eyes to do gave his mind something
to do. Something that took his mind away from the many
things bothering him.

- Such as his wound. He had ripped away the putrescent bandage to find a blanket of black tics crawling across
the puffy, greenish flesh. Gangrene had not wasted any
time in settling into his unclean wound.
- Such as his mouth. It had not had a drop of water
since he was wounded—twenty-four hours before. To go
that long without water was not new to Ju-Chao. Many
campaigns had dictated lack of water as a normal course
of events, and he had grown accustomed to going without,
but his system had not been invaded by a piece of metal
then, nor had he been slipping from consciousness into
unconsciousness. Nor had pain and fever wracked his
body, drying up his small reserve of liquid.
- Such as his memories. They were nightmares.

brought on by delirium—a terrible blend of reality and un-reality. Monsters and mortals mixed into a single tableau of life forms. Dragons were a-wing, things floated languidly in gastric juices in bottles, moths fluttered around light bulbs and turned into gargantuan insects which devastated cities and destroyed entire columns of Chinese soldiers.

• Such as his failures. He had attempted the chant of misery, and then had gone the full gamut: remorse, happiness, gaiety, horniness, love, hate, and other emotions, some of which he had never experienced before. Every device at his disposal had failed to put him in a frame of mind to accept his plight and give him the strength to survive it. Unless he could accept these things, he would surely die before the day was over.

Therefore, for the first time in his life, Ju-Chao prayed for a miracle.

Buddha stretched his fire-scarred arms, yawned, and picked at His nostrils. "Boo," he said.

EPILOGUE
Communiqués

BROWN COAT FILE 34266
SUBJECT: PHASE APEKILL

TO: FIELD COMMANDER ARTHUR L. CONNOLLY
THIRD BATTALION, SIXTH REGIMENT
NINTH BATTLE GROUP, ASIATAC

*STILL AWAITING EXPLANATION OF C-323
SIGNAL RECEIVED BY YOUR STAFF LATE
WEDNESDAY XXX WHY HAVEN'T YOUR BOYS
TRANSLATED YET? XXX PENTAGON/CAPITOL
HILL BREATHING FIRE/BRIMSTONE IN HASTE TO
RELEASE ADDITIONAL APEKILL POWER IN YOUR
SECTOR FOR MOP-UP ACTION/SEARCH OUT AND
DESTROY PATROLS XXX DON'T NEED TO TELL
YOU BY NOW THIS IS URGENT XXX GENERAL
HOWARD T. STEPMANN, COMMANDING, NATSEC
HQ, WASHINGTON D.C.*

X X X

BROWN COAT FILE 34267
SUBJECT: PHASE APEKILL

TO: GENERAL HOWARD T. STEPMANN
    CMMDNG NATSEC HQ
    WASHINGTON D.C.

STAFF OF TRANSLATORS WORKING ROUND
CLOCK TO DECIPHER LAST SIGNAL FROM C-
323 XXX SOMETHING DEFINITELY OUT OF
ORDINARY HERE XXX FAILURE OF C-323 TO
RETURN AT DESIGNATED TIME PUTS ENTIRE
OPERATION IN DOUBT XXX REALIZE YOUR PRE-
DICAMENT CAN ONLY ADVISE ALL PLANS FOR
CONTINUATION OF OPERATION BROWNCOAT BE
DELAYED UNTIL STRAIGHTENED OUT ON THIS
END XXX FIELD COMMANDER ARTHUR L. CON-
NOLLY, THIRD BATTALION, SIXTH REGIMENT,
NINTH BATTLE GROUP ASIATAC

XXX

BROWN COAT FILE 34268
SUBJECT: PHASE APEKILL

TO: FIELD COMMANDER ARTHUR L. CONNOLLY
    THIRD BATTALION, SIXTH REGIMENT
    NINTH BATTLE GROUP, ASIATAC

WHAT ARE THOSE TRANSLATORS DOING? XXX
MUST HAVE IMMEDIATE EXPLANATION OF C-
323 OR PENTAGON/CAPITOL HILL MAY BLOW
ALL GASKETS XXX REPEAT ALL GASKETS XXX
EFFECTIVENESS OF C-323 VITAL TO CURRENT
CONGRESSIONAL SESSION XXX APPROPRIATIONS
ONLY FORTHCOMING ON GUARANTEE OF C-
323'S SUCCESS XXX GENERAL HOWARD T.
STEPMANN, COMMANDING, NATSEC HQ, WASH-
INGTON D.C.

XXX

BROWN COAT FILE 34269
SUBJECT: PHASE APEKILL

TO: GENERAL HOWARD T. STEPMANN
CMMDNG NATSEC HQ
WASHINGTON D.C.

ALL BROWN COAT OPERATIONS STOP XXX RE-
PEAT ALL BROWN COAT OPERATIONS STOP XXX
EFFECTIVE IMMEDIATELY XXX DESPITE CONDI-
TIONING AND TRAINING OF C-323, DECODED
SIGNAL FROM C-323 WEDNESDAY NIGHT INDI-
CATES COMPLETE BREAKDOWN XXX C-323
DESERTED IN FACE OF ENEMY XXX LOCATION
NOW UNKNOWN XXX CARCASS OF SON OF
KONG (CH 345 67 230) LOCATED XXX DEATH
BY LAND MINE XXX WHEREABOUTS OF OTHERS
STILL UNKNOWN XXX POSSIBLE COWARDICE
FOLLOWING DEATH OF MEMBER XXX ALL EVI-
DENCE POINTS TO COMPLETE BREAKDOWN OF
APEKILL XXX UNKNOWN FACTOR IN SUBJECTS
XXX SORRY IT HAS TO BE YOUR BRAINCHILD,
HOWIE XXX PHASE APEKILL BOONDOGGLE XXX
GLAD I'M NOT THE ONE WHO HAS TO TELL
CAPITOL HILL/PENTAGON BOYS XXX FIELD
COMMANDER ARTHUR L. CONNOLLY, THIRD
BATTALION, SIXTH REGIMENT, NINTH BATTLE
GROUP ASIATIC.

X X X

BROWN COAT FILE 34270
SUBJECT: PHASE APEKILL

TO: FIELD COMMANDER ARTHUR L. CONNOLLY
THIRD BATTALION, SIXTH REGIMENT
NINTH BATTLE GROUP, ASIATAC

HAVE SUSPENDED ALL TRAINING OPERATIONS
XXX MOJAVE BASE CLOSED DOWN XXX APPRO-

PRIATION BILL DEAD XXX NATSEC HQ PHASE
APEKILL BEING PHASED OUT XXX BEING REAS-
SIGNED PARAMEDIC COMBAT UNIT, WHERE I
BELONGED IN FIRST PLACE XXX MAY SEE YOU
IN SIX WEEKS XXX ASSIGNED YOUR AREA OF
OPERATIONS XXX OFF RECORD, WHAT THE
HELL WAS THE DECODING? XXX GENERAL
HOWARD T. STEPMANN, CMMDNG, NATSEC HQ,
WASHINGTON D.C.

X X X

BROWN COAT FILE 34271
SUBJECT: PHASE APEKILL

TO: GENERAL HOWARD T. STEPMANN
    CMMDNG NATSEC HQ
    WASHINGTON D.C.

READ AND DESTROY XXX IMPERATIVE REPEAT
IMPERATIVE NO COPIES OF THIS DOCUMENT
MUST REMAIN IN EXISTENCE AFTER ORIGINAL
SCAN XXX YOU ASK OFF RECORD, THAT'S WHY
THIS REPLY XXX SIGNAL FROM C-323 IMPOS-
SIBLE TO DECIPHER LITERALLY XXX HOWEVER,
APPROXIMATE TRANSLATION BASED ON PAT-
TERN OF PAST MESSAGES XXX "FUCK-OFF" XXX
DESTROY, REPEAT, DESTROY XXX FIELD COM-
MANDER ARTHUR L. CONNOLLY, THIRD BATTAL-
ION, SIXTH REGIMENT, NINTH BATTLE GROUP
ASIATAC.

X X X

THE BIG BESTSELLERS
ARE AVON BOOKS!

A CHILLING DETECTIVE STORY OF MURDER AND MADNESS

AN EX-COP MUST FIND A CRAZED KILLER . . . BEFORE THE COPS CATCH UP WITH HIM!

NATIONAL BOOK AWARD NOMINEE

THE DEATH OF THE DETECTIVE

MARK SMITH

This is a novel about murder, corruption, defilement and violence—every seamy reality you have ever read about in the daily papers . . .

The Detective is an ex-cop who left the force because he was too honest. Now, he must find an escaped mental patient with a terrible grudge who will kill anyone in his way. Here are two human beings, stalking each other in the American hell called Chicago, the city where people suffer and bleed; love and die. One is the pursuer, one the pursued; one the murderer, one the avenger; one the madman, one the detective.

"A COMPLETE SUCCESS . . . ABSOLUTELY WORTH READING . . ." *The New York Times Book Review*

AVON ◆ 26567 $1.95

Where better paperbacks are sold, or directly from the publisher. Include 25¢ per copy for mailing; allow three weeks for delivery. Avon Books, Mail Order Dept., 250 West 55th Street, New York, N.Y. 10019.   DDet 12-75